New Casebooks

WUTHERING
HEIGHTS

New Casebooks

PUBLISHED
Hamlet
Middlemarch
Tristram Shandy
Macbeth
Villette
Emma
Waiting for Godot and *Endgame*
Shakespeare's History Plays: Richard II to Henry V
King Lear
Wordsworth
Tess of the d'Urbervilles
Wuthering Heights
Mrs Dalloway and *To the Lighthouse*

FORTHCOMING
Sense and Sensibility and *Pride and Prejudice*
Jane Eyre
Great Expectations
Jude the Obscure
Sons and Lovers
Ulysses
Chaucer
Metaphysical Poetry
Blake
Antony and Cleopatra

New Casebooks

WUTHERING
HEIGHTS

EMILY BRONTË

EDITED BY PATSY STONEMAN

St. Martin's Press　　　New York

823.09
BRONTE, E
WUTHGRING

3 1257 00875 2197

First published in the United States of America in 1993

Printed in Hong Kong

ISBN 0–312–09689–5

Library of Congress Cataloging-in-Publication Data
Wuthering Heights : Emily Brontë / edited by Patsy Stoneman.
p.   cm. — (New casebooks)
Includes bibliographical references and index.
ISBN 0–312–09689–5
1. Bronte, Emily, 1818–1848.   Wuthering Heights.   I. Stoneman,
Patsy.   II. Series.
PR4172.W73W88   1993
823'.8—dc20   93–14830
                                                                      CIP

Contents

Acknowledgements

I have, with the authors' agreement, shortened most of the essays in the way the editorial note after each essay indicates. Individual cuts in the text, however, are not marked.

The editor and publishers wish to thank the following for permission to use copyright material:

Terry Eagleton, 'Wuthering Heights' in Myths of Power: A Marxist Study of the Brontës (1976), by permission of Macmillan Press Ltd; Stevie Davies, 'The Language of Familial Desire' in Emily Brontë (1988) Harvester Key Women Writers Series, by permission of Harvester Wheatsheaf and Indiana University Press; Sandra Gilbert, 'Looking Oppositely: Emily Brontë's Bible of Hell' from The Madwoman in the Attic; the Woman Writer and the Nineteenth-Century Literary Imagination by Sandra Gilbert and Susan Gubar (1979). Copyright © 1979 by Sandra Gilbert and Susan Gubar, by permission of Yale University Press; N. M. Jacobs, 'Gender and Layered Narrative in Wuthering Heights and The Tenant of Wildfell Hall', Journal of Narrative Technique, 16 (1986), by permission of the Journal of Narrative Technique and the author; Frank Kermode, extract from The Classic: T. S. Eliot Memorial Lectures (1975), by permission of Faber & Faber Ltd and Peters Fraser and Dunlop Group Ltd on behalf of the author; Q. D. Leavis, 'A Fresh Approach to Wuthering Heights' in Lectures in America, vol. 1 (1969), by permission of G. Singh, executor of Q. D. Leavis's Estate; Michael S. Macovski, 'Wuthering Heights and the Rhetoric of Interpretation', English Literary History, 54(2) (Summer 1987), by permission of the Johns Hopkins University Press; John T. Matthews, 'Framing in Wuthering Heights', Texas Studies in Literature and Language, 27(1) (Spring 1985), by permission of University of Texas Press; Patricia

Parker, 'The (Self-) Identity of the Literary Text: Property, Proper Place and Proper Name in *Wuthering Heights*' in *Literary Fat Ladies: Rhetoric, Gender, Property* (1987), Methuen and Co., by permission of Routledge; Lyn Pykett, 'Gender and Genre in *Wuthering Heights*' in *Emily Brontë* (1989), Macmillan Women Writers Series, by permission of Macmillan Education Ltd.

General Editors' Preface

The purpose of this series of New Casebooks is to reveal some of the ways in which contemporary criticism has changed our understanding of commonly studied texts and writers and, indeed, of the nature of criticism itself. Central to the series is a concern with modern critical theory and its effect on current approaches to the study of literature. Each New Casebook editor has been asked to select a sequence of essays which will introduce the reader to the new critical approaches to the text or texts being discussed in the volume and also illuminate the rich interchange between critical theory and critical practice that characterises so much current writing about literature.

In this focus on modern critical thinking New Casebooks aim not only to inform but also to stimulate, with volumes seeking to reflect both the controversy and the excitement of current criticism. Because much of this criticism is difficult and often employs an unfamiliar critical language, editors have been asked to give the reader as much help as they feel is appropriate, but without simplifying the essays or the issues they raise. Again, editors have been asked to supply a list of further reading which will enable readers to follow up issues raised by the essays in the volume.

The project of New Casebooks, then, is to bring together in an illuminating way those critics who best illustrate the ways in which contemporary criticism has established new methods of analysing texts and who have reinvigorated the important debate about how we 'read' literature. The hope is, of course, that New Casebooks will not only open up this debate to a wider audience, but will also encourage students to extend their own ideas, and think afresh about their responses to the texts they are studying.

John Peck and Martin Coyle
University of Wales, Cardiff

Introduction

PATSY STONEMAN

Wuthering Heights is not a comfortable book; it invites admiration rather than love. In the nineteenth century, when readers tended to regard novels as personal communications from the author, even critics who acknowledged its power found it crude and alien.[1] By the 1930s two things had happened to change this response. Firstly, a new kind of literary criticism, called the 'New Criticism' in England and America, and 'Formalism' in Russia, encouraged readers to look at works of literature not as 'messages' but as artifacts, 'verbal icons' to be valued for the skill with which they are constructed. Secondly, in the crisis situation of the inter-war period, intellectuals who might previously have looked to religion increasingly turned to literature to 'teach us how to live'. These movements – one formalistic, the other moral – seem to be opposed, but they came together in the critics associated with the English journal *Scrutiny*, who believed that the inspirational power of literature was produced by its formal perfection.

Although this New Casebook is devoted to essays written during the last twenty years, it is important to look back at this earlier period, because the habits of reading established then are still what most academic readers find natural. Most teachers still discuss books in terms of their unity of construction and assume that they can 'do us good' even if we don't quite understand them. A poem like *The Waste Land* is valued because we *don't* understand it; its gaps and difficulties are accepted as parts of a structure designed to tease us into thought, and its self-conscious allusions act as clues to its hidden truth.[2] Its breadth of symbolic reference seems a guarantee that its meanings are universal, beyond time.

In this new climate of criticism, *Wuthering Heights* could also be revalued; its tight structure was recognised and its mysteriousness of meaning became a sign of greatness.[3] Something, however, was missing; the novel was too individual, not, apparently, part of a literary heritage with clear ancestors and descendants. F. R. Leavis, the central figure in the *Scrutiny* circle, could not admit *Wuthering Heights* to the 'Great Tradition' of English novelists because, he said, 'that astonishing work seems to me a kind of sport'.[4]

Most of the essays in this collection challenge one or more of the assumptions behind the judgements of this earlier period. Those written from a poststructuralist position argue that there *is* no ultimate 'meaning', or 'wholeness' that we can reach by 'interpreting' the text, only an infinite play of meanings. Those written from an acknowledged political position argue that the apparently 'universal' meanings are actually those favoured by politically dominant groups, and that the 'great tradition' is a concept which excludes culturally marginal groups such as women and the working class. Because these challenging essays are written in the atmosphere of debate, as 'answers' to an existing orthodoxy, readers of this volume will do well to look back at the original Casebook edited by Miriam Allott in 1970.

The first essay in this New Casebook, however, provides a link with the *Scrutiny* circle. This is Q. D. Leavis's 'Fresh Approach to *Wuthering Heights*'. Q. D. Leavis is less concerned than her husband with issues of 'major' and 'minor' talent, but she shares his assumption that there are self-evident aesthetic and moral values.[5] She is certain 'that Emily Brontë intended to create a coherent, deeply responsible novel whose wisdom should be recognised as useful', and she sees the critic's job as to mediate between the text and the reader, helping us to see the intention behind the text. She wants readers to focus on 'the human truths' of the novel.[6] Her essay thus stands as an important example of the liberal humanist position which many of the other contributors to this volume wish to question.

On the other hand, her essay is far from bland. She argues that much of the 'mysteriousness' of *Wuthering Heights* is the result of muddle rather than profundity, and that Heathcliff 'is an enigmatic figure only by reason of his creator's indecision'.[7] The novel's greatness lies not in its perfection of form, therefore, but in its truthfulness. Leavis's 'fresh approach' involves detailed social-historical contextualisation which sets her apart from the more formalistic *Scrutiny* critics even while her aesthetic exclusiveness and moral urgency mark her as one of them.[8] Another new aspect of the essay is its feminism; Q. D. Leavis was one of the first critics to argue that the 'truths' of the novel lie in Catherine's story, rather than Heathcliff's.[9]

One of the aims of this collection of essays is to demonstrate the variety of critical positions which have proliferated during the last twenty years – positions to which we assign labels such as 'liberal', 'deconstructive' and 'feminist' – and I have suggested that Q. D. Leavis's essay in some senses represents a norm from which the other essays dissent. The discussion above, however, should alert us to the dangers of labels. Q. D. Leavis's essay might be labelled 'liberal humanist', but this would ignore the fact that it veers towards the sociological rather than the formalist and that it includes a feminist (and even a 'vulgar Marxist') perspective. Each of the essays which follows is in the same way multiple and complex in its theoretical bases; the labels I have attached cannot be definitive, and each essay should be seen as part of a debate among critics. Because the debate ranges much more widely than the ten essays reproduced in this volume, I have tried in this Introduction not only to place the chosen essays in their theoretical context, but also to describe some other important essays which are not reprinted here.

The second essay in this collection, by Frank Kermode, engages directly with Q. D. Leavis and, like hers, looks back to a pre-war climate of debate. In particular, Kermode is concerned with the question of what constitutes a 'classic' work of literature and its relation to a literary tradition. These are questions raised by T. S. Eliot's famous essays, 'Tradition and the Individual Talent' (1919) and 'What is a Classic?' (1944). In one way, therefore, Kermode locates himself in a long tradition of English criticism. On the other hand his appeal to 'the new French criticism' marks a new direction.

Unlike Q. D. Leavis, Kermode is not prepared to intuit the author's intention or to privilege one reading of the text. He thus challenges the 'hermeneutic' conception of criticism.[10] 'We don't', he says, 'think of the novel as a code, or a nut, that can be broken; which contains or refers to a meaning all will agree upon if it can once be presented *en clair*.'[11] Whereas Leavis creates 'a hierarchy of elements' within the novel, Kermode proposes 'a plurality of significances', accepting Leavis's 'fine awareness of human relations' alongside his own and other readings. His essay is a meditation on the patterns of names in the novel, and hence on family relations, property relations, personal identities. He is concerned with structures, not only of genealogy but of 'generic opposites – daylight and dream . . . life and death', and he argues that the significance we find in the novel derives from these structures.

Though it looks back to Leavis, Kermode's reading thus clearly shows the influence of structuralism. Structuralism was a movement combining linguistics with anthropology; structuralists showed that cultural behaviours of all kinds have a pattern analogous to language and that the meanings we find in these patterns are socially constructed.[12] The structural linguist Ferdinand de Saussure argues that meanings are not inherent in words (there is nothing dog-like about the word 'dog') but are constructed, within cultures, by people who *learn* to recognise the difference between 'dog', 'bog', 'dig' and 'doll'.[13] For a structuralist, there is no point in trying to reach the true nature of 'dogness', although the difference between 'dog' and 'hound' is interesting. Meaning is produced in the gaps between words, not in the words themselves, and users of language are alert to differences, not essences. All meanings depend on binary oppositions ('dog' versus 'not-dog'), and although most such meanings are culture-specific,[14] cultures share certain 'primary oppositions' such as night/day, life/death.

A humanist such as Leavis can base her claim for the classic status of *Wuthering Heights* on 'its truly human centrality'[15] because she is confident that we all have intuitive knowledge of what is 'human' and 'good'. Kermode, on the other hand, argues that we have no way of arriving at such 'central' understanding. He explains the sense (which many readers feel) of some 'ultimate' truth underlying *Wuthering Heights* by pointing to the extreme nature of its oppositional structures. 'The mingling of generic opposites', he argues, 'creates a need . . . for something that will mediate between them.'[16] This 'something', is experienced as 'the answer', but each reader supplies a different answer.

For structuralists, words are 'signifiers' which are only precariously attached to their 'signified'. Not only can each signifier float between several possible signifieds,[17] but because no signifier can ever fuse with its signified, the signified always seems to be slipping away, calling for supplementary definition.[18] A novel like *Wuthering Heights* provides a superfluity of signifiers, more than any reader can cope with. The 'indeterminacies of meaning' which for Q. D. Leavis are flaws, only to be explained by the author's confused intentions, are, for Kermode, what makes *Wuthering Heights* a classic. A classic must, he says, 'always signify more than is needed by any one interpreter or any one generation of interpreters'.[19] In this liberal acceptance of 'pluralities', however, Kermode also manages to imply that different readings 'add up' to something greater than themselves, and his essay concludes with the suggestion that the old image of the classic, 'beyond time . . . had perhaps, after all, a measure of authenticity'.

Kermode's residual sympathy with 'universal values' becomes more obvious in contrast with a deconstructionist reading such as that of John T. Matthews (whose essay is the third in this collection). Crudely speaking, Leavis says, 'there is one truth'; Kermode says, 'there are many truths'; Matthews says, 'there is no truth'.[20]

'Deconstruction' is a critical practice invented by the French philosopher Jacques Derrida, based on but challenging structuralism. Derrida points out that although structuralists claimed to analyse language and culture scientifically, in terms of binary oppositions, in effect there are hidden value-judgements which always privilege one element of a primary opposition ('light' is preferred to 'dark', for instance) and that this unexamined weighting makes it easy to slip back into the idea of a 'central' truth. There may be good reasons for this preference, but it is a human *choice*, not an innate quality. It cannot be arrived at 'scientifically'.[21] Derrida demonstrates this by means of an argument about 'supplements'. In the example I have given, 'dark' seems supplementary to the more 'primary' concept, 'light'. On examination, however, the 'supplement' always proves to be essential (you cannot conceive of 'light' without the notion of 'dark'). Hence there is no way of objectively determining which element is 'original' or 'central'; the element which *seems* more important seems so because of cultural agreement.

In the case of *Wuthering Heights*, John T. Matthews argues that the 'core story' of Catherine and Heathcliff *requires* the 'framing narrative' which most readers take as 'supplementary'.[22] This argument challenges not only Leavis's assumption that the 'core story' is 'humanly central', but also Kermode's feeling that meaning accumulates somewhere between such oppositions. For Matthews, 'core' and 'frame' are reflections which endlessly dissolve into one another, and it is this recognition which 'deconstructs' the privilege usually accorded to Catherine and Heathcliff.

Another deconstructive reading of *Wuthering Heights* (not included here) which can be matched against Kermode is that of J. Hillis Miller, one of the first generation of American followers of Derrida. Like Kermode, Miller reads *Wuthering Heights* as a 'heterogeneous' text for which any act of interpretation always leaves something 'over'. Like Kermode again, he recognises 'the invitation to believe that some invisible or transcendent cause, some origin, end or underlying ground, would explain all the enigmatic incongruities of what is visible'. Miller, however, cannot accept this invitation. For him, *Wuthering Heights* is an 'uncanny text' because it not only compels but simultaneously prohibits readers from identifying this 'secret truth'. He is using the word 'uncanny' in Freud's sense, as indicating something which is familiar, but unspeakable (in both senses).[23]

'Uncanny' well describes the unsettling effect of *Wuthering Heights*; although we seem to recognise what it is saying, we are never able to look squarely at its meaning (it is both obscure and frightening). It baffles conventional criticism, in other words, because it *deconstructs itself*. Deconstructive critics argue, in fact, that deconstruction is not something that you *do* to a text, but something that you can *find happening* in it. The unity we find in texts is only a reflection of our need for things to make sense; our readings fix for a moment a play of words in which meaning is always dissolving into something else. It may be that we fight shy of deconstruction not because it is difficult, but because it is frightening – like the echo in the Marabar Caves, it seems to reduce everything to the same value and us to despair.[24] In a 'pure' form, deconstructive criticism is incompatible with any moral or political commitment. 'Words promise to be the portals to what we desire', Matthews says, but in fact 'can only keep us moving in the passages of communication'.[25] Its compensations lie in the excitement of reading itself. Deconstruction at its best is so intelligent, witty and provoking that 'moving on' proves more enjoyable and (in a paradoxical way) more 'human' and 'truthful' than 'arriving'.[26]

Derrida himself, however, acknowledges that 'pure' deconstruction is impossible, like forever sawing off the branch on which you are sitting. Carol Jacobs's essay, '*Wuthering Heights*: At the Threshold of Interpretation', demonstrates the potential bleakness of this unceasingly self-referential analysis, which ends by deconstructing itself and swallowing its own tail.[27] It is more common, however, for critics to use deconstructive techniques as a tool rather than a final position. Readers taking a political stance other than the dominant one can use deconstruction to undermine the assumptions behind liberal humanism in order to assert some alternative priority such as Marxism or feminism. This is not to make nonsense of deconstruction, since it is the *hidden* nature of dominant value-systems which Derrida sought to 'undo'.[28] One might argue that the aim of deconstruction is not to reduce us to despair but to force us to acknowledge that our judgements are a question of choice and not of 'truth'. As Terry Eagleton puts it, 'it is not a matter of starting from certain theoretical or methodological problems: it is a matter of starting from what we want to *do*, and then seeing which method and theories will best help us to achieve these ends'.[29]

Feminist criticism often takes this instrumental attitude to theories and methods. I have placed Naomi Jacobs's feminist essay, 'Gender and Layered Narrative in *Wuthering Heights*', after Matthews not because she owes anything explicitly to deconstruction but because she arrives at a position which corroborates Matthews's frame/reverse argument by quite a different route. Her title links narrative technique with gender in a way which announces a political intention, and her argument about the form of the novel is substantiated both by sociological evidence about the position of nineteenth-century women and by 'literary history' – the contemporary reception of the Brontë novels. In reading *Wuthering Heights*, Jacobs argues,

> we approach a horrific private reality only after passing through and then discarding the perceptual structures of a narrator – significantly a male narrator – who represents the public world that makes possible and tacitly approves the excesses behind the closed doors of these pre-Victorian homes.

The 'framing' technique thus shows that the 'official standards of morality' are 'in part the cause of the shocking reality they encounter'.[30] This, then, is a 'politicised' version of Matthews's more philosophical essay on 'Framing'. Although she does not use the word, Jacobs's essay is just as 'deconstructive' as his; like him she argues that 'frame' and 'core' are intimately connected, so that neither can be discarded or privileged over the other. Unlike him, however, she exposes this structure in the hope of changing it.

Other feminist critics also make connections between the form of the novel and the historical position of women. They are exposing the fact that literary form is not politically innocent, but that 'discourses, sign-systems and signifying practices of all kinds . . . are closely related to the maintenance or transformation of our existing systems of power'. The word 'discourse' in this quotation from Terry Eagleton[31] suggests that he is invoking the theories of the French historian Michel Foucault, sometimes called 'discourse theory'. Foucault argues that power is maintained through the control of 'discourse' – accepted ways of describing and evaluating experience, such as religious or medical discourses. It is a theory with immediate implications for literary criticism.[32]

Heather Glen gives an excellent practical analysis of how three such discourses – of Methodism, Romanticism and folklore – inter-twine in *Wuthering Heights*.[33] Nancy Armstrong argues that the 'enigmatic' character of Heathcliff is the result of his crossing be-tween literary *genres* – the Romantic *genres* of the early nineteenth century (which account for the 'core' story) and early Victorian domestic realism (which accounts for the 'second-generation' story). These *genres* are themselves related to economic and thus to political changes, so that she is able to develop an argument in which formal analysis is continuous with the political.[34]

Lyn Pykett's essay, which appears fifth in this collection, draws on several studies of this kind. Pykett finds Armstrong's work 'difficult, tendentious and overstated', but she also recognises 'the connections that [Armstrong] makes, or implies, between gender, class, culture, literature, society and politics'.[35] Pykett's essay, which does not mention Foucault or use the word 'discourse', reminds us that theory is there to be *used*. Behind the scenes, as it were, discourse theory has allowed Pykett quietly to discount the idea that great literature is outside history and to make her own strongly political reading of *Wuthering Heights* as an 'experiment with alternative visions of reality in which dominance, power, and energy are not exclusively masculine qualities, and nor do they necessarily prevail'.[36]

Fifty years before Foucault, in the 1920s, the Russian critic Mikhail Bakhtin was already arguing that literary texts are constructed from different discourses in dialogue with one another. Where the Russian formalists saw works of art as organic 'unities', complete in them-selves, Bakhtin insists that meaning always depends on context because language itself is 'dialogic'. Every utterance is part of a dialogue, dependent on previous statements and expecting a sub-sequent response. Bakhtin is best known for his writing on the novel, in which he distinguishes a 'monologic' form such as that of Tolstoy, where the author claims control of the various 'voices' of the text, from a 'dialogic' or 'polyphonic' form such as Dostoevski's, where 'heteroglossia' – a multiplicity of voices – prevails.[37]

Peter Garrett is one of several critics who have applied this theory to *Wuthering Heights*. He argues that 'to consider *Wuthering Heights* and other Victorian multiplot novels as dialogical forms requires us to follow the movement in which meaning is continually produced and effaced'.[38] Patricia Yaeger, in 'Violence in the Sitting Room: *Wuthering Heights* and the Woman's Novel', uses Bakhtin's view of the novel as 'a multi-voiced, multi-languaged form' to oppose other feminist critics such as Myra Jehlen and Rachel Brownstein, who see novel-reading as a 'danger' for women. Exploiting the dynamism of Bakhtin's model, Yaeger sees the novel as 'an emancipatory form which permits the woman novelist to refuse and revise other literary genres'.[39]

Dialogism and discourse theory, like deconstruction, build on some basic premises of structuralism – for instance the arbitrary nature of meaning – but they depart from it in stressing the *dynamic* nature of language – the fact that it is always in process. Theories which share this ambiguous relationship with structuralism are often called 'poststructuralist'. The other theory usually included under this umbrella is psychoanalysis, and although there is no 'straight-forwardly' psychoanalytic essay in this collection, psychoanalytic ideas are pervasive in most of the remaining essays.

Freudian psychoanalysis frustrates the ambitions of science by recognising that the human mind is not completely accessible to conscious understanding. There is, Freud says, an unconscious sector which motivates our actions in ways that can only be guessed at through 'unguarded' mental activities such as dreams. The unconscious is the repository for memories and ideas which are not accept-able to the culture an infant finds itself in, and Freud's theory is that adult human beings reach a state of 'adjustment' to society by a process of *repressing* those unacceptable elements. The most im-portant of these are sexual, and Freud scandalised his early readers by insisting that infants live a vivid sexual life and reach adulthood by mentally repeating the ancient Greek drama in which Oedipus blinds himself as punishment for killing his father and marrying his mother. The 'Oedipus complex' is Freud's name for the process by which children learn to situate themselves and acquire social identity by repressing desire for the parent of the opposite sex.[40] Where this repression is traumatic, it may produce symptoms in later life which are not intelligible to the sufferer. Freud's 'cure' was to encourage the patient to talk until the 'unspeakable' memory emerged into consciousness.

As a tool in literary criticism, psychoanalysis has gone through several phases. Because it is itself a kind of interpretation, it lends

itself to a hermeneutic approach to literature in which the critic, like
the analyst, searches the text for clues to its repressed meanings. The
mental state of the author or its principal character(s) may be seen as
the key to the text. Thomas Moser, for instance, in 'What is the
Matter with Emily Jane?' concludes that the author of *Wuthering
Heights* was suffering from sexual frustration.[41]

Carol Ohmann deals briskly with Moser in her essay, 'Emily
Brontë in the Hands of Male Critics',[42] but several feminist studies
from the 1960s and 70s also use psychoanalysis to 'interpret' the text
in a different way. Juliet Mitchell argues persuasively that psychoanalysis explains why the severely limited world of *Wuthering Heights*
strikes readers as having a 'cosmic' quality: 'the universe has become
the family, and a microcosm has become the cosmos.' For her,

> the nature and actions of every character in the drama are fully
> intelligible because they are always related to the total biographical
> development of the person and, above all, to what we now know to be
> the most critical phase of life: childhood.[43]

Juliet Mitchell's essay demonstrates how strong is our need for
intelligibility and thus why poststructuralist theories seem difficult.
Just as Kermode embraces a structuralist theory which says, 'there is
no central truth' and yet arrives at the conclusion, 'perhaps, after all
. . .', so Juliet Mitchell embraces Freudian theory, which says that
part of the mind is unknowable, and arrives at the conclusion that
the characters in *Wuthering Heights* are 'fully intelligible'.

Juliet Mitchell, however, later abandoned this position under the
influence of Jacques Lacan, the poststructuralist reinterpreter of
Freud. Lacan combined psychoanalysis with structural linguistics to
elaborate the reasons why our sense of individual 'wholeness' is an
illusion. We can only define our sense of self, he says, by leaving
behind the 'Imaginary' stage in which infants identify with an image
– of themselves, the mother or another child – and entering what he
calls the Symbolic realm, adopting a language which is always already there. I learn to express myself by saying 'I', by adopting a
pronoun which is equally available to you; my 'self' is therefore split
between the I who speaks and the 'I' who is the subject of the
sentence. The meaning of 'I' slips away between signifier and signified. Poststructuralist critics, therefore, do not expect psychoanalysis
to make the text 'fully intelligible'. They do use it, however, to point
to certain obsessively repetitive structures in literature, especially the
compulsive regression to what Lacan calls the 'mirror-phase' of

infancy, where the self is defined not through language but through the reflecting gaze of an other who 'is more myself than I am'.[44]

Michael Macovski, in the sixth essay in this collection, combines Lacanian psychoanalysis with Bakhtinian dialogism. He notes the unusual number of 'interpretive' situations in *Wuthering Heights*, each involving a teller and a listener who has to 'make sense' of a narrative, and suggests that the novel thus conforms to Bakhtin's account of dialogic self-creation, in which 'dialogue with the "existence . . . beyond" ' is necessary for self-definition. Macovski's combination of dialogism ('*speaking* to another') with Lacan's mirror-phase theory is not entirely straightforward, since for Lacan, the mirror-phase is, precisely, 'infantile' (Latin 'infans' means ' not speaking').[45] He argues, however, that the adult dialogues in *Wuthering Heights* 'initiate an interpretive re-enactment of past voices – a regress that ultimately extends back to that original dialogue with the self, that confrontation with the other which we experience during the "mirror stage" '.[46]

The novel does call for some such combination of theories to account for our sense that what the novel 'says' is somehow 'beyond words'. For most readers, the fascination of *Wuthering Heights* lies in its evocation of Romantic love, the state of being-in-another which psychoanalysis identifies as a powerful nostalgic re-enactment of the pre-linguistic symbiosis of mother and child.[47] Yet the novel is, necessarily, a structure of words; it can only gesture towards this pre-linguistic state in what is, strictly, linguistic nonsense: 'I *am* Heathcliff'.

Psychoanalytic critics believe that this desperate desire to recover a wholeness experienced as 'lost' explains not only why we fall in love, but also why we look for 'unity' in works of art and yearn for 'universal values'. As theorists come to recognise its importance in human motivation, they have increasingly focused attention on what Freud called the pre-Oedipal and Lacan the pre-Symbolic. Marxists and feminists in particular, who are concerned with discourse as a source of power, have wrestled with the problem of theorising how language articulates a pre-linguistic desire.

Bakhtin was a Marxist. He was interested in language because he recognised that words are the carriers of values, a 'site of struggle' between the classes. Unlike earlier Marxists, who assumed that literature simply 'reflects' a social reality, he recognised that the dialogue of discourses which constitutes literature *makes* history instead of describing it.[48] The later Marxist Louis Althusser, however, tried combining Bakhtin's idea of multiple discourses with

Lacanian psychoanalysis in an attempt to explain the hypnotic power of what he calls 'ideologies'. He argues that discourses give people an identity in a process analogous to the powerful 'mirror-phase' of infancy. Thus the discourse of Christianity, imagined as the gaze of God, 'identifies' the willing participant as 'a Christian'. Althusser argues that ideology reconciles people to their economic role by providing an 'imaginary' relationship to the real conditions of their existence.[49] Thus Christianity makes a virtue of affliction while the liberal humanist ideology of personal freedom conceals our economic bondage to capitalism. This is not a conspiracy theory; ideologies do not need to be imposed on people because we need them to 'make sense' of the world. It does, however, explain why we cling on to value-systems which do not always serve us well – they seem 'more myself than I am'.

Literature has a complex relationship with ideology. In so far as a text seeks to 'make sense', it is ideological, that is, working within a recognised discourse. All texts, however, contain contradictions which ideology cannot conceal, and it is for this reason that Marxist critics now see literature as 'semi-autonomous', not tied either to the economic 'base' of society or to its dominant ideologies. Criticism which looks for 'unity' in the text, however, obscures this dynamic potential, papering over the cracks to produce what is itself an ideological reading. The Marxist critic Pierre Macherey therefore argues that we should read the gaps and silences in texts not as clues to their potential 'wholeness' but as symptoms of the failure of ideology.[50]

At the beginning of his chapter on *Wuthering Heights*, which forms the seventh essay in this collection, Terry Eagleton distinguishes between Charlotte and Emily Brontë in ideological terms. Whereas Charlotte aims to resolve contradictions (such as Jane Eyre's simultaneous defiance *and* acceptance of social conventions) by recourse to the dominant ideology of individualism, Emily refuses this resolution by insisting that there is a dimension to life outside 'society'. Eagleton does give us an orthodox Marxist reading of Heathcliff's life as 'an extreme parody of capitalist activity', aping an ideology of self-help, enterprise and industry;[51] this is the equivalent of the 'sociological novel' which Q. D. Leavis rejects in favour of the 'human core'. Unlike Leavis, however, Eagleton is not prepared to discard the bits of the novel that do not 'fit' his reading, because it is here that, following Macherey, he finds the text's ideological resistance.

Eagleton argues that although Heathcliff can be read as participating in an economic structure, he can also, because of his unknown origins, be read as 'a purely atomised individual . . . outside the family and society in[ ] an opposing realm which can be adequately imaged only as "Nature" '. The novel thus offers a 'dialectical vision' in which two contradictory versions of reality are held in suspension; 'Heathcliff cannot represent at once an absolute metaphysical refusal of an inhuman society and a class which is intrinsically part of it'. It forces us to recognise that if 'available social languages are too warped and constrictive to be the bearers of love, freedom and equality . . . those values can be sustained only in the realms of myth and metaphysics'.[52] By recognising the ideology of 'escape to nature' as a response to an imprisoning society, Eagleton gives a social value to that ideology without endorsing it as 'truth'.[53] Implicit in this position is the idea that if society were less restrictive, this 'myth' would not be necessary. Like Matthews, therefore, Eagleton is arguing that the 'core' story (the 'myth') is causally related to the 'frame' (the social structure); but like Naomi Jacobs, he exposes the relation in the hope of changing it.[54]

Eagleton, despite his impeccably materialist analysis, still takes Heathcliff as the novel's central character, and he was famously taken to task for this by the Marxist-Feminist Literature Collective in 1977. The Collective argued that a Marxist analysis alone could not account for the oppression of women. While Marxism assumes that all social formations are determined by the relations of production as demonstrated in the workplace, feminism argues that the family constitutes a separate power-structure in which women are oppressed in the relations of *re*production.[55] It is, however, indicative of the uncertain position of *Wuthering Heights* in the developing feminist consciousness that the Collective chose *Jane Eyre* and *Shirley*, not *Wuthering Heights*, to represent 'Women's Writing' of 1848.[56] Similarly, Jenni Calder's *Women and Marriage in the Victorian Novel* (1976)[57] gives *Wuthering Heights* the merest mention, while Elaine Showalter, in a book dedicated to 'establishing a more . . . accurate and systematic literary history for women writers',[58] also deals with Charlotte but not Emily Brontë. It is as if these feminist critics are establishing their own 'great tradition', different from F. R. Leavis's, but still tending to see *Wuthering Heights*, as he did, as 'a kind of sport'.[59]

All this changes in 1979 with Sandra Gilbert and Susan Gubar's *The Madwoman in the Attic*.[60] Although its title derives, once more, from Charlotte rather than Emily, *The Madwoman* is an inclusive text. Whereas Showalter's *A Literature of Their Own* aimed at defining a female literary tradition, Gilbert and Gubar look at women writers in relation to the male mainstream. In particular they take issue with the American critic Harold Bloom, who, in *The Anxiety of Influence*, explains literary history as 'the crucial warfare of fathers and sons', in which younger writers struggle to resist the influence of their elders. Gilbert and Gubar point out that a woman writer in this context suffers 'an even more primary "anxiety of authorship" – a radical fear that she cannot create . . . not fight a male precursor on "his" terms and win'.[61] They read nineteenth-century texts by women as split between a (semi-)conforming heroine (like Jane Eyre) and a repressed and marginalised 'other' (like the first Mrs Rochester) who cannot be allowed to occupy centre stage, but who nevertheless registers the author's 'unspeakable' anger.

Identifying Milton's *Paradise Lost* as a culturally definitive 'story of woman's secondness',[62] *The Madwoman in the Attic* sees *Wuthering Heights* as a series of strategies for negotiating 'Milton's bogey'. Sandra Gilbert, who is the author of the chapter on *Wuthering Heights* which forms the eighth essay in this collection, argues that like *Paradise Lost*, 'the story of *Wuthering Heights* is built around a central fall'. The novel is thus in part 'a *Bildungsroman* about a girl's passage from "innocence" to "experience" '.[63] Unlike *Paradise Lost*, however, 'this fall . . . is not a fall into hell. It is a fall from "hell" into "heaven" '.[64] Because 'Emily Brontë thought in polarities',[65] it is easy for Gilbert to use structuralist techniques, reading Milton's theological 'hell and heaven' in terms of Lévi-Strauss's anthropological 'raw and cooked'.[66] Heaven, the 'cooked', is associated with patriarchy (the rule of the father, or male dominance in general), represented in *Wuthering Heights* by Edgar Linton. 'In Freudian terms', Gilbert argues, 'he would . . . be described as her superego, the internalised guardian of morality and culture, with Heathcliff, his opposite, functioning as her childish and desirous id'.[67]

Gilbert reads *Wuthering Heights* as an 'anti-Miltonic myth' in which an 'Original Mother (Catherine), a daughter of nature. . . . fell into a decline' and fragmented into several selves. The two generations of the novel offer us two possible outcomes of this myth. In the first, 'the fierce primordial selves [Catherine and Heathcliff] disappeared into nature, the perversely hellish heaven which was their home'. In the second, 'the more teachable and docile selves [Catherine II and Hareton] . . . moved into the fallen cultured world of parlours and parsonages, the Miltonic heaven which, from the Original

Mother's point of view, is really hell'.[68] For Gilbert, the second-generation story is a capitulation to an undesirable 'reality' which is undercut by angry rumbling echoes from the 'primordial selves' in the wilderness.

Although obviously influenced by structuralist and psychoanalytic theories, *The Madwoman in the Attic* does not advertise its theoretical underpinnings. By contrast, Margaret Homans's chapter on *Wuthering Heights* in *Bearing the Word* depends on a theoretical introduction in which she collates Lacanian psychoanalysis and object-relations theory, a variety of psychoanalysis heavily focused on the pre-Oedipal stage. Homans's version of Gilbert and Gubar's 'fall' into culture is the child's 'fall' into Lacan's Symbolic order. In the Lacanian version of Freud's Oedipus complex, the prohibition of incest opens a gap between child and mother which is bridged by the father's symbolic language. Language is thus 'a system for generating substitutes for the forbidden mother'.[69] Lacan sees girls as disadvantaged in the process of acquiring language, because they are less motivated than boys to give up the (incestuous) relationship with the mother. Homans, however, invokes the feminist object-relations psychologist Nancy Chodorow in order to argue that, on the contrary, daughters have the advantage of speaking 'two languages at once'.[70] Without quite confronting the problem that one of these 'languages' is strictly 'pre-linguistic', Homans reads women's texts as dramatising 'the hope that the father's law might cease to be the exclusive language of literary culture'.[71]

Like Gilbert, Homans finds 'the first Cathy's . . . refusal to enter . . . the Lacanian symbolic order' more inspiring than the second Cathy's acceptance of 'the father's law',[72] though a number of feminists have made more positive readings of the second generation story.[73] It is, however, Stevie Davies who provides a startling contrast to both Gilbert and Homans in her two books on Emily Brontë, and a chapter from the later of these books forms the penultimate essay in this collection.[74] It is now almost feminist orthodoxy to see nineteenth-century women writers as excluded and repressed by masculine culture, yet Davies argues that Emily Brontë was a 'free woman'. Like Juliet Mitchell, Davies sees *Wuthering Heights* as preoccupied with childhood and the family, and like Gilbert she acknowledges its story as 'stages of the fall'. She differs from them, however, in asserting the novel's positive strength, which she finds in its iconoclastic protest against the (father) God who has 'orphaned' his children, and in its celebration of 'a spiritual home

identifiable with the mother'. Drawing on protestant theology and
Emily Brontë's poetry, Davies argues that 'uniquely among mythopoeic
works of fiction *Wuthering Heights* raises the mother-principle . . . to
the status of deity, presenting it as the focal object of human aspira-
tion and the final end of Emily Brontë's language of desire'. In an
implicit answer to Homans, Davies argues that 'the tonality of the
novel's voices . . . is joyous'. Recognising (again implicitly) Lacan's
definition of language as a sign of loss (of mother-child bliss), she
argues that in *Wuthering Heights*, nevertheless, 'the act of writing
appears as the unique means of immortalising and authorising the
energies of childhood'. Words thus become 'a homeopathic . . .
remedy' for the very loss which they record.[75]

As the various theories interact with one another, it becomes
increasingly difficult to categorise critics, and Patricia Parker's essay,
the last in this collection, is perhaps best described simply as
poststructuralist. Its very title – 'The (Self-) Identity of the Literary
Text: Property, Proper Place, and Proper Name in *Wuthering Heights*'
– gestures towards many of the other essays we have discussed here.
Like Kermode she finds significance in proper names; like Eagleton
she looks at private property; like Leavis she recognises the humanist
'centrality' (identity) of the text and like Matthews she sees it as
meaning nothing but itself (self-identity). The essay is taken from a
book whose subtitle is 'Rhetoric, Gender, Property', terms which
again bring together discourse theory, feminism and Marxism. She
attends both to the philosophical and historical context of the novel
and to its textual detail.

We would be wrong, however, to look to this essay for a 'summing up' either of the novel or of recent criticism. Following Foucault,
Parker reads *Wuthering Heights* as functioning through older forms
of discourse, but following Derrida, she insists that the novel evokes
categories only to transgress them, becoming literally a 'preposterous' text which upsets our sense of what is 'proper'.[76] Recent criticism of *Wuthering Heights* is, perhaps, most clearly defined by this
unsettling quality which it shares with the novel, challenging us to
read in new ways and for purposes other than reaching fixed conclusions. The last sentence of Parker's essay is still 'moving us on'.
Wuthering Heights, it says, 'demands a reading which seeks to raise
more demons than it casts out'. This collection of essays aims to
provoke this kind of interrogative reading, in which readers are not
passive consumers but active participators in the construction of the
text.

NOTES

1. See Miriam Allott (ed.), *The Brontës: The Critical Heritage* (London, 1974), for criticism up to 1900.

2. The process of 'interpreting' texts through 'clues' is sometimes called 'hermeneutics'. The 'hermeneutic circle' is the interpretative process in which the details make sense only in relation to a (guessed-at) whole, while the whole is only knowable through the detail.

3. See C. P. Sanger, *The Structure of Wuthering Heights* (London, 1926) and Lord David Cecil, 'Emily Brontë', in *Early Victorian Novelists* (London, 1934).

4. F. R. Leavis, *The Great Tradition: George Eliot, Henry James, Joseph Conrad* (London, 1948; reprinted Harmondsworth, 1962), p. 38. Leavis is using the word 'sport' in the sense that a shoot of briar-rose growing from a cultivated garden plant is a sport – it is a reversion to nature, not breeding true.

5. G. Singh (ed.), in Q. D. Leavis, *Collected Essays*, vol. 1 (Cambridge, 1983), p. 1.

6. See p. 34 below.

7. See p. 30 below. Unlike Leavis, Robert Kiely, in *The Romantic Novel in England* (Cambridge, Mass., 1972), sees *Wuthering Heights* as 'perfect'; and Keith Sagar also sees the novel as 'marvellously coherent . . . like printing when all the colours are overlaid in perfect register' ('The Originality of *Wuthering Heights*', in *The Art of Emily Brontë*, ed. Anne Smith [London, 1976], p. 137). Although Kiely and Sagar seem to disagree with Leavis, however, these critics are all working within the same tradition of humanist criticism; they disagree about the success of this particular novel, but they are all using the same criteria of 'wholeness' and 'integrity'.

8. The result is what Ronald Frankenberg calls 'a fascinating combination of vulgar Marxism and elite sensitivity' ('Styles of Marxism, Styles of Criticism: *Wuthering Heights*: A Case Study', in *The Sociology of Literature: Applied Studies*, Monograph No. 26 [Keele, Staffs, 1978], p. 109).

9. See p. 34 below. Leavis argues that previous criticism, from Charlotte Brontë's 'Biographical Notice to *Wuthering Heights*' (1850) to Miriam Allott's essay, 'The Rejection of Heathcliff?' (1958), had too often assumed that Heathcliff was the centre of the novel.

10. See note 2, above.

11. See p. 39 below.

12. One of the most accessible structuralist works is Roland Barthes,

Mythologies (1957), trans. Annette Lavers (London, 1973), in which he 'reads' non-linguistic sign-systems such as fashion or cooking.

13. The huge significance which cultures invest in minute differences is demonstrated by the joke about the dyslexic agnostic insomniac, who lay awake wondering if there was a dog.

14. Eskimos distinguish between many different substances which for us are the same, because we have only one word for it – 'snow'. See Terence Hawkes, *Structuralism and Semiotics* (London, 1977).

15. See p. 34 below.

16. See p. 48 below.

17. 'Dog' can mean a person, or a kind of metal tool, as well as a four-legged animal, for instance – so what does 'Heathcliff' 'mean'?

18. So that the signifier 'Heathcliff' is 'supplemented' by 'man', 'beast', 'devil', 'rock', 'more myself than I am', etc.

19. See p. 51 below.

20. See Terry Eagleton, *Literary Theory* (Oxford, 1983), pp. 199ff., for a discussion of 'pluralism' in a political context.

21. The value-judgement becomes more obvious with a politically sensitive opposition such as 'masculine:feminine'; in every culture 'masculine' is the preferred term, the norm against which feminine things are measured. This example is taken from Terry Eagleton, *Literary Theory*, p. 132.

22. Film-makers, for instance, generally ignore or drastically reduce the 'frame' element and I myself have cut the sections of Matthews's essay which relate to the frame more heavily than those relating to the 'core'.

23. J. Hillis Miller, '*Wuthering Heights*: Repetition and the "Uncanny" ', in *Fiction and Repetition in Seven English Novels* (Cambridge, Mass., 1982), pp. 52, 68, 69. See Sigmund Freud, 'The Uncanny' (1919).

24. In E. M. Forster's novel, *A Passage to India*, ch. 14 (1924; reprinted Harmondsworth, 1971), p. 147.

25. P. 68 below.

26. Linda H. Peterson gives a useful introduction to deconstructionist criticism in her critical edition of *Wuthering Heights* ([New York; Basingstoke and London, 1992], pp. 359–70).

27. Carol Jacobs, '*Wuthering Heights*: At the Threshold of Interpretation', *boundary 2*, 7 (Spring 1979); reprinted in *Emily Brontë's Wuthering Heights*, ed. Harold Bloom (New York, 1987), pp. 99–118. Carol Jacobs offers yet another deconstructive critique of Kermode. Kermode reads the proper names of *Wuthering Heights* as a 'hermeneutic prom-

ise' which the text seems to fulfil (it begins and ends with 'Hareton Earnshaw') at the same time as it opens up a 'plurality of significances'. In place of this 'largesse of liberalism' (p. 103), Jacobs argues that the 'reality' promised by the text always proves to be another text; 'the name . . . eliminates its referent, leaving room neither for plurality nor significance' (p. 106). Finally, 'no limits [can be] set to the voracious realm of fiction . . . [which] threatens to . . . assimilate the "real" ' (p. 118).

28. Such a double procedure is in fact suggested by the two terms ('destruction'/'construction') which Derrida sought to hold in tension in his invented word 'deconstruction'.

29. See Terry Eagleton, *Literary Theory* (Oxford, 1983), p. 210.

30. See p. 74 below.

31. Terry Eagleton, *Literary Theory* (Oxford, 1983), p. 210.

32. See Paul Rabinow (ed.), *The Foucault Reader* (1986; reprinted Harmondsworth, 1991); also Chris Weedon, *Feminist Practice and Poststructuralist Theory* (Oxford, 1987). Criticism of Renaissance texts from this perspective is sometimes called 'New Historicist', but most critics of the nineteenth century prefer to call themselves 'materialist' or 'cultural' critics. Terry Eagleton revives the ancient term 'rhetoric' to describe the practice of analysing linguistic activity which he, like Foucault, sees as 'a form of power'. (Terry Eagleton, *Literary Theory* [Oxford, 1983], p. 206.)

33. Heather Glen (ed.), 'Introduction', *Wuthering Heights* (Routledge English Texts Series [London, 1988]).

34. Nancy Armstrong, 'Emily Brontë in and out of her time', *Genre*, 15 (1982), 243–64. Carol Senf, in 'Emily Brontë's Version of Feminist History: *Wuthering Heights*', *Essays in Literature*, 12 (1985), 204–14, argues that the 'domestic' ending to the novel represents 'a softening – a feminising – of patriarchal history' as represented by the violent world of the 'core' story.

35. Lyn Pykett, *Emily Brontë* (Basingstoke and London, 1989), p. 133. She is referring to Nancy Armstrong's later book, *Desire and Domestic Fiction* (New York, 1987), which does not deal extensively with *Wuthering Heights*.

36. Lyn Pykett, *Emily Brontë* (Basingstoke and London, 1989), p. 17.

37. Mikhail Bakhtin, *Problems of Dostoevski's Poetics* (1929); see Raman Selden, *A Reader's Guide to Contemporary Literary Theory* (Hemel Hempstead, 1989). Even Q. D. Leavis acknowledges the play of discourses in *Wuthering Heights*, though for her this is a fault, so that only 'candour obliges us to admit' it (see p. 25 below).

38. Peter Garrett, *The Victorian Multi-Plot Novel: Studies in Dialogical Form* (New Haven, Conn., 1980), p. 20.

39. Patricia Yaeger, 'Violence in the Sitting Room: *Wuthering Heights* and the Woman's Novel', *Genre*, 21 (1988), 203, 209. (See Myra Jehlen, 'Archimedes and the Paradox of Feminist Criticism', in *The Signs Reader*, ed. Abel and Abel [1983]; and Rachel Brownstein, *Becoming a Heroine* [Harmondsworth, 1984].)

40. The structuralist anthropologist Claude Lévi-Strauss also argues that the ultimate social structure is the incest taboo, which forbids marriage with close kin, and produces a basic binary opposition between groups of people who can and cannot marry. An analysis of *Wuthering Heights* using Lévi-Strauss's theories about incest can be found in William R. Goetz, 'Genealogy and Incest in *Wuthering Heights*', *SNNTS: Studies in the Novel* (North Texas State University), 14 (Winter 1982), 359–76.

41. Thomas Moser, 'What is the Matter with Emily Jane?', *Nineteenth-Century Fiction*, 17 (1962), 1–19.

42. Carol Ohmann, 'Emily Brontë in the Hands of Male Critics', *College English*, 32 (1971), 906–13.

43. Juliet Mitchell, '*Wuthering Heights*: Romanticism and Rationality', in *Women: the Longest Revolution* (1966; reprinted London, 1984), pp. 128, 143–4. See also Helen Moglen, 'The Double Vision of *Wuthering Heights*: A Clarifying View of Female Development', *Centennial Review*, 15 (Fall 1971), 391–405; Carolyn Heilbrun, 'The Woman as Hero', in *Toward a Recognition of Androgyny* (New York, 1973), pp. 49–112; and Ellen Moers, who reads the novel 'as a statement of a very serious kind about a girl's childhood and the adult woman's tragic yearning to return to it. . . . The gratuitous cruelties of the novel thus are justified as realistic attributes of the nursery world – and as frankly joyous memories of childhood eroticism' (Ellen Moers, *Literary Women* [London, 1978], p. 106).

44. Perhaps because the 'mirror-phase' theory fits Catherine and Heathcliff so perfectly, no one seems to have made this 'obvious' analysis. Philip Wion, in 'The Absent Mother in Emily Brontë's *Wuthering Heights*', *American Imago*, 42 (1985), 143–64, argues that the Catherine–Heathcliff relationship is 'a displaced version of the symbiotic relationship between mother and child' (p. 146), but he argues from the position of object-relations theory, not the Lacanian Imaginary. (See Judith Kegan Gardiner, 'Mind Mother: psychoanalysis and feminism', in *Making a Difference: Feminist Literary Criticism*, ed. Gayle Greene and Coppélia Kahn [London, 1985], pp. 113–45 for an account of object relations theory.) Leo Bersani, in *A Future for Astyanax: Character and Desire in Literature* (Boston, 1976), uses Lacan to investigate 'the deconstructed self'; he reads the repetitions of *Wuthering Heights*

as representing 'the danger of being haunted by alien versions of the self' (p. 208).

45. Macovski argues that because Emily Brontë's characters define themselves in dialogue with others, her 'concept of self is thus essentially plural, social in the broadest sense' (see below, p. 109). Other critics, however, have used the mirror-phase as a way of defining not the social breadth, but the self-enclosure, of the Romantic theories Macovski also refers to. (See, for instance, Diane Long Hoeveler, *Romantic Androgyny: The Women Within* [University Park and London, 1990].) Barbara Schapiro argues that it is only the second Catherine who achieves a social definition of self, because her 'dialogue' with Hareton is explicitly linguistic. ('The Rebirth of Catherine Earnshaw: Splitting and Reintegration of Self in *Wuthering Heights*', *Nineteenth-Century Studies*, 3 [1989], 37–51.)

46. See below, p. 107.

47. Heather Glen gives a good, non-technical description of this process in the 'Critical Commentary' in her edition of *Wuthering Heights* (London, 1988), pp. 360–1.

48. See Terry Eagleton, *Marxism and Literary Criticism* (London, 1976); and Linda H. Peterson (ed.), *Wuthering Heights* (Boston; Basingstoke and London, 1992), pp. 385–99, for comment on Marxist literary criticism.

49. See Louis Althusser, *Essays on Ideology* (London, 1984); also Catherine Belsey, *Critical Practice* (London, 1980).

50. Pierre Macherey, trans. G. Wall, *A Theory of Literary Production* (London, 1978).

51. Terry Eagleton, *Myths of Power* (London and Basingstoke, 1975), p. 114.

52. See pp. 120–1, 128–9 below.

53. Though he implicitly endorses 'love, freedom and equality'. Heather Glen writes illuminatingly about the persistence of such 'universals' in apparently 'historicist' criticism in the Introduction to her edition of *Wuthering Heights* (London, 1988), p. 12 and *passim*.

54. The Marxist concept of 'dialectics' means that where Matthews sees oppositions (frame and core) endlessly dissolving into one another (see above, p. 5), Eagleton sees the opposed elements eventually giving rise to a new order.

55. Ten years after *Myths of Power*, Eagleton wrote the editorial introduction to James Kavanagh's *Emily Brontë* (Oxford, 1985), an idiosyncratic (some would say outrageous) book which demonstrates how far Marxist criticism has come since then. It is an ambitious attempt to

combine the insights of Marxism, feminism, psychoanalysis and poststructuralism. Kavanagh makes the link between class and gender through the concept of 'desire', which is both sexual and economic. The 'peculiar power' of the novel, according to Kavanagh, 'derives from its reluctance to imagine any stable, "compromise" resolution that would deny the integrity and tenacity of the psycho-sexual and socio-ideological tensions that constitute the novel' (p. 96). Although Kavanagh adopts Marxist and feminist categories of analysis, his book is not political in the sense of urgently advocating change.

56. Marxist-Feminist Literature Collective, 'Women's Writing', in *The Sociology of Literature: 1848*, ed. Francis Barker *et al.* (Essex, 1978).

57. Jenni Calder, *Women and Marriage in the Victorian Novel* (London, 1976).

58. Elaine Showalter, *A Literature of Their Own* (London, 1978), p. 8.

59. F. R. Leavis, *The Great Tradition* (London, 1948), p. 27.

60. Sandra Gilbert and Susan Gubar, *The Madwoman in the Attic: The Woman Writer and the Nineteenth-Century Literary Imagination* (Yale, 1979).

61. Ibid., pp. 47–9.

62. Ibid., p. 191.

63. See below, p. 132. A *Bildungsroman* is a novel of 'upbringing' or youthful development.

64. See below, p. 133.

65. See below, p. 142.

66. One of Claude Lévi-Strauss's binary oppositions is between nature and culture, the raw and the cooked (*The Raw and the Cooked: Introduction to A Science of Mythology* (New York, 1969).

67. See below, p. 145. Freud uses the Latin 'id' (it) to mean a person's instinctual drives as opposed to the 'ego' (Latin for 'I'), which is constructed from the need to regulate these drives. See Terry Eagleton, *Literary Theory* (Oxford, 1983), for an account of Freudian terminology.

68. See p. 156 below. The 'split selves' which are treated mythically by Sandra Gilbert are explained more technically by Barbara Schapiro in 'The Rebirth of Catherine Earnshaw: Splitting and Reintegration of Self in Wuthering Heights', *Nineteenth-Century Studies*, 3 (1989), 37–51.

69. Margaret Homans, 'The Name of the Mother in *Wuthering Heights*', in *Bearing the Word: Language and Female Experience in Nineteenth-Century Women's Writing* (London and Chicago, 1986), p. 7.

70. See Judith Kegan Gardiner, 'Mind Mother: psychoanalysis and fem-

inism', in *Making a Difference: Feminist Literary Criticism*, ed. Gayle Greene and Coppélia Kahn (London, 1985), pp. 113–45 for an account of Chodorow's theories.

71. Margaret Homans, *Bearing the Word: Language and Female Experience in Nineteenth-Century Women's Writing* (London and Chicago, 1986), p. 33.

72. Ibid., p. 68. Leo Bersani, in *A Future for Astyanax* (Boston, 1976), also sees the ending of the novel as a capitulation to the conventional 'novelistic tradition' (p. 221).

73. See, for instance, Carol Senf, 'Emily Brontë's Version of Feminist History: *Wuthering Heights*', *Essays in Literature*, 12 (1985), 204–14; and Barbara Schapiro, 'The Rebirth of Catherine Earnshaw: Splitting and Reintegration of Self in *Wuthering Heights*', *Nineteenth-Century Studies*, 3 (1989), 37–51.

74. Stevie Davies, *Emily Brontë: The Artist as a Free Woman* (Manchester, 1983); *Emily Brontë* (Key Women Writers Series) (Hemel Hempstead, 1988).

75. See below, pp. 162, 171, and also Stevie Davies, *Emily Brontë* (Hemel Hempstead, 1988), pp. 25, 89–90.

76. Latin 'pre-' means 'before', 'post-' means 'after'. 'Preposterous' therefore means 'putting things back-to-front'.

1

A Fresh Approach to 'Wuthering Heights'

Q. D. LEAVIS

After its initial adverse reception ('too odiously and abominably pagan to be palatable to the most vitiated class of English reader' – *The Quarterly Review*) and its subsequent installation as a major English classic (of such mystic significance that while its meaning transcends criticism adverse comment on any concrete features would be in the worst taste), *Wuthering Heights*, to my knowledge as a university teacher of English Literature, seems to be coming under attack from a new generation. To those who find the novel mainly melodrama, complain that the violence is factitious or sadistic, or object (with justice) to the style as often stilted and uneven, and to those who can see no coherent intention but find incompatible fragments and disjointed intentions at different levels of seriousness, an answer that the novel's greatness is unquestionable is useless. Some of these charges cannot be altogether refuted, though they can be generally accounted for as inevitable features of the kind of undertaking by such a writer at such a date, and some agreement reached about the nature of the success of the book on the whole: for that *Wuthering Heights* is a striking achievement of some kind, candid readers can and do feel. The difficulty of establishing that a literary work is a classic is nothing compared to the difficulty of establishing *what kind* of a classic it is – what is in fact the nature of its success, what kind of creation it represents. One has only to read the admiring critics of *Wuthering Heights*, even more the others, to see that there is no agreed reading of this novel at all. Desperate attempts to report a flawless work of art lead to a dishonest ignoring of recalcitrant elements or an interpretation of them which is sophistical; other and more sustained sophistry has resulted from such academic bright ideas as the one confidently asserted to me in an American university by a professor of English Literature who had discovered that 'The clue to *Wuthering Heights* is that Nelly Dean is Evil'.

Of course, in general one attempts to achieve a reading of a text which includes all its elements, but here I believe we must be satisfied with being able to account for some of them and concentrate on what remains. It is better to admit that some of the difficulties of grasping what is truly creative in *Wuthering Heights* are due to the other parts – to the author in her inexperience having made false starts, changing her mind (as tone and style suggest) probably because of rewriting from earlier stories with themes she had lost interest in and which have become submerged, though not assimilated, in the final work.[1] Another source of confusion to the reader is that she tried to do too much, too many different things (a common trouble in first novels and in most Victorian novels) and that some of these interfere with her deeper intentions – though of course this is also one source of the richness of this novel and we wouldn't care to sacrifice many of these, I think. The novel has all the signs of having been written at different times (because in different styles) and with varying intentions; we must sort these out in order to decide what *is* the novel. In spite of the brilliantly successful timeshifts and what has been called, not very happily, the 'Chinese box' ingenuity of construction, it certainly isn't a seamless 'work of art', and candour obliges us to admit ultimately that some things in the novel are incompatible with the rest, so much so that one seems at times to find oneself in really different novels.

I would first like to clear out of the way the *confusions* of the plot and note the different levels on which the novel operates at different times. It seems clear to me that Emily Brontë had some trouble in getting free of a false start – a start which suggests that we are going to have a regional version of the sub-lot of *Lear* (Shakespeare being generally the inspiration for those early nineteenth-century novelists who rejected the eighteenth-century idea of the novel). In fact, the Lear-world of violence, cruelty, unnatural crimes, family disruption and physical horrors remains the world of the household at Wuthering Heights, a characteristic due not to sadism or perversion in the novelist (some of the physical violence is quite unrealised)[2] but to the

Shakespearian intention. The troubles of the Earnshaws started when the father brought home the boy Heathcliff (of which he gives an unconvincing explanation and for whom he shows an unaccountable weakness) and forced him on the protesting family; Heathcliff 'the cuckoo' by intrigue soon ousts the legitimate son Hindley and, like Edmund, Gloucester's natural son in *Lear*, his malice brings about the ruin of two families (the Earnshaws and the Lintons, his rival getting the name Edgar by attraction from *Lear*). Clearly, Heathcliff was originally the illegitimate son and Catherine's half-brother, which would explain why, though so attached to him by early associations and natural sympathies, Catherine never really thinks of him as a possible lover either before or after marriage;[3] it also explains why all the children slept in one bed at the Heights till adolescence, we gather (we learn later from Catherine [ch. 12] that being removed at puberty from this bed became a turning point in her inner life, and this is only one of the remarkable insights which *Wuthering Heights* adds to the Romantic poets' exploration of childhood experience). The favourite Romantic theme of incest therefore must have been the impulsion behind the earliest conception of *Wuthering Heights*. Rejecting this story for a more mature intention, Emily Brontë was left with hopeless inconsistencies on her hands, for while Catherine's feelings about Heathcliff are never sexual (though she feels the bond of sympathy with a brother to be more important to her than her feelings for her young husband), Heathcliff's feelings for her are always those of a lover. As Heathcliff has been written out as a half-brother, Catherine's innocent refusal to see that there is anything in her relation to him incompatible with her position as a wife, becomes preposterous and the impropriety which she refuses to recognise is translated into social terms – Edgar thinks the kitchen the suitable place for Heathcliff's reception by Mrs Linton while she insists on the parlour. Another trace of the immature draft of the novel is the fairy-tale opening of the Earnshaw story, where the father, like the merchant in *Beauty and the Beast*, goes off to the city promising to bring his children back the presents each has commanded: but the fiddle was smashed and the whip lost so the only present he brings for them is the Beast himself, really a 'prince in disguise' (as Nelly tells the boy he should consider himself rightly); Catherine's tragedy then was that she forgot her prince and he was forced to remain the monster, destroying her; invoking this pattern brought in much more from the fairy-tale world of magic folk-lore and ballads, the oral tradition of the folk, that the Brontë children learnt principally from their nurses and their servant Tabby.[4] This element surges up in chapter 12, the important scene of Catherine's illness, where the dark superstitions about premonitions of death, about ghosts and primitive beliefs about the soul, come into play so significantly;[5] and again in the excessive attention given to Heathcliff's goblin-characteristics and especially to the prolonged account of his uncanny obsession and death. That this last should have an air of being infected by Hoffmann too is not surprising in a contemporary of Poe's; Emily is likely to have read Hoffmann when studying German at the Brussels boarding-school and certainly read the ghastly supernatural stories by James Hogg and others in the magazines at home. It is a proof of her immaturity at the time of the original conception of *Wuthering Heights* that she should express real psychological insights in such inappropriate forms.

In the novel as we read it Heathcliff's part either as Edmund in *Lear* or as the Prince doomed to Beast's form, is now suspended in boyhood while another influence, very much of the period, is developed, the Romantic image of childhood,[6] with a corresponding change of tone. Heathcliff and Catherine are idyllically and innocently happy together (and see also the end of chapter 5) roaming the countryside as hardy, primitive Wordsworthian children, 'half savage and hardy and free'. Catherine recalls it longingly when she feels she is dying trapped in Thrushcross Grange. (This boy Heathcliff is of course not assimilable with the vicious, scheming and morally heartless – 'simply insensible' – boy of chapter 4 who plays Edmund to old Earnshaw's Gloucester.) Catherine's dramatic introduction to the genteel world of Thrushcross Grange – narrated with contempt by Heathcliff who is rejected by it as a plough-boy unfit to associate with Catherine – is the turning point in her life in *this* form of the novel; her return, got up as a young lady in absurdly unsuitable clothes for a farmhouse life, and 'displaying fingers wonderfully whitened with doing nothing and staying indoors'[7] etc. visibly separates her from the 'natural' life, as her inward succumbing to the temptations of social superiority and riches parts her from Heathcliff. Heathcliff's animus against his social degradation by his new master Hindley is barbed by his being made to suffer (like Pip at the hands of Estella in *Great Expectations*)[8] taunts and insults – mainly from Edgar Linton – based on class and externals alone. They are suffered again (thus making Emily Brontë's point inescapable) in the second half of the novel by Hindley's son Hareton at the hands of Catherine's and Edgar's daughter Cathy as well as from his other cousin Linton

Heathcliff, Isabella's son. And this makes us sympathetic to Heathcliff as later to Hareton; we identify here with Nelly who with her wholesome classlessness and her spontaneous maternal impulses supports Heathcliff morally while he is ill-used (and even tries to persuade Catherine not to let Edgar supplant him in her life) – she retains this generous sympathy for him until she transfers it to her foster-child Hareton when in turn he becomes a victim (of Heathcliff's schemes). Her sympathy for Heathcliff's hard luck, even when she sees that his return is a threat to the Lintons' happiness, is at odds with her loyalty to her new master Edgar, and leads her to consent to some ill-advised interviews between Catherine and the desperate Heathcliff – though she also feels that to consent to help him there is the lesser of two evils (as it probably was), and she has no doubts about her duty to protect Isabella from becoming Heathcliff's victim.

Nelly Dean is most carefully, consistently and convincingly created for us as the normal woman, whose truly feminine nature satisfies itself in nurturing all the children in the book in turn.[9] To give this salience we have the beginning of chapter 8 when the farm-girl runs out to the hayfield where Nelly is busy to announce the birth of 'a grand bairn' and to give her artless (normal feminine) congratulations to Nelly for being chosen to nurse it since it will soon be motherless: 'I wish I were you, because it will be all yours when there is no missus.' Nelly's greater sensibility in realising that from the bairn's point of view this is not altogether a matter for rejoicing is shown in the next chapter when she says 'I went into the kitchen, and sat down to lull my little lamb to sleep . . . I was rocking Hareton on my knee, and humming a song that began

"It was far in the night, and the bairnies grat,
The mither beneath the mools heard that . . ." '

The ballad is evidently one expressing the widespread belief, in folk-song and folk-tale, that a prematurely dead mother cannot rest in the grave but returns to suckle the babe or help her child in the hour of need,[10] an indication of what is going on in Nelly's compassionate mind. But the whole episode of Hareton's birth and childhood exposes Catherine's insensibility, that her self-centred nature is essentially loveless. (Her only reference to her own pregnancy later is the hope that a son's birth will 'erase Isabella's title' to be Edgar's heir.) Yet Nelly's limitations are made clear and the novelist's distinct position of true insight, where necessary. Like Dolly in *Anna Karenina*

who is also the normal maternal woman, Nelly is inevitably too
terre-à-terre (Vronsky's complaint about Dolly), therefore unable to
sympathise with difficulties that seem to her the result only of will,
and a perverse will at that ('I should not have spoken so, if I had
known her true condition, but I could not get rid of the notion that
she acted a part of her disorder'). These limitations and not ill-will
are of course the reason why Nelly makes some mistakes in trying to
act for the best in situations where no easy or right solution offered
itself. But in doing Catherine full justice ('she was not artful, never
played the coquette') and giving her sound advice in her 'perplexities
and untold troubles', Nelly convinces us of her right to take a
thoroughly disenchanted view of Catherine's disposition. In fact,
both Heathcliff and Edgar know the truth about Catherine and
Hindley is under no illusions – 'You lie, Cathy, no doubt' he remarks
(correctly) of her explanation of Edgar Linton's visit in his absence.
One of the most successful indications of the passage of time is Nelly
Dean's change, from the quick-moving and quick-witted girl who for
little Hareton's sake copes with the drunken murderous Hindley, to
the stout, breathless, middle-aged woman who, though still spirited,
cannot save Cathy from a forced marriage.

   To hark back to Heathcliff: it follows from this 'social' development of the theme that Heathcliff should go out into the world to
make his fortune and come back to avenge himself, 'a cruel hard
landlord', 'near, close-handed' and given over to 'avarice, meanness
and greed', plotting to secure the property of both Earnshaws and
Lintons and also to claim equality with them socially – we are now
in the Victorian world of *Great Expectations* where money, as
Magwitch the convict learnt, makes a gentleman. Emily Brontë took
no trouble to explain the hiatus in Heathcliff's life – irrelevant to her
purposes – and in fact it is enough for us to gather that he comes
back a professional gambler at cards; a real flaw however is wholly
inadequate illustration of the shared life and interests of himself and
Catherine that makes it plausible that on his return she should be so
absorbed in conversing with him as to cut out immediately and
altogether her young husband. After all, we reflect, they couldn't
always have been talking about their childhood escapades – that is to
say, we recognise a failure in creative interest here in the novelist; nor
do we ever hear what they talk about till Catherine attacks him over
Isabella and they quarrel, when it becomes clear even to Catherine
that he can be only the monster he has been made by his history. This
aspect of him is kept before us from now till the end and accounts for

his brutalities and violent outbreaks. For various reasons, therefore, after envisaging several alternative conceptions of Heathcliff, Emily Brontë ended by keeping and making use of them all, so that like Dostoievski's Stavrogin he is an enigmatic figure only by reason of his creator's indecision, like Stavrogin in being an unsatisfactory composite with empty places in his history and no continuity of character. And like Iago and Stavrogin, Heathcliff has been made the object of much misdirected critical industry on the assumption that he is not merely a convenience. There is nothing enigmatic about either Catherine, we note, and this points to the novelist's distribution of her interest.

There are various signs that the novelist intended to stress the aspect of her theme represented by the corruption of the child's native goodness by Society and to make this part of the explanation of Catherine's failure in life. She evidently had in mind the difficulties and dangers inevitable in civilising children to enter the artificial world of class, organised religion, social intercourse and authoritarian family life. This is the point of Catherine's childhood journal that Lockwood reads, which gives a caricature of the torments suffered by children in the enforcement of the Puritan Sabbath, and another caricature is the account given by the boy Heathcliff of the parlour life of the broken-in Linton children as seen from the other side of the window by a Noble Savage whose natural good instincts have not been destroyed like theirs. More impressive is the beautifully rendered exemplary relation between the child Catherine and the adults as reported by Nelly in chapter 5. Her father's attempts to improve her, or tame her to an approved pattern,[11] resulted only in 'a naughty delight to provoke him: she was never so happy as when we were all scolding her at once, and she defying us with her bold, saucy look, and her ready words; turning Joseph's religious curses into ridicule, baiting me, and doing just what her father hated most' – 'Mr Earnshaw did not understand jokes from his children', Nelly notes, 'he had always been strict and grave with them'.

> After behaving as badly as possible all day, she sometimes came fondling to make it up at night. 'Nay, Cathy' the old man would say, 'I cannot love thee; go, say thy prayers, child, and ask God's pardon. I doubt thy mother and I must rue that we ever reared thee!' That made her cry, at first; and then, being repulsed continually hardened her, and she laughed if I told her to say she was sorry for her faults, and beg to be forgiven . . . It pleased the master rarely to see her gentle – saying 'Why canst thou not always be a good lass, Cathy?' And she

turned up her face to his, and laughed, and answered, 'Why cannot you always be a good man, father?'

We note that the child is allowed the last word – and a very telling rejoinder it is. Emily Brontë, the girl in the family most sympathetic to the black-sheep brother, was the most recalcitrant to the domestic training of her rigid aunt, to schooling, and to orthodox religion; she had plainly thought about the psychological effects of conventional disciplines and taken this opportunity to report adversely in the strongest terms a novelist can use – by showing their part in destroying the possibilities of a happy childhood and maturity.

But this originally naïve and commonplace subject – the Romantics' image of childhood in conflict with society – becomes something that in this novel is neither superficial nor theoretic because the interests of the responsible novelist gave it, as we have seen above, a new insight, and also a specific and informed sociological content. The theme is here very firmly rooted in time and place and richly documented: we cannot forget that Gimmerton and the neighbourhood are so bleak that the oats are always green there three weeks later than anywhere else, and that old Joseph's Puritan preachings accompany his 'overlaying his large Bible with dirty bank-notes, the produce of the day's transactions' at market; and we have a thoroughly realistic account of the life indoors and outdoors at Wuthering Heights as well as at the gentleman's residence at the Grange. In fact, there would be some excuse for taking this, the pervasive and carefully maintained sociological theme which fleshes the skeleton, for the real novel. This novel, which could be extracted by cutting away the rest, was deliberately built, to advance a thesis, on the opposition between Wuthering Heights and Thrushcross Grange, two different cultures of which the latter inevitably supersedes the former. The point about dating this novel as ending in 1801 (instead of its being contemporary with the Brontës' own lives) – and much trouble was taken to keep the dates, time-scheme and externals such as legal data, accurate[12] – is to fix its happenings at a time when the old rough farming culture based on a naturally patriarchal family life, was to be challenged, tamed and routed by social and cultural changes that were to produce the Victorian class consciousness and 'unnatural' idea of gentility.[13]

The inspiration for this structure, based on a conflict between, roughly speaking, a wholesome primitive and natural unit of a healthy society and its very opposite, felt to be an unwholesome refinement of the parasitic 'educated', comes from observation – in the Brontës' youth and county the old order visibly survived.[14] But the clue to making such perceptions and sympathies into a novel was found, I suspect, in Scott, whose novels and poetry were immensely admired by Charlotte and Emily. His own sympathies were with the wild rough Border farmers, not only because they represented a romantic past of balladry. He felt that civilisation introduced there entailed losses more than gains, and a novel where – before, with characteristic lack of staying power, he divagated from a serious theme into tushery – he made some effort to express this, *The Black Dwarf*, has long been known as the source for surnames used in *Wuthering Heights*. Scott's Earnscliffe (= Eaglescliff) and Ellieslaw suggested Heathcliff[15] and Earnshaw no doubt, but more important is their suggesting, it seems to me, that Emily Brontë found part of her theme in that novel's contrast between a weak, corrupt, refined upper-class, and the old-style Border farmers' 'natural' or socially primitive way of life in which feuds and violence were a recognised part of the code (though transacted for the most part strictly according to rule and tradition and quite compatible with good-humour and a generous humanity); there, the rich and great live in their castles, are treacherous, and come to grief, the rough Borderers, eking out subsistence farming by hunting, suffer drastic ups and downs with hardihood and survive; the setting is on the moors and hills, and an essential element in establishing the primitive social condition of the Borderers is the superstition and folk-lore believed in by them all. Now the Yorkshire moors with the hardy yeomen farmers of pre-Victorian times who had lived thereabouts and whose histories Tabby used to tell the Brontë children[16] in her broad dialect, must have seemed to them not essentially different from Scott's Border farmers. Emily and Charlotte were genuinely attached to their moorland country but Scott's example was what made it usable for them as literature and gave it rich associations, so it is natural that in her first attempt at a novel Emily should draw on even a poor fiction like *The Black Dwarf* to give meaning and purpose to her feelings about what was happening or had happened recently to the world she lived in. It is proof of her development out of her day-dream world of the Gondals that she was thus interested in the real world and roused to the need to enquire into the true nature of the change, perhaps as a way to alert her own (Early Victorian) generation to what this was. From being a self-indulgent storytelling, *Wuthering Heights* thus became a responsible piece of work, and the writer thought herself into the positions, outlooks, sufferings and tragedies of the actors in these typical events as an *artist*.

But if we were to take the sociological novel as the real novel and relegate the Heathcliff–Catherine–Edgar relationship and the corresponding Cathy–Linton–Hareton one, as exciting but ex-centric dramatic episodes, we should be misconceiving the novel and slighting it, for it is surely these relationships and their working out that give all the meaning to the rest. For instance, though Cathy has in the second half to unlearn, very painfully, the assumptions of superiority on which she has been brought up at the Grange, this is only part of her schooling; it is only incidental to the process by which we see her transcend the psychological temptations and the impulses which would have made her repeat her mother's history; and this is not a question of sociology or social history but is timeless.

Another misconception for which the novelist gives little excuse is to attribute a mystique to the moor; the moor is not meaningful like Hawthorne's forests that surround the Puritan settlements in the wild, it is not even powerful over man's destiny like Egdon Heath. The moor is a way of pointing a distinction: to the child Cathy brought up in the gentleman's park at the Grange, the moor means freedom from restraint, and romantic Nature to which she longs to escape, and in which she delights, but to the people who live there of necessity it is something they have to wrest a living out of: in the long run man lives by farming, and the farmhouse at the Heights is braced against the challenge the extreme conditions there represent (for instance, on our first sight of it we see that the architecture is determined by the violence of the winds). Lockwood (characteristically) demands that the farm should provide him with a guide home when, though snow threatened, he foolishly paid a call, and he thinks, as we at first do, that the refusal is brutal and wanton; but there is no guide to spare – the hands are needed to get in the sheep before the animals are snowed under and to see to the horses. Similarly, when Cathy in her thoughtlessness uses her new power over Hareton to get him to pull up the fruit-bushes to make her a flower-garden, old Joseph, who has worked all his life at the Heights and meant to die there, is so outraged that he gives notice rather than stay to witness such a sinful proceeding as to sacrifice food to flowers. Unattractive as Joseph usually is, his disinterested identification with the family's well-being is impressive and as so often he is the vehicle for expressing a truth to which we need to have our attention called: here, that where fertile soil is precious, flower-gardens are an unjustified self-indulgence. Another example (there are plenty) is Linton Heathcliff's selfishness, due like Cathy's to ignorance of the facts of life on such a farm: Zillah complains 'he must always have sweets and dainties, and always milk, milk for ever – heeding naught how the rest of us are pinched in winter'. The novelist knows that thrift as well as austerity is a necessary virtue in such a context, so that old Joseph's indignation when the feckless Isabella flings down the tray of porridge is wholly respectable: 'yah desarve pining froo this tuh Churstmas, flinging t'precious gifts uh God under fooit i' yer flaysome rages!'

The clearest light is thrown on the moor by Catherine's likening Heathcliff to 'an arid wilderness of furze and whinstone' when trying to make the romantic Isabella understand the basic irreducibility of the nature of the man Isabella fancies she is in love with. But Catherine has also said to Nelly, in trying to explain her own 'love' for Heathcliff, that it is like 'the eternal rocks: a source of little visible delight, but necessary', in fact it is not love but a need of some fundamental kind that is quite separate from her normal love for Edgar Linton, a love which leads to a happily consummated marriage and the expectation of providing an heir.[17]

The plight of Catherine Earnshaw is thus presented as at once a unique personal history, a method of discussing what being a woman means, and a tragedy of being caught between socially incompatible cultures, for each of which there is much to be said for and against. That Emily Brontë intended to create a coherent, deeply responsible novel whose wisdom should be recognised as useful we can have no doubt.

I would make a plea, then, for criticism of *Wuthering Heights* to turn its attention to the human core of the novel, to recognise its truly human centrality. How can we fail to see that the novel is based on an interest in, concern for, and knowledge of, real life? We cannot do it justice, establish what the experience of reading it really is, by making analyses of its lock and window imagery, or by explaining it as being concerned with children of calm and children of storm, or by putting forward such bright ideas as that '*Wuthering Heights* might be viewed at long range as a variant of the demon-lover motif' (*The Gates of Horn*, H. Levin) or that 'Nelly Dean is Evil' – these are the products of an age which conceives literary criticism as either a game or an industry, not as a humane study. To learn anything of this novel's true nature we must put it into the category of novels it belongs to – *Women in Love, Jules et Jim, Anna Karenina* and *Great*

Expectations – and recognise its relation to the social and literary history of its own time. The human truths *Wuthering Heights* is intended to establish are, it is necessary to admit, obscured in places and to varying degrees by discordant trimmings or leftovers from earlier writings or stages of its conception; for these, stylistic and other evidence exists in the text. Nor could we expect such complexity and such technical skill to have been achieved in a first novel otherwise; it is necessary to distinguish what is genuine complexity from what is merely confusion. That there is the complexity of accomplished art we must feel in the ending, ambiguous, impersonal, disquieting but final. And when we compare the genius devoted to creating Nelly Dean, Joseph, Zillah, Frances, Lockwood, the two Catherines, and to setting them in significant action, with the very perfunctory attention given to Heathcliff and Hareton as wholes (attention directed only when these two are wheeled out to perform necessary parts at certain points in the exposition of the theme to which – like Isabella and Edgar Linton – they are subsidiary) then we can surely not misinterpret the intention and the nature of the achievement of *Wuthering Heights*.

From Q. D. Leavis, *Collected Essays*, ed. G. Singh, vol. 1 (Cambridge, 1983), pp. 228–40 *passim*, 260–1 *passim*, 263–4, 343–5 *passim*.

NOTES

[Q. D. Leavis's essay on *Wuthering Heights* is composed from material which (despite her lack of official university status) she had been using with Cambridge undergraduates over a number of years. It was first put together in the form of two lectures which she delivered at the American Universities of Harvard and Cornell in 1966 and first published in *Lectures in America* (with F. R. Leavis [London, 1969]). The Leavises are both identified with the journal *Scrutiny* (1932–53), which made broad and urgent claims for the moral influence of literature. One of F. R. Leavis's most famous books was *The Great Tradition: George Eliot, Henry James, Joseph Conrad* (London, 1948), in which he selected the 'pre-eminent few' for the 'human awareness they promote' (Penguin edition [Harmondsworth, 1962], p. 10).

Q. D. Leavis's essay on *Wuthering Heights* appeared, in 1969, just too late for inclusion in the original Casebook on *Wuthering Heights*, but Miriam Allott comments in her Introduction that Mrs Leavis's essay likewise values 'renewal, consolidation and commitment to the central currents of human life' (Miriam Allott [ed.], *Wuthering Heights*, The Casebook Series

[London, 1970], p. 30). This moral aspect of the *Scrutiny* position was, however, linked to some of the assumptions of the 'New Criticism' associated with I. A. Richards. This formalist school of criticism encouraged readers to engage with 'the words on the page', arguing that through a thorough engagement with the ambiguities, ironies and contradictions of the text we can arrive at ever more complete understanding. This position assumes that works of literature are 'organic' and at least potentially, whole, and that the work of the reader is to move towards an understanding of this 'wholeness'.

Q. D. Leavis's essay is thus an important example of the liberal humanist position which many of the other contributors to this volume wish to question, and many of them refer specifically to it (see, for instance, Kermode, Matthews, Gilbert, below). It is, however, by no means an outdated essay and in a survey of academic readers' preferences I found a large number of devotees. Nor is it a straightforward example of *Scrutiny* criticism. Formalist critics, for instance, tend to ignore the biographical or historical context of a text, but 'A Fresh Approach to *Wuthering Heights*' is distinguished by 'the unusually varied scholarship – historical, biographical, sociological and anthropological – that she brought to bear' on the text (G. Singh [ed.], Q. D. Leavis, *Collected Essays* [Cambridge, 1983], p. 1).

With the agreement of Professor G. Singh, the editor of Q. D. Leavis's *Collected Essays*, the essay presented here has been cut to less than one-third of its original length. I have reproduced the introductory section of Q. D. Leavis's argument and her conclusion, which state the broad principles of her reading, omitting most of the detailed commentary on Catherine's story, which takes the form of an extended comparison between *Wuthering Heights* and Henri-Pierre Roché's novel, *Jules et Jim* (later filmed by François Truffaut). The complete essay also includes four useful Appendices, on 'The Northern Farmer, Old Style', on 'Violence', on 'Superstitions and Folk-lore' and on '*Wuthering Heights* and *The Bride of Lammermoor*'. Ed.]

1. Mr Justice Vaisey, giving a legal opinion of the text ('The Authorship of *Wuthering Heights*', *Brontë Society Publications* [1946]), notes such a distinction in 'diction, style and taste' between 'the introductory portion' and the rest of the book, that he believed it to indicate two authors; which would give ground to an old theory or tradition that Emily worked from a manuscript of Branwell's at the start (joint composition being probably a practice of the Brontë children, and Emily and [Branwell] are said to have written practically indistinguishable minute hands). Writing at two different periods by Emily alone, and at the earlier under the influence of Branwell or in deliberate imitation of his style (as Lockwood) would, however, account for such a disparity.

2. See Appendix B, 'Violence'. [Not reprinted here. Ed.]

3. The speech (ch. 9) in which Catherine explains to Nelly why she couldn't marry Heathcliff – on social grounds – belongs to the sociological *Wuthering Heights*. But even then she intends, she declares, to

keep up her old (sisterly) relations with him, to help him get on in the world – 'to *rise*' as she significantly puts it in purely social terms.

4. Tabby had, Mrs Gaskell reports, 'known the "bottom" or valley in those primitive days when the faeries frequented the margin of the "beck" on moonlight nights, and has known folk who had seen them. But that was when there were no mills in the valleys, and when all the wool-spinning was done by hand in the farm-houses round. "It wur the factories as had driven 'em away", she said.'

5. See Appendix C, 'Superstitions and Folk-lore'. [Not reprinted here. Ed.]

6. I am referring to the invaluable book, *The Image of Childhood*, by P. Coveney, though this does not in fact deal with *Wuthering Heights*.

7. This very evident judgement of Nelly's on the gentility with which Catherine has been infected by her stay at Thrushcross Grange (lavishly annotated in the whole scene of her return home in ch. 7) is clearly endorsed by the author, since it is based on values that are fundamental to the novel and in consonance with Emily's Wordsworthian sympathies. It is supplemented by another similar but even more radical judgement, put into old Joseph's mouth, the indispensable Joseph who survives the whole action to go on farming the Heights and who is made the vehicle of several central judgements, as well as of many disagreeable Calvinistic attitudes. Resenting the boy Linton Heathcliff's contempt for the staple food, porridge, made, like the oat-cake, from the home-grown oats, Joseph remembers the boy's fine-lady mother: 'His mother were just soa – we wer a'most too mucky tuh sow t'corn fur makking her breead.' There are many related judgements in the novel. We may note here the near-caricature of Lockwood in the first three chapters as the town visitor continually exposing his ignorance of country life and farming.

8. A regular Victorian theme, springing from the consciousness and resentment by creative artists of a new class snobbery and expressed in such widely different novels as *Alton Locke*, *North and South*, *Felix Holt*, *Dombey and Son*, *Great Expectations*, as well as *Wuthering Heights* which is earlier than all these.

9. David Copperfield's Peggotty is the same type, registered through the nursling's eyes (she is supplemented, as he grows out of her, by his great-aunt Betsy Trotwood) and Dickens's testimony to such truths is important. It will be noticed that Peggotty has to mother not only David but also his permanently immature mother. Our nineteenth-century fiction and memoirs are full of such nurses (sometimes they are spinster aunts), bearing witness to the living reality (see, e.g. Lord Shaftesbury's nurse, the Strachey nurse, and the Darwin nurse in Gwen Raverat's autobiography *Period Piece*). Nelly Dean seems to have incurred a good deal of unjustified ill-will, and perverse misrepresentation in consequence, from Catherine's defenders. That Peggotty and Miss Trotwood haven't

(so far – or so far as I know) must be due less to Dickens's fairly unambiguous presentation of David's Dora and (but to a lesser degree) of David's mother, than to the fact that Doras are not now in esteem.

10. Hence Nelly's indignant rebuke to Hareton's father in ch. 9 takes the form of telling him: 'Oh! I wonder his mother does not rise from her grave to see how you use him.'

11. Significantly, because old Joseph 'was relentless in worrying him about ruling his children rigidly', as religion required.

12. C. P. Sanger's *The Structure of 'Wuthering Heights'* (a Hogarth Press pamphlet).

13. Other pre-Victorian novelists noted and resented the effects on children too. In the original preface to her children's classic *Holiday House* (1839), Catherine Sinclair wrote: 'In these pages the author has endeavoured to paint that species of noisy, frolicsome, mischievous children, now almost extinct, wishing to preserve a sort of fabulous remembrance of days long past, when young people were like wild horses on the prairies, rather than like well-broken hacks on the road.'

14. See Appendix A, 'The Northern Farmer, Old Style'. [Not reprinted here. Ed.]

15. With the added force of Scott's dark and violent *Ravenswood* who both in name-pattern and type of hero suggests Heathcliff. See Appendix D, '*Wuthering Heights* and *The Bride of Lammermoor*'. [Not reprinted here. Ed.]

16. Mrs Gaskell says she told 'of bygone days of the countryside; old ways of living, former inhabitants, decayed gentry who had melted away, and whose places knew them no more; family tragedies, and dark superstitious dooms; and in telling these things, without the least consciousness that there might ever be anything requiring to be softened down, would give at full length the bare and simple details.' This is evidence of external, real life, sources for *Wuthering Heights* which cannot be dismissed.

17. [In the full version of the essay there follows an extended analysis of the novel in comparison with Henri-Pierre Roché's novel, *Jules et Jim*, filmed by François Truffaut. Ed.]

2

'Wuthering Heights' as Classic

FRANK KERMODE

In Charlotte Brontë's Biographical Notice of her sisters, she singles out a contemporary critic as the only one who got Emily's book right. 'Too often,' she says, 'do reviewers remind us of the mob of Astrologers, Chaldeans and Soothsayers gathered before the "writing on the wall", and unable to read the characters or make known the interpretation.' One, however, has accurately read 'the Mene, Mene, Tekel, Upharsin of an original mind' and 'can say with confidence, "This is the interpretation thereof" '. This latterday Daniel was Sidney Dobell, but a modern reader who looks him up in the hope of coming upon what would after all be a very valuable piece of information is likely to be disappointed. Very few would dream of doing so; most would mistrust the critic for whom such claims were made, or the book which lent itself to them. Few would believe that such an interpretation exists, however frequently the critics produce new 'keys'. For we don't think of the novel as a code, or a nut, that can be broken; which contains or refers to a meaning all will agree upon if it can once be presented *en clair*. We need little persuasion to believe that a good novel is not a message at all. We assume in principle the rightness of the plurality of interpretations to which I now, in ignorance of all the others, but reasonably confident that I won't repeat them, now contribute.

When Lockwood first visits Wuthering Heights he notices, among otherwise irrelevant decorations carved above the door, the date *1500* and the name *Hareton Earnshaw*. It is quite clear that everybody read and reads this as a sort of promise of something else to come. It is part of what is nowadays called a 'hermeneutic code'; something that promises, and perhaps after some delay provides, explanation. There is, of course, likely to be some measure of peripeteia or trick; you would be surprised if the explanation were not, in some way, surprising, or at any rate, at this stage unpredictable. And so it proves. The expectations aroused by these inscriptions are strictly *generic*; you must know things of this kind before you can entertain expectations of the sort I mention. Genre in this sense is what Leonard Meyer (writing of music) calls 'an internalised probability system'.[1] Such a system could, but perhaps shouldn't, be thought of as constituting some sort of contract between reader and writer. Either way, the inscriptions can be seen as something other than simple elements in a series of one damned thing after another, or even of events relative to a story as such. They reduce the range of probabilities, reduce randomness, and are expected to recur. There will be 'feedback'. This may not extinguish all the informational possibilities in the original stimulus, which may be, and in this case is, obscurer than we thought, 'higher', as the information theorists say, 'in entropy'. The narrative is more than merely a lengthy delay, after which a true descendant of Hareton Earnshaw reoccupies the ancestral house; though there is little delay before we hear about him, and can make a guess if we want.

When Hareton is first discussed, Nelly Dean rather oddly describes him as 'the late Mrs Linton's nephew'. Why not 'the late Mr Earnshaw's son'? It is only in the previous sentence that we have first heard the name Linton, when the family of that name is mentioned as having previously occupied Thrushcross Grange. Perhaps we are to wonder how Mrs Linton came to have a nephew named Earnshaw. At any rate, Nelly's obliquity thus serves to associate Hareton, in a hazy way, with the house on which his name is *not* carved, and with a family no longer in evidence. Only later do we discover that he is in the direct Earnshaw line, in fact, as Nelly says, 'the last of them'. So begins the provision of information which both fulfils and qualifies the early 'hermeneutic' promise; because, of course, Hareton, his inheritance restored, goes to live at the Grange. The two principal characters remaining at the end are Mr and Mrs Hareton Earnshaw. The other names, which have intruded on Earnshaw – Linton and Heathcliff – are extinct. In between there have been significant recursions to the original inscription – in chapter XX Hareton cannot read it; in XXIV he can read the name but not the date.

We could say, I suppose, that this so far tells us nothing about *Wuthering Heights* that couldn't, with appropriate changes, be said of most novels. All of them contain the equivalent of such inscriptions; indeed all writing is a sort of inscription, cut memorably into the uncaused flux of event; and inscriptions of the kind I am talking about are interesting secondary clues about the nature of the writing in which they occur. They draw attention to the literariness of what we are reading, indicate that the story is a story, perhaps with beneficial effects on our normal powers of perception; above all they distinguish a *literary* system which has no constant relation to readers with interests and expectations altered by long passages of time. Or, to put it another way, Emily Brontë's contemporaries operated different probability systems from ours, and might well ignore whatever in a text did not comply with their generic expectations, dismissing the rest somehow – by skipping, by accusations of bad craftsmanship, inexperience, or the like. In short, their internalised probability systems survive them in altered and less stringent forms; we can read more of the text than they could, and of course read it differently. In fact, the only works we value enough to call classic are those which, and they demonstrate by surviving, are complex and indeterminate enough to allow us our necessary pluralities. That 'Mene, Mene, Tekel, Upharsin' has now many interpretations. It is in the nature of works of art to be open, in so far as they are 'good'; though it is in the nature of authors, and of readers, to close them.

The openness of *Wuthering Heights* might be somewhat more extensively illustrated by an inquiry into the passage describing Lockwood's bad night at the house, when, on his second visit, he was cut off from Thrushcross Grange by a storm. He is given an odd sort of bed in a bedroom-within-a-bedroom; Catherine Earnshaw slept in it and later Heathcliff would die in it. Both the bed and the lattice are subjects of very elaborate 'play'; but I want rather to consider the inscriptions Lockwood examines before retiring. There is writing on the wall, or on the ledge by his bed: it 'was nothing but a name repeated in all kinds of characters, large and small – *Catherine Earnshaw*, here and there varied to *Catherine Heathcliff*, and then again to *Catherine Linton*'. When he closes his eyes Lockwood is assailed by white letters 'which started from the dark, as vivid as spectres – the air swarmed with Catherines'. He has no idea whatever to whom these names belong, yet the expression 'nothing but a name' seems to suggest that they all belong to one person. Waking from a doze he finds the name *Catherine Earnshaw* inscribed in a book his candle has scorched.

It is true that Lockwood has earlier met a Mrs Heathcliff, and got into a tangle about who she was, taking first Heathcliff and then Hareton Earnshaw for her husband, as indeed, we discover she, in a different sense, had also done or was to do. For she had a merely apparent kinship relation with Heathcliff – bearing his name as the wife of his impotent son and having to tolerate his ironic claim to fatherhood – as a prelude to the restoration of her true name, Earnshaw; it is her mother's story reversed. But Lockwood was not told her first name. Soon he is to encounter a ghost called Catherine Linton; but if the scribbled names signify one person he and we are obviously going to have to wait to find out who it is. Soon we learn that Mrs Heathcliff is Heathcliff's daughter-in-law, *née* Catherine Linton, and obviously not the ghost. Later it becomes evident that the scratcher must have been Catherine Earnshaw, later Linton, a girl long dead who might well have been Catherine Heathcliff, but wasn't.

When you have processed all the information you have been waiting for you see the point of the order of the scribbled names, as Lockwood gives them: *Catherine Earnshaw, Catherine Heathcliff, Catherine Linton*. Read from left to right they recapitulate Catherine Earnshaw's story; read from right to left, the story of her daughter, Catherine Linton. The names Catherine and Earnshaw begin and end the narrative. Of course some of the events needed to complete this pattern had not occurred when Lockwood slept in the little bedroom; indeed the marriage of Hareton and Catherine is still in the future when the novel ends. Still, this is an account of the movement of the book: away from Earnshaw and back, like the movement of the house itself. And all the movement must be *through* Heathcliff.

Charlotte Brontë remarks, from her experience, that the writer says more than he knows, and was emphatic that this was so with Emily. 'Having formed these beings, she did not know what she had done.' Of course this strikes us as no more than common sense; though Charlotte chooses to attribute it to Emily's ignorance of the world. A narrative is not a transcription of something pre-existent. And this is precisely the situation represented by Lockwood's play with the names he does not understand, his constituting, out of many scribbles, a rebus for the plot of the novel he's in. The situation indicates the kind of work we must do when a narrative opens itself to us, and contains information in excess of what generic probability requires.

Consider the names again; of course they reflect the isolation of the society under consideration, but still it is remarkable that in a story whose principal characters all marry there are effectively only three surnames, all of which each Catherine assumes. Furthermore, the Earnshaw family makes do with only three Christian names, Catherine, Hindley, Hareton. Heathcliff is a family name also, but parsimoniously, serving as both Christian name and surname; always lacking one or the other, he wears his name as an indication of his difference, and this persists after death since his tombstone is inscribed with the one word *Heathcliff*. Like Frances, briefly the wife of Hindley, he is simply a sort of interruption in the Earnshaw system.

Heathcliff is then as it were between names, as between families (he is the door through which Earnshaw passes into Linton, and out again to Earnshaw). He is often introduced, as if characteristically, standing outside, or entering, or leaving, a door. He is in and out of the Earnshaw family simultaneously; servant and child of the family (like Hareton, whom he puts in the same position, he helps to indicate the archaic nature of the house's society, the lack of sharp social division, which is not characteristic of the Grange). His origins are equally betwixt and between: the gutter or the royal origin imagined for him by Nelly; prince or pauper, American or Lascar, child of God or devil. This betweenness persists, I think: Heathcliff, for instance, fluctuates between poverty and riches; also between virility and impotence. To Catherine he is between brother and lover; he slept with her as a child, and again in death, but not between latency and extinction. He has much force, yet fathers an exceptionally puny child. Domestic yet savage like the dogs, bleak yet full of fire like the house, he bestrides the great opposites: love and death (the necrophiliac confession), culture and nature ('half-civilised ferocity') in a posture that certainly cannot be explained by any generic formula ('Byronic' or 'Gothic').

He stands also between a past and a future; when his force expires the old Earnshaw family moves into the future associated with the civilised Grange, where the insane authoritarianism of the Heights is a thing of the past, where there are cultivated distinctions between gentle and simple – a new world in the more civil south. It was the Grange that first separated Heathcliff from Catherine, so that

Earnshaws might eventually live there. Of the children – Hareton, Cathy, and Linton – none physically resembles Heathcliff; the first two have Catherine's eyes (ch. XXXIII) and the other is, as his first name implies, a Linton. Cathy's two cousin-marriages, constituting an endogamous route to the civilised exogamy of the south – are the consequence of Heathcliff's standing between Earnshaw and Linton, north and south; earlier he had involuntarily saved the life of the baby Hareton. His ghost and Catherine's, at the end, are of interest only to the superstitious, the indigenous now to be dispossessed by a more rational culture.

If we look, once more, at Lockwood's inscriptions, we may read them thus (see facing page).

Earnshaws persist, but they must eventually do so within the Linton culture. Catherine burns up in her transit from left to right. The quasi-Earnshaw union of Heathcliff and Isabella leaves the younger Cathy an easier passage; she has only to get through Linton Heathcliff, who is replaced by Hareton Earnshaw, Hareton has suffered part of Heathcliff's fate, moved, as it were, from Earnshaw to Heathcliff, and replaced him as son-servant, as gratuitously cruel; but he is the last of the Earnshaws, and Cathy can both restore to him the house on which his name is carved, and take him on the now smooth path to Thrushcross Grange.

Novels, even this one, were read in houses more like the Grange than the Heights, as the emphasis on the ferocious piety of the Earnshaw library suggests. The order of the novel is a civilised order; it presupposes a reader in the midst of an educated family and habituated to novel reading; a reader, moreover, who believes in the possibility of effective ethical choices. And because this is the case, the author can allow herself to meet his proper expectations without imposing on the text or on him absolute generic control. She need not, that is, know all that she is saying. She can, in all manner of ways, invite the reader to collaborate, leave to him the supply of meaning where the text is indeterminate or discontinuous, where explanations are required to fill narrative lacunae.

Instances of this are provided by some of the dreams in the book.[2] Lockwood's brief dream of the spectral letters is followed by another about an interminable sermon, which develops from hints about Joseph in Catherine's Bible. The purport of this dream is obscure. The preacher Jabes Branderham takes a hint from his text and expands the seven deadly sins into seventy times seven plus one. It is when he reaches the last section that Lockwood's patience runs out,

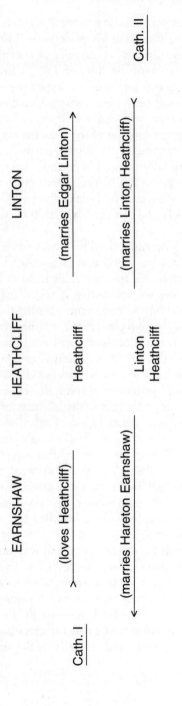

N.B. Heathcliff stands between Earnshaw and Linton as having Earnshaw origins but marrying Isabella Linton. He could also be represented as moving from left to right and right to left – into the Linton column, and then back to the Earnshaw when he usurps the hereditary position of Hareton. Hareton himself might be represented as having first been forced out of the Earnshaw column into the intermediate position when Heathcliff reduces him to a position resembling the one he himself started from, a savage and inferior member of the family. But he returns to the Earnshaw column with Cath. II. Finally they move together (without passing through the intermediate position, which has been abolished) from left to right, from Wuthering Heights to Thrushcross Grange.

and he protests, with his own allusion to the Bible: 'He shall return no more to his house, neither shall his place know him any more.' Dreams in stories are usually given a measure of oneiric ambiguity, but stay fairly close to the narrative line, or if not, convey information otherwise useful; but this one does not appear to do so, except in so far as that text may bear obscurely and incorrectly on the question of where Hareton will end up. It is, however, given a naturalistic explanation: the rapping of the preacher on the pulpit is a dream version of the rapping of the fir tree on the window.

Lockwood once more falls asleep, but dreams again, and 'if possible, still more disagreeably than before'. Once more he hears the fir-bough, and rises to silence it; he breaks the window and finds himself clutching the cold hand of a child who calls herself Catherine Linton.

He speaks of this as a dream, indeed he ascribes to it 'the intense horror of nightmare', and the blood that runs down into the bed-clothes may be explained by his having cut his hand as he broke the glass; but he does not say so, attributing it to his own cruelty in rubbing the child's wrist on the pane; and Heathcliff immediately makes it obvious that of the two choices the text has so far allowed us the more acceptable is that Lockwood was not dreaming at all.

So we cannot dismiss this dream as 'Gothic' ornament or commentary, or even as the kind of dream Lockwood has just had, in which the same fir-bough produced a comically extended dream-explanation of its presence. There remain all manner of puzzles: why is the visitant a child and, if a child, why Catherine *Linton*? The explanation, that this name got into Lockwood's dream from a scribble in the Bible is one even he finds hard to accept. He hovers between an explanation involving 'ghosts and goblins', and the simpler one of nightmare; though he has no more doubt than Heathcliff that 'it' – the child – was trying to enter. For good measure he is greeted, on going downstairs, by a cat, a brindled cat, with its echo of Shakespearian witchcraft.

It seems plain, then, that the dream is not simply a transformation of the narrative, a commentary on another level, but an integral part of it. The Branderham dream is, in a sense, a trick, suggesting a measure of rationality in the earlier dream which we might want to transfer to the later experience, as Lockwood partly does. When we see that there is a considerable conflict in the clues as to how we should read the second tapping and relate it to the first we grow aware of further contrasts between the two, for the first is a comic treatment of 491 specific and resistible sins for which Lockwood is about to be punished by exile from his home, and the second is a more horrible spectral invasion of the womb-like or tomb-like room in which he is housed. There are doubtless many other observations to be made; it is not a question of deciding which is the single right reading, but of dealing, as reader, with a series of indeterminacies which the text will not resolve.

Nelly Dean refuses to listen to Catherine's dream, one of those which went through and through her 'like wine through water'; and of those dreams we hear nothing save this account of their power. 'We're dismal enough without conjuring up ghosts and visions to perplex us,' says Nelly – another speaking silence in the text, for it is implied that we are here denied relevant information. But she herself suffers a dream or vision. After Heathcliff's return she finds herself at the signpost: engraved in its sandstone – with all the permanence that Hareton's name has on the house – are 'Wuthering Heights' to the north, 'Gimmerton' to the east, and 'Thrushcross Grange' to the south. Soft south, harsh north, and the rough civility of the market town (something like that of Nelly herself) in between. As before, these inscriptions provoke a dream apparition, a vision of Hindley as a child. Fearing that he has come to harm, she rushes to the Heights and again sees the spectral child, but it turns out to be Hareton, Hindley's son. His appearance betwixt and between the Heights and the Grange was proleptic; now he is back at the Heights, a stone in his hand, threatening his old nurse, rejecting the Grange. And as Hindley turned into Hareton, so Hareton turns into Heathcliff, for the figure that appears in the doorway is Heathcliff.

This is very like a real dream in its transformations and displacements. It has no simple narrative function whatever, and an abridgement might leave it out. But the confusion of generations, and the double usurpation of Hindley by his son and Heathcliff, all three of them variants of the incivility of the Heights, gives a new relation to the agents, and qualifies our sense of all narrative explanations offered in the text. For it is worth remarking that no naturalistic explanation of Nelly's experience is offered; in this it is unlike the treatment of the later vision, when the little boy sees the ghost of Heathcliff and 'a woman', a passage which is a preparation for further ambiguities in the ending. Dreams, visions, ghosts – the whole pneumatology of the book is only indeterminately related to the 'natural' narrative. And this serves to muddle routine 'single' readings, to confound explanation and expectation, and to make necessary a full recognition of the intrinsic plurality of the text.

Would it be reasonable to say this: that the mingling of generic opposites – daylight and dream narratives – creates a need, which we must supply, for something that will mediate between them? If so, we can go on to argue that the text in our response to it is a provision of such mediators, between life and death, the barbaric and the civilised, family and sexual relations. The principal instrument of mediation may well be Heathcliff: neither inside nor out, neither wholly master nor wholly servant, the husband who is no husband, the brother who is no brother, the father who abuses his changeling child, the cousin without kin. And that the chain of narrators serve to mediate between the barbarism of the story and the civility of the reader – making the text itself an intermediate term between archaic and modern – must surely have been pointed out.

What we must not forget, however, is that it is in the completion of the text by the reader that these adjustments are made; and each reader will make them differently. Plurality is here not a prescription but a fact. There is so much that is blurred and tentative, incapable of decisive explanation; however we set about our reading, with a sociological or a pneumatological, a cultural or a narrative code uppermost in our minds, we must fall into division and discrepancy; the doors of communication are sometimes locked, sometimes open, and Heathcliff may be astride the threshold, opening, closing, breaking. And it is surely evident that the possibilities of interpretation increase as times goes on. The constraints of a period culture dissolve, generic presumptions which concealed gaps disappear, and we now see that the book, as James thought novels should, truly 'glories in a gap', a hermeneutic gap in which the reader's imagination must operate, so that he speaks continuously in the text. For these reasons the rebus – *Catherine Earnshaw, Catherine Heathcliff, Catherine Linton* – has exemplary significance. It is a riddle that the text answers only silently; for example it will neither urge nor forbid you to remember that it resembles the riddle of the Sphinx – what manner of person exists in these three forms? – to which the single acceptable and probable answer involves incest and ruin.

I have not found it possible to speak of *Wuthering Heights* in this light without, from time to time, hinting – in a word here, or a trick of procedure there – at the new French criticism. I am glad to acknowledge this affinity, but it also seems important to dissent from the opinion that such 'classic' texts as this – and the French will call them so, but with pejorative intent – are essentially naïve, and become in a measure plural only by accident. The number of choices is simply too large; it is impossible that even two competent readers should agree on an authorised naïve version. It is because texts are so naïve that they can become classics. It is true, as I have said, that time opens them up; if readers were immortal the classic would be much closer to changelessness; their deaths do, in an important sense, liberate the texts. But to attribute the entire *potential* of plurality to that cause (or to the wisdom and cunning of later readers) is to fall into a mistake. The 'Catherines' of Lockwood's inscriptions may not have been attended to, but there they were in the text, just as ambiguous and plural as they are now. What happens is that methods of repairing such indeterminacy change; and, as Wolfgang Iser's neat formula has it, 'the repair of indeterminacy' is what gives rise 'to the generation of meaning'.[3]

Having meditated thus on *Wuthering Heights* I passed to the second part of my enterprise and began to read what people have been saying about the book. I discovered without surprise that no two readers saw it exactly alike; some seemed foolish and some clever, but whether they were of the party that claims to elucidate Emily Brontë's intention, or libertarians whose purpose is to astonish us, all were different. This secondary material is voluminous, but any hesitation I might have had about selecting from it was ended when I came upon an essay which in its mature authority dwarfs all the others: Q. D. Leavis's 'A Fresh Approach to *Wuthering Heights*'.[4]

Long-meditated, rich in insights, this work has a sober force that nothing I say could, or is intended to, diminish. Mrs Leavis remarks at the outset that merely to *assert* the classic status of such a book as *Wuthering Heights* is useless; that the task is not to be accomplished by ignoring 'recalcitrant elements' or providing sophistical explanations of them. One has to show 'the nature of its success'; and this, she at once proposes, means giving up some parts of the text. 'Of course, in general one attempts to achieve a reading of a text which includes all its elements, but here I believe we must be satisfied with being able to account for some of them and concentrate on what remains.' And she decides that Emily Brontë through inexperience, and trying to do too much, leaves in the final version vestiges of earlier creations, 'unregenerate writing', which is discordant with the true 'realistic novel' we should attend to.

Now it seems very clear to me that the 'real novel' Mrs Leavis describes *is* there, in the text. It is also clear that she is aware of the danger in her own procedures, for she explains how easy it would be to account for *Wuthering Heights* as a sociological novel by discarding certain elements and concentrating on others, which, she says, would be 'misconceiving the novel and slighting it'. What she will not admit is that there is a sense in which all these versions are not only present but have a claim on our attention. She creates a hierarchy of elements, and does so by a peculiar archaeology of her own, for there is no *evidence* that the novel existed in the earlier forms which are supposed to have left vestiges in the only text we have, and there is no reason why the kind of speculation and conjecture on which her historical argument depends could not be practised with equal right by proponents of quite other theories. Nor can I explain why it seemed to her that the only way to establish hers as the central reading of the book was to explain the rest away; for there, after all, the others *are*. Digging and carbon-dating simply have no equivalents here; there is no way of distinguishing old signs from new; among readings which attend to the text it cannot be argued that one attends to a truer text than all the others.

A recognition of plurality relieves us of the necessity of a *Wuthering Heights* without a Heathcliff, just as it does of a *Wuthering Heights* that 'really' ends with the death of Catherine, or for that matter an *Aeneid* which breaks off, as some of the moral allegorists would perhaps have liked it to, at the end of Book VI. A reading such as that with which I began Chapter 1 is of course extremely selective, but it has the negative virtue that it does not excommunicate from the text the material it does not employ; indeed, it assumes that it is one of the very large number of readings that may be generated from the text of the novel. They will of course overlap, as mine in some small measure does with that of Mrs Leavis.

And this brings me to the point: Mrs Leavis's reading is privileged; what conforms with it is complex, what does not is confused; and presumably all others would be more or less wrong, in so far as they treated the rejected portions as proper objects of attention. On the other hand, the view I propose does not in any way require me to reject Mrs Leavis's insights. It supposes that the reader's share in the novel is not so much a matter of knowing, by heroic efforts of intelligence and divination, what Emily Brontë really meant – knowing it, quite in the manner of Schleiermacher, better than she did – as of responding creatively to indeterminacies of meaning inherent in the text and possibly enlarged by the action of time. When we say now that the writer speaks more than he knows we are merely using an archaism; what we mean is that the text is under the absolute control of no thinking subject, or that it is not a message from one mind to another.

The classic, we may say, has been secularised by a process which recognises its status as a literary text; and that process inevitably pluralised it, or rather forced us to recognise its inherent plurality. We have changed our views on change. We may accept, in some form, the view proposed by Michel Foucault, that our period-discourse is controlled by certain unconscious constraints, which make it possible for us to think in some ways to the exclusion of others. However subtle we may be at reconstructing the constraints of past *epistèmes*, we cannot ordinarily move outside the tacit system of our own; it follows that except by extraordinary acts of divination we must remain out of close touch with the probability systems that operated for the first readers of the *Aeneid* or of *Wuthering Heights*. And even if one argues, as I do, that there is clearly less epistemic discontinuity than Foucault's crisis-philosophy proposes, it seems plausible enough that earlier assumptions about continuity were too naïve. The survival of the classic must therefore depend upon its possession of a surplus of signifier; as in *King Lear* or *Wuthering Heights* this may expose them to the charge of confusion, for they must always signify more than is needed by any one interpreter or any one generation of interpreters. We may recall that, rather in the manner of Mrs Leavis discarding Heathcliff, George Orwell would have liked *King Lear* better without the Gloucester plot, and with Lear having only one wicked daughter – 'quite enough', he said.

If, finally, we compare this sketch of a modern version of the classic with the imperial classic that occupied me earlier, we see on the one hand that the modern view is necessarily tolerant of change and plurality whereas the older, regarding most forms of pluralism as heretical, holds fast to the time-transcending idea of Empire. Yet the new approach, though it could be said to secularise the old in an almost Feuerbachian way, may do so in a sense which preserves it in a form acceptable to changed probability systems. For what was thought of as beyond time, as the angels, or the *majestas populi Romani*, or the *imperium* were beyond time, inhabiting a fictive perpetuity, is now beyond time in a more human sense; it is here, frankly vernacular, and inhabiting the world where alone, we might say with Wordsworth, we find our happiness – our felicitous readings – or not at all. The language of the new Mercury may strike us as harsh after the songs of Apollo; but the work he contemplates stands there, in all its native plurality, liberated not extinguished by death, the death of writer and reader, unaffected by time yet offering itself to be read under our particular temporal disposition. 'The work proposes; man disposes.' Barthes's point depends upon our recalling that the proverb originally made God the disposer. The implication remains that the classic is an essence available to us under our dispositions, in the aspect of time. So the image of the imperial classic, beyond time, beyond vernacular corruption and change, had perhaps, after all, a measure of authenticity; all we need do is bring it down to earth.

From Frank Kermode, *The Classic* (London, 1975), pp. 118–31, 132–4 *passim*, 139–41.

NOTES

[In its original form, this essay was delivered as the fourth and final address of the 1973 T. S. Eliot Memorial Lectures presented at the University of Canterbury. It was first published as 'A Modern Way with the Classic' in *New Literary History*, 5 (Spring 1974), 415–34, and later as the last chapter to Kermode's book, *The Classic*. Kermode reads *Wuthering Heights* in the context of the Greek and Latin classics; his definition of a classic is a book which is still read a hundred years after the death of the author. His thoughts about the novel were prompted by T. S. Eliot's paper, 'What is a Classic?', which he delivered to the Virgil Society in 1944 (Frank Kermode, *The Classic* [London, 1975], p. 11). On the other hand he refers extensively to 'the new French critics' – i.e. Claude Lévi-Strauss, Roland Barthes, and other 'structuralists'. (See Terence Hawkes, *Structuralism and Semiotics* [London, 1977] for an account of these thinkers.)

It is perhaps useful to see Kermode as an 'Anglo-structuralist', occupying a compromise position; willing, like the structuralists, to read texts as open and ambiguous in meaning, but unwilling to accept the common structuralist assumption that what are known as 'classic' texts are 'essentially naïve'. Kermode's position is clarified by the extended critique of Q. D. Leavis's 'Fresh Approach to *Wuthering Heights*' (reprinted above), with which his essay ends.

I have tried to retain the sense of Kermode's essay as pivoted between different critical positions, but I have, with his permission, cut some of the detail of his engagement with both Q. D. Leavis and the structuralists. Ed.]

1. Leonard B. Meyer, *Music, the Arts and Ideas* (Chicago, 1967), p. 8 (speaking of musical styles).

2. My subsequent reading in *Wuthering Heights* criticism (which has
    certainly substantiated my vague sense that there was a lot of it about)
    has taught me that the carved names, and Lockwood's dreams, have
    attracted earlier comment. Dorothy Van Ghent's distinguished essay
    asks why Lockwood, of all people, should experience such a dream as
    that of the ghost-child, and decides that the nature of the dreamer – 'a
    man who has shut out the powers of darkness' – is what gives force to
    our sense of powers 'existing autonomously' both without and within
    (*The English Novel: Form and Function* [New York 1953]). Ronald E.
    Fine suggests that the dreams are 'spasms of realism' and that Emily
    Brontë arranged the story to fit them, or as he says, lets the dreams
    generate the story. He emphasises their sexual significance, and the
    structural relations between them, explained by the generative force of
    a basic dream of two lovers seeking to be reunited ('Lockwood's Dream
    and the Key to *Wuthering Heights*', *Nineteenth Century Fiction*, 24
    [1969–70], 16–30). Ingeborg Nixon suggests that 'the names must have
    been written by Catherine after her first visit to Thrushcross Grange as
    a child . . . but they form a silent summary of the whole tragic dilemma';
    they indicate three possibilities for Catherine, who of course chooses
    Linton. This is to give the inscriptions the most limited possible
    'hermeneutic' sense, reading them back into a possible chronology and
    ignoring their larger function as literary or defamiliarising signs ('A
    Note on the Pattern of *Wuthering Heights*', *English Studies*, 45 [1964]).
    Cecil W. Davies notices that 'Heathcliff' is an Earnshaw name, and
    argues that this makes him 'in a real, though non-legal sense, a true
    inheritor of Wuthering Heights' ('A Reading of *Wuthering Heights*',
    Essays in Criticism, 19 [1969]). Doubtless C. P. Sanger's justly cel-
    ebrated essay ('The Structure of *Wuthering Heights*' [London, 1926]) is
    partly responsible for the general desire to fit everything that can be
    fitted into legal and chronological schemes; but the effect is often to
    miss half the point. All these essays are reprinted, in whole or in part,
    in the Penguin Critical Anthology, *Emily Brontë*, ed. J.-P. Petit
    (Harmondsworth, 1973). Other collections include one by Miriam
    Allott in the Macmillan Casebook Series (London, 1970), Thomas A.
    Vogler's *Twentieth-Century Interpretations of 'Wuthering Heights'*
    (Englewood Cliffs, NJ, 1968) and William M. Sale's Norton edition
    (New York, 1963).

3. 'Indeterminacy and the Reader's Response', in *Aspects of Narrative*, ed.
    J. Hillis Miller (New York, 1971), p. 42.

4. F. R. Leavis and Q. D. Leavis, *Lectures in America* (London, 1969),
    pp. 83–152. [A shortened version of this essay is reprinted in this
    volume – see p. 24 Ed.]

3

Framing in 'Wuthering Heights'

JOHN T. MATTHEWS

THE SINKING FRAME

Wuthering Heights is a novel preoccupied with the idea of boundary.[1] In vast variations of single-mindedness, it haunts the sites of division – between self and other, individual and family, nature and culture, mortality and immortality.[2] It is not surprising, then, that Emily Brontë should be drawn to a formal expression of her concern with boundaries by enclosing her 'central' story in an outlying narrative episode. What is the relation of the story *itself* – the chronicle of Earnshaw–Linton transactions crowned by Catherine and Heathcliff's love – to the story's *other* in its frame – Nelly Dean's entertaining account to her convalescent master Lockwood? Brontë means us to cross this question repeatedly in her deployment of the frame, in part because *Wuthering Heights* broods both at its centre and in its margins on the problem of articulation. As in its structure, the novel's imagery and diction are saturated to the same purpose by the rhetoric of framing.

Dorothy Van Ghent and others have written insightfully on the prominence of doors and windows as representations of the mind's and spirit's grasp of interior and exterior.[3] We will come to see, in addition, that the narrative frame is required by the incapacity of the central lovers to utter their relation. Perpetually frustrated, they cannot articulate the relation that would bind them, and so they leave a gap to be framed and filled by the loquacity of the narrators. Accordingly, Brontë brings into play a subtle and widespread terminology of framing that sounds almost all of its senses: to frame is to set off, to encompass, to edge, but also to invent, to lie, even – in the idiomatic 'frame-off' – to cease, to leave off, to escape. Likewise, a frame may be a border, but also one's state of mind, skeletal build, or bodily condition. Brontë invites us to entertain the agreements between these kinds of framing as she considers how establishing a ground for the story's figure is indistinguishable from inventing the story 'itself'. Disclosure is enclosure. The discreteness of the frame wavers under the labour of setting off the story.

The frame portion of *Wuthering Heights* sinks into the background of the monumental passion which it discloses. Unsurprisingly, interpretations of the novel readily ignore the circumstances of storytelling that appear in the opening and concluding pages and intermittently throughout. When Ellen Dean and Lockwood are discussed at all, their effects are confined largely to their status as characters *in* their story, not as its confabulators. Lockwood's 'normalcy' or priggishness and Nelly's meddlesomeness or salt-of-the-earthness do bear on a few points of the central story – the moments of Lockwood's admiration for Heathcliff and attraction to Catherine the younger, or Nelly's protection of the innocent and censure of the indulged.[4] In those few instances in which their roles as narrators are taken up, however, what is emphasised is their passivity. The usual paradigm for Lockwood's part is as the dreamer of the story.[5] Nelly, perhaps because of her subservient marginality to the culture she describes and to the cultured gentleman for whom she describes it, typically comes across as a transparent narrator. But the transparency of narratorial disinterest we scarcely grant any more, even to professionally objective narrators like historians.[6] There is little reason to expect that the equivocations of Lockwood's tremulous misanthropy or the gnarls of Nelly's ambivalence toward her supportive oppressors should not condition the story one transcribes as the other tells. My contention goes beyond the view that the narrators' personalities simply colour the story they relate; rather, in this novel so absorbed by the instabilities of identity,[7] story becomes the only mode of being, a temporary shelter which permits the transient sense of stilled, collected selfhood for its telling tenants. Having encountered themselves in the passages of *Wuthering Heights* – the house of the narrative – the narrators sink back into the greater oblivion of all that is unframed.

The two principal narrators of *Wuthering Heights* are actively interested in their story, and thus they are intimated by it. Although their position as frame narrators implies that they simply transmit events that have already taken place. Brontë never wholly gives those narrators over to the dictates of the story. They re-emerge regularly to remind us of their agency and the requirements of the telling scenes. In accepting the substance of the past, each narrator measures, revises, and preserves what he or she sees fit. Lockwood refers to his willingness to record the essence of Nelly's account: 'I'll continue it in her own words, only a little condensed' (p. 132); but condensation is a form of composition. Elsewhere he accents the actual vigilance of the listener's apparent passivity; he is so intent on following the details of Nelly's narration that he will abide no leaping over spaces in the story. Nelly is impressed by the laziness of such a mood, but Lockwood protests that it is 'a tiresomely active one. It is mine, at present, and, therefore, continue minutely' (p. 52). Lockwood's engagement with the story draws him into a version of a strenuously contemplative life, one he thinks Nelly enjoys in her isolated condition ('You have been compelled to cultivate your reflective faculties', p. 52). And she agrees that both experience and her reading have made her wise ('I have read more than you would fancy', p. 53). Both Lockwood and Nelly are careful to describe their states of mind during the reveries stimulated by the story as grounded in waking reality: Lockwood's dreams early in the novel and Nelly's fantasies on Heathcliff's behalf are varieties of 'imaging' (p. 280),[8] a practice suggesting active creation, or framing. As Nelly, encouraging the rude foundling Heathcliff, once puts it: 'Were I in your place, I would frame high notions of my birth; and the thoughts of what I was should give me courage and dignity to support the oppressions of a little farmer!' (p. 48). How Nelly specifically manages to frame herself is a question I shall take up shortly, but at this point we note that 'imaging' requires exertion. Whatever impulses toward self-fulfilment and self-restraint Lockwood and Nelly exhibit, they emerge most forcefully in the aims and strategies of their narrating. An interpretation of the frame in *Wuthering Heights* must account not only for how the narrators take their story but what they make of it. The energies of desire, imaginative compensation, revenge, subversiveness, and ambivalence toward moral and social rectitude – the very stuff of the core story – have already been set off, are already under way, in the novel's frame. Brontë associates imagination with marginality (as the insinuation of Catherine's diary into the margins of Branderham's sermons confirms); what is imagined is the outside of what is possessed – the frame is for framing. If, as so many readers are willing to have it, Catherine and Heathcliff's passion involves a yearning for self-possession by means of the passage through the other,[9] then central to that passion is the sense of lack, of an interiority yearning for completion by (or through) its exterior. The structure of the core story is a synecdoche for the novel's structure, then, since the existence of the frame narrative signals that the central story lacks self-sufficiency, just as each of the lovers defines love as lack. The central story's compromised self-sufficiency actually constitutes its unity by calling forth the encircling frame. A silence, a reticence, some stunted power of speech in the lovers' relation requires the supplement of Nelly's telling and Lockwood's writing. The frame's preliminary nature requires completion by the central story it serves, but the self-insufficiency of the enframed story returns us to the required frame. This conceptual cycle is doubled by our actual reading experience of the novel, since we sink past the circumstances of the narrating scene only to rise back into the frame at the conclusion.

AN EXISTENCE OF YOURS BEYOND YOU

Perhaps the millions of interpretive words which have come to encase this love story measure the incapacity of Catherine and Heathcliff to speak for themselves. Most readers register the ferocious privacy and thick silence which close off Catherine and Heathcliff from the rest of their world. Such remoteness surely deepens our impression of their mysterious, suprapersonal passion, and it rallies our discontent with the oppressive institutions of civilisation that conspire to frustrate their happiness. Yet it is the lovers' own powers of expression that fail to find a form or even to name the nature of their relation, and not merely the commonsensical incomprehension of Nelly and Lockwood or Brontë's respectful reticence. Catherine recognises that somehow her need of Heathcliff involves his representation of all that she is not, including her language: 'I cannot express it; but surely you and everybody have a notion that there is, or should be an existence of yours beyond you. What were the use of creation if I were entirely contained here?' (p. 70). Catherine wants to get at the notion that selfhood is distributed between one's contained identity and all it is not.[10] The 'I' is also elsewhere, not 'entirely here'. In part, such a conception of selfhood stuns the potency of language because it blocks the clear passage of the word into the outer realm of the signified; that is, the zone of mind or experience that would complete Catherine, the 'existence of yours beyond you', is not separate from her present state and so cannot simply be named as something else. Her words for it cannot break into that imagined space and represent it, since that space has no place of its own; instead, the conjoined self haunts the threshold of self and other, inside and outside, as if it were a site, though it is nothing more than the placeless line of differentiation. The lovers ceaselessly survey and traverse the line between themselves. Catherine resorts to the vocabulary virtually of figure and ground to elaborate this unutterable notion: 'my love for Heathcliff resembles the eternal rocks beneath – a source of little visible delight, but necessary. Nelly, I am Heathcliff – he's always, always in my mind – not as a pleasure, any more than I am always a pleasure to myself – but as my own being – so, don't talk of our separation again – it is impracticable' (p. 70). Ostensibly the separation but also the talk are 'impracticable' in this situation, for there is no term, no form, for the relationship that would fulfil Catherine's and Heathcliff's wants. Like both sorts of framing, Heathcliff serves Catherine as the ground for her figure – the necessary foundation against which she distinguishes herself – and also as the imaged otherwise of herself – 'the use of creation'. In both regards he is the container that gives shape to the contained.

For all of the differences in Heathcliff's management of passion, he shares Catherine's grasp of an unspeakable edge of interlocking unity. When Catherine's death finally makes their incessant separations incurable, Heathcliff offers his own version of love's meaning: 'You said I killed you – haunt me then! . . . Be with me always – take any form – drive me mad! only *do* not leave me in this abyss, where I cannot find you! Oh, God! it is unutterable! I *cannot* live without my life! I *cannot* live without my soul!' (p. 143). Heathcliff's words, like Catherine's, disappear into the abyss of the inexpressible, which is the lovers' boundary. Each is the other's ground and life, being and soul; each is the other's essence experienced as external, one's core the other's frame, and that frame the first's sought centre. Nelly finds the suitable image for their state when they reunite on the eve of Catherine's passing: 'An instant they held asunder; and then how they met I hardly saw, but Catherine made a spring, and he caught her, and they were locked in an embrace from which I thought my mistress would never be released alive' (p. 137). The parts of the lock are indistinguishable to Nelly's modest eyes, but the configuration of interlockedness is what signifies their love to her.

It is this configural nature of Catherine and Heathcliff's attachment that stays them on the threshold of fulfilment throughout the novel, whether we employ the vocabulary of metaphysics, theology, psychology, sociology, or grammatology to characterise that nature. As the figure–ground relation might suggest, and the lock image might embody, the current that draws together Catherine and Heathcliff runs from the arbitrary opposition of their polarity rather than from any literal circumstances dividing them. What keeps them apart as it attracts them is less the simple facts of class discrepancy, or the conflict of natural appetite and social repression, or the incest prohibition, or the irretrievability of childhood's innocence – less these than the plain unavailability of a form for their bond. If we subscribe, for example, to the simple view that Catherine betrays her heart by marrying Edgar instead of Heathcliff, we ignore the lovers' own unquestioned devotion to *maintaining* the very barriers that keep them apart.[11] The kinds of prohibitions that seem to forestall their merging acquire force from being respected as actual obstacles when they are only virtual ones. It must strike every reader, for instance, that Catherine's prediction that marrying Heathcliff would degrade them seems a rationalisation of some other reluctance to articulate their attachment in a common form: out of Heathcliff's hearing she elaborates that her love for him is fundamental to her 'because he's more myself than I am' (p. 68), as if mere marriage were somehow simply beside the point of their relationship. Catherine thinks that she can concentrate on the strictly practical advantages of marriage because to her the potency of their love escapes confinement to any recognised container. Conversely, Catherine's match with Edgar is the soul of conventional romantic love; she furnishes a nice litany of the ordinary attributes of the beloved when she explains to Nelly her decision to marry him and concludes that she loves him 'as anybody loves' (p. 66).

In other ways Catherine and Heathcliff are balked by their powerlessness to represent the union they crave. If the prospect of marriage is no answer, neither is the recovery of childhood. It has become one of the truisms of the novel's critical edifice that Catherine and Heathcliff suffer exile from a world of pre-conscious, natural intimacy which they struggle ever after to recover or recall.[12] But *Wuthering Heights* steadfastly resists picturing either such original moments themselves or even sharp memories of them. In childhood the times of companionship that Catherine and Heathcliff enjoy are always the *products* and *not* the *predecessors* of discord, violence, and the often brutal re-establishment of social order. Catherine and

Heathcliff are never closer than when one has been momentarily hurt or banished by the family, against which they can maintain their separation. Lockwood's acquaintance with the character of their love comes in the diary entry he happens upon in Catherine's former bed, and its first passage shows that the two children are thrown together by their rebellion against Hindley's 'tyranny' and their mourning for old Earnshaw's patronage. The two are inclined to defy and mime the patriarchal order of the family, and yet they depend upon it to solidify their intimacy and purpose. Heathcliff's irruption into the Earnshaw household, of course, occasions his celebrated ostracism and objectification (he is 'it'), and Nelly remarks that 'from the very beginning, he bred bad feeling in the house' (p. 31). Heathcliff's very place in the family is the product of its rending, and his maintenance of his authority – from Earnshaw's favouritism through Hindley's oppressiveness to the foundling's eventual mastery – depends on his manipulation of the legalised violence of domestic arrangements. Likewise, his intimacies with Catherine, scrupulously concealed by the novel as they are, are indicated only by the constraints they habitually defy. The so-called fullness of childhood innocence rarely if ever appears in *Wuthering Heights*; it is a virtual condition made palpable by the incessant flights and breakings out of the two children as they seek 'to have a ramble at liberty' (p. 39), liberty meaningful only in the context of tyranny. Even the paradisiacal state of unity, then, is already a curative ghost called forth by what was an intolerable present. The remembered wholeness of childhood is the memory of a dream that was to have redeemed what was already lost. Nelly's account of the earliest phases of Heathcliff's and Catherine's positions in the family (the fourth and following chapters) invariably demonstrates that separation is the condition of their attraction, displacement the location of their alliance, exile the origin of their union.

Neither marriage in the future nor memory of their past will serve to denominate the state sought by Catherine and Heathcliff. Instead, the object of desire owes its mass to the velocity with which it recedes before the pursuit of the lovers. The collapse of the distinction between natural and cultural forms contributes to this same air of desire without namable content. One of the murkiest restraints on Heathcliff's and Catherine's relationship is the simulated incest prohibition that periodically grows legible. Q. D. Leavis has been the most emphatic champion of the taboo's evocation in the novel,[13] and though the evidence is striking, Brontë meticulously prevents it from being conclusive. Throughout *Wuthering Heights* it is always *as if* Catherine and Heathcliff were brother and sister: though he is named for the deceased, perhaps oldest, Earnshaw son, Heathcliff is not that son (and his missing surname forever declares the family's willingness to bring him in, but not all the way into, its lineage). Even the hint of Heathcliff's bastardy only draws half a line between brother and sister. Edgar identifies the nature of their relationship as all but siblings when he pouts to Catherine about 'the sight of your welcoming a runaway servant as a brother' (p. 81). For reasons that may escape them, Catherine and Heathcliff often behave as if the barriers they take to separate themselves are the terms for their intimacy.

Our impression that their love constantly drives them to the moors from the drawing room may make us forget that the lovers strictly observe the structuring codes of society. As they accept the burden of class dictates and the restrictions of consanguinity, so their instincts have been made highly conventional. Since Heathcliff is so regularly misrepresented as the thrust of stormy nature at the foundations of culture, it might be worth pointing out that Heathcliff, having survived the Earnshaws' instinctive equation of his swarthiness with bestiality, constantly surprises Nelly by being more refined, better mannered, and more amply furnished than the loutish gentry at which he takes aim. In the later, vaster stages of his revenge, Heathcliff leaves no doubt about the lawfulness of his design – from confining himself to the regulations of gaming in order to acquire Hindley's fortune to mastering the ins and outs of inheritance law.[14] Throughout his avenging career, Heathcliff follows the letter of the law, as he gives notice in warning Edgar through Nelly not to interfere with his marriage to Isabella: 'But tell him also, to set his fraternal and magisterial heart at ease, that I keep strictly within the limits of the law' (p. 129). Heathcliff's patient study of the ways of the world and Isabella's careless forfeiture of privilege for passion seem to create a reversal; in Nelly's view, 'He was the only thing there that seemed decent, and I thought he never looked better. So much had circumstances altered their positions, that he would certainly have struck a stranger as a born and bred gentleman, and his wife as a thorough little slattern!' (p. 125). Nelly has an unconscious reason for repeatedly forgetting Heathcliff's advanced culture too (and I will take it up shortly), but even if she had simply remembered their shared childhood, she might have had a fuller appreciation of Heathcliff's polish.

Even when Heathcliff behaves at his most despicable, he invariably turns out to be reflecting the violence inherent to the structure of social order. In the aftermath of Heathcliff's nearest disregard of the law, the kidnapping of Catherine the younger and her forced marriage to Linton, Brontë is careful to show that power, often exerted violently, is the condition of lawful order. Though Heathcliff detains Catherine against her will, she negotiates her own release by deciding that marrying Linton, a prospect she earlier pursues (with her father's belated approval, moreover), is an acceptable price to pay for rejoining Edgar before he dies. If Heathcliff is fiendish in holding her to her earlier promises, his monstrosity in part just magnifies the flimsiness of one's word in common society and the coercive selfishness of affectional relations. When Nelly evaluates the state of Catherine's dispossession, furthermore, she is forced to conclude that Heathcliff's occupation of the Heights cannot be opposed 'I suppose legally[;] at any rate Catherine, destitute of cash and friends, cannot disturb his possession' (p. 250). Nelly exposes how fully the protection of the law depends upon the exercise of simple power – cash and friends.

Brontë's strategy is folded, then, in a way too readily ignored by readers who want to identify the contents of the opposing wings of *Wuthering Heights*. The realms of nature and culture, person and family, and male and female, for example, bear features which seem to divide them on the basis of intrinsic content; but the force of Brontë's writing simultaneously evacuates the contents by showing that each realm is at once the outer zone defining the other and also the required, essential, central, interior supplement to the other's lack. The namelessness of Catherine and Heathcliff's relationship accents this situation and helps explain the odd pointlessness of the characters' schemes for satisfaction. Many critics imply that Catherine and Heathcliff simply miss or renounce possibilities for contentment available to them out there – as if with Heathcliff grinning at her side, Catherine might have had the roof removed from the Heights and set up an authentically natural household, with Nelly serving them supper on the moors.[15] I have sought to show instead how their longing cannot abide the congealment of representation.

However, Brontë does allow the narrative to propose two modes of being for the lovers' sought union that accord more exactly with their inexpressible nature: the image of the border and the gesture of effacement. Given the fusion that desire seeks, it is not surprising that the imagery of the margin, the shared boundary, the dividing line, rules the lovers' vision of their merging. Heathcliff's most spectacular description of uniting with Catherine depicts the confusion of their remains in the graveyard. Heathcliff demands of Nelly that his burial arrangements be respected; he threatens to haunt her if she does not see to it that the sexton performs the service he has agreed to:

> I got the sexton, who was digging Linton's grave, to remove the earth off her coffin lid, and I opened it. I thought, once, I would have stayed there, when I saw her face again – it is hers yet – he had hard work to stir me; but he said it would change, if the air blew on it, and so I struck one side of the coffin loose – and covered it up – not Linton's side, damn him! I wish he'd been soldered in lead – and I bribed the sexton to pull it away, when I'm laid there, and slide mine out too, I'll have it made so, and then, by the time Linton gets to us, he'll not know which is which!
>
> (p. 244)

Heathcliff makes central the space of the barrier between them, the interval that both interferes with and makes possible a site for their reunion. The thickness of the missing coffin boards corresponds to the emptied forms of desire throughout the novel; the disfigured coffin frames open a virtual space that is the trace of the missing borderline.

That the space between desire and its object has been made a fetish in *Wuthering Heights* helps explain other prominent images to which the lovers resort. Catherine, for example, interpreting her dream about exile from childhood, concentrates less on her innocent pleasures or marital sufferings than on the gap opened by the sundering 'stroke': 'the whole last seven years of my life grew a blank' (p. 107). The imagery of her dream elaborates the derangement of being lost in that gaping blankness, the placeless line that cuts adulthood out of childhood: 'But, supposing at twelve years old, I had been wrenched from the Heights, and every early association, and my all in all, as Heathcliff was at that time, and been converted, at a stroke into Mrs Linton, the lady of Thrushcross Grange, and the wife of a stranger; an exile, and outcast, thenceforth, from what had been my world – You may fancy a glimpse of the abyss where I grovelled!' (p. 107). The abyss is the space that measures and makes the margin of desire, the barrier literally imaged in the window frame through which Catherine looks as she says this sentence and contemplates her return to her 'all in all'. She looks from the Grange's bedroom into 'the outer darkness' (p. 109), where her home in the kirkyard lies; yet she also sees her candlelit room at the Heights, another home that awaits her. As throughout the novel, it is the 'journey', 'a way', the passage, that preoccupies the lovers, and not any destination privileged in its own right.

In that each lover thinks of the other as, paradoxically, an essential supplement to himself or herself, each encounters that other as a kind of pressing blankness that gives contour to the self. In *Wuthering Heights* the blankness of desire also attaches to the desired, and Catherine and Heathcliff each become, as lovers, the haunting spectre of the other. Catherine promises that she will never rest 'till you are with me' (p. 108), and Heathcliff welcomes just such a possession: 'haunt me then! . . . Be with me always' (p. 143). The odd, satisfying change that seems to overtake Heathcliff at the end of the novel arises from closer approach to Catherine's blankness; having arranged for the communication of their remains underground, Heathcliff begins to 'see' Catherine. At breakfast soon after, 'he cleared a vacant space in front' of him and 'gazed at something within two yards distance' (p. 281). According to my argument, such an emanation is as full a representation of the beloved as may be drawn; Catherine's haunting Heathcliff simply perpetuates the spacing and separation which constitute desire.

IN A HOLIER FRAME, OR FRAMING A BIT OF A LIE

Nelly may be entranced by the unfathomable devotion of the lovers to each other, but she rejoices when their lives finally quiet down in death. Beholding Catherine's now smooth brow, Nelly extols the consolations of the deathbed: 'My mind was never in a holier frame, than while I gazed on that untroubled image of Divine rest' (p. 140). Both Nelly and Lockwood are relieved that the destination of their story turns out to be the restoration of tranquillity, with its conclusion that unquiet slumbers can no longer be imagined. What propels the tellers' craving for release from the narrative, however, is finally not the story's strangeness – for all its monstrosity, its characters of nearly another species – but the intimate resemblances of the frame and the enframed. At first, as in so many reaches of *Wuthering Heights*, we might take the tellers as the opposites of their protagonists; yet the novel suggests that here, as throughout, what seems contrary is actually complementary. Just as Catherine and Heathcliff serve as both exterior and essence to each other, so the fiction erects imaginary desires beyond, yet within, its framers. Inquiring into Heathcliff's cracked antics at the end, Nelly allows mildly that 'he might have had a monomania on the subject of his departed idol; but on every other point his wits were as sound as mine' (p. 275).

Early in the novel Catherine reminds Nelly that the 'use of creation' is to represent 'an existence of yours beyond you' (p. 70). As we have already for the lovers, we might apply this formulation to the tellers in order to characterise the purposes of imaginative (not only natural) creation. In the interval of their narrative, Nelly and Lockwood both occupy manners of being otherwise inadmissible by them. Through their exacting conventionality, Nelly and Lockwood evoke the spectral satisfactions and transgressions that haunt the repressive order of society. Catherine and Heathcliff's love is the ghost of the prohibitions that structure society: it has the air of unspeakably natural passion, even incest, the spaciousness of escape from tyrannous convention, the heedlessness of self-abandon, the dark allure of disease and deathliness. Toward this representation of an existence beyond the numbing containments of their lives, the narrators grope as they pass into the story. And yet the mysterious 'ideal' of Catherine and Heathcliff's passion fails finally to sustain its perfect otherness. Inexorably the script of the framers' hands grows legible in the novel's palimpsest: the subversiveness of passion in the core story – whether we focus on the romantic or social facet of that passion – reverts into subservience to convention, representation, reason, health. The central love is stained, then, from the outset by the strains of its creators' imaginations. Catherine and Heathcliff end up reinforcing the dictates of class, family, the law, and mortality. What they seem to defy they actually verify. And it is in this swerve toward a holier, sanctioned frame that Lockwood and Nelly escape (with) themselves,[16] for the survival of the narrators at the cost of their protagonists defines the triumph of framing this fiction. 'Imaging' transcendence, innocence, regression, and naturalness – the zone projected by the novel's fantasy of a perfected society – imaging them is losing them and accepting their loss. When critics speak of Brontë's vision of a world in which authentic values might hold sway, they comply with the very process that Brontë unsettles in *Wuthering Heights*.[17] Brontë shows that – helpless as we are to stop longing for a corrective transformation of our present circumstances – those circumstances determine the very nature of the ideal. The oppressions of society not only compromise our present, they condition the dreams of its reversal and defeat. The 'subversive' exterior ends up being seen as the representation of the spectral interior, a conflation of outside and inside that we have noted in every region of the novel. All that beckons to us as the beyond is the blank inverse of what is within. Brontë sees that these versions of personal and social desire are the shapes of their own repression, pressing in to keep the configuration of the boundary in force. Nelly points to this effect of her involvement when she tries to interpret Catherine's outlandish declaration of love for Heathcliff: ' "If I can make any sense out of your nonsense, Miss," I said, "it only goes to convince me that you are ignorant of the duties you undertake in marrying" ' (p. 70). The nonsense of Catherine and Heathcliff's behaviour always carries the sense of Nelly's containment of it.

Nelly and Lockwood cooperate in the contrary motions of their narration: on the one hand, raising the spectre of 'something else'; on the other, laying that spectre to rest. The ends of the story can accommodate the uncertain end of its characters: Nelly can entertain her lovers' haunting perpetuation at the same time that Lockwood can insist on their quiet slumbers, for the consequence of telling their story arises from both evoking and revoking the ghosts' potential. The resting place for the lovers predictably secures their suspension across boundaries:

> The place of Catherine's interment, to the surprise of the villagers, was neither in the chapel, under the carved monument of the Lintons, nor yet by the tombs of her own relations, outside. It was dug on a green slope, in a corner of the kirkyard, where the wall is so low that heath and bilberry plants have climbed over it from the moor.
>
> (p. 144)

Neither inside nor outside, the site of the wall's rupture, the obliteration of nature's and culture's demarcation. Like the holy frame of the kirkyard wall, Nelly and Lockwood's frame story aspires to bring the remains of the enframed story within safe confines. In a telling phrase that carries beyond the immediate circumstance, Nelly once confesses that to get rid of Heathcliff she is forced into 'framing a bit of a lie' (p. 99). To vacate the story they tell, she and Lockwood likewise must traffic in deception: Nelly convincing herself that the restitution of social order (the oppression she supports) in the marriage of Catherine the younger and Hareton will assure that 'there won't be a happier woman than myself in England' (p. 268); Lockwood satisfied that he can return to the arms of tranquillity leaving a world well lost behind.

Lockwood the diarist succeeds in keeping his hand out of the way. Although he is earlier startled that the ghostly product of his reading and writing might come to demand entry and seek intimacy, he knows too that he must himself break the pane of the locked casement in order to quiet the noise. The frame remains locked but penetrable, the very figure for the writer's situation in *Wuthering Heights*. Lockwood would lock the interior story in the wooden lock of his frame, attempting to contain the characters within the bound space of representation. But to do so he must also break through the frame, displaying for the reader that the threshold of the novel's frame (figured in the window's ledge) provides the space for sought but feared intimacy. Lockwood's writing everywhere frames that bit of a lie to his created spectres: 'Let *me* go, if you want me to let you in!' (p. 20).

FRAME OFF

Wuthering Heights would be unimaginable without its framing. Although its frame portions always appear preliminary and subliminal to its central story, we have seen that *Wuthering Heights* interferes with the division and ranking of opposites on the basis of content alone. The urge to establish identity drives the characters – whether they are the protagonists or the narrators – to consider how the articulation of self is a process which sets one apart by setting one within a system of differences. The relation of figure to ground, which we have seen as a prominent motif in both the enframed and framing parts of the novel, suggests one way in which Brontë comprehends the conditions of representation in her book. Each of the lovers seeks to supplement an interior lack by representing it as an other who becomes the 'all in all'. The lack in each, then, constitutes the unifying lock of their love; each frames and is enframed by the other. At the next remove, the unity of the core story is secured by a lack to be filled by the frame story. The lovers' inability to grasp a form, a word, for their attachment requires the labours of their tellers; yet we have seen that the lack in the core is also the lack of the frame story, since the authors conjure up the emanations of their own and society's discontents. *Wuthering Heights* does not offer us a regulated structural whole; rather, it displays mutually embracing structures that despair of perfected unity while simulating its effect.

I have kept my terminology abstract in this closing account because I wish it to touch the diverse registers of the novel that we have looked at serially. The point of my analysis is not to displace one centre of *Wuthering Heights* in order to substitute another; I am not arguing that the frame narrative is 'actually' the more important part of the novel, nor that readers must begin with it and see it as the origin of the work's meaning. Instead, I have sought to follow the novel's own leading as it proceeds through the passages of representation, constantly turning us back at the point we take to be the centre of significance, our attainment of the 'penetralium'. For Brontë shows us how the nature of narrative is all frame and framing, the articulation of thresholds meaningful as they conduct our passing through them, and not our passing by or over them. Throughout the novel, doors bear words, and words serve as doors. Lockwood notices at the outset that the threshold to Wuthering Heights demands reading.[18] And toward the end Hareton signals his crossing (back) into literacy by reading his (ancestor's) name inscribed on the lintel: 'he moved off to open the door, and, as he raised the latch, he looked up to the inscription above' (p. 211). Words promise to be the portals to what we desire and imagine. They offer access to what we do not possess: the perfected self, the object of longing, the exiled regions of the mind. Yet Nelly only once agrees to 'leaving the door of communication open' (p. 60); more often she insists on keeping doors closed. Though language promises to conduct us to what it signifies, it can only keep us moving in the passages of communication. Since the readers and tellers of the story all are only passing through, any passage might be taken as introductory to any other, any frame actually the enframed. We step immediately into Lockwood's story, which also is to be taken as the novel's 'central' subject. It is this incessant dissolving of figure into ground and back that I contend organises our spellbinding admiration for *Wuthering Heights* and our remarkable inability to agree on what it means.

When Isabella offers her friendship to young Hareton, she says he curses her and threatens to 'set Throttler on me if I did not "frame off" ' (p. 117). As the word does when Joseph uses it to tell the children to vacate the room at Earnshaw's death ('frame upstairs, and make little din', p. 36), 'frame' carries the sense of ceasing or vanishing. Framing comes round, then, to be seen as that which invents some existence of yours beyond you by encompassing it, but in so doing lets the framer disappear. Frames are meant, to be forgotten.

From *Texas Studies in Literature and Language*, 27 (Spring 1985), 26–37 *passim*, 53–61 *passim*.

NOTES

[John T. Matthews locates his critical position in this essay by means of very helpful summaries (mostly in the endnotes) of previous readings by Q. D. Leavis, Frank Kermode, Carol Jacobs, J. Hillis Miller, Leo Bersani, Terry Eagleton, Sandra Gilbert and many others. (Those by Leavis, Kermode, Eagleton and Gilbert will be found elsewhere in this volume.) He offers a deconstructive reading of the text following the French philosopher Jacques Derrida. Very briefly, deconstruction is a way of challenging whatever position you may adopt to make a judgement. Its point is that there is no way of deciding, objectively or scientifically, the 'truth' about anything. In *Wuthering Heights*, Matthews argues, there is no way of deciding whether the 'core story' or the 'frame' is more important; but we are nevertheless endlessly fascinated by the connections between them.

A brief account of deconstruction will be found in the Introduction (see p. 5 above), and a fuller account in Christopher Norris, *Deconstruction: Theory and Practice* (London, 1982). Linda H. Peterson gives a useful introduction to deconstructionist criticism in her critical edition of *Wuthering Heights* (New York; Basingstoke and London, 1992), pp. 359–70.

Matthews's essay as it appears here has, with his permission, been cut to less than half its original length; much of the omitted material relates to Lockwood and Nelly as 'framing' narrators. References in the essay are to *Wuthering Heights*, ed. V. S. Pritchett (Boston, 1956). Ed.]

1. Although my argument proceeds without mentioning Jacques Derrida, my approach is indebted to his project in both spirit and letter. In spirit because Derrida inspects indefatigably the marginal, the secondary, the derived. (Among other titles, see 'LIVING ON: *Border Lines*', in *Deconstruction and Criticism*, comp. Geoffrey Hartman [New York, 1979].) In letter because of Derrida's remarks on the frame as philosophical framework and as aesthetic ornament in 'The Parergon' (*October*, 9 [Summer 1979], 3–41), a translation of 'Le parergon', part 2 of *La Verité en peinture* (Paris, 1978). Derrida concentrates on Kant's preface to the third *Critique* in order to show that Kant's attempt to establish a foundation in philosophy for art has already been subverted by the preface, which founds philosophy in art (through recourse to the aesthetic registers of metaphor and imagery). The content and category of aesthetics, then, determine the ground of the metaphysics that will subsequently be made the ground for aesthetic criteria. This knot occasions a Derridean meditation on the particular disjunctions of philosophical frameworks. I have carried several of Derrida's observations into my approach to *Wuthering Heights*, but I have sought to let

Brontë's text suggest its own involvement with the problematics of framing and textual production.

2. Two central examples are J. Hillis Miller's study of the opposition in *Wuthering Heights* of virtue and joy in his chapter on Emily Brontë in *The Disappearance of God* (New York, 1965) and Dorothy Van Ghent's consideration of the unconscious and the conscious, or nature and culture, in *The English Novel: Form and Function* (New York, 1953).

3. Van Ghent's essay on *Wuthering Heights* is in many respects still the most perceptive and capacious we have. She isolates the importance of the imagery of thresholds to argue that the novel concerns the 'tension between two kinds of reality: the raw, inhuman reality of anonymous natural energies, and the restrictive reality of civilised habits, manners, and codes' (p. 157). I take issue with Van Ghent by maintaining that the opposition of natural innocence and civilised corruption is a false dichotomy in Catherine and Heathcliff's desire and that Lockwood manages – through his narrative procedures – to evade the glimpse of nature within him (a recognition Van Ghent points to in passing). Moreover, Van Ghent specifies the content of the other as dark, savage instincts while I think that the novel shows the radical arbitrariness of all that is other.

4. See, for example, John K. Mathison, 'Nelly Dean and the Power of *Wuthering Heights*', *Nineteenth-Century Fiction*, 11 (September 1956), 106–29, and James Haffey, 'The Villain of *Wuthering Heights*', *Nineteenth-Century Fiction*, 13 (December 1958), 199–215.

5. An example is Edgar F. Shannon, Jr, 'Lockwood's Dreams and the Exegesis of *Wuthering Heights*', *Nineteenth-Century Fiction*, 14 (September 1959), 95–110. Even in a recent and shrewd application of Derridean deconstruction to *Wuthering Heights*, Carol Jacobs emphasises the narrators' passivity before the requirements of interpretation and the intractable nature of language ('*Wuthering Heights*': At the Threshold of Interpretation', *boundary 2*, 7 (Spring 1979), 49–71). This article represents an early stage in deconstructive reading as it follows the dislocating effects of *écriture*: the conditions of imperfect repetition, usurpation, homelessness, and wandering that yoke the central characters and their interpreters. But Jacobs ignores the creative work of reading and the spectral products of writing in her deconstruction. Brontë's text confronts the kind of haunting presences produced by textual exertions, and not the absolutes of absence.

6. Consider Hayden White's study of the narrative tropes that organise the writing of history in *Tropics of Discourse* (Baltimore, 1978).

7. See Leo Bersani, *A Future for Astyanax: Character and Desire in Literature* (New York, 1969), pp. 197–229, for a study of the self as the other and the subversion of identity in *Wuthering Heights*.

8. Emended by Charlotte Brontë in the 1850 edition to 'imagining' (*Wuthering Heights*, ed. Hilda Marsden and Ian Jack [Oxford, 1976], p. 476).

9. In addition to Bersani, see Miller's *Disappearance of God* (New York, 1965).

10. My focus on the alterity of selfhood differs from both Miller's and Bersani's treatments by concentrating on the prominence of the border or the space between the lovers' desire. Miller, somewhat like Van Ghent, probes the paradox that 'a person is most himself when he participates most completely in the life of something outside himself. This self outside the self is the substance of a man's being. . . . It is the intimate stuff of the self, and it is also that which "stands beneath" the self as its foundation and support' (p. 172). Miller goes on to situate this alienation in a theological context: the individual's estrangement from God. In a second essay on the novel, Miller finds a similar dismantling of unitary identity in the register of textual meaning (*Fiction and Repetition* [Cambridge, Mass., 1982]). *Wuthering Heights* demonstrates, according to Miller, that interpretation produces multiple valid readings, not a single master reading. Though he contributes to our understanding of how the struggles of interpretation are one of Brontë's themes, Miller does neglect the scenes of narration in which Lockwood and Nelly focus these issues.

Besides several studies of the textuality of *Wuthering Heights* that I shall cite in the course of my argument, a recent exchange in *Critical Inquiry* explored the problematics of interpretation by centring on the novel. See James R. Kincaid, 'Coherent Readers, Incoherent Texts', *Critical Inquiry*, 3 (Summer 1977), 781–802; Robert Denham, 'The No-Man's Land of Competing Patterns', *Critical Inquiry*, 4 (Autumn 1977), 194–202; and James R. Kincaid, 'Pluralist Monism', *Critical Inquiry*, 4 (Summer 1978), 839–45.

Bersani extends the line on the alterity of identity by arguing that an individual's sense of an essential other destabilises the possibility of unitary identity. Eve Kosofsky Sedgwick proposes the importance of the barrier and the equivalence of the states it divides in her examination of *Wuthering Heights* in *The Coherence of Gothic Conventions* (New York, 1980), pp. 104–27, and in her more general study of veil imagery in Gothic Fiction, 'The Character in the Veil: Imagery of the Surface in the Gothic Novel', *PMLA*, 96 (March 1981), 255–67.

11. See Sandra M. Gilbert and Susan Gubar, *The Madwoman in the Attic* (New Haven and London, 1979), for an account of Catherine's suffering under patriarchal domination. Although their feminist analysis of Catherine's predicament is occasionally insightful, Gilbert and Gubar seem to me to subvert the power of their critique of repressive social institutions by implying that Catherine should have married Heathcliff (pp. 278ff.). It is not the person of Edgar which disappoints Catherine;

it is the very contamination with repression of all social forms – along with their ameliorative future forms – that blocks Catherine's hope to fulfil her true desire. As I go on to argue, the very ideology of desire's fulfilment depends on the mechanism of repression and testifies to the deepseatedness of discontentment as the condition of civilisation. [Extracts from *The Madwoman in the Attic* are reprinted in this volume – see p. 131 Ed.]

12. Miller typifies the view: 'The violence of Emily Brontë's characters is a reaction to the loss of an earlier state of happiness' (*The Disappearance of God* [New York, 1965], p. 170).

13. Q. D. Leavis, 'A Fresh Approach to *Wuthering Heights*', *Lectures in America* (with F. R. Leavis) (New York, 1969), pp. 85–138, as reprinted in *Wuthering Heights*, ed. William M. Sale, Jr (New York, 1972), pp. 306–21. William R. Goetz ('Genealogy and Incest in *Wuthering Heights*', *Studies in the Novel*, 14 [Winter 1982], 359–76) perceptively studies the novels from the standpoint of kinship systems. He argues that the story of Catherine and Heathcliff is shaped by the incest taboo to determine so-called free choice; the first part of the novel is based, then, on Catherine's rejection of Heathcliff as 'the renunciation of incest' (p. 363). Goetz also analyses the distinction between nature and culture that is represented by the authority of the incest taboo, finding (after Lévi-Strauss) that the apparent succession of nature by culture in *Wuthering Heights* is illusory and that society for Brontë is constantly threatened by the collapse into incest and nature.

14. C. P. Sanger, *The Structure of Wuthering Heights* (London, 1926).

15. This is the point of Gilbert and Gubar's analysis. Their championing of Heathcliff as the man who might have filled Catherine's dreams re-entrenches the dependence on masculine energy and on patriarchal models of self-realisation that they want to challenge. They make a belated attempt to correct this drift by claiming that Heathcliff is feminine in his attractiveness; aside from having little textual support, this strategy further consolidates the stereotypes of gender.

16. From the standpoint purely of the contradictory nature of all texts, Jacobs discusses Lockwood's efforts to deny its textuality and turn *Wuthering Heights* into a good book, a univocal work that can be understood and concluded.

17. I am thinking of Gilbert and Gubar's hypothesis of a satisfactory marriage, or Eagleton's vision of an alternative society free of oppression. [Both these essays are reprinted in this volume – see pp. 131, 118 Ed.]

18. Frank Kermode looks at the question of reading in the novel as he makes a case for an unlimited pluralism in critical interpretation ('A Modern Way with the Classic', *New Literary History*, 5 [Spring 1974],

415–34). [A later version of this essay is reprinted in this volume – see p. 39 Ed.]

4

Gender and Layered Narrative in 'Wuthering Heights'

N. M. JACOBS

What tenants haunt each mortal cell,
What gloomy guests we hold within –
Torments and madness, tears and sin!
(Emily Brontë)

In thinking of the Brontës as a group – something it is difficult not to do – we have tended to see Anne and Emily at opposite ends of the clan's continuum: Emily the wild pagan, Anne the mild Christian, with Charlotte somewhere in between. But in fact, Branwell's portrait of his sisters, with Emily and Anne close together on the left and Charlotte keeping company with the ghost of Branwell's face on the right, is a true one. Though the twinship of the younger sisters faltered as Anne went into the world and tired of Gondal, a certain kinship of mind remained, which shows itself in the structures of their major works. In both *Wuthering Heights* and *The Tenant of Wildfell Hall*, we approach a horrific private reality only after passing through and then discarding the perceptual structures of a narrator – significantly, a male narrator – who represents the public world that makes possible and tacitly approves the excesses behind the closed doors of these pre-Victorian homes. This structure, appropriated and modified from the familiar gothic frame-tale, here serves several functions that are strongly gender-related: it exemplifies a process, necessary for both writer and reader, of passing through or going behind the official version of reality in order to approach a truth that the culture prefers to deny; it exemplifies the ways in which domestic reality is obscured by layers of conventional ideology; and it replicates a cultural split between male and female spheres that is shown to be at least one source of the tragedy at the centre of the fictional world.

Unlike Charlotte, whose novels also critiqued the myth of domestic bliss but who eroticised the very dominance/submission dynamic from which she longed to escape, Emily and Anne seem to have moved beyond any faith in categories of gender as formulated by their culture. To them, gender is a ragged and somewhat ridiculous masquerade concealing the essential sameness of men and women. Each expressed direct opposition to the establishment of separate moral standards for men and women. According to Charlotte, nothing moved Emily 'more than any insinuation that the faithfulness and clemency, the long-suffering and loving-kindness which are esteemed virtues in the daughters of Eve, become foibles in the sons of Adam';[1] and in the Preface to her novel Anne wrote, 'I am at a loss to conceive how a man should permit himself to write anything that would be really disgraceful to a woman, or why a woman should be censured for writing anything that would be proper and becoming for a man'.[2] Yet both sisters, in approaching subjects they must have known would be controversial, seemed to find it necessary first to become that constructed creature, a man, to appropriate and delegitimise his power, before telling their anti-patriarchal truths. Each of these books depicts an unpleasant and often violent domestic reality completely at odds with the Victorian ideal of the home as a refuge from the harshly competitive outside world. And each shows that those with social power inflict violence on the powerless, including children, women, and landless men. Any observers who might attempt to intervene are equally powerless, aware of that fact, and concomitantly fatalistic about the occurrence of violence. This reality, hidden beneath layers of narration in the two novels, was as well-hidden in mid-century English society as it often is today. As late as 1878, when Frances Power Cobbe wrote 'Wife-Torture in England', she found it more politic to suggest that Englishmen of the middle and upper classes were unlikely to perpetrate domestic abuse of a really serious sort.[3]

Similarly, many early critics of both *Wuthering Heights* and *The Tenant of Wildfell Hall* preferred to attribute domestic abuse solely to yokels and ruffians.[4] The reviewer for the *Examiner* wrote, 'it is with difficulty that we can prevail upon ourselves to believe in the appearance of such a phenomenon [as Heathcliff], so near our own dwellings as the summit of a Lancashire or Yorkshire moor'.[5] The *Britannia* reviewer was equally determined to differentiate the world of the book from the world of its readers: 'The uncultured freedom of native character . . . knows nothing of those breakwaters to the fury of tempest which civilised training establishes to subdue the harsher workings of the soul'.[6] Lewes in the *Leader* granted the story a certain truth, but maintained a similar distance: 'such brutes we should all be, or the most of us, were our lives as insubordinate to law; were our affections and sympathies as little cultivated, our imaginations as undirected'.[7] Even Charlotte, in the Preface to the 1850 edition of *Wuthering Heights*, assured readers that they had nothing in common with its characters:

> Men and women who . . . have been trained from their cradle to observe the utmost evenness of manner and guardedness of language, will hardly know what to make of the rough, strong utterance, the harshly manifested passions, the unbridled aversions, and headlong partialities of unlettered moorland hinds and rugged moorland squires.[8]

These reviewers sought to reassure themselves and their readers that education, cultivation, and civilisation will preclude brutal behaviour, and objected to powerful fictional representations contradicting this premise. Yet the novels quite pointedly locate the brutality, sometimes physical and sometimes psychological, in civilised families, the 'best' in their neighbourhoods. Even Heathcliff, the Liverpool orphan, commits his worst crimes only after he has acquired the manners and resources of a gentleman.

The narrative structure of both of these novels represents an authorial strategy for dealing with the unacceptability of the subject matter, a strategy drawn but significantly modified from the familiar framing narrator of the gothic tales. According to MacAndrew, the gothic frame-tale creates a 'closed-off region within an outer world . . . The mind is turned in on itself'.[9] This internal or closed world approximates the hidden self within the social world, the dark side of the psyche. The framing narrator or fictional editor generally belongs to the world of the reader, and is a conventional and pragmatic sort who is shocked by the gothic evils he encounters. Anne Brontë's Markham and Emily Brontë's Lockwood serve in a somewhat analogous way to 'define the limits of propriety and to measure observed events against the official standards of morality',[10] but differ from their gothic predecessors in that they and the official standards they represent are shown to be in part the cause of the shocking reality they encounter. In fact, the metaphor of a framed picture implies a static two-dimensionality that is nothing like the experience of reading these novels. In looking at a picture we are only peripherally aware of the frame, which marks the limits beyond which our eyes need not stray: it is not a presence but the boundary between an artifice which deserves our attention and a surrounding mundane reality which does not. But the Brontës' framing narratives are more like competing works of art, or outer rooms in a gallery, or even the picture painted over a devalued older canvas. We cannot see or experience the buried reality of the 'framed' story without first experiencing the 'framing' narrative. There is no other way in.

In these novels, the outer reality is male and the inner reality is largely female; it is perhaps not entirely irrelevant to this conceptual structure that the laws of the Victorian age classified married women or underage unmarried women such as Helen Huntingdon, Catherine Earnshaw, and Catherine Linton as 'femmes couvertes'; their legal identities were 'covered' by and subsumed into that of the husband or father. I would contend that for Emily and Anne Brontë, there was no other way into the tabooed realities at the cores of their novels than through the satirical miming and disempowering of a masculine authority which 'covered' and often profited from those realities. Notwithstanding Heathcliff's ghoulish fancies, the evil hidden at the centre of these pseudo-gothic narratives is not supernatural or even particularly diabolical; it is mundane, vulgar, and grounded in the legal and economic structures of the time and the effects of those structures on the consciousness of both those in power (the 'covering' narrators) and those without power (the 'covered' narrators).

Taylor has discussed the use of a female persona as a 'literary masquerade' through which certain classic male authors have expressed vulnerabilities and emotions that the culture denies to men. Many female writers use male personae and particularly male pseudonyms in the same way. But the comic qualities of the Brontës' male personae suggest that they are using them less to enlarge themselves than to free themselves from the restrictive ideology and consciousness for which the personae speak. This mockery of conventional masculinity involves also mocking the conventional or 'male' element in the authors themselves, and thus is not so cheerful as the gaming with gender that Gilbert has described in female modernists such as Woolf and Barnes.[11]

There are a number of intriguing similarities between Victorian male impersonation in fiction and modern female impersonation on stage, for writing, particularly that dealing with 'coarse' subject matters, was seen by the Victorians as a masculine activity, unnatural to women. Gilbert and Gubar have described the anxiety created in the nineteenth-century woman writer by participation in an art dominated by male writers and male-oriented metaphors of creation. In one sense, becoming a writer meant becoming a man, or at least something other than what the culture considered to be a woman. By contrast with the relatively innocuous masquerade of a male pseudonym – a common enough ploy, and one justified by ladylike modesty as well as economic prudence – the extended assumption of a male persona must have required a great deal of courage in a time almost obsessively concerned with defining the differences in consciousness between men and women.[12] Nevertheless, Emily and Anne Brontë seem to have found their male impersonations necessary, as a way to silence the dominant culture by stealing its voice, to exorcise the demon of conventional consciousness and male power by holding it up to ridicule. Only by first discrediting views that the readers of these novels were likely to share – and from which the writers themselves, as products of their culture, could not entirely be free – could they hope to make the reality clear to themselves and to their readers.

Wuthering Heights, though much more complex in its narrative structure than *Wildfell Hall*, follows an essentially similar process of approaching a pervasively violent private reality through a narrator who embodies an ideology that justifies the violence. From the opening scene, when Heathcliff tells Lockwood to 'walk in!' through a locked gate, this novel stresses the boundaries between public and private realities as well as the parallels between the two. Though known as a great love story, the book focuses less on the relationship between Catherine and Heathcliff than on the ways in which that relationship and others are distorted by the power structure of the characters' world. Class differences certainly are a major issue here, as Marxist analyses of Heathcliff's career have shown. But what is less often recognised is the way in which most of the violence and abuse in this fictional world is made possible by the vestiture of total power in the patriarch of the home and by the psychic fragmentation this concept of male power imposes on both men and women. To discipline the members of the household as he sees fit is both the legal and moral right of the master of the house, and in the Earnshaw family – 'a respectable house, the next best in the neighbourhood' (p. 168) – this right leads to frequent abuse. Mr Earnshaw, though kind-hearted enough to take up a starving orphan, freely uses his power as master. When six-year-old Cathy spits at Heathcliff, she earns 'for her pains a sound blow from her father to teach her cleaner manners' (p. 39). Heathcliff warns that if Mr Earnshaw knows of the blows Hindley has dealt to the younger boy, he'll pay Hindley back 'with interest' (p. 41). After illness confines him to inactivity, Earnshaw becomes extremely sensitive to 'suspected slights of his authority' and trembles with rage when he cannot reach Hindley to strike him with a stick (pp. 41–2).

Thus, the Earnshaw children understand very early that social power legitimises violence. Even as a child, Cathy likes 'to act the little mistress; using her hands freely and commanding her companions' (p. 43). Hindley beats Heathcliff several times a week, taunting him as a 'gipsy' and 'beggarly interloper' (p. 41). This abuse escalates after Hindley becomes head of the household; when Cathy and Heathcliff defy him, he says, 'You forget you have a master here . . . I'll demolish the first who puts me out of temper' (p. 26). When Hindley threatens to murder Nelly, he says, 'no law in England can hinder a man from keeping his house decent' (p. 67). As master, Hindley tends to delegate the actual infliction of punishment; when ordered to flog Heathcliff for missing church, Joseph accepts the task with relish, thrashing Heathcliff 'till his arm ached' (p. 46). Significantly, Heathcliff never returns Hindley's violence or, in fact, perpetrates violence until he himself has gained the legal and economic status of paterfamilias. But he has learned very well not only how to exercise his power but how to justify that exercise. He imagines with pleasure bruising Isabella's face 'and turning the blue eyes black, every day or two' (p. 93), for nothing more than her resemblance to her brother. Imprisoning his wife, he says, 'you're not fit to be your own guardian, Isabella, now; and I, being your legal protector, must retain you in my custody' (p. 128). He refers to his son as his 'property' and as 'it' (p. 169). When the younger Catherine defies him, he administers 'a shower of terrific slaps on both sides of the head' and says, 'I know how to chastise children, you see . . . you shall have a daily taste, if I catch such a devil of a temper in your eyes again!' (pp. 215–16). He teaches Linton to regard such 'chastisement' as a husband's prerogative, promising that the boy will be able to 'pay her back her present tyrannies, with a vigorous hand' once they are married (p. 217). Edgar Linton is certainly not a violent man, but he is equally ready to assert control over his household, both in ceasing to 'humour' Catherine by allowing her friend to enter the house and in disinheriting his sister when she marries against his wishes. Learning of Isabella's misery with Heathcliff, he says only, 'Trouble me no more about her' (p. 113), and refuses, with self-righteous mildness, to help: 'I am not *angry*, but I'm *sorry* to have lost her . . . My communication with Heathcliff's family shall be as sparing as his with mine. It shall not exist' (p. 123). Clearly, to Edgar, Isabella now belongs to Heathcliff and is no longer his concern.

Lockwood is a product and beneficiary of the social structure that justifies the oppression and abuse at the Heights. Much like the readers and reviewers of the Brontë novels in the 1840s, he is a 'civilised man', who 'likes . . . to shut out the possibilities of darkness and violence'.[13] He closes himself into that panelled bed hoping to secure himself 'against the vigilance of Heathcliff and everyone else' (p. 25); but by thus isolating and, as it were, concentrating his own self, he finds himself at the epicentre of the house's demonic energy. In the violence of his attempt to keep out the wailing child, he 'pulled its wrist on to the broken pane, and rubbed it to and fro till the blood ran down and soaked the bedclothes' (p. 30), showing that the 'polite, civilised gentleman, is capable, albeit in a dream, of greater cruelty than any of the savage inhabitants of Wuthering Heights'.[14] And just as he stops his ears 'to exclude the lamentable prayers' (p. 30) of the ghost-Cathy, he stops his eyes, in a sense, to exclude knowledge of the plight of the living Cathy. The agency of his self-blinding is the ideology of domestic harmony. His fatuous courtesies are completely inappropriate to the scene before him, but he has no other vocabulary for describing what he sees. Observing the 'ferocious gaze' and savage tone with which Heathcliff addresses Cathy, and the universal grim silence at the tea-table, he nevertheless offers the platitudinous opinion that Heathcliff must be happy, 'surrounded by your family and with your amiable lady as the presiding genius over your home and heart' (p. 20). Learning that Cathy is not Heathcliff's 'amiable lady', he assumes that Hareton is the 'favoured possessor of the beneficent fairy' (p. 21). The real meaning of this sentimental language is clarified by Heathcliff, who echoes sarcastically, 'We neither of us have the privilege of owning your good fairy' (p. 21). That the 'favoured possessor' of a woman owns her is a fact of the law, which Isabella learns most painfully and which Anne Brontë's Helen Huntingdon recognised when she warned a young friend, 'You might as well sell yourself into slavery at once, as marry a man you dislike' (p. 380).

Lockwood realises, of course, that this 'pleasant family circle' (p. 21) does not live up to the ideals expressed by his own language, but his only response is repression or avoidance. When Cathy informs him that she is a prisoner, not allowed outside the garden wall, he sidesteps this fact by gallantry: 'I should be sorry to ask you to cross the threshold, for my convenience, on such a night' (p. 23). It becomes clear that she is the subject of both verbal and physical abuse, but when Lockwood sees Heathcliff lift his hand against her, he trivialises the exchange: 'Having no desire to be entertained by a cat and dog combat, I stepped forward briskly . . . Each had enough decorum to suspend further hostilities' (p. 34). Understanding that his presence merely interrupts the violence, he prefers to imagine its continuance as a mildly comic barnyard spat. He says that he hears 'not altogether disapprovingly' (p. 239) a blow she receives during a quarrel with Hareton, and he attributes her sullenness to a bad nature rather than to the treatment she receives. Fantasising that marriage to him would be 'more romantic than a fairy tale' for Catherine, Lockwood imagines such a change primarily as a move to more glamorous surroundings and more stimulating society (p. 241). He is unable to imagine the very grim fairy tale of her life as prisoner to the monstrous Heathcliff.

As in *The Tenant of Wildfell Hall*, the opposition of male and female worlds that is reflected in the structure of the novel is shown to be one source of the brutality depicted. Cathy's transition into adulthood is a diminution of her powers, signalled by her reappearance, after a period of invalidism, in the garb of a lady and by the resultant forced change in her behaviour. Her years as Mrs Linton before Heathcliff's return pass in a sort of somnolence, a most un-Cathylike acquiescence and calm, as she acts out the ideal of a flower-like woman without desires or passions. At Heathcliff's reappearance, her 'male' traits of anger, desire, and the power to harm resurface, as if evoked by the presence of her 'other half'. She feels that Heathcliff is 'more myself than I am' because he represents her lost self, the asexual 'girl . . . half savage, and hardy, and free' (p. 107). Her anger at Linton, who is probably more androgynous than any other character in the novel, is anger at him for refusing to complete her yet demanding that she remain only half herself.

Similarly, we might say that Heathcliff's years away from Cathy make him into a man in the terms of the age: he has gone out into the world, has done battle and conquered, but has also been hardened. He returns violent, ruthlessly exploitive, and dangerous to those around him, particularly when Cathy is no longer there to keep him in check. Yet his egotism is only a less civilised version of Lockwood's (or of Arthur Huntingdon's), as his hatred for Isabella because she loves him is a harsher version of Lockwood's rejection of the 'goddess' who returned his interest (p. 15). After Cathy's death, Heathcliff is incapable of any 'feminine' or soft emotion, except perhaps for the affection he sometimes shows Nelly. Thus, when he describes Cathy as his soul, and her death as the death of his soul, he is describing the death of a part of himself that he had needed her to act out, because that part had been projected onto her as they stepped into the simplified roles of adulthood.

Like Helen Huntingdon, Nelly Dean serves as recorder or uncoverer of a hidden reality of the novel, and her story is also one of impotence and suppression. Despite her dependence on the families she serves, she attempts to protest or correct the injustices she sees, to soften Hindley's and Heathcliff's anger, to reconcile Edgar and Isabella, to moderate Catherine's outbursts, and later to protect the second Catherine from Heathcliff's schemes. But none of her white lies, manipulations, or even mistakes is successful in changing the structure of her world, and by the time that Lockwood encounters her she has been co-opted to the extent that she is working for the tyrant Heathcliff and only sighing a bit over his mistreatment of Cathy and his deception of Hareton, quite aware that nothing she says or does can make a difference. Only the death of Heathcliff can free those in his 'family' from their degradation and semi-slavery, for Cathy is restrained by fear and Hareton by love from taking steps to escape. But Cathy and Hareton promise to escape the destructive dynamic of the previous generation, for they each possess strength and tenderness, light and dark, all the qualities polarised in their parents and in the novel. The slap that Cathy gives Hareton for not attending to his lessons is a love-tap, a playful remnant of the blows he has given her in the past, and that diminution of force suggests the waning of the violence that had inhabited the house they will soon abandon. The novel's concluding image of fluttering moths and soft winds around the graves of those who had perpetrated the violence of the past, then, underlines the resolution of that violence, which occurs with the reunion of Catherine and Heathcliff and the new union of the younger lovers. Lockwood seeks the graves, seeks the knowledge that those sufferers are indeed at rest – and whether or not they do walk the moors, it is clear that they are at peace. As in *The Tenant of Wildfell Hall*, we return to the world of normality, as Hareton and Cathy will return to Thrushcross Grange and some version of the domestic bliss that was the Victorian ideal. But we have seen an under-world or other-world that is still latent in the structures of that comfortable reality.

Charlotte Brontë described both of her sisters' characters as consisting of layers much like those of their novels. Emily was a person whose mind and feelings had 'recesses' on which not 'even those nearest and dearest to her could, with impunity, intrude unlicensed', a person who concealed under an 'unpretending outside . . . a secret power and fire'.[15] Anne had a reserve that 'covered her mind, and especially her feelings, with a sort of nunlike veil, which was rarely lifted'.[16] But in their novels, they projected a process of removing those veils, revealing those secrets. In her Preface to the so-called 'Second Edition' of *Wildfell Hall*, Anne Brontë describes 'that precious gem', the truth, as something one must 'dive' for, sometimes becoming rather muddy in the process. And certainly the devotion to unsavoury truths brought upon her and her sister 'misconstruction and some abuse'.[17] Neither could have been unaware of the likelihood that their truths would not be welcomed by polite society, which could more comfortably deny them. But they were nevertheless compelled to make that deep dive into themselves, beneath their own layers of conventional consciousness, to see, as Adrienne Rich would write a century later, 'the damage that was done / and the treasures that prevail', to seek 'the wreck and not the story of the wreck / the thing itself and not the myth'. The structures of their novels reflect that intrepid search.

From *Journal of Narrative Technique*, 16 (1986), 204–8 *passim*, 213–19 *passim*.

NOTES

[This article appeared in the *Journal of Narrative Technique* as 'Gender and Layered Narrative in *Wuthering Heights* and *The Tenant of Wildfell Hall*', and has been cut, with the author's assistance, to exclude reference to Anne's novel. It provides an example of the fruitful eclecticism of much feminist criticism, combining formal analysis with social and literary history. By showing a relationship between the 'frame-narrative' of the novel and the gendered power-structures of Victorian England, Naomi Jacobs gives us a 'politicised' version of John T. Matthews's philosophical essay on 'Framing' (reprinted above). References are to *Wuthering Heights*, ed. William M. Sale, Jr (New York, 1972). Ed.]

1. Charlotte Brontë, 'Editor's Preface to the New Edition of *Wuthering Heights*', in *Wuthering Heights*, ed. William M. Sale, Jr (New York, 1972), p. 11.

2. Anne Brontë, *The Tenant of Wildfell Hall*, ed. G. D. Hargreaves (Harmondsworth, 1979), p. 31.

3. '"A Husband Is A Beating Animal": Frances Power Cobbe Confronts the Wife-Abuse Problem in Victorian England', *International Journal of Women's Studies*, 6 (1983), 99–108, p. 106.

4. Unless otherwise noted, all citations of contemporary reviews are to the most widely available source: Miriam Allott (ed.), *The Brontës: The Critical Heritage* (London and Boston, 1974).

5. Ibid., p. 221.

6. Ibid., p. 223.

7. Ibid., p. 292.

8. Charlotte Brontë, 'Editor's Preface to the New Edition of *Wuthering Heights*', in *Wuthering Heights*, ed. William M. Sale, Jr (New York, 1972).

9. Elizabeth MacAndrew, *The Gothic Tradition in Fiction* (New York, 1979), p. 110.

10. Anne Robinson Taylor, *Male Novelists and Their Female Voices: Literary Masquerades* (New York, 1981), p. 22.

11. The Brontës' use of male pseudonyms can be seen as a masquerade of the merry variety, freeing them to write and gain a fair hearing. Charlotte Brontë wrote to Hartley Coleridge, 'I am pleased that you cannot quite decide whether I am an attorney's clerk or a novel-reading dressmaker' (Elizabeth Gaskell, *The Life of Charlotte Brontë* [1857; reprinted Harmondsworth, 1975], p. 201), and Mrs Gaskell thought that 'her sense of humour was tickled by the perplexity which her correspondent felt' (ibid., p. 202). Though Charlotte wrote that she and her sisters felt 'a sort of conscientious scruple at assuming Christian names positively masculine' (Charlotte Brontë, 'Editor's Preface to the New Edition of *Wuthering Heights*', in *Wuthering Heights*, ed. William M. Sale, Jr [New York, 1972], p. 4), she quite positively directed Smith and Elder to address 'Mr Currer Bell' and referred to 'Mr Bell' by the male pronoun when acting as 'his' agent. This use of male pseudonyms generally resembles the comfortable 'male impersonation' of George

Sand, who loved to stroll Paris in the freedom and safety of her male trousers and cigar; it provides a certain degree of protection without much affecting the narrative voice. The emphatic maleness of George Eliot's early narrator, on the other hand, became progressively more ironic and self-parodic as readers learned that 'George Eliot' was really a woman, and a woman known to some as 'Madonna'!

12. Some of the responses to Charlotte Brontë's *Shirley* showed the dangers facing a female writer willing to impersonate or intimately examine male characters. G. B. Lewes wrote that literary women have too often 'written from the man's point of view . . . women have too often thought but of rivalling men. It is their boast to be mistaken for men, – instead of speaking sincerely and energetically as women.' He went on to apply to Brontë, whose work he generally admired, Schiller's criticism of Madame de Staël: 'She steps out of her sex – without elevating herself above it' (Miriam Allott [ed.], *The Brontës: The Critical Heritage* [London and Boston, 1974], pp. 162, 163, 169). Another reviewer wrote of *Shirley*, 'Not one of its men are genuine. There are no such men . . . Let Currer Bell get some one else to paint men, and herself do none but the female figures, or dissect at least none save female hearts' (ibid., p. 118).

13. Tony Tanner, 'Passion, Narrative and Identity in *Wuthering Heights* and *Jane Eyre*', in *Teaching the Text*, ed. Susanne Kappeler and Norman Bryson (London, 1983), pp. 109–25, p. 111.

14. Terence McArthy, 'The Incompetent Narrator of *Wuthering Heights*', *Modern Language Quarterly*, 42 (1981), 54.

15. Charlotte Brontë, 'Editor's Preface to the New Edition of *Wuthering Heights*', in *Wuthering Heights*, ed. William M. Sale, Jr (New York, 1972), pp. 4, 8.

16. Anne Brontë, *The Tenant of Wildfell Hall*, ed. G. D. Hargreaves (Harmondsworth, 1979), p. 8.

17. Charlotte Brontë, 'Editor's Preface to the New Edition of *Wuthering Heights*', in *Wuthering Heights*, ed. William M. Sale, Jr (New York, 1972), p. 6.

5

Gender and Genre in 'Wuthering Heights': Gothic Plot and Domestic Fiction

LYN PYKETT

> In spite of much power and cleverness, in spite of its truth to life in
> the remote corners of England – *Wuthering Heights* is a disagreeable
> story. The Bells seem to affect painful and exceptional subjects – the
> misdeeds or oppression of tyranny, the eccentricities of 'woman's
> fantasy'.[1]

Most commentators on *Wuthering Heights*, whether critics or devotees, have been struck by the novel's extraordinary power and idiosyncratic nature, its 'eccentricities of "woman's fantasy" '. Many
have followed Charlotte Brontë's lead, attributing its strange power
to the mysterious vision of an isolated Romantic genius. The novel,
wrote Charlotte Brontë in her Preface to the second edition,

> was hewn in a wild workshop, with simple tools, out of homely
> materials. The statuary found a granite block on the moor; gazing
> thereon, he saw how from the crag might be elicited a head, savage,
> swart, sinister; a form modelled with at least one element of grandeur
> – power. He wrought with a rude chisel, and from no model but the
> vision of his meditations.[2]

This mythologising of the novel's origins, which seems to have been
designed to explain it to a genteel, Southern audience, presents

Wuthering Heights as the fortuitous conjunction of nature and intense visionary experience in which the shaping process of art plays little part.

There are, however, more mundane sources for this novel than those suggested by Charlotte Brontë. Emily Brontë's bizarre narrative, with its intense passions, inter-familial rivalries, and revenge plot, may have originated in actual family histories of which she knew. Brontë's plot has a number of similarities to the stories which she would have heard, during her brief stay at Law Hill school, about Jack Sharp, its sometime owner, and the Walkers of Walterclough Hall. The rivalry between the usurping adopted son, Jack Sharp, and a natural son; Sharp's systematic degradation of a Walker nephew, and his subsequent decline and bankruptcy are all echoed in the plot of *Wuthering Heights*.[3]

Others have suggested that the novel owes a great deal to the strange Irish stories with which Patrick Brontë diverted his children at breakfast. In particular, Edward Chitham in *The Brontës' Irish Background* (1986) has argued that the story of the orphan's vengeance is derived from the story of Hugh Brunty, Patrick Brontë's father, who was adopted and subsequently ill-treated by an uncle called Welsh. Welsh himself is a sort of Heathcliff figure: an orphan, discovered on a boat travelling from Liverpool, and adopted by Hugh's grandfather, he later ousted the legitimate heirs from their home and married the daughter of the house.

The tale of 'The Bridegroom of Barna', published in *Blackwood's* in 1840, may also have been a source for Emily Brontë's novel. Certainly it has a very similar plot to *Wuthering Heights*, and concerns the star-crossed love of the children of rival families. Ellen Nugent and Hugh Lawlor, the heroine and hero of this violent tale are, like Catherine and Heathcliff, united only in death when they are finally buried in a single grave. If Emily Brontë's plot did not spring fully formed from the isolated depths of her imagination, neither did her broader themes and techniques. The fictional transformation of the late eighteenth-century histories which supply some of the elements of the novel's plot, has much in common with other recent and contemporary literature. This is partly a matter of direct influence from Emily Brontë's own reading, but it is also indicative of the ways in which individual artists (no matter how geographically isolated, nor how idiosyncratic) participate in a shared cultural language, and work with shared forms and patterns.

One of my concerns in this chapter will be to suggest that *Wuthering*

Heights is not, as F. R. Leavis argues in *The Great Tradition*, 'a kind of sport' – an interesting but minor divergence from the high road of the mainstream English Novel. Instead I want to look at *Wuthering Heights* in the context of the developing traditions of late eighteenth- and early nineteenth-century fiction, and to suggest that the peculiar generic mix of this novel offers a number of interesting perspectives on the whole question of the relationship of the woman writer to the history and tradition of fiction.

Wuthering Heights straddles literary traditions and genres. It combines elements of the Romantic tale of evil-possession, and Romantic developments of the eighteenth-century Gothic novel, with the developing Victorian tradition of Domestic fiction in a realist mode. Its use of the ballad and folk material, romance forms and the fantastic, its emphasis on the passions, its view of childhood, and the representation of the romantic quest for selfhood and of aspiring individualism, all link the novel with Romanticism. On the other hand, the novel's movement towards a renewed emphasis on community and duty, and towards an idealisation of the family seem to be more closely related to the emerging concerns of Victorian fiction. Emily Brontë's novel mixes these various traditions and genres in a number of interesting ways, sometimes fusing and sometimes juxtaposing them. I want to direct attention to the ways in which the novel's mixing of genres may be related to issues of gender by examining some of the ways in which specific historic genres may be related to particular historic definitions of gender.

If Emily Brontë's poems are, as her sister suggested, 'not at all like the poetry women generally write', her novel is at once both very similar to and very different from, the kinds of fiction generally written by women in the early nineteenth century. Indeed, much of the distinctiveness of Emily Brontë's novel may be attributed to the particular ways in which it negotiates different literary traditions, and both combines and explores two major fictional genres – the Gothic and Domestic fiction – which are usually associated with the female writers of the period, although by no means confined to them.

Wuthering Heights has proved impossible to categorise, and continues to confront its readers with a sometimes alarming sense of disorientation, a feeling of finding themselves in 'really different novels'.[4] The novel begins in fictional territory which is reasonably familiar to readers of the eighteenth- and nineteenth-century Domestic novel: a date (1801), the genteel narrator's ironic description of a social visit, the careful description of the domestic interior at the Heights, and the beginnings of an investigation of a code of manners and a particular way of life. However, even in the opening chapter the codes and conventions of polite fiction do not seem adequate either to comprehend or represent life at the Heights. For example, Lockwood's description focuses on the *absence* of the *expected* 'glitter of saucepans and tin cullenders on the walls' (p. 47), and the presence of 'villainous old guns, and a couple of horse pistols'. Certainly, by the second and third chapters, the genteel narrator and the reader find their generic and social expectations increasingly at odds with the literary genre and social world into which the narrative has moved. The appearance of Catherine's ghost, and Heathcliff's passionate response, take the novel into the literary genre of Gothic and the forms of the fantastic which provide much of its extraordinary power.

The Earnshaw–Heathcliff–Linton plot is a legend-like tale of an old family disrupted by the arrival of Heathcliff, a dark child of mysterious origins who is brought from Liverpool to the Heights by Mr Earnshaw. Nelly Dean's version of this history is almost literally a 'family romance:' a story of changing familial and inter-familial relationships; of sibling rivalry between Heathcliff and Hindley; of the intensely close brother–sister relationship of Catherine and Heathcliff, the children of nature and comrades-in-arms against the adult tyranny of Joseph and later of Hindley, the new owner of the Heights.

The theme of active male competition begun in Heathcliff and Hindley is continued beyond the Earnshaw family in Edgar Linton and Heathcliff's rivalry for the attentions of Catherine. Catherine's preference for the more cultivated Edgar precipitates Heathcliff's disappearance, and when he subsequently returns in the guise of a fine and prosperous gentleman he once more disrupts family stability, threatening C therine and Edgar's fragile marriage, setting in train an elaborate plan of revenge against both the Earnshaw and the Linton families, and eloping with Edgar's sister Isabella. Nelly's account of Heathcliff's destruction of Hindley and his brutalisation of Hindley's son Hareton, the almost parodic violence of his hanging of Isabella's dog, and his callous treatment of his wife and son represents him as a Gothic villain, a demonic, almost otherworldly figure. This fantastic, demonic version of Heathcliff is reinforced by the melodramatic scenes surrounding Catherine's death, and in the final stages of the narrative when he appears to be communing with the spirit of the dead Catherine in preparation for a removal to her sphere.

Embedded within this Gothic framework, however, is a second narrative, which seems to move progressively in the direction of Victorian Domestic Realism. The second half of the novel's double plot – the second generation story of Linton Heathcliff, Hareton Earnshaw and Catherine Linton – appears to move from Gothic beginnings, in which a monstrous Hareton implicitly collaborates in the abduction of Catherine, her forced marriage to Linton and her effective imprisonment at the Heights, to the conventional closure of a dominant form of the Victorian Domestic novel, in which the hero (Hareton) and heroine (Catherine) overcome the obstacles of an obstructive society and withdraw into a private realm of domesticity, where social, co-operative values are renewed within the bosom of the family. In this case the pattern of closure is completed by the planned removal of Hareton and Catherine from the Heights to Thrushcross Grange.

Gothic is usually taken to be the dominant genre of the first generation plot of *Wuthering Heights*, and is associated with its Romanticism, its mystical, fantastic and supernatural elements, and its portrayal of wild nature. In the eighteenth and nineteenth centuries Gothic was a genre particularly identified with women writers, and many recent feminist critics have argued that Female Gothic may be seen as a complex genre which simultaneously represents women's fears and offers fantasies of escape from them.[6] Female Gothic enacts fantasies of female power in the heroine's courage and enterprise, while simultaneously, or by turns, representing the female condition as both confinement and refuge. Many of the Gothic elements of *Wuthering Heights* may be seen as examples of Female Gothic's representation and investigation of women's fears about the private domestic space which is at once refuge and prison. Indeed, Catherine Earnshaw's story might almost be read as an archetypal example of the genre. After a childhood which alternates between domestic confinement and freely roaming the unconfined spaces of the moors, Catherine's puberty is marked by her confinement to the couch of Thrushcross Grange. Womanhood and marriage to Edgar further confine her within the genteel household, and the denouement of her particular Gothic plot involves her imprisonment in increasingly confined spaces: the house, her room, and finally 'this shattered prison' (p. 196), her body, from which she longs to escape as she does from womanhood itself.

Similarly the story of Isabella Linton focuses on the female lot as a choice between degrees and varieties of imprisonment, as Isabella flees the stifling confinement of the genteel household for a more brutal domestic incarceration at the Heights, now a stronghold of male violence (ch. 17). The first two stages of the history of Catherine Linton follow a similar pattern to Isabella's. Although as a spirited young woman she chafes against the bonds of gentility and the over-protected environment of the Grange, Catherine comes to reassess her former prison as a shelter after her enforced marriage to Linton Heathcliff. The Cathy whom Lockwood observes in the early stages of his narrative is, effectively, a household prisoner, constrained not simply by her own terror and Heathcliff's brute force, but also by contemporary matrimonial laws and her father-in-law's financial power. In changing her role from that of dependent daughter to wife she has ceased to be the legal property of her father and has become instead the property of her husband. When she is both widowed and orphaned she comes under the legal control of her father-in-law, Heathcliff. This legal control of women plays an important part in the novel's plot, and is vividly illustrated in a scene from the marriage of Heathcliff and Isabella.

> If you are called upon in a court of law you'll remember her language Nelly! And take a good look at that countenance – she's near the point which would suit me. No, you're not fit to be your own guardian, Isabella, now; and I, being your legal protector, must retain you in my custody, however distasteful the obligation may be.
>
> (pp. 188–9)

Female Gothic explores women's power and powerlessness, their confinement within the domestic space, their role in the family, and their regulation by marriage and property laws not of their own making and, at this point in history, beyond their power to alter. Many of these concerns are represented, from a different perspective, in the increasingly dominant female genre of Domestic fiction. In a fascinating study of twentieth-century popular Gothics Tania Modleski has suggested that these similarities make for a continuity between Gothic and Domestic, since both are 'concerned with the (often displaced) relationships among family members and with driving home to women the importance of coping with enforced confine-ment and the paranoid fears it generates'.[7]

Certainly, in *Wuthering Heights* Gothic and Domestic are continuous, not simply because of this shared project, but also because the genres are mixed so as to produce a structural continuity. For example, although the Gothic is usually associated with the first generation plot and the Domestic with the second (or even with the last phase of the second generation plot), the novel's narrative structure, and particularly its dislocated chronology, tends to blur the boundaries between generations and genres. Emily Brontë's adaptation of the conventions of the Gothic frame tale is a particularly important element in this process. In earlier Gothic novels the central narrative is approached by way of diaries, letters and other documents which are transcribed or edited by the narrator(s) of the story. Similarly, the reader approaches the central narrative of *Wuthering Heights* via an outsider, Lockwood, who transmits or mediates Nelly's inner (and insider) narrative. To gain access to the extraordinary stories of the families of Wuthering Heights and Thrushcross Grange the reader must thus pass through, and ultimately pass beyond, the perceptual structures of a bemused genteel male narrator who mediates between the public world he shares with his readers and the inner, private, domestic world conveyed to him by Nelly's stories.

Lockwood's mediation of Nelly's narrative reproduces, as N. M. Jacobs points out, that separation between the male and female spheres which lies at the heart of the novel's action, and also actively involves the reader in the process by which 'domestic reality is obscured by layers of conventional ideology'.[8] This narrative layering also serves to close the gap between inner and outer, private and public, domestic and Gothic. Lockwood's framing narrative is particularly important here, since many of the Gothic horrors displayed to and by Lockwood are in fact supported by the ideology of the culture he represents. His own views of marriage and of women, shown in his romantic fantasies about Cathy, and his cold withdrawal from his flirtation with the young lady at the Spa town, reveal this genteel commentator to be just as manipulative and selfish as the apparently demonic Heathcliff. Lockwood's own genteel ideology in fact sanctions the domestic tyranny whose everyday details he appears to find so foreign and extraordinary as he reports them.

The reader's perception of what Lockwood reports is persistently at odds with what the narrator himself sees or expects to see. For example, when he visits the Heights and attempts to engage politely with its owner, Lockwood converses in platitudes derived from the Victorian ideology of the home as refuge from the harsh competitive outside world. The scene he reports is quite at odds with the language in which he congratulates Heathcliff on being 'surrounded by your family and with your amiable lady as the presiding genius over your home and heart' (p. 55). When he is disabused of this particular conventionalised domestic framework Lockwood's second attempt at comprehending the domestic scene is equally wide of the mark: he assumes that Hareton is the 'favoured possessor of the beneficent fairy'. Heathcliff's bitterly amused riposte, 'We neither of us have the privilege of owning your good fairy', of course goes right to the ideological heart of the matter, since legally Heathcliff does own his daughter-in-law.

Although there is a lack of perceptual fit between Lockwood's language and the domestic reality at the Heights, there is no essential lack of fit between the domestic scene he describes and the ideology of domesticity. Lockwood's expectations emphasise one side of the domestic ideal – the harmonious family presided over by the beneficent fairy who submits to her husband's (father's, brother's or father-in-law's) legal and financial control, in exchange for domestic power as the presiding genius of the tea table. However, the domestic reality of the Heights (as witnessed by Lockwood, or experienced by the two Catherines and Isabella) emphasises the other side of this ideal – the inequalities of the exchange and the implicit tyranny of the structure. One major effect of Brontë's adaptation of the Gothic frame tale in this novel is to locate the domestic as the source of the Gothic.

The structural continuity of Gothic and Domestic is also seen in the way in which the second generation plot supposedly replays the first generation story. *Wuthering Heights* tells the same story twice. Leo Bersani is not alone in feeling that the story is diminished in the retelling, and that the novel declines into a 'rather boring second half . . . the cosy and conventionalised romance between the young Catherine and Hareton Earnshaw'.[9] Others, most notably recent feminist critics, have argued that the novel does not simply repeat the same story, but that it revises it, rewriting the Gothic first generation plot as a Domestic novel.

What is involved in the retelling, and what is the significance of the rewriting? Some feminist critics offer an analysis of the revision which in essence seems to reach the same conclusions as Bersani but via a different route. Rosemary Jackson, for example, sees the revision as a loss of power which signifies inauthenticity and a retreat into compromise as *Wuthering Heights* harnesses Gothic 'to serve and not subvert a dominant ideology' and ultimately silences its fantastic or Gothic elements 'in the name of establishing a normative bourgeois realism'.[10] Similarly, Sandra Gilbert and Susan Gubar argue that by the end of the novel, 'The Heights – hell – has been converted into the Grange – heaven –; and with patriarchal history redefined, renovated, restored, the nineteenth century can truly begin'.[11] Carol Senf, on the other hand, interprets the revision, more affirmatively, as offering an evolutionary 'version of history that is both more feminine and more egalitarian, a history in which women are no longer the victims of patriarchal authority'.[12] Read in these ways *Wuthering Heights* is either a novel of conformity to dominant ideologies of class and gender, or a novel of protest against, or reformation of, those ideologies.

However, more complex and inclusive possibilities are offered if we read *Wuthering Heights*' movement from Gothic to Domestic Romance in relation to the rise of 'feminine authority' in the novel and the feminisation of nineteenth-century literary culture in general. Nancy Armstrong, in *Desire and Domestic Fiction* (1987), and Jane Spencer in *The Rise of the Woman Novelist* (1986), have both attempted to trace the development of 'a view of writing that links it to the feminine role rather than opposing [it]', and which 'encouraged the expansion of women's professional writing'.[13] Both Spencer and Armstrong argue that women novelists gained acceptance and 'authority' only 'at the price of agreeing to keep within the feminine sphere'[14] as defined by their culture. This process of feminisation, which began with the eighteenth-century novel, increasingly defined literature 'as a special category supposedly outside the political arena, with an influence on the world as indirect as women's was supposed to be'.[15] In particular the emergence of the novel of courtship and domestic life gave a new value and meaning to the female experience and sensibility. In almost a single move women's experience becomes both absolutely central (to literature) and utterly marginal (to politics).

Clearly this view of literature positioned women writers in a particular way. Any woman who attempted to enter this discourse of literature was faced with a choice of responses: she could accept the dominant definitions of the feminine and write within them; or she could refuse those definitions and attempt either to escape or transcend them, or to engage with and rebel against them. In its mixing and juxtaposing of genres *Wuthering Heights*, perhaps, employs or acknowledges all of these strategies. The revisionary double plotting of this novel does not simply involve a straightforward change of genre from Gothic (the genre of escape or protest) to Domestic (the genre of conformity), but rather its generic and generational shifts are also the structural embodiment of that tendency of Female Gothic – noted by Tania Modleski – which serves to 'convince women that they will not be victims the way their mothers were'.[16]

The closing stages of the narrative seem to move towards the conventional closure of the Victorian Domestic novel: the restitution of family fortunes, the restoration of disrupted stability, and intimations of protracted domestic bliss in the protected space of the ideal nuclear family. However, as with so many aspects of this novel, appearances are deceptive. Although the second generation story revises the Gothic plot of the first generation in the direction of Domestic fiction, the Gothic is not simply written out or obliterated in the process. The Gothic persists in the person of Heathcliff who spans both generations. Indeed, his necrophilia and otherworldliness become more pronounced as the Domestic plot reaches its resolution. The Gothic persists too in the power of Catherine and Heathcliff which remains in the outer narrative, beyond the closure of the Catherine–Hareton plot.

Moreover the 'conventional' Domestic romance with which the novel ends not only revises the initial Gothic plot but is also a revisionary form of the genre in which it purports to be written. In the closing stages of the narrative Catherine Linton, who has previously suffered from the powerlessness imposed on her by a patriarchal legal system, family structures, and dominant views of the feminine, learns to use some of the power that lies in her own abilities. Her book-knowledge (gained from her relatively and unusually free access to her father's library) empowers her against Heathcliff. She can both conduct a witty war of words with him, and can signify her imaginative freedom by taking refuge in a book. In turn she empowers Hareton by helping him to read, and thus both civilises him and imparts practical skills which enable him to reclaim his birthright. Catherine's civilising of Hareton is an interesting variant of a common scene in eighteenth- and nineteenth-century fiction in which a male character offers improving reading to an 'ignorant' (but improvable) female. It is also interesting to note that Catherine's cultivation or 'feminisation' of her cousin coincides with Heathcliff's final decline into an otherworldliness which diverts him from completing his plans to gain total control of the Heights and the Grange. As the novel ends Catherine is about to regain control of her inheritance, and although at this period she would have been legally required to hand all her property back to Hareton when he became her husband, it is nevertheless at least of symbolic importance that Hareton's patrimony is returned to him via the female line. Like Jane Eyre's legacy, the restoration of Catherine's property equalises the balance of power between marriage partners. A degree of financial independence for the female partner seems to be a prerequisite for the companionate marriages with which both these novels end.

In its transition from patriarchal tyranny, masculine competition, domestic imprisonment and the Gothic to the revised Domestic romance of the courtship and companionate marriage of Catherine and Hareton, *Wuthering Heights* both participates in, and engages with, the feminisation of literature and the wider culture noted by Armstrong and Spencer. However, I would suggest that Emily Brontë's novel does not simply reflect or represent this process, but that it also investigates and explores it. The narrative disruptions, the dislocations of chronology, the mixing of genres and Brontë's historical displacement of her story, published in 1847 but set in a carefully dated period leading up to and just beyond 1801, combine to produce a novel which goes back and traces both changing patterns of fiction and the emergence of new forms of the family.

Wuthering Heights traces the emergence of the characteristic form of Victorian fiction – the Domestic novel in realist mode. Its own mixing of genres emphasises the links of this newly dominant form with Gothic and also foregrounds the romance elements of the realistic Domestic novel. The 'cosy conventionalised romance' of Catherine and Hareton is an extremely simplified version of the Domestic romance, which exposes and explores the mechanisms of the form. In other words, the self-conscious idealisation of the Catherine–Hareton story exposes the ideological component of both Emily Brontë's story and of the genre in which it is written.

In its movement between generations and genres *Wuthering Heights* also traces the emergence of the modern family in idealised form. It traces the process, minutely documented by Leonore Davidoff and Catherine Hall in *Family Fortunes* (1987), by which the modern nuclear family (represented by Catherine and Hareton) replaced the larger and more loosely related household (as exemplified by various stages of domestic life at the Heights), withdrawing to a private domestic space removed from the workplace. Catherine and Hareton are shown as inhabiting this newly privatised domestic realm even before their marriage and removal to the Grange. Their cultivation of the flower garden and Hareton's primrose-strewn porridge (p. 348) are emblematic of their transformation of the Heights into a domain of feminine values, a haven of tranquillity to which men retire from a workaday world of business and competition, in order to cultivate their gardens, their hobbies and the domestic ideal.

However, at the same time as *Wuthering Heights* traces the emergence of the modern family and its hegemonic fictional form of Domestic realism, other elements of the novel – its disrupted chronology, its dislocated narrative structure, and the persistence of the disturbing power of Catherine and Heathcliff – work together to keep other versions of domestic life before the reader: the domestic space as prison, the family as site of primitive passions, violence, struggle and control. In its mixing of genres and in the particular genres it chooses to mix *Wuthering Heights* may, perhaps, be placed with those female fictions which, as Judith Lowder Newton argues 'both support and resist ideologies which have tied middle-class women to the relative powerlessness of their lot and which have prevented them from having a true knowledge of their situation'.[17]

From Lyn Pykett, *Emily Brontë*, Macmillan Women Writers Series, (Basingstoke and London, 1989), pp. 71–85, 137–8.

NOTES

[Lyn Pykett's essay originally appeared as chapter 5 of her *Emily Brontë*, a book with a feminist orientation intended primarily for undergraduate readers, and to some extent it is thus a summing up of previous work. She draws on several genre-based studies in order to argue that *Wuthering Heights* spans two distinct phases of the 'woman's novel' in the nineteenth century – the 'Gothic' and the 'domestic'. Like Carol Senf and Naomi Jacobs, whose essays she refers to, Pykett demonstrates the political implications of this formal analysis, seeing a correlation between the change from 'Gothic' to 'domestic' novels and the position of women in society, while insisting that *Wuthering Heights* is never straightforward in its relationship to these genres.

It is not easy to put a label on Pykett's critical position, but her emphasis on the novel as constructed from and constructing historically-specific discourses means that her essay has much in common with the New Historicist or 'cultural' criticism which draws its inspiration from the writings of Michel Foucault. (See Paul Rabinow [ed.], *The Foucault Reader* [1986; reprinted Harmondsworth, 1991].)

Lyn Pykett's chapter is reproduced here without cuts. N. M. Jacobs's essay, referred to above, is also partly reprinted in this volume – see p. 74.

References are to *Wuthering Heights*, ed. David Daiches (Harmondsworth, 1967). Ed.]

1. *Athenaeum* (25 December 1847), in Miriam Allott (ed.), *The Brontës: The Critical Heritage* (London, 1974), p. 218.

2. Charlotte Brontë, Preface to the second edition of *Wuthering Heights* (1850; reprinted in *Wuthering Heights*, ed. David Daiches [Harmondsworth, 1967], p. 41).

3. See Winifred Gérin, *Emily Brontë: A Biography* (Oxford, 1972), pp. 76ff. and 220ff.

4. Q. D. Leavis, 'A Fresh Approach to *Wuthering Heights*', in F. R. Leavis and Q. D. Leavis, *Lectures in America* (London, 1969), p. 87.

5. Freud uses this term to describe the familial fantasies by means of which children attempt to resolve their confusions about identity and the boundaries of the self. Leo Bersani offers a sustained Freudian reading of *Wuthering Heights* in *A Future for Astyanax: Character and Desire in Literature* (London, 1978).

6. See Ellen Moers, *Literary Women* (London, 1978) and Eva Figes, *Sex and Subterfuge: Women Novelists to 1850* (London, 1982). Also Tania Modleski, *Loving With A Vengeance: Mass Produced Fantasies for Women* (London, 1984), and Jane Spencer, *The Rise of the Woman Novelist: From Aphra Behn to Jane Austen* (Oxford, 1986).

7. Tania Modleski, *Loving With A Vengeance: Mass Produced Fantasies for Women* (London, 1984), p. 20.

8. N. M. Jacobs, 'Gendered and Layered Narrative in *Wuthering Heights* and *The Tenant of Wildfell Hall*', *Journal of Narrative Technique*, 16 (1986), 204.

9. Leo Bersani, *A Future for Astyanax: Character and Desire in Literature* (London, 1978), p. 221.

10. Rosemary Jackson, *Fantasy: The Literature of Subversion* (London, 1981), p. 124.

11. Sandra Gilbert and Susan Gubar, *The Madwoman in the Attic: The Woman Writer and the Nineteenth-Century Literary Imagination* (New Haven, 1978), p. 302.

12. Carol Senf, 'Emily Brontë's Version of Feminist History: *Wuthering Heights*', *Essays in Literature*, 12 (1985), 209.

13. Jane Spencer, *The Rise of the Woman Novelist: From Aphra Behn to Jane Austen* (Oxford, 1986), p. ix.

14. Ibid., p. 107.

15. Ibid., p. xi.

16. Tania Modleski, *Loving With A Vengeance: Mass Produced Fantasies for Women* (London, 1984), p. 83.

17. Judith Lowder Newton, *Women, Power and Subversion: Social Strategies in British Fiction, 1778–1860* (London, 1985), p. 13.

6

Voicing a Silent History: 'Wuthering Heights' as Dialogic Text

MICHAEL MACOVSKI

> For storytelling is always the art of repeating stories, and this art is lost when the stories are no longer retained. It is lost because there is no more weaving and spinning to go on while they are being listened to.
> (Walter Benjamin, 'The Storyteller')

> I want you to *tell* me my way, not to *show* it; or else to persuade Mr Heathcliff to give me a guide.
> (Lockwood in *Wuthering Heights*)

I

Ever since F. R. Leavis first characterised it as a 'kind of sport' – an anomaly with 'some influence of an essentially undetectable kind' – critics have attempted to locate *Wuthering Heights* within various schools of literary interpretation or detection. To the 'barred' doors of the Heights world have come those who see the novel as an allegory of class conflict, a microcosm of generational tension, or a response to Romantic tradition.[1] The last fifteen years, however, have seen a determined, if inconsistent, turn away from this legacy of attempted interpretation, of what J. Hillis Miller calls our need 'to satisfy the mind's desire for logical order', to 'indicate the right way to read the novel as a whole'.[2] These latter critics accordingly cite what they variously refer to as the 'misinterpretation', 'crisis of interpretation', or 'conflicting possibilities of interpretation' that allegedly distinguish the novel.[3] Of course, such approaches differ among themselves: while some attribute this misinterpretation to a particular narrator's unreliable point of view, others maintain that *any* path through the novel leads to a 'reader's quandary' – since its 'multiplicity of outlook' and 'surplus of signifiers' demonstrate an 'intrinsic plurality'. Still others deny even the potential import of such signifiers, insisting that the very language of the novel presents us with a 'missing centre': hence even the name of a given character 'despotically eliminates its referent, leaving room neither for plurality nor for significance'.[4] Although these recent critics hardly constitute a consensus, they would seem to agree that, in Miller's words, 'however far inside [the "penetralium"] the reader gets', he will find only 'enigmatic signs', 'bewilderment', and 'ultimate bafflement'. 'The secret truth about *Wuthering Heights* is', Miller goes on, 'that there is no secret truth.'[5]

Thus, the present generation of critics seems inclined to let the problematic mysteries and open questions of *Wuthering Heights* live a life of their own, and indeed there is much to be said for this approach to interpretation. The tortured relationship, for instance, between Catherine and Heathcliff is inimical to any recognisable casuistic standard; and if some alien morality stands behind Heathcliff's own inconsistent actions, it has yet to be defined. Yet despite the reader's 'bewilderment' and even 'ultimate bafflement' at such mysteries, it is difficult to deny that the novel is about the act of interpretation itself. Despite its disturbing 'crisis of interpretation', we must still recognise that Brontë presents the entire novel as a rendering, as a story reported at one, two, or three removes. The interpretive valuations of characters like Lockwood, Nelly, and Zillah distort almost every episode of the story we hear – thereby implicating the reader as the last in a framed succession of interpreters.

Much has been made of this peculiarly framed form of *Wuthering Heights*: several critics, for instance, have suggested that the listeners embedded in the novel are in many ways analogous to actual readers. Such studies attempt to liken our interpretations to those of the 'normal sceptical reader', and to insist that Nelly and Lockwood, the primary witnesses to the events of the novel, serve to represent this reader.[6] Yet the question of reading in *Wuthering Heights* is surely more complex than this comparison would suggest: we must, for instance, ask how any reader who apprehends the novel can resemble

Lockwood, a character universally acknowledged to be an effete bungler, insensitive to the dramatic power of the story he hears. We must also take into account that we hear Nelly's perspective during most of the novel, and sense that she too is not an observer worth emulating. Finally, we must consider what these models of audition say about the possibility for interpreting such characters as Heathcliff and Catherine Earnshaw.

What the foregoing studies have not considered is that the issue of interpretation and response is addressed directly within the text of *Wuthering Heights* – most explicitly by interrogative exchanges between characters, but also by the rhetorical form of the novel itself. For the substance of the novel is in effect a succession of addresses directed to designated listeners, a series of witnessed narratives. These addresses include not only Nelly Dean's narrative to Lockwood, but the two climactic exchanges in which Heathcliff and Catherine respectively describe their preternatural union to Nelly (pp. 72–4, 255–6). The novel accordingly foregrounds the act of interpretation by framing both characters' experiences within the context of sustained audition.

In fact, in order for these two characters to 'let out' (in Catherine's words) their secrets, the presence of an interpreter appears to be vital (p. 70). At the beginning of one interchange, Catherine actually proceeds to restrain Nelly, her auditor (p. 72). Furthermore, Catherine seems determined to incorporate a listener's response into her own evaluation of self. Again and again, she begs Nelly to corroborate her decision to marry Edgar. When Nelly mocks the question, Catherine again demands, 'Be quick, and say whether I was wrong'; still later, Catherine pleads, 'say whether I should have done so – do!' (p. 70). Finally, at the end of this broken colloquy Catherine says to Nelly, 'yet you have not told me whether I'm right' (p. 71). Thus, the impetus behind rhetorical interchange here appears to be interpretation: to 'let out' one's 'secret' is to need it received and judged.

Even Heathcliff displays the need to express his inmost feelings before another, to break his solitude, at least momentarily. During his most extended attempt to describe his relation to Catherine, he says to Nelly, 'you'll not talk of what I tell you, and my mind is so eternally secluded in itself, it is tempting, at last, to turn it out to another' (p. 255). Here again, the purpose of audition is to draw out the 'eternally secluded' self: to delineate the ego according to social or dialogic correlates. Much as Catherine seeks to 'let out' her buried 'secret', Heathcliff too attempts to 'turn [his mind] out to another' in order to interpret it. In this sense, his request to 'turn out' his self to Nelly resembles his earlier plea to Catherine's ghost: 'Oh! my heart's darling, hear me *this* time' (p. 33). In both cases, Heathcliff enjoins his listener to 'hear' or comprehend the broken 'heart' – the fragmented self. And although he eventually attains a form of union with the deceased Catherine, Heathcliff still spends the final days of his life endeavouring to address her beyond the grave and thus transcend both his rhetorical and social isolation.

II

Yet audition ultimately fails Heathcliff, as it does nearly all would-be interlocutors in *Wuthering Heights*; within the dialogic framework of the novel, they must remain 'eternally secluded'. No sooner has Heathcliff begun his attempt to 'turn out' his mind 'to another' than he breaks off, saying, 'it is frenzy to repeat these thoughts to you' (p. 255). He then concludes: 'My confessions have not relieved me' (p. 256). And such an outpouring to Nelly does indeed resemble an undirected 'frenzy', since she proves incapable of any reciprocal response. In recounting Heathcliff's earlier efforts to depict his attendant 'spectre', Nelly says, 'He only half addressed me, and I maintained silence – I didn't like to hear him talk!' (p. 230).

Nelly's silence here indicates a larger pattern of failed audition, for it implies an inability to apprehend those ghosts and visions which represent revelation in the novel. When Catherine, for instance, begins to speak of her vision of heaven, Nelly insists, 'Oh! don't, Miss Catherine. . . . We're dismal enough without conjuring up ghosts and visions to perplex us' (p. 72). When Catherine goes on, Nelly cries, 'I tell you I won't harken to your dreams, Miss Catherine!' Yet by refusing to 'harken' to these revelatory visions, Nelly also misses the pivotal revelation of the novel: the spectral bond between Catherine and Heathcliff, a bond represented primarily by sightings and visions. As one critic has written in describing this mystic union, 'To deny Heathcliff's assurance of Catherine's presence is to deny the novel'.[7]

Such denials amount to a kind of analytic deafness: both Nelly and Lockwood attempt to discount what they cannot understand. Thus when Nelly first bungles this auricular role, Catherine responds, in effect, to every interpretive process in the novel: 'that's not what I intend', she says, 'that's not what I mean!' (p. 73). Even

Heathcliff has become a deceived auditor after he 'listened till he heard Catherine say it would degrade her to marry him, and then he stayed to hear no farther' (p. 73). We thus begin to see that this failure of interpretation runs deeper than any local misunderstandings of Heathcliff and Catherine on the part of Nelly. Although revelations are 'half-addressed' to listeners, they repeatedly encounter interpretive silence. Whereas exposure may be possible in this novel, colloquy is not.[8]

We are left, then, with the question of why this novel would incorporate a self-consciously flawed model of listening. What is more, why would Brontë emphasise these flawed interpretations by making them the central point of view, the irregular lens through which we see every character in the novel? Why would she actually dramatise a frustrated interchange seen from the position of an uncomprehending observer – as if she had built an intentionally skewed frame of reference into her novel? And if this distorting frame does leave us in what Miller calls 'ultimate bafflement', how might Brontë have expected us to respond to such an exegetical predicament? That is, what are we to make of those longstanding critical dilemmas which continue to dog the novel: the unaccountable cruelty and other Gothic events; the frame narrative and representations of reading; the import of Catherine's climactic statement, 'I *am* Heathcliff'?[9] Finally, if these critical problems are inseparable from the elusive beauty of the novel, we must still ask what they say about the status of interpretive possibility in Brontë's world.

We can start to answer these questions of interpretation and response by re-examining what is certainly the most immediate audience for Heathcliff's and Catherine's story – those incorporated auditors who first witness the narrative. I will argue that many of these unresolved questions are a result of what I consider the vital structure of the novel: an epistemological disjunction between listeners and speakers. It is, moreover, precisely this disjunction that blurs the line between speakers and listeners. Indeed, the question of who interprets and who narrates becomes a complex one in this novel, since it is actually built around a pair of speaker/listener paradigms. We have noted, for instance, that while Nelly clearly directs her tale to Lockwood, the most crucial scenes of the novel centre around those dialogues in which she herself must play the listener to Heathcliff's and Catherine's revelatory confessions. Nelly must therefore be both teller and listener, for she acts as an interpreter positioned between an unexplained character and an uncomprehending audience. Though she is a storyteller in her own right, she is also a listener attempting to fathom the 'history' of an enigmatic Heathcliff (pp. 37, 139). And once again, the final listeners in this succession of audiences are the readers: we receive Lockwood's journal of uncertain destination.

We can thus reconsider *Wuthering Heights* as a convergence of apostrophes, a chain of rhetorical exposures. Indeed, I would suggest that when the speakers of *Wuthering Heights* address a listener, they in effect expose a hidden part of the self – expose it to the interpretation not only of the other, but of themselves as well. While most of these interpretations break down during the novel, I ultimately reject the notion that Brontë leaves us with only circumscribed vision and misinterpretation. Instead, I will argue that the novel continually keeps the possibility of interpretation open *by sustaining a rhetorical process of understanding*, by enacting a series of hermeneutic forms. For even when these addresses come up against inadequate audition, they nevertheless establish models of ongoing comprehension and interpretation for the reader. What is more, these rhetorical exposures before an other come to represent not only the separate interpretation of self and other, but the actual fashioning of this self in terms of the other. In this sense, the listener's function is both interpretive and ontological.

It is not surprising, then, that these narrative exposures take on different functions at various points in the novel. On one level, I argue that when Brontë uses the narrative address to an auditor as a mode of interpretation, she in effect re-enacts the nineteenth-century transformation of confession into self-decipherment. On another level, I show how, elsewhere in *Wuthering Heights*, this narrative exposure takes on attributes of an interpretive dialogue, and is accordingly analogous to such psychoanalytic processes as reconstructing the past and transferring onto the other. I then expand on Brontë's view of self-interpretation, taking as my model the child's method of mirroring his ego onto an other, and showing how this method illuminates the literary speaker's establishment of his or her own self before an addressee. At other points in the novel, this self-creation results from a character's 'dialogic' interchanges with a listener, which I go on to consider in light of Bakhtin's paradigm of multiple voices. Lastly, I suggest that this nineteenth-century desire to inspirit the self through an other is best explained by Coleridge's concept of 'outness' – that state in which he can define the 'Boundary' of his external 'Self'.

III

The role of the speaker/confessee in Brontë's novel reflects the nineteenth-century view of confession as self-examination, as opposed to the earlier injunction to provide evidence for external judgement. In Michel Foucault's formulation, 'the nineteenth century altered the scope of the confession; it tended no longer to be concerned solely with what the subject wished to hide [from another], but with what was hidden from himself' (p. 66). Earlier religious encounters had stressed an outside witness's role in both interpretation and absolution; now, confessional rhetoric was also seen as enabling a speaker to structure his own self-knowledge, his process of learning what was 'hidden from himself'. Hence in *Wuthering Heights*, when Heathcliff and Catherine deliberately seek to confess their secrets, each is framing these mysteries within a mode of discourse that demands as much decipherment from the speaking confessee as it does from the listening confessor (pp. 39, 70). Thus when Brontë depicts both characters deploying the rhetoric of confession, she suggests that each is engaged in a process of revealing the self. Such revelation is not only exposure of self (to another), but disclosure within self as well.

IV

Narrative addresses in *Wuthering Heights* thus make use of confessional tropes, and thereby enact a rhetorical search for unorthodox notions of relief and pardon. In other passages, however, the addresses in the novel represent a more overt form of interpretation – an enactment of that narrative form which is intrinsically self-analytical. In rhetorical terms, the recurrence of this attempted colloquy in *Wuthering Heights* signifies a proleptic method of interpreting the self, a method best explained in terms of the psychoanalytic dialogue. This heuristic again demands the presence of a listener, even an agonistic one, for he or she is the rhetorical equivalent of the analytic or interpretive figure. Even Lockwood can hold this rhetorical place in the novel, especially since his early request to play the listener to Nelly's narrative actually initiates the analytic form of the novel. Accordingly, it is Lockwood who voices the novel's analytic intention, its interpretive quest to fathom Heathcliff's 'curious conduct' and 'character' (pp. 19, 37), 'decypher' Catherine's 'faded hieroglyphics' (p. 26), and uncover, in Lockwood's words, 'something of my neighbours' (p. 37).

What distinguishes this analytic rhetoric is that it allows characters like Heathcliff and Catherine to effect the kind of projective self-understanding sought during the psychoanalytic exchange.

According to this view, the recreation of dialogue gives voice to a silent history and thereby allows for its reinterpretation. If Heathcliff's truncated dialogues with Nelly represent his desire to hear his earliest historic voice, Catherine's flawed addresses attempt to invoke her father and Heathcliff, the auditors of her first linguistic era. Even Nelly, by sustaining her own narrative address before Lockwood, attempts to impose some contrived order on her past dialogues with both Heathcliff and Catherine. In each case, these characters initiate an interpretive re-enactment of past voices – a regress that ultimately extends back to that original dialogue with the self, that confrontation with the other which we experience during the 'mirror stage'.[10]

This stage is, of course, Jacques Lacan's term for the child's clarification of selfhood by focusing on an other with whom he can identify. The child thereby defines his ego by projecting his own separateness onto an other. Lacan sees this process of self-identification as a mirroring, 'a veritable capture by the other . . . "as in a mirror", in the sense that the subject identifies his sentiment of Self in the image of the other'.[11] It is this mirror stage confrontation that lies at the heart of many sustained addresses in *Wuthering Heights*, for only in being recognised by the autochthonous other can characters like Heathcliff and Catherine extract their own identities. Indeed, 'the first object of desire is to be recognised by the other' (p. 31), and it is precisely this desire for recognition of self in other that in turn prompts Catherine to envision her identity in Heathcliff: 'He's more myself than I am', she says to Nelly; 'Whatever our souls are made of, his and mine are the same' (p. 72). Later, she adds, 'so, don't talk of our separation again – it is impracticable' (p. 74). In *Wuthering Heights*, moreover, this primal recognition also takes place in rhetorical terms, which again accounts for the self-defining other's repeatedly taking the form of an addressee. Accordingly, establishing self in the novel must necessarily be a linguistic act, since only through language can the other both manifest itself and provide 'recognition'.[12]

V

Thus the analytic addressee serves not only to represent the past interlocutors of Heathcliff and Catherine, but to provide them with recognition – the self imaged in the other. In what is perhaps the most explicit account of this projected selfhood, Catherine says to Nelly, 'surely you and everybody have a notion that there is, or should be, an existence of yours beyond you. What were the use of my creation if I were entirely contained here?' (pp. 73–4). On one level, of course, Catherine's 'existence . . . beyond' refers to Heathcliff: she is explaining a union that eventually defies 'separation'. Yet on another level, this passage also alludes to a more vital capacity to move outside of one's contained existence, to establish creation and being through an other. Later, Heathcliff too seeks this externalised identification when, upon learning of Catherine's death, he cries to her, 'take any form . . . only *do* not leave me . . . Oh, God! it is unutterable! I *cannot* live without my life! I *cannot* live without my soul!' (p. 139). Heathcliff recognises that life inheres in the form of the other, the surrogate soul.

The critic who has most thoroughly formulated this ontological connection between speaker and other is Mikhail Bakhtin. To speak of that 'existence . . . beyond' the 'contained' self, that object who informs being, is to speak at once of what Bakhtin calls 'self-consciousness'. He writes, 'I am conscious through another, and with the help of another. The most important acts constituting self-consciousness are determined by a relationship toward another consciousness (toward a *thou*).'[13] For Bakhtin, this '*thou*' hypostatises self-consciousness, which is to say that only this dialogic relationship can make the self aware of its own distinctness, can actually unveil the self to itself. He goes on: 'in dialogue a person not only shows himself outwardly, *but he becomes for the first time that which he is* – and, we repeat, not only for others but for himself as well. *To be means to communicate dialogically*'.[14] Thus dialogue with the 'existence . . . beyond' enacts the ego.

In *Wuthering Heights*, moreover, this other can also manifest itself collectively. Catherine, for instance, in seeking union with Heathcliff, is actually striving to orient her existence, to place it within the social world. She attempts to locate her consciousness within a human order, to eschew (in Lockwood's words) the 'perpetual isolation' of being 'banished from the world' (pp. 17, 240). Hence this need for social intercourse recalls Bakhtin's notion of polyphonic discourse, in which one 'invests his entire self in discourse, and this discourse enters into the dialogic fabric of human life'.[15] Brontë's concept of self is thus essentially plural, social in the broadest sense.

We must further bear in mind that if characters establish being through social intercourse, they also stress this delineation of self as vocal or spoken. The ego must be overheard in the form of a voice. 'Life', Bakhtin writes, 'by its very nature is dialogic. To live means to *participate* in dialogue: to ask questions, to heed, to respond, to agree, and so forth.'[16]

> To find one's own voice and to orient it among other voices, to combine it with some and to oppose it to others, to separate one's voice from another voice with which it has inseparably merged – these are the tasks that the heroes solve in the course of the novel. And this determines the hero's discourse. It must find itself, reveal itself among other words.[17]

In *Wuthering Heights*, then, the dream narratives of Heathcliff and Catherine must also 'orient [themselves] among other voices'; each must 'find itself, reveal itself among' the spoken responses of inadequate listeners. Only such interchanges – including the listening which underlies them – can resonate the social self.

VI

Bakhtin's discussions of the dialogic consciousness of self thus serve to clarify Brontë's concepts of existence and social intercourse. Yet we need not rely solely on modern commentary to expand on this notion of consciousness-in-other. Indeed, the writer who best exemplifies the nineteenth-century concern with the externally-defined self, with plural self-consciousness, is Coleridge, whose aesthetics are cited by the many critics who insist on the Romantic quality of *Wuthering Heights*.[18] Catherine herself might have said, as Coleridge did, 'Self in me derives its sense of Being from having this one absolute Object'.[19] Her 'Object' thus defines a mental 'Neighbourhood', which in turn defines her place in 'the Universe'. When she momentarily loses this 'Boundary' (during Heathcliff's absence), she necessarily loses her 'being' and perishes (p. 85). She falls victim to what Coleridge calls 'the *incorporeity* of true love in absence' – that 'incorporeity' of 'Self' which follows from the loss of 'Definition'.[20]

Catherine's apparent need for this projected existence or 'Definition' is further explicable in light of what Coleridge elsewhere refers to as 'outness', that state in which he can expose or 'withdraw' his 'painful Peculiarities . . . from the dark Adyt of [his] own Being'.[21] And once again, this outness emerges even in the form of the feckless listeners in *Wuthering Heights*: they provide not corroboration by others so much as an exposure before conscience. In Coleridge's terms, the sole 'Impulse' for establishing 'Outness' is to unveil or 'withdraw' the hidden self – and 'not the wish for others to see it'.[22] It is the symbolic and rhetorical presence of such listeners that enables Catherine to expose her self, to demarcate 'existence', to 'continue to be'.

Here, I would say, we are addressing what is perhaps the most perplexing critical dilemma surrounding *Wuthering Heights*: the status of Catherine's cryptic statement, 'I *am* Heathcliff' (p. 74). For we can now account for this equation by reflecting on what we have been calling Catherine's avowed need for outness, that desire to define being in terms of an 'existence . . . beyond' one's 'contained' self. Thus, in the statement 'I *am* Heathcliff', Catherine essentially delimits her existence by locating it in another, by making her outness one with Heathcliff's. It is this notion of outness that also accounts for Heathcliff's last visions of Catherine's spectre, for he is essentially living out her stated description of her externality: 'If all else perished, and *he* remained, I should continue to be' (p. 14). And it is this depiction of self-defining, moreover, which also underlies the novel's last ghostly images of Catherine and Heathcliff; by the time of his death, they have at last established this externally hypostatised self-through-other.

As the novel closes, it is this projection of self that finally accounts for the attenuated image of the second generation union – for in this couple, not only do part of Catherine and Heathcliff 'continue to be', but a symbol of their rhetorical process of outness necessarily lives on. And when the younger Cathy ultimately asks Hareton to listen, she necessarily provides a vehicle for her own 'affection & duties towards others', her own 'Definition' of 'Conscience' and 'Self', her own outness. The legacy of the auditor is thus confirmed.

From *ELH*, 54 (Summer 1987), 363–8, 370–2 *passim*, 374–5, 377–84 *passim*.

NOTES

[Although Macovski offers a psychoanalytic reading of *Wuthering Heights*, his is not a conventional Freudian reading but one based on a combination of Jacques Lacan's poststructuralist revisions of Freud and Mikhail Bakhtin's theory of dialogism.

Bakhtin (1895–1975) wrote from within Soviet Russia and his works became available in English in the 1970s. During the 1920s he wrote in opposition to the influential Russian formalists, arguing that works of art cannot be organic 'unities' because language is essentially 'dialogic'. A text is always part of a 'dialogue' with previous and following texts, and is always composed of several 'voices' in dialogue within the text. Some of the implications of this position are discussed in the Introduction (see p. 8 above). Bakhtin's ideas have been popular with recent materialist or cultural critics, since they encourage a dynamic concept of the relationship between texts and history.

The combination of Bakhtin with Lacan raises some problems. Briefly, while Bakhtin argues that people define themselves by *talking* to each other, Lacan's 'mirror-phase' theory refers to a pre-linguistic stage of human development in which infants define themselves by looking at an image. Macovski, however, argues that the dialogue in *Wuthering Heights* 'gives voice to a silent history'.

A number of feminist writers have also tried to 'retrieve' the pre-linguistic phase of mother–child bliss to which women, they feel, have privileged access (see, for instance, Margaret Homans, *Bearing the Word* [Chicago, 1986], discussed in the Introduction [above, p. 15]; and Elaine Millard, 'New French Feminisms', in *Feminists Reading; Feminist Readings*, ed. Sara Mills *et al.* [Hemel Hempstead, 1989]).

Macovski's essay is reprinted here, with his permission, in a shortened version. References are to *Wuthering Heights*, ed. William M. Sale, Jr (New York, 1963). Ed.]

1. For an indication of this extraordinary range of readings – a range so contradictory that it begins to suggest a problematic approach to interpretation – see Richard Lettis and William E. Morris (eds), *A Wuthering Heights Handbook* (New York, 1961); Miriam Allott (ed.), *The Brontës: The Critical Heritage* (London and Boston, 1974); Miriam Allott, 'The Brontës' in *The English Novel: Select Bibliographical Guides*, ed. A. E. Dyson (London, 1974), pp. 218–45; Alastair G. Everitt, *Wuthering Heights: An Anthology of Criticism* (London, 1967); as well as the criticism selected in William M. Sale, Jr (ed.), *Wuthering Heights: An Authoritative Text, with Essays in Criticism* (New York, 1963). See p. 17 of this edition for the reference to the 'barred' doors of the Heights World. (I have also adopted the critical practice of using 'Catherine' to designate Catherine Earnshaw, and 'Cathy' to refer to her daughter by Edgar Linton.)

Regarding the novel's Romantic characteristics, I have summarised research on this aspect of *Wuthering Heights* in note 18.

Finally, Leavis's observation also accounts for the unusually disparate attempts to approach this novelistic 'sport' and trace its 'undetectable' influence; he briefly mentions the novel in *The Great Tradition* (1948; reprinted New York, 1973), p. 27.

2. See J. Hillis Miller's *Fiction and Repetition* (Cambridge, Mass., 1983), pp. 52–3, 49. The remainder of Miller's comments cited in this section are from an earlier version of his chapter on the novel: '*Wuthering Heights* and the Ellipses of Interpretation', *Notre Dame English Journal*, 12 (1980), 85–100.

    For a survey of what I see as the prevailing approach to the novel during the last fifteen years, see note 3.

3. The three phrases are, respectively, from Allan R. Brick, '*Wuthering Heights*: Narrators, Audience, and Message', *College English*, 21 (November 1959), 81 (reprinted in Richard Lettis and William E. Morris [eds], *A Wuthering Heights Handbook* [New York, 1961], pp. 219–20); Carol Jacobs, '*Wuthering Heights*: At the Threshold of Interpretation', *boundary 2*, 7 (1979), 68; and Peter K. Garrett, 'Double Plots and Dialogic Form in Victorian Fiction', *Nineteenth-Century Fiction*, 32 (1977), 8. Although Brick's essay pre-dates the period I am discussing, it too partakes of the hermeneutical approach that has prevailed during the last fifteen years. A brief glance at the titles of these studies – see Donoghue, Jacobs, and Sonstroem (cited in notes 4 and 18) – again suggests this approach. See also Elizabeth R. Napier, 'The Problem of Boundaries in *Wuthering Heights*', *Philological Quarterly*, 63 (1984), 96, 97; and Peter Widdowson, 'Emily Brontë: the Romantic Novelist', *Moderna Sprak*, 66 (1972), who notes that his essay 'is not intended to circumscribe the range of interpretation of *Wuthering Heights* (which is splendidly impossible anyway)' (p. 3).

4. Those studies that attribute the novel's problems of interpretation to its narrators' 'unreliability' include Gideon Shumani, 'The Unreliable Narrator in *Wuthering Heights*', *Nineteenth-Century Fiction*, 27 (1973), 449–68; and Jacqueline Viswanathan, 'Point of View and Unreliability in Brontë's *Wuthering Heights*, Conrad's *Under Western Eyes*, and Mann's *Doktor Faustus*',*Orbis Litterarum*, 29 (1974), 42–60.

    The phrases 'reader's quandary' and 'multiplicity of outlook' are from David Sonstroem, '*Wuthering Heights* and the Limits of Vision', *PLMA*, 86 (1971), 59, 61; the phrases 'surplus of signifiers' and 'intrinsic plurality' are from Frank Kermode, 'A Modern Way with the Classic', *New Literary History*, 5 (1974), 434, 425. See also J. Hillis Miller, *Fiction and Repetition* (Cambridge, Mass., 1983), who writes that the 'act of interpretation always leaves something over. . . . This something left out is clearly a significant detail. There are always in fact a group of such significant details which have been left out of any reduction to order. The text is over-rich' (p. 52).

Both Miller (p. 67) and Carol Jacobs, ('*Wuthering Heights*: At the Threshold of Interpretation', *boundary 2*, 7 [1979]), argue that the language of the novel leaves us with a 'missing centre' (p. 56). [A shortened version of Frank Kermode's essay referred to above is reprinted in this volume – see p. 39 Ed.]

5. J. Hillis Miller, '*Wuthering Heights* and the Ellipses of Interpretation', *Notre Dame English Journal*, 12 (1980), 92. Miller goes on to revise this sentence in *Fiction and Repetition*, where he writes that 'there is no secret truth which criticism might formulate' as a 'principle of explanation which would account for everything in the novel' (p. 51). Despite this revision, however, he then goes on to say that 'it is impossible to tell whether there is any secret at all hidden in the depths' of *Wuthering Heights* (p. 69). And although he speaks of the reader's 'process' and 'effort of understanding', he repeatedly stresses the 'baffling of that effort' – since an 'interpretive origin . . . cannot be identified for *Wuthering Heights*' (pp. 53, 63). Yet if Miller dwells on that 'remnant of opacity which keeps the interpreter dissatisfied' (p. 51), I argue that the rhetorical force of those hermeneutic forms enacted in the novel counterbalances this opacity. Although such concerns are finally distinct from Miller's, he is clearly aware of them when he writes that opacity keeps 'the process of interpretation still able to continue' (pp. 51–2) and that 'the situation of the reader of *Wuthering Heights* is inscribed within the novel in the situations of all those characters who are readers [and] tellers of tales' (p. 70).

6. See, for instance, Carl R. Woodring, 'The Narrators of *Wuthering Heights*', *Nineteenth-Century Fiction*, 11 (1957), 298–305, reprinted in William M. Sale, Jr (ed.), *Wuthering Heights: An Authoritative Text, with Essays in Criticism* (New York, 1963), pp. 338–43. See especially pp. 315, 338, 340. Woodring comes closest to the concerns of this study when he writes: 'If he [Lockwood] seems inane, he suffers from the inanity his author attributes to the average London reader into whose hands her book will fall. In his introduction to the Rinehart College Edition, Mark Schorer follows Garrod in interpreting the original plan of the novel as the edification of a sophisticated and sentimental prig, Lockwood, in the natural human values of grand passion. Rather, Lockwood reacts for the normal sceptical reader in appropriate ways at each stage of the story and its unfolding theme' (p. 340). Woodring, however, never explains his use of the term 'normal sceptical reader', nor does he mention why Brontë would feel the need to represent such a reader's reaction in this particular novel. We must also ask how readers since 1847 have read the novel: do they share reactions which have been widely recognised to be inadequate to the novel? Such questions, I would say, can only be addressed if we consider the status of listeners in the novel. See also Clifford Collins, 'Themes and Conventions in *Wuthering Heights*', *The Critic*, 1 (Autumn 1947), 43–50, reprinted in William M. Sale, Jr (ed.), *Wuthering Heights: An Author-*

itative Text, with Essays in Criticism (New York, 1963), pp. 309–18. Collins maintains that 'Lockwood not only exhibits the reactions that may be expected from the ordinary reader (thereby invalidating them, for his commentary is carefully shown to be neither intelligent nor sensitive), but he is representative of urban life and by origin unfitted for the tempo of life about the Heights' (p. 315). Yet I would say that, for reasons which I will make clear, the reactions of more than just the 'ordinary reader' inform the frame structure of the novel. And I would add that *Wuthering Heights* is less about the incompatibility of 'urban life' and the Heights than about interpretive rhetoric and the epistemological chasm between listeners and narrators.

7. See Walter E. Anderson, 'The Lyrical Form of *Wuthering Heights*', *University of Toronto Quarterly*, 47 (1977–8), 120.

Of course, most characters in this novel *do* deny its visionary premises (as represented by its spectral symbols) and in doing so they deny not only the novel, but the very possibility of interpretive audition. Lockwood, for instance, not only repulses the ghostly Catherine's return to Heathcliff (p. 30), but also fails to understand how this vision of Catherine resonates throughout the narration he hears from Nelly. He seems unaware of the connection between his waif-haunted nightmare and the later 'confession' by Heathcliff: 'the moment I closed my eyes, she was either outside the window, or sliding back the panels' (p. 230). On an earlier occasion, Lockwood calls Heathcliff's belief in Catherine's ghost 'folly' (p. 33) – a term that Nelly later uses to describe Catherine's revelations (p. 74). Indeed, when Catherine herself begins to describe her phantasmal union with Heathcliff, Nelly can only respond, 'I won't hear it, I won't hear it! . . . I was superstitious about dreams then, and am still' (p. 72). Later, Heathcliff's encounters with 'ghosts and visions' prompt the same fearful response from Nelly: 'Mr Heathcliff! master!' she cries, 'Don't, for God's sake, stare as if you saw an unearthly vision' (p. 261). And when Nelly encounters the child who claims to have glimpsed the deceased lovers, she insists that 'he probably raised the phantoms from thinking' (p. 265). By the end of the novel, Nelly regards even her own dreams as lapses into 'superstition', which, as she says, continued until 'dawn restored me to common sense' (p. 260).

We should also note that Lockwood's general incapacity for response precludes reaction not only to the visionary mysteries of Heathcliff and Catherine, but even to the 'fascinating creature' who earlier shows interest in him (p. 15). 'I "never told my love" vocally', he says; and when he finally does prompt a 'return' from her, he reports. 'I . . . shrunk icily into myself, like a snail; at every glance retired colder and farther' (p. 15). Once again, Lockwood's silence obviates any rhetorical return.

Finally, Edgar too becomes the victim of broken colloquy when he demands of Catherine, 'answer my question. . . . You *must* answer it. . . . I absolutely *require* to know' – only to hear her order him from the room (pp. 101–2).

8. As I go on to argue, it is this exposure which sustains both the ongoing process of interpretation and the vitality of the rhetorical form. This is not to say, though, that the novel discounts the fallibility of the interpretive process, including its potential for flawed judgement and moral caprice. Even Nelly seems at times to recognise this possible failure, for after condemning one of Catherine's explanations, she adds, 'though I'm hardly a judge' (p. 73). And indeed, the entire issue of judgement as interpretation is a questionable one within *Wuthering Heights*: the Branderham episode, for example, erupts into a chain-reaction of misfired auditions. First Lockwood renounces his listening role and attacks the offending narrator; then the congregation itself appears to misjudge its leader's account of Lockwood and falls upon one another. And response in *Wuthering Heights* is patterned after Lockwood's audition during this sermon – a botched audition which Branderham, with appropriate inclusiveness, refers to as 'human weakness' (p. 29). In the end, the Reverend's casuistry also proves to be flawed, for his 'judgement' is actually retribution when he cries, 'execute upon him the judgement written' (p. 29).

Generally speaking, the listeners of *Wuthering Heights* indulge in seemingly arbitrary moral judgements; like Branderham, each has 'his private manner of interpreting' (p. 29). Because of this moral subjectivity, no interpretation can transcend another: as Nelly puts it to Lockwood, 'you'll judge as well as I can, all these things; at least, you'll think you will, and that's the same' (p. 152). Without interpretive standards, then, audition becomes a punishment with narration the trial. Listeners accordingly become the objects of judgement in this novel; like Lockwood, they are 'condemned to hear' what they can never understand (p. 29).

9. See Walter E. Anderson, 'The Lyrical Form of *Wuthering Heights*', *University of Toronto Quarterly*, 47 (1977–8), for a reading of Catherine's celebrated statement. For discussion of the other critical dilemmas mentioned here, see the anthologies listed in note 1 (especially Lettis and Morris).

10. See Jacques Lacan, 'Le Stade du miroir', reprinted in *Ecrits* (Paris, 1966). I am applying Lacan's model selectively here, with particular emphasis on his discussion of the infant's ontological development. See also Lacan, *The Language of the Self*, trans. Anthony Wilden (Baltimore, 1968), especially pp. 100, 163, 166, 172–4, 200. Unless otherwise noted, all references to Lacan are to Wilden's edition.

11. See Lacan, 'Propos sur la causalité psychique' (1950), p. 45; quoted in Wilden, p. 100, note 27.

12. Ibid., p. 9. In Lacan's terms, such linguistic recognition is a function of what he calls the 'Word' – that abstract sign of the analysand's individual 'response', his discreteness. 'What I seek in the Word', he writes, 'is the response of the other' (p. 63). In *Wuthering Heights*, I would say that the interpretive listener represents this linguistic 'response of the

other': when characters like Catherine, Nelly, and Heathcliff seek out listeners, they seek that linguistic interpretation ('response') which identifies the self ('recognition'). Many studies, of course, have cited examples of such linguistic interpretation in *Wuthering Heights*, including the instances of Hareton's reading, Nelly's censorship, and Lockwood's decipherment and naming process; see, for instance, Carol Jacobs, '*Wuthering Heights*: At the Threshold of Interpretation', *boundary 2*, 7 (1979), 99; Ian Gregor, 'Reading a Story: Sequence, Pace, and Recollection', in *Reading the Victorian Novel: Detail into Form*, ed. Ian Gregor (Totowa, NJ, 1980); and J. Hillis Miller, *Fiction and Repetition* (Cambridge, Mass., 1983). What these studies have not noted, though, is that such linguistic interactions can use the 'response of the other' to establish the self. In Lacan's words, 'Language, before signifying *something*, signifies for someone' (pp. 76–7). Self-affirmation in *Wuthering Heights* is literally the articulation of the self to the other.

13. Mikhail Bakhtin, *Problems of Dostoevsky's Poetics*, trans. and ed. Caryl Emerson (Minneapolis, 1984), p. 287. All further citations of Bakhtin are to this edition. Although for Bakhtin dialogues between self and '*thou*' often take place internally, he nevertheless depicts them in terms of the spoken word.

14. Ibid., p. 252, emphasis added.

15. Ibid., p. 16.

16. Ibid., p. 293, emphasis added.

17. Ibid., p. 239.

18. For studies which apply Coleridge's theory and poetry directly to the novel, see, for instance, Denis Donoghue, 'Emily Brontë: On the Latitude of Interpretation', in Morton W. Bloomfield (ed.), *The Interpretation of Narrative: Theory and Practice* (Cambridge, Mass., 1970), pp. 105–33, especially p. 114; and Peter Widdowson, 'Emily Brontë: the Romantic Novelist', *Moderna Sprak*, 66 (1972), 1–9 (especially p. 4 on the 'Rime'). My references to Coleridgean theory are from Kathleen Coburn, *The Notebooks of Samuel Taylor Coleridge* (New York, 1957–61), and will be cited by volume and page number.

The most provocative applications of general Romantic ideology to the novel include Alan S. Loxterman, '*Wuthering Heights* as Romantic Poem and Victorian Novel', in Frieda Elaine Penninger (ed.), *A Festschrift for Professor Marguerite Roberts* (Richmond, 1976), pp. 87–100; and Peter Widdowson, 'Emily Brontë: the Romantic Novelist', *Moderna Sprak*, 66 (1972). For more theoretical treatment of Romanticism in relation to the novel see J. Hillis Miller, *The Disappearance of God* (New York, 1965), p. 160; Walter L. Reed, *Meditations on the Hero: A Study of the Romantic Hero in Nineteenth-Century Fiction* (New Haven and London, 1974); Judith Weissman, ' "Like a Mad Dog": The Radical Romanticism of *Wuthering Heights*', *Midwest Quarterly*, 19

(1978); Alain Blayac, 'A Note on Emily Brontë's Romanticism in *Wuthering Heights*', *Cahiers Victoriens et Edouardiens*, 3 (1976), 1–6; and Denis Donoghue, 'Emily Brontë: On the Latitude of Interpretation', in Morton W. Bloomfield (ed.), *The Interpretation of Narrative: Theory and Practice* (Cambridge, Mass., 1970), pp. 113, 115. Studies that discuss the novel directly in the context of Romantic poetry include John Hewish, *Emily Brontë: A Critical and Biographical Study* (New York, 1969); and Miriam Allott, *Novelists on the Novel* (London, 1968), p. 169. Other research briefly notes this Romantic context for the novel, but chooses not to dwell on its particular implication: see Q. D. Leavis, 'Introduction to Charlotte Brontë's *Jane Eyre*' (Harmondsworth, 1966), p. 25; Patricia Meyer Spack, *The Female Imagination* (New York, 1975), p. 134; Muriel Spark and Derek Stanford, *Emily Brontë: Her Life and Work* (New York, 1959); and E. A. Baker, *The History of the English Novel*, vol. 8 (New York, 1968), especially pp. 11–29, 64–77, and preface.

Still other approaches cite the Romantic qualities of the novel, but then go on to characterise it as transitional to (or indicative of) the Victorian era; see, for instance, David Sonstroem, '*Wuthering Heights* and the Limits of Vision', *PLMA*, 86 (1971); Alan S. Loxterman, '*Wuthering Heights* as Romantic Poem and Victorian Novel', in Frieda Elaine Penninger (ed.), *A Festschrift for Professor Marguerite Roberts* (Richmond, 1976), p. 93; and even Arnold Shapiro, '*Wuthering Heights* as a Victorian Novel', *Studies in the Novel*, 1 (1969), 284–95. I would stress that those who see the novel as a response to Romanticism also serve to locate the work within the general rhetorical and philosophical currents I am discussing (see, for instance, Nancy Armstrong, 'Emily Brontë In and Out of Her Time', *Genre*, 15 (1982), 243–64, especially pp. 260, 262, 259.

19. Kathleen Coburn, *The Notebooks of Samuel Taylor Coleridge* (New York, 1957–61), vol. 2, p. 3148.

20. Ibid., vol. 3, p. 4036.

21. Ibid., vol. 3, p. 4166.

22. Ibid., vol. 3, pp. 4166, 3624.

7

Myths of Power in 'Wuthering Heights'

TERRY EAGLETON

If it is a function of ideology to achieve an illusory resolution of real contradictions, then Charlotte Brontë's novels are ideological in that they exploit fiction and fable to smooth the jagged edges of real conflict, and the evasions which that entails emerge as aesthetic unevennesses – as slanting, overemphasis, idealisation, structural dissonance. *Wuthering Heights*, on the other hand, confronts the tragic truth that the passion and society it presents are not fundamentally reconcilable – that there remains at the deepest level an ineradicable contradiction between them which refuses to be unlocked, which obtrudes itself as the very stuff and secret of experience. It is, then, precisely the imagination capable of confronting this tragic duality which has the power to produce the aesthetically superior work – which can synchronise in its internal structures the most shattering passion with the most rigorous realist control. The more authentic social and moral recognitions of the book, in other words, generate a finer artistic control; the unflinchingness with which the novel penetrates into fundamental contradictions is realised in a range of richer imaginative perceptions.

The primary contradiction I have in mind is the choice posed for Catherine between Heathcliff and Edgar Linton. That choice seems to me the pivotal event of the novel, the decisive catalyst of the tragedy; and if this is so, then the crux of *Wuthering Heights* must be conceded by even the most remorselessly mythological and mystical of critics to be a social one. In a crucial act of self-betrayal and bad

118

faith, Catherine rejects Heathcliff as a suitor because he is socially
inferior to Linton; and it is from this that the train of destruction
follows. Heathcliff's own view of the option is not, of course, to be
wholly credited: he is clearly wrong to think that Edgar 'is scarcely a
degree dearer [to Catherine] than her dog, or her horse'.[1] Linton
lacks spirit, but he is, as Nelly says, kind, honourable and trustful, a
loving husband to Catherine and utterly distraught at her loss. Even
so, the perverse act of *mauvaise foi* by which Catherine trades her
authentic selfhood for social privilege is rightly denounced by
Heathcliff as spiritual suicide and murder:

> *Why* did you betray your own heart, Cathy? I have not one word of
> comfort. You deserve this. You have killed yourself. Yes, you may kiss
> me, and cry; and ring out my kisses and tears: they'll blight you –
> they'll damn you. You loved me – then what *right* had you to leave
> me? What right – answer me – for the poor fancy you felt for Linton?
> Because misery and degradation, and death, and nothing that God or
> Satan could inflict would have parted us, *you*, of your own will, did it.
> I have not broken your heart – *you* have broken it; and in breaking it,
> you have broken mine.[2]

Like Lucy Snowe, Catherine tries to lead two lives: she hopes to
square authenticity with social convention, running in harness an
ontological commitment to Heathcliff with a phenomenal relationship to Linton. 'I *am* Heathcliff!' is dramatically arresting, but it is
also a way of keeping the outcast at arm's length, evading the
challenge he offers. If Catherine is Heathcliff – if identity rather than
relationship is in question – then their estrangement is inconceivable,
and Catherine can therefore turn to others without violating the
timeless metaphysical idea Heathcliff embodies. She finds in him an
integrity of being denied or diluted in routine social relations; but to
preserve that ideal means reifying him to a Hegelian essence, sub-
limely untainted by empirical fact. Heathcliff, understandably, refuses
to settle for this: he would rather enact his essence in existence by
becoming Catherine's lover. He can, it seems, be endowed with
impressive ontological status only at the price of being nullified as a
person.

   The uneasy alliance of social conformity and personal fulfilment
for which Charlotte's novels work is not, then, feasible in the world
of *Wuthering Heights*; Catherine's attempt to compromise unleashes
the contradictions which will drive both her and Heathcliff to their
deaths. One such contradiction lies in the relation between Heathcliff

and the Earnshaw family. As a waif and orphan, Heathcliff is inserted into the close-knit family structure as an alien; he emerges from that ambivalent domain of darkness which is the 'outside' of the tightly defined domestic system. That darkness is ambivalent because it is at once fearful and fertilising, as Heathcliff himself is both gift and threat. Earnshaw's first words about him make this clear: 'See here, wife! I was never so beaten with anything in my life: but you must e'en take it as a gift of God; though it's as dark almost as if it came from the devil.'[3] Stripped as he is of determinate social relations, of a given function within the family, Heathcliff's presence is radically gratuitous; the arbitrary, unmotivated event of his arrival at the Heights offers its inhabitants a chance to transcend the constrictions of their self-enclosed social structure and gather him in. Because Heathcliff's circumstances are so obscure he is available to be accepted or rejected simply for himself, laying claim to no status other than a human one. He is, of course, proletarian in appearance, but the obscurity of his origins also frees him of any exact social role; as Nelly Dean muses later, he might equally be a prince. He is ushered into the Heights for no good reason other than to be arbitrarily loved; and in this sense he is a touchstone of others' responses, a liberating force for Cathy and a stumbling-block for others. Nelly hates him at first, unable to transcend her bigotry against the new and non-related; she puts him on the landing like a dog, hoping he will be gone by morning. Earnshaw pets and favours him, and in doing so creates fresh inequalities in the family hierarchy which become the source of Hindley's hatred. As heir to the Heights, Hindley understandably feels his social role subverted by this irrational, unpredictable intrusion.

Catherine, who does not expect to inherit, responds spontaneously to Heathcliff's presence; and because this antagonises Hindley she becomes after Earnshaw's death a spiritual orphan as Heathcliff is a literal one. Both are allowed to run wild; both become the 'outside' of the domestic structure. Because his birth is unknown, Heathcliff is a purely atomised individual, free of generational ties in a novel where genealogical relations are of crucial thematic and structural importance; and it is because he is an internal *émigré* within the Heights that he can lay claim to a relationship of direct personal equality with Catherine who, as the daughter of the family, is the least economically integral member. Heathcliff offers Catherine a friendship which opens fresh possibilities of freedom within the internal system of the Heights; in a situation where social determinants are insistent, freedom can mean only a relative independence of given blood-ties, of the settled, evolving, predictable structures of kinship. Whereas in Charlotte's ·fiction the severing or lapsing of such relations frees you for progress up the class-system, the freedom which Cathy achieves with Heathcliff takes her down that system, into consorting with a 'gypsy'. Yet 'down' is also 'outside', just as gypsy signifies 'lower class' but also asocial vagrant, classless natural life-form. As the eternal rocks beneath the woods, Heathcliff is both lowly and natural, enjoying the partial freedom from social pressures appropriate to those at the bottom of the class-structure. In loving Heathcliff, Catherine is taken outside the family and society into an opposing realm which can be adequately imaged only as 'Nature'.

The loving equality between Catherine and Heathcliff stands, then, as a paradigm of human possibilities which reach beyond, and might ideally unlock, the tightly dominative system of the Heights. Yet at the same time Heathcliff's mere presence fiercely intensifies that system's harshness, twisting all the Earnshaw relationships into bitter antagonism. He unwittingly sharpens a violence endemic to the Heights – a violence which springs both from the hard exigencies imposed by its struggle with the land, and from its social exclusiveness as a self-consciously ancient, respectable family. The violence which Heathcliff unwittingly triggers is turned against him: he is cast out by Hindley, culturally deprived, reduced to the status of farm-labourer. What Hindley does, in fact, is to invert the potential freedom symbolised by Heathcliff into a parody of itself, into the non-freedom of neglect. Heathcliff is robbed of liberty in two antithetical ways: exploited as a servant on the one hand, allowed to run wild on the other; and this contradiction is appropriate to childhood, which is a time of relative freedom from convention and yet, paradoxically, a phase of authoritarian repression. In this sense there is freedom for Heathcliff neither within society nor outside it; his two conditions are inverted mirror-images of one another. It is a contradiction which encapsulates a crucial truth about bourgeois society. If there is no genuine liberty on its 'inside' – Heathcliff is oppressed by work and the familial structure – neither is there more than a caricature of liberty on the 'outside', since the release of running wild is merely a function of cultural impoverishment. The friendship of Heathcliff and Cathy crystallises under the pressures of economic and cultural violence, so that the freedom it seems to signify ('half-savage and hardy, and free'[4]) is always the other face of oppression, always exists in its shadow. With Heathcliff and Catherine, as in Charlotte's fiction, bitter social reality breeds Romantic escapism; but whereas Charlotte's novels try to trim the balance between them, *Wuthering Heights* shows a more dialectical interrelation at work. Romantic intensity is locked in combat with society, but cannot wholly transcend it; your freedom is bred and deformed in the shadow of your oppression, just as, in the adult Heathcliff, oppression is the logical consequence of the exploiter's 'freedom'.

Just as Hindley withdraws culture from Heathcliff as a mode of domination, so Heathcliff acquires culture as a weapon. He amasses a certain amount of cultural capital in his two years' absence in order to shackle others more effectively, buying up the expensive commodity of gentility in order punitively to re-enter the society from which he was punitively expelled. This is liberty of a kind, in contrast with his previous condition; but the novel is insistent on its ultimately illusory nature. In oppressing others the exploiter imprisons himself; the adult Heathcliff's systematic tormenting is fed by his victims' pain but also drains him of blood, impels and possesses him as an external force. His alienation from Catherine estranges him from himself to the point where his brutalities become tediously perfunctory gestures, the mechanical motions of a man who is already withdrawing himself from his own body. Heathcliff moves from being Hindley's victim to becoming, like Catherine, his own executioner.

Throughout *Wuthering Heights*, labour and culture, bondage and freedom, Nature and artifice appear at once as each other's dialectical negations and as subtly matched, mutually reflective. Culture – gentility – is the opposite of labour for young Heathcliff and Hareton; but it is also a crucial economic weapon, as well as a product of work itself. The delicate spiritless Lintons in their crimson-carpeted drawing-room are radically severed from the labour which sustains them; gentility grows from the production of others, detaches itself from that work (as the Grange is separate from the Heights), and then comes to dominate the labour on which it is parasitic. In doing so, it becomes a form of self-bondage; if work is servitude, so in a subtler sense is civilisation. To some extent, these polarities are held together in the yeoman-farming structure of the Heights. Here labour and culture, freedom and necessity, Nature and society are roughly complementary. The Earnshaws are gentlemen yet they work the land; they enjoy the freedom of being their own masters, but that freedom moves within the tough discipline of labour; and because the social unit of the Heights – the family – is both 'natural' (biological) and an economic system, it acts to some degree as a mediation between Nature and artifice, naturalising property relations and socialising blood-ties. Relationships in this isolated world are turbulently face-to-face, but they are also impersonally mediated through a working relation with Nature. This is not to share Mrs Q. D. Leavis's view of the Heights as 'a wholesome primitive and natural unit of a healthy society';[5] there does not, for instance, seem much that is wholesome about Joseph. Joseph incarnates a grimness inherent in conditions of economic exigency, where relationships must be tightly ordered and are easily warped into violence. One of *Wuthering Heights'* more notable achievements is ruthlessly to de-mystify the Victorian notion of the family as a pious, pacific space within social conflict. Even so, the Heights does pin together contradictions which the entry of Heathcliff will break open. Heathcliff disturbs the Heights because he is simply superfluous: he has no defined place within its biological and economic system. (He may well be Catherine's illegitimate half-brother, just as he may well have passed his two-year absence in Tunbridge Wells.) The superfluity he embodies is that of a sheerly human demand for recognition; but since there is no space for such surplus within the terse economy of the Heights, it proves destructive rather than creative in effect, straining and overloading already taut relationships. Heathcliff catalyses an aggression intrinsic to Heights society; that sound blow Hindley hands out to Catherine on the evening of Heathcliff's first appearance is slight but significant evidence against the case that conflict starts only with Heathcliff's arrival.

The effect of Heathcliff is to explode those conflicts into antagonisms which finally rip the place apart. In particular, he marks the beginnings of that process whereby passion and personal intensity separate out from the social domain and offer an alternative commitment to it. For farming families like the Earnshaws, work and human relations are roughly coterminous: work is socialised, personal relations mediated through a context of labour. Heathcliff, however, is set to work meaninglessly, as a servant rather than a member of the family; and his fervent emotional life with Catherine is thus forced outside the working environment into the wild Nature of the heath, rather than Nature reclaimed and worked up into significant value in the social activity of labour. Heathcliff is stripped of culture in the sense of gentility, but the result is a paradoxical intensifying of his fertile imaginative liaison with Catherine. It is fitting, then, that their free, neglected wanderings lead them to their adventure at Thrushcross Grange. For if the Romantic childhood culture of Catherine and Heathcliff exists in a social limbo divorced from the minatory world of working relations, the same can be said in a different sense of the genteel culture of the Lintons, surviving as it does on the basis of material conditions it simultaneously conceals. As the children spy on the Linton family, that concealed brutality is unleashed in the shape of bulldogs brought to the defence of civility. The natural energy in which the Lintons' culture is rooted bursts literally through to savage the 'savages' who appear to threaten property. The underlying truth of violence, continuously visible at the Heights, is momentarily exposed; old Linton thinks the intruders are after his rents. Culture draws a veil over such brute force but also sharpens it: the more property you have, the more ruthlessly you need to defend it. Indeed, Heathcliff himself seems dimly aware of how cultivation exacerbates 'natural' conflict, as we see in his scornful account of the Linton children's petulant squabbling; cultivation, by pampering and swaddling 'natural' drives, at once represses serious physical violence and breeds a neurasthenic sensitivity which allows selfish impulse free rein. 'Natural' aggression is nurtured both by an excess and an absence of culture – a paradox demonstrated by Catherine Earnshaw, who is at once wild and pettish, savage and spoilt. Nature and culture, then, are locked in a complex relation of antagonism and affinity: the Romantic fantasies of Heathcliff and Catherine, and the Romantic Linton drawing-room with its gold-bordered ceiling and shimmering chandelier, both bear the scars of the material conditions which produced them – scars visibly inscribed on Cathy's ankle. Yet to leave the matter there would be to draw a purely formal parallel. For what distinguishes the two forms of Romance is Heathcliff: his intense communion with Catherine is an uncompromising rejection of the Linton world.

The opposition, however, is not merely one between the values of personal relationship and those of conventional society. What prevents this is the curious impersonality of the relationship between Catherine and Heathcliff. Edgar Linton shows at his best a genuine capacity for tender, loving fidelity; but this thrives on obvious limits. The limits are those of the closed room into which the children peer – the glowing, sheltered space within which those close, immediate encounters which make for both tenderness and pettishness may be conducted. Linton is released from material pressures into such a civilised enclave; and in that sense his situation differs from that of the Heights, where personal relations are more intimately entwined with a working context. The relationship of Heathcliff and Catherine, however, provides a third term. It really is a personal relationship, yet seems also to transcend the personal into some region beyond it. Indeed, there is a sense in which the unity the couple briefly achieve is narrowed and degutted by being described as 'personal'. In so far as 'personal' suggests the liberal humanism of Edgar, with his concern (crudely despised by Heathcliff) for pity, charity and humanity, the word is clearly inapplicable to the fierce mutual tearings of Catherine and Heathcliff. Yet it is inadequate to the positive as well as the destructive aspects of their love. Their relationship is, we say, 'ontological' or 'metaphysical' because it opens out into the more-than-personal, enacts a style of being which is more than just the property of two individuals, which suggests in its impersonality something beyond a merely Romantic-individualist response to social oppression. Their relationship articulates a depth inexpressible in routine social practice, transcendent of available social languages. Its impersonality suggests both a savage depersonalising and a paradigmatic significance; and in neither sense is the relationship wholly within their conscious control. What Heathcliff offers Cathy is a non- or pre-social relationship, as the only authentic form of living in a world of exploitation and inequality, a world where one must refuse to measure oneself by the criteria of the class-structure and so must appear inevitably subversive. Whereas in Charlotte's novels the love-relationship takes you into society, in *Wuthering Heights* it drives you out of it. The love between Heathcliff and Catherine is an intuitive intimacy raised to cosmic status, by-passing the mediation of the 'social'; and this, indeed, is both its strength and its limit. Its non-sociality is on the one hand a revolutionary refusal of the given language of social roles and values; and if the relationship is to remain unabsorbed by society it must therefore appear as natural rather than social, since Nature is the 'outside' of society. On the other hand, the novel cannot realise the meaning of that revolutionary refusal in social terms; the most it can do is to *universalise* that meaning by intimating the mysteriously impersonal energies from which the relationship springs.

Catherine, of course, *is* absorbed: she enters the civilised world of the Lintons and leaves Heathcliff behind, to become a 'wolfish, pitiless' man. To avoid incorporation means remaining as unreclaimed as the wild furze: there is no way in this novel of temporising between conformity and rebellion. But there is equally no way for the revolutionary depth of relationship between Heathcliff and Catherine to realise itself as a historical force; instead, it becomes an elusive dream of absolute value, an incomparably more powerful version of Charlotte's myth of lost origins. Catherine and Heathcliff seek to preserve the primordial moment of pre-social harmony, before the fall into history and oppression. But it won't do to see them merely as children eternally fixated in some Edenic infancy: we do not see them merely as children, and in any case to be 'merely' a child is to endure the punitive pressures of an adult world. Moreover, it is none of Heathcliff's fault that the relationship remains 'metaphysical': it is Catherine who consigns it to unfulfilment. Their love remains an unhistorical essence which fails to enter into concrete existence and can do so, ironically, only in death. Death, indeed, as the ultimate outer limit of consciousness and society, is the locus of Catherine and Heathcliff's love, the horizon on which it moves. The absolutism of death is prefigured, echoed back, in the remorseless intensity with which their relationship is actually lived; yet their union can be achieved only in the act of abandoning the actual world.

Catherine and Heathcliff's love, then, is pushed to the periphery by society itself, projected into myth; yet the fact that it seems *inherently* convertible to myth spotlights the threshold of the novel's 'possible consciousness'. I take that phrase from Lukács and Goldmann to suggest those restrictions set on the consciousness of a historical period which only a transformation of real social relations could abolish – the point at which the most enterprising imagination presses against boundaries which signify not mere failures of personal perception but the limits of what can be historically said. The force Heathcliff symbolises can be truly realised only in some more than merely individualist form; *Wuthering Heights* has its roots not in that narrowed, simplified Romanticism which pits the lonely rebel against an anonymous order, but in that earlier, more authentic Romantic impulse which posits its own kind of 'transindividual' order of value, its own totality, against the order which forces it into exile. Heathcliff may be Byronic, but not in the way Rochester is: the novel counterposes social convention not merely with contrasting personal life-styles but with an alternative world of meaning. Yet it is here that the limits of 'possible consciousness' assert themselves: the offered totalities of Nature, myth and cosmic energy are forced to figure as asocial worlds unable to engage in more than idealist ways with the society they subject to judgement. The price of universality is to be fixed eternally at a point extrinsic to social life – fixed, indeed, at the moment of death, which both manifests a depth challengingly alien to the Lintons and withdraws the character from that conventional landscape into an isolated realm of his own.

Nature, in any case, is no true 'outside' to society, since its conflicts are transposed into the social arena. In one sense the novel sharply contrasts Nature and society; in another sense it grasps civilised life as a higher distillation of ferocious natural appetite. Nature, then, is a thoroughly ambiguous category, inside and outside society simultaneously. At one level it represents the unsalvaged region beyond the pale of culture; at another level it signifies the all-pervasive reality of which culture itself is a particular outcropping. It is, indeed, this ambiguity which supplies the vital link between the childhood and adult phases of Heathcliff's career. Heathcliff the child is 'natural' both because he is allowed to run wild and because he is reduced as Hindley's labourer to a mere physical instrument; Heathcliff the adult is 'natural' man in a Hobbesian sense: an appetitive exploiter to whom no tie or tradition is sacred, a callous predator violently sundering the bonds of custom and piety. If the first kind of 'naturalness' is anti-social in its estrangement from the norms of 'civilised' life, the second involves the unsociality of one set at the centre of a world whose social relations are inhuman. Heathcliff moves from being natural in the sense of an anarchic outsider to adopting the behaviour natural to an insider in a viciously competitive society. Of course, to be natural in both senses is at a different level to be unnatural. From the viewpoint of culture, it is unnatural that a child should be degraded to a savage, and unnatural too that a man should behave in the obscene way Heathcliff does. But culture in this novel is as problematical as Nature. There are no cool Arnoldian touchstones by which to take the measure of natural degeneracy, since the dialectical vision of *Wuthering Heights* puts culture into question in the very act of exploring the 'naturalness' which is its negation. Just as being natural involves being either completely outside or inside society, as roaming waif or manipulative landlord, so culture signifies either free-wheeling Romantic fantasy or that well-appointed Linton drawing-room. The adult Heathcliff is the focus of these contradictions: as he worms his way into the social structure he becomes progressively detached in spirit from all it holds dear. But *contradiction* is the essential emphasis. Heathcliff's schizophrenia is symptomatic of a world in which there can be no true dialectic between culture and Nature – a world in which culture is merely refuge from or reflex of material conditions, and so either too estranged from or entwined with those conditions to offer a viable alternative.

Heathcliff's social relation to both Heights and Grange is one of the most complex issues in the novel. Lockwood remarks that he looks too genteel for the Heights; and indeed, in so far as he represents the victory of capitalist property-dealing over the traditional yeoman economy of the Earnshaws, he is inevitably aligned with the world of the Grange. Heathcliff is a dynamic force which seeks to destroy the old yeoman settlement by dispossessing Hareton; yet he does this partly to revenge himself on the very Linton world whose weapons (property deals, arranged marriages) he deploys so efficiently. He does this, moreover, with a crude intensity which is a quality of the Heights world; his roughness and resilience link him culturally to *Wuthering Heights*, and he exploits those qualities to destroy both it and the Grange. He is, then, a force which springs out of the Heights yet subverts it, breaking beyond its constrictions into a new, voracious acquisitiveness. His capitalist brutality is an extension as well as a negation of the Heights world he knew as a child; and to that extent there is continuity between his childhood and adult protests against Grange values, if not against Grange weapons. Heathcliff is subjectively a Heights figure opposing the Grange, and objectively a Grange figure undermining the Heights; he focuses acutely the contradictions between the two worlds. His rise to power symbolises at once the triumph of the oppressed over capitalism and the triumph of capitalism over the oppressed.

He is, indeed, contradiction incarnate. The contradiction of the *novel*, however, is that Heathcliff cannot represent at once an absolute metaphysical refusal of an inhuman society and a class which is intrinsically part of it. Heathcliff is both metaphysical hero, spiritually marooned from all material concern in his obsessional love for Catherine, and a skilful exploiter who cannily expropriates the wealth of others. It is a limit of the novel's 'possible consciousness' that its absolute metaphysical protest can be socially articulated only in such terms – that its 'outside' is in this sense an 'inside'. The industrial bourgeoisie is outside the farming world of both Earnshaws and Lintons; but it is no longer a *revolutionary* class, and so provides no sufficient social correlative for what Heathcliff 'metaphysically' represents. He can thus be presented only as a conflictive unity of spiritual rejection and social integration; and this, indeed, is his personal tragedy.

Wuthering Heights has been alternately read as a social and a metaphysical novel – as a work rooted in a particular time and place, or as a novel preoccupied with the eternal grounds rather than the shifting conditions of human relationship. That critical conflict mirrors a crucial thematic dislocation in the novel itself. The social and metaphysical are indeed ripped rudely apart in the book: existences only feebly incarnate essences, the discourse of ethics makes little creative contact with that of ontology. So much is apparent in Heathcliff's scathing dismissal of Edgar Linton's compassion and moral concern: 'and that insipid, paltry creature attending her from *duty* and *humanity*! From *pity* and *charity*! He might as well plant an oak in a flower-pot, and expect it to thrive, as imagine he can restore her to vigour in the soil of his shallow cares!' The novel's dialectical vision proves Heathcliff both right and wrong. There *is* something insipid about Linton, but his concern for Catherine is not in the least shallow; if his pity and charity are less fertile than Heathcliff's passion, they are also less destructive. But if ethical and ontological idioms fail to mesh, if social existence negates rather than realises spiritual essence, this is itself a profoundly social fact. The novel projects a condition in which the available social languages are too warped and constrictive to be the bearers of love, freedom and equality; and it follows that in such a condition those values can be sustained only in the realms of myth and metaphysics. It is a function of the metaphysical to preserve those possibilities which a society cancels, to act as its reservoir of unrealised value. This is the history of Heathcliff and Catherine – the history of a wedge driven between the actual and the possible which, by estranging the ideal from concrete existence, twists that existence into violence and despair. The actual is denatured to a mere husk of the ideal, the empty shell of some tormentingly inaccessible truth. It is an index of the dialectical vision of *Wuthering Heights* that it shows at once the terror and the necessity of that denaturing, as it shows both the splendour and the impotence of the ideal.

From Terry Eagleton, *Myths of Power: A Marxist Study of the Brontës* (London and Basingstoke, 1976), pp. 97, 100–11, 112–15, 116–21, 142–3.

NOTES

[Terry Eagleton's Marxist study of the Brontës, from which this essay is taken, was written before the more thorough adoption of poststructuralism represented by his *Literary Theory* (1983). It is, however, a sophisticated reading in literary terms, distinguished from that of earlier 'vulgar' Marxists by its analysis of ideology in terms suggested by the French Marxist Louis Althusser.

Whereas earlier Marxists saw literature as 'reflecting' a social reality, Althusser argued that literature was best analysed in relation to ideology. His concept of ideology was itself innovatory; drawing on Lacanian psychoanalysis, he argued that ideology (for instance religion, or patriotism, or duty) provided people with an 'Imaginary' relationship to the real conditions of their existence. Althusser's writings on ideology are a more explicitly political version of discourse theory; like Bakhtin, he saw literature as in a dynamic relationship with ideology, both constructed and constructing. (See Raman Selden, *A Reader's Guide to Contemporary Literary Theory* [Hemel Hempstead, 1985], for an account of Althusser and of Eagleton's evolving theoretical position.)

Terry Eagleton's essay is reproduced here, with the author's permission, in a shortened version. References are to *Wuthering Heights*, ed. Mrs H. Ward and C. K. Shorter (London, 1899–1900). Ed.]

1. *Wuthering Heights*, ed. Mrs H. Ward and C. K. Shorter (London, 1899–1900), ch. 14, p. 155.

2. Ibid., ch. 15, p. 168.

3. Ibid., ch. 4, p. 36.

4. Ibid., ch. 12, p. 130.

5. F. R. and Q. D. Leavis, *Lectures in America* (London, 1969), p. 131. [A shortened version of Q. D. Leavis's essay referred to here is reprinted in this volume – see p. 24 Ed.]

8

Looking Oppositely: Emily Brontë's Bible of Hell

SANDRA GILBERT

> It indeed appear'd to Reason as if Desire was cast out, but the Devils account is, that the Messiah fell, & formed a heaven of what he stole from the Abyss
>
> (William Blake)

> A loss of something ever felt I –
> The first that I could recollect
> Bereft I was – of what I knew not
> Too young that any should suspect
>
> A Mourner walked among the children
> I notwithstanding went about
> As one bemoaning a Dominion
> Itself the only Prince cast out –
>
> Elder, Today, a session wiser
> And fainter, too, as Wiseness is –
> I find myself still softly searching
> For my Delinquent Palaces –
>
> And a Suspicion, like a Finger
> Touches my Forehead now and then
> That I am looking oppositely
> For the site of the Kingdom of Heaven –
>
> (Emily Dickinson)

That *Wuthering Heights* is in some sense about a fall has frequently been suggested, though critics from Charlotte Brontë to Mark Schorer, Q. D. Leavis, and Leo Bersani have always disputed its exact nature and moral implications. Is Catherine's fall the archetypal fall of the *Bildungsroman* protagonist? Is Heathcliff's fall, his perverted 'moral teething', a shadow of Catherine's? Which of the two worlds of *Wuthering Heights* (if either) does Brontë mean to represent the truly 'fallen' world? These are just some of the controversies that have traditionally attended this issue. Nevertheless, that the story of *Wuthering Heights* is built around a central fall seems indisputable, so that a description of the novel as in part a *Bildungsroman* about a girl's passage from 'innocence' to 'experience' (leaving aside the precise meaning of those terms) would probably also be widely accepted. And that the fall in *Wuthering Heights* has Miltonic over-tones is no doubt culturally inevitable. But even if it weren't, the Miltonic implications of the action would be clear enough from the 'mad scene' in which Catherine describes herself as 'an exile, and outcast . . . from what had been my world', adding 'Why am I so changed? Why does my blood rush into a hell of tumult at a few words?' (ch. 12). Given the metaphysical nature of *Wuthering Heights*, Catherine's definition of herself as 'an exile and outcast' inevitably suggests those trail-blazing exiles and outcasts Adam, Eve, and Satan. And her Romantic question – 'Why am I so changed?' – with its desperate straining after the roots of identity, must ultimately refer back to Satan's hesitant (but equally crucial) speech to Beelzebub, as they lie stunned in the lake of fire: 'If thou be'est he; But O . . . how chang'd' (*Paradise Lost*, 1. 84).

Of course, *Wuthering Heights* has often, also, been seen as a subversively visionary novel. Indeed, Brontë is frequently coupled with Blake as a practitioner of mystical politics. Usually, however, as if her book were written to illustrate the enigmatic religion of 'No coward soul is mine', this visionary quality is related to Catherine's assertion that she is tired of 'being enclosed' in 'this shattered prison' of her body, and 'wearying to escape into that glorious world, and to be always there' (ch. 15). Many readers define Brontë, in other words, as a ferocious pantheist/transcendentalist, worshipping the manifestations of the One in rock, tree, cloud, man and woman, while manipulating her story to bring about a Romantic *Liebestod* in which favoured characters enter 'the endless and shadowless here-after'. And certainly such ideas, like Blake's *Songs of Innocence*, are 'something heterodox', to use Lockwood's phrase. At the same time, however, they are soothingly rather than disquietingly neo-Miltonic, like fictionalised visions of *Paradise Lost's* luminous Father God. They are, in fact, the ideas of 'steady, reasonable' Nelly Dean, whose denial of the demonic in life, along with her commitment to the angelic tranquillity of death, represents only one of the visionary alternatives in *Wuthering Heights*. And, like Blake's metaphor of the lamb, Nelly's pious alternative has no real meaning for Brontë outside of the context provided by its tigerish opposite.

The tigerish opposite implied by *Wuthering Heights* emerges most dramatically when we bring all the novel's Miltonic elements together with its author's personal concerns in an attempt at a single formulation of Brontë's metaphysical intentions: the sum of this novel's visionary parts is an almost shocking revisionary whole. Heaven (or its rejection), hell, Satan, a fall, mystical politics, metaphysical romance, orphanhood, and the question of origins – disparate as some of these matters may seem, they all cohere in a rebelliously topsy-turvy retelling of Milton's and Western culture's central tale of the fall of woman and her shadow self, Satan. This fall, says Brontë, is not a fall *into* hell. It is a fall *from* 'hell' into 'heaven', not a fall from grace (in the religious sense) but a fall into grace (in the cultural sense). Moreover, for the heroine who falls it is the loss of Satan rather than the loss of God that signals the painful passage from innocence to experience. Emily Brontë, in other words, is not just Blakeian in 'double' mystical vision, but Blakeian in a tough, radically political commitment to the belief that the state of being patriarchal Christianity calls 'hell' is eternally, energetically delightful, whereas the state called 'heaven' is rigidly hierarchical, Urizenic, and 'kind' as a poison tree. But because she was metaphorically one of Milton's daughters, Brontë differs from Blake, that powerful son of a powerful father, in reversing the terms of Milton's Christian cosmogony for specifically feminist reasons.

* * *

Because Emily Brontë was looking oppositely not only for heaven (and hell) but for her own female origins, *Wuthering Heights* is one of the few authentic instances of novelistic myth-making, myth-making in the functional sense of problem-solving. Where writers from Charlotte Brontë and Henry James to James Joyce and Virginia Woolf have used mythic material to give point and structure to their novels, Emily Brontë uses the novel form to give substance – plausibility, really – to her myth. It is urgent that she do so because, as we shall see, the feminist cogency of this myth derives not only from its daring corrections of Milton but also from the fact that it is a distinctively nineteenth-century answer to the question of origins: it is the myth of how culture came about, and specifically of how nineteenth-century society occurred, the tale of where tea-tables, sofas, crinolines, and parsonages like the one at Haworth came from.

Because it is so ambitious a myth, *Wuthering Heights* has the puzzling self-containment of a *mystery* in the old sense of that word – the sense of mystery plays and Eleusinian mysteries. Locked in by Lockwood's uncomprehending narrative, Nelly Dean's story, with its baffling duplication of names, places, events, seems endlessly to re-enact itself, like some ritual that must be cyclically repeated in order to sustain (as well as explain) both nature and culture. At the same time, because it is so prosaic a myth – a myth about crinolines! – *Wuthering Heights* is not in the least portentous or self-consciously 'mythic'. On the contrary, like all true rituals and myths, Brontë's 'cuckoo's tale' turns a practical, casual, humorous face to its audience. One of her most famous adolescent diary papers juxtaposes a plea for culinary help from the parsonage housekeeper, Tabby – 'Come Anne pilloputate' – with 'The Gondals are discovering the interior of Gaaldine' and 'Sally Mosely is washing in the back kitchen'.[1] Significantly, no distinction is made between the heroic exploits of the fictional Gondals and Sally Mosely's real washday business.

No doubt, however, it is this deep-seated tendency of Brontë's to live literally with the fantastic that accounts for much of the critical disputation about *Wuthering Heights*, especially the quarrels about the novel's genre and style. Q. D. Leavis and Arnold Kettle, for instance, insist that the work is a 'sociological novel', while Mark Schorer thinks it 'means to be a work of edification [about] the nature of a grand passion'. Leo Bersani sees it as an ontological psychodrama, and Elliot Gose as a sort of expanded fairytale.[2] And strangely there is truth in all these apparently conflicting notions, just as it is also true that (as Robert Kiely has affirmed) 'part of the distinction of *Wuthering Heights* [is] that it has no "literary" aura about it', and true at the same time that (as we have asserted) *Wuthering Heights* is an unusually literary novel because Brontë approached reality chiefly through the mediating agency of literature.[3] In fact, Kiely's comment illuminates not only the uninflected surface of the diary papers but also the controversies about their author's novel, for Brontë is 'unliterary' in being without a received sense of what the eighteenth century called literary decorum. As one of her better-known poems declares, she follows 'where [her] own nature would be leading', and that nature leads her to an oddly literal

– and also, therefore, unliterary – use of extraordinarily various literary works, ideas, and genres, all of which she refers back to herself, since 'it vexes [her] to choose another guide'.[4]

The world of *Wuthering Heights*, in other words, like the world of Brontë's diary papers, is one where what seem to be the most unlikely opposites coexist without, apparently, any consciousness on the author's part that there is anything unlikely in their coexistence. The ghosts of Byron, Shakespeare, and Jane Austen haunt the same ground. People with decent Christian names (Catherine, Nelly, Edgar, Isabella) inhabit a landscape in which also dwell people with strange animal or nature names (Hindley, Hareton, Heathcliff). Fairy-tale events out of what Mircea Eliade would call 'great time' are given a local habitation and a real chronology in just that historical present Eliade defines as great time's opposite.[5] Dogs and gods (or goddesses) turn out to be not opposites but, figuratively speaking, the same words spelled in different ways. Funerals are weddings, weddings funerals. And of course, most important for our purposes here, hell is heaven, heaven hell, though the two are not separated, as Milton and literary decorum would prescribe, by vast aeons of space but by a little strip of turf, for Brontë was rebelliously determined to walk

> . . . not in old heroic traces
> And not in paths of high morality.
> And not among the half-distinguished faces,
> The clouded forms of long-past history.

On the contrary, surveying that history and its implications, she came to the revisionary conclusion that 'the earth that wakes *one* human heart to feeling / Can centre both the worlds of Heaven and Hell'.[6]

* * *

If we identify with Lockwood, civilised man at his most genteelly 'cooked' and literary, we cannot fail to begin Brontë's novel by deciding that hell is a household very like Wuthering Heights. Lockwood himself, as if wittily predicting the reversal of values that is to be the story's central concern, at first calls the place 'a perfect misanthropist's Heaven' (ch. 1). But then what is the traditional Miltonic or Dantesque hell if not a misanthropist's heaven, a site that substitutes hate for love, violence for peace, death for life, and in consequence the material for the spiritual, disorder for order? Certainly Wuthering Heights rings all these changes on Lockwood's first two visits. Thus just as Milton's hell consists of envious and (in the poet's view) equality-mad devils jostling for position, so these inhabitants of Wuthering Heights seem to live in chaos without the structuring principle of heaven's hierarchical chain of being, and therefore without the heavenly harmony God the Father's ranking of virtues, thrones, and powers makes possible. For this reason Catherine sullenly refuses to do anything 'except what I please' (ch. 4), the servant Zillah vociferously rebukes Hareton for laughing, and old Joseph – whose viciously parodic religion seems here to represent a hellish joke at heaven's expense – lets the dogs loose on Linton without consulting his 'maister', Heathcliff.

In keeping with this problem of 'equality', a final and perhaps definitive sign of the hellishness that has enveloped Wuthering Heights at the time of Lockwood's first visits is the blinding snowfall that temporarily imprisons the by now unwilling guest in the home of his infernal hosts. Engulfing the Earnshaws' ancestral home and the Lintons', too, in a blizzard of destruction, hellish nature traps and freezes everyone in the isolation of a 'perfect misanthropist's heaven'. And again, as in *Lear* this hellish nature is somehow female or associated with femaleness, like an angry goddess shaking locks of ice and introducing Lockwood (and his readers) to the female rage that will be a central theme in *Wuthering Heights*. The femaleness of this 'natural' hell is suggested, too, by its likeness to the 'false' material creation Robert Graves analysed so well in *The White Goddess*. Female nature has risen, it seems, in a storm of protest, just as the Sin-like dog Juno rises in a fury when Lockwood 'unfortunately indulge[s] in winking and making faces' at her while musing on his heartless treatment of a 'goddess' to whom he never 'told' his love (ch. 1). Finally, that the storm is both hellish and female is made clearest of all by Lockwood's second visionary dream. Out of the tapping of branches, out of the wind and swirling snow, like an icy-fingered incarnation of the storm rising in protest against the patriarchal sermon of 'Jabes Branderham', appears that ghostly female witch-child the *original* Catherine Earnshaw, who has now been 'a waif for twenty years'.

* * *

Why is Wuthering Heights so Miltonically hellish? And what happened to Catherine Earnshaw? Why has she become a demonic, storm-driven ghost? The 'real' aetiological story of *Wuthering Heights* begins, as Lockwood learns from his 'human fixture' Nelly Dean, with a random weakening of the fabric of ordinary human society. Once upon a time, somewhere in what mythically speaking qualifies as pre-history or what Eliade calls 'illo tempore', there is/was a primordial family, the Earnshaws, who trace their lineage back at least as far as the paradigmatic Renaissance inscription '1500 Hareton Earnshaw' over their 'principal doorway'. And one fine summer morning toward the end of the eighteenth century, the 'old master' of the house decides to take a walking tour of sixty miles to Liverpool (ch. 4). His decision, like Lear's decision to divide his kingdom, is apparently quite arbitrary, one of those mystifying psychic *données* for which the fictional convention of 'once upon a time' was devised. Perhaps it means, like Lear's action, that he is half-consciously beginning to prepare for death. In any case, his ritual questions to his two children – an older son and a younger daughter – and to their servant Nelly are equally stylised and arbitrary, as are the children's answers. 'What shall I bring you?' the old master asks, like the fisherman to whom the flounder gave three wishes. And the children reply, as convention dictates, by requesting their heart's desires. In other words, they reveal their true selves, just as a father contemplating his own ultimate absence from their lives might have hoped they would.

Strangely enough, however, only the servant Nelly's heart's desire is sensible and conventional: she asks for (or, rather, accepts the promise of) a pocketful of apples and pears. Hindley, on the other hand, the son who is destined to be next master of the household, does not ask for a particularly masterful gift. His wish, indeed, seems frivolous in the context of the harsh world of the Heights. He asks for a fiddle, betraying both a secret, soft-hearted desire for culture and an almost decadent lack of virile purpose. Stranger still is Catherine's wish for a whip. 'She could ride any horse in the stable', says Nelly, but in the fairy-tale context of this narrative that realistic explanation hardly seems to suffice,[7] for, symbolically, the small Catherine's longing for a whip seems like a powerless younger daughter's yearning for power.

Of course, as we might expect from our experience of fairy tales, at least one of the children receives the desired boon. Catherine gets her whip. She gets it figuratively – in the form of a 'gypsy brat' – rather than literally, but nevertheless 'it' (both whip and brat) functions just as she must unconsciously have hoped it would, smashing her rival-brother's fiddle and making a desirable third among the children in the family so as to insulate her from the pressure of her brother's domination. (That there should always have been three children in the family is clear from the way other fairy-tale rituals of three are observed, and also from the fact that Heathcliff is given the name of a dead son, perhaps even the true oldest son, as if he were a reincarnation of the lost child.)

Having received her deeply desired whip, Catherine now achieves, as Hillis Miller and Leo Bersani have noticed, an extraordinary fullness of being.[8] The phrase may seem pretentiously metaphysical (certainly critics like Q. D. Leavis have objected to such phrases on those grounds)[9] but in discussing the early paradise from which Catherine and Heathcliff eventually fall we are trying to describe elusive psychic states, just as we would in discussing Wordsworth's visionary childhood, Frankenstein's youth before he 'learned' that he was (the creator of) a monster, or even the prelapsarian sexuality of Milton's Adam and Eve. And so, like Freud who was driven to grope among such words as *oceanic* when he tried to explain the heaven that lies about us in our infancy, we are obliged to use the paradoxical and metaphysical language of mysticism: phrases like *wholeness*, *fullness of being*, and *androgyny* come inevitably to mind.[10] All three, as we shall see, apply to Catherine, or more precisely to Catherine-Heathcliff, because as Catherine's whip he is (and she herself recognises this) an alternative self or double for her, a complementary addition to her being who fleshes out all her lacks the way a bandage might staunch a wound. Thus in her union with him she becomes, like Manfred in his union with his sister Astarte, a perfect androgyne. As devoid of sexual awareness as Adam and Eve were in the prelapsarian garden, she sleeps with her whip, her other half, every night in the primordial fashion of the countryside. And if Heathcliff's is the body that does her will – strong, dark, proud, and a native speaker of 'gibberish' rather than English – she herself is an 'unfeminine' instance of transcendently vital spirit. For she is never docile, never submissive, never ladylike. On the contrary, her joy – and the Coleridgean word is not too strong – is in what Milton's Eve is never allowed: a tongue 'always going – singing, laughing, and plaguing everybody who would not do the same', and 'ready words: turning Joseph's religious curses into ridicule . . . and doing just what her father hated most' (ch. 5).

* * *

Catherine's sojourn in the earthly paradise of childhood lasts for six years, according to C. P. Sanger's precisely worked-out chronology, but it takes Nelly Dean barely fifteen minutes to relate the episode.[11] Prelapsarian history, as Milton knew, is easy to summarise. Since happiness has few of the variations of despair, to be unfallen is to be static, whereas to fall is to enter the processes of time. Thus Nelly's account of Catherine's fall takes at least several hours, though it also covers six years. And as she describes it, that fall – or process of falling – begins with Hindley's marriage, an event associated for obvious reasons with the young man's inheritance of his father's power and position. Hindley and Frances seem to Catherine like transformed or alien parents, and since this is as much a function of her own vision as of the older couple's behaviour, we must assume that it has something to do with the changes wrought by the girl's entrance into adolescence.

Why do parents begin to seem like step-parents when their children reach puberty? The ubiquitousness of step-parents in fairy tales dealing with the crises of adolescence suggests that the phenomenon is both deepseated and widespread. One explanation – and the one that surely accounts for Catherine Earnshaw's experience – is that when the child gets old enough to become conscious of her parents as sexual beings they really do begin to seem like fiercer, perhaps even (as in the case of Hindley and Frances) younger versions of their 'original' selves. Certainly they begin to be more threatening (that is, more 'peevish' and 'tyrannical') if only because the child's own sexual awakening disturbs them almost as much as their sexuality, now truly comprehended, bothers the child. Thus the crucial passage from Catherine's diary which Lockwood reads even before Nelly begins her narration is concerned not just with Joseph's pious oppressions but with the cause of those puritanical onslaughts, the fact that she and Heathcliff must shiver in the garret because 'Hindley and his wife [are basking] downstairs before a comfortable fire . . . kissing and talking nonsense by the hour – foolish palaver we should be ashamed of'. Catherine's defensiveness is clear. She (and Heathcliff) are troubled by the billing and cooing of her 'step-parents' because she understands, perhaps for the first time, the sexual nature of what a minute later she calls Hindley's 'paradise on the hearth' and – worse – understands its relevance to her.

Flung into the kitchen, 'where Joseph asseverated, "owd Nick" would fetch us', Catherine and Heathcliff each seek 'a separate nook to await his advent'. For Catherine-and-Heathcliff – that is, Catherine and Catherine, or Catherine and her whip – have already been separated from each other, not just by tyrannical Hindley, the *deus* produced by time's *machina*, but by the emergence of Catherine's own sexuality, with all the terrors which attend that phenomenon in a puritanical and patriarchal society. And just as peevish Frances incarnates the social illness of ladyhood, so also she quite literally embodies the fearful as well as the frivolous consequences of sexuality. Her foolish if paradisaical palaver on the hearth, after all, leads straight to the death her earlier ghostliness and silliness had predicted. Her sexuality's destructiveness was even implied by the minor but vicious acts of injustice with which it was associated – arbitrarily pulling Heathcliff's hair, for instance – but the sex-death equation, with which Milton and Mary Shelley were also concerned, really surfaces when Frances's and Hindley's son, Hareton, is born. At that time, Kenneth, the lugubrious physician who functions like a medical Greek chorus throughout *Wuthering Heights*, informs Hindley that the winter will 'probably finish' Frances.

To Catherine, however, it must appear that the murderous agent is not winter but sex, for as she is beginning to learn, the Miltonic testaments of her world have told woman that 'thy sorrow I will greatly multiply / By thy Conception . . . ' (*Paradise Lost*, 10. 192–5) and the maternal image of Sin birthing Death reinforces this point. That Frances's decline and death accompany Catherine's fall is metaphysically appropriate, therefore. And it is dramatically appropriate as well, for Frances's fate foreshadows the catastrophes which will follow Catherine's fall into sexuality just as surely as the appearance of Sin and Death on earth followed Eve's fall. That Frances's death also, incidentally, yields Hareton – the truest scion of the Earnshaw clan – is also profoundly appropriate. For Hareton is, after all, a resurrected version of the original patriarch whose name is written over the great main door of the house, amid a 'wilderness of shameless little boys'. Thus his birth marks the beginning of the historical as well as the psychological decline and fall of that Satanic female principle which has temporarily usurped his 'rightful' place at Wuthering Heights.

* * *

Realistically speaking, Catherine and Heathcliff have been driven in the direction of Thrushcross Grange by their own desire to escape not only the pietistic tortures Joseph inflicts but also, more urgently, just that sexual awareness irritatingly imposed by Hindley's romantic paradise. Neither sexuality nor its consequences can be evaded, however, and the farther the children run the closer they come to the very fate they secretly wish to avoid. Racing 'from the top of the Heights to the park without stopping', they plunge from the periphery of Hindley's paradise (which was transforming their heaven into a hell) to the boundaries of a place that at first seems authentically heavenly, a place full of light and softness and colour, a 'splendid place carpeted with crimson . . . and [with] a pure white ceiling bordered by gold, a shower of glass-drops hanging in silver chains from the centre, and shimmering with little soft tapers' (ch. 6). Looking in the window, the outcasts speculate that if they were inside such a room 'we should have thought ourselves in heaven!' From the outside, at least, the Lintons' elegant haven appears paradisaical. But once the children have experienced its Urizenic interior, they know that in their terms this heaven is hell.

Because the first emissary of this heaven who greets them is the bulldog Skulker, a sort of hellhound posing as a hound of heaven, the wound this almost totemic animal inflicts upon Catherine is as symbolically suggestive as his role in the girl's forced passage from Wuthering Heights to Thrushcross Grange. Barefoot, as if to emphasise her 'wild child' innocence, Catherine is exceptionally vulnerable, as a wild child must inevitably be, and when the dog is 'throttled off, his huge, purple tongue hanging half a foot out of his mouth . . . his pendant lips [are] streaming with bloody slaver'. 'Look . . . how her foot bleeds', Edgar Linton exclaims, and 'She may be lamed for life', his mother anxiously notes (ch. 6). Obviously such bleeding has sexual connotations, especially when it occurs in a pubescent girl. Crippling injuries to the feet are equally resonant, moreover, almost always signifying symbolic castration, as in the stories of Oedipus, Achilles, and the Fisher King. Additionally, it hardly needs to be noted that Skulker's equipment for aggression – his huge purple tongue and pendant lips, for instance – sounds extraordinarily phallic. In a Freudian sense, then, the imagery of this brief but violent episode hints that Catherine has been simultaneously catapulted into adult female sexuality *and* castrated.

Certainly the hypothesis that Catherine Earnshaw has become in some sense a 'social castrate', that she has been 'lamed for life', is borne out by her treatment at Thrushcross Grange – and by the treatment of her alter ego, Heathcliff. For, assuming that she is a 'young lady', the entire Linton household cossets the wounded (but

still healthy) girl as if she were truly an invalid. Indeed, feeding her
their alien rich food – negus and cakes from their own table –
washing her feet, combing her hair, dressing her in 'enormous slip-
pers', and wheeling her about like a doll, they seem to be enacting
some sinister ritual of initiation, the sort of ritual that has traditionally weakened mythic heroines from Persephone to Snow White. And
because he is 'a little Lascar, or an American or Spanish castaway',
the Lintons banish Heathcliff from their parlour, thereby separating
Catherine from the lover/brother whom she herself defines as her
strongest and most necessary 'self'. For five weeks now, she will be
at the mercy of the Grange's heavenly gentility.

To say that Thrushcross Grange is genteel or cultured and that it
therefore seems 'heavenly' is to say, of course, that it is the opposite
of Wuthering Heights. And certainly at every point the two houses
are opposed to each other, as if each in its self-assertion must
absolutely deny the other's being. Like Milton and Blake, Emily
Brontë thought in polarities. Thus, where Wuthering Heights is
essentially a great parlourless room built around a huge central
hearth, a furnace of dark energy like the fire of Los, Thrushcross
Grange has a parlour notable not for heat but for light, for 'a pure
white ceiling bordered by gold' with 'a shower of glass-drops' in the
centre that seems to parody the 'sovran vital Lamp' (*Paradise Lost*,
3. 22) which illuminates Milton's heaven of Right Reason. Where
Wuthering Heights, moreover, is close to being naked or 'raw' in
Lévi-Strauss' sense – its floors uncarpeted, most of its inhabitants
barely literate, even the meat on its shelves open to inspection –
Thrushcross Grange is clothed and 'cooked': carpeted in crimson,
bookish, feeding on cakes and tea and negus.[12] It follows from this,
then, that where Wuthering Heights is functional, even its dogs
working sheepdogs or hunters, Thrushcross Grange (though guarded
by bulldogs) appears to be decorative or aesthetic, the home of
lapdogs as well as ladies. And finally, therefore, Wuthering Heights
in its stripped functional rawness is essentially anti-hierarchical and
egalitarian as the aspirations of Eve and Satan, while Thrushcross
Grange reproduces the hierarchical chain of being that Western
culture traditionally proposes as heaven's decree. Divided from each
other, the once androgynous Heathcliff-and-Catherine are now conquered by the concerted forces of patriarchy, the Lintons of Thrushcross Grange acting together with Hindley and Frances, their
emissaries at the Heights.

It is, appropriately enough, during this period, that Frances gives birth to Hareton, the new patriarch-to-be, and dies, having fulfilled her painful function in the book and in the world. During this period, too, Catherine's education in ladylike self-denial causes her dutifully to deny her self and decide to marry Edgar. For when she says of Heathcliff that 'he's more myself than I am', she means that as her exiled self the nameless 'gipsy' really does preserve in his body more of her original being than she retains: even in his deprivation he seems whole and sure, while she is now entirely absorbed in the ladylike wishing and denying Dickinson's poem describes. Thus, too, it is during this period of loss and transition that Catherine obsessively inscribes on her windowsill the crucial writing Lockwood finds, writing which announces from the first Emily Brontë's central concern with identity: 'a name repeated in all kinds of characters, large and small – Catherine Earnshaw, here and there varied to Catherine Heathcliff, and then again to Catherine Linton' (ch. 3). In the light of this repeated and varied name it is no wonder, finally, that Catherine knows Heathcliff is 'more myself than I am', for he has only a single name, while she has so many that she may be said in a sense to have none. Just as triumphant self-discovery is the ultimate goal of the male *Bildungsroman*, anxious self-denial, Brontë suggests, is the ultimate product of a female education. What Catherine, or any girl, must learn is that she does not know her own name, and therefore cannot know either who she is or whom she is destined to be.

It has often been argued that Catherine's anxiety and uncertainty about her own identity represents a moral failing, a fatal flaw in her character which leads to her inability to choose between Edgar and Heathcliff. Heathcliff's reproachful 'Why did you betray your own heart, Cathy?' (ch. 15) represents a Blakeian form of this moral criticism, a contemptuous suggestion that 'those who restrain desire do so because theirs is weak enough to be restrained'.[13] The more vulgar and commonsensical attack of the Leavisites, on the other hand – the censorious notion that 'maturity' means being strong enough to choose not to have your cake and eat it too – represents what Mark Kinkead-Weeks calls 'the view from the Grange'.[14] To talk of morality in connection with Catherine's fall – and specifically in connection with her self-deceptive decision to marry Edgar – seems pointless, however, for morality only becomes a relevant term where there are meaningful choices.

As we have seen, Catherine has no meaningful choices. Driven from Wuthering Heights to Thrushcross Grange by her brother's marriage, seized by Thrushcross Grange and held fast in the jaws of reason, education, decorum, she cannot do otherwise than as she does, must marry Edgar because there is no one else for her to marry and a lady must marry. Indeed, her self-justifying description of her love for Edgar – 'I love the ground under his feet, and the air over his head, and everything he touches, and every word he says' (ch. 9) – is a bitter parody of a genteel romantic declaration which shows how effective her education has been in indoctrinating her with the literary romanticism deemed suitable for young ladies, the swooning 'femininity' that identifies all energies with the charisma of fathers/ lovers/husbands. Her concomitant explanation that it would 'degrade' her to marry Heathcliff is an equally inevitable product of her education, for her fall into ladyhood has been accompanied by Heathcliff's reduction to an equivalent position of female powerlessness, and Catherine has learned, correctly, that if it is degrading to be a woman it is even more degrading to be *like* a woman. Just as Milton's Eve, therefore, being already fallen, had no meaningful choice despite Milton's best efforts to prove otherwise, so Catherine has no real choice. Given the patriarchal nature of culture, women must fall – that is, they are already fallen because doomed to fall.

* * *

Catherine Earnshaw Linton's decline follows Catherine Earnshaw's fall. Slow at first, it is eventually as rapid, sickening, and deadly as the course of Brontë's own consumption was to be. And the long slide toward death of the body begins with what appears to be an irreversible death of the soul – with Catherine's fatalistic acceptance of Edgar's offer and her consequent self-imprisonment in the role of 'Mrs Linton, the lady of Thrushcross Grange'. It is, of course, her announcement of this decision to Nelly, overheard by Heathcliff, which leads to Heathcliff's self-exile from the Heights and thus definitively to Catherine's psychic fragmentation. And significantly, her response to the departure of her true self is a lapse into illness which both signals the beginning of her decline and foreshadows its mortal end. Her words to Nelly the morning after Heathcliff's departure are therefore symbolically as well as dramatically resonant: 'Shut the window, Nelly, I'm starving!' (ch. 9).

But Heathcliff's mysterious reappearance six months after her wedding intensifies rather than cures her symptoms. For his return does not in any way suggest a healing of the wound of femaleness that was inflicted at puberty. Instead, it signals the beginning of 'madness', a sort of feverish infection of the wound. Catherine's marriage to Edgar has now inexorably locked her into a social system that denies her autonomy, and thus, as psychic symbolism, Heathcliff's return represents the return of her true self's desires without the rebirth of her former powers. And desire without power, as Freud and Blake both knew, inevitably engenders disease.

Because Edgar is so often described as 'soft', 'weak', slim, fair-haired, even effeminate-looking, the specifically patriarchal nature of his feelings toward Heathcliff may not be immediately evident. Certainly many readers have been misled by his almost stylised angelic qualities to suppose that the rougher, darker Heathcliff incarnates masculinity in contrast to Linton's effeminacy. The returned Heathcliff, Nelly says, 'had grown a tall, athletic, well-formed man, beside whom my master seemed quite slender and youthlike. His upright carriage suggested the idea of his having been in the army' (ch. 10). She even seems to acquiesce in his superior maleness. But her constant, reflexive use of the phrase 'my master' for Edgar tells us otherwise, as do some of her other expressions. At this point in the novel, anyway, Heathcliff is always merely 'Heathcliff' while Edgar is variously 'Mr Linton', 'my master', 'Mr Edgar', and 'the master', all phrases conveying the power and status he has independent of his physical strength.

In fact, as Milton also did, Emily Brontë demonstrates that the power of the patriarch, Edgar's power, begins with words, for heaven is populated by '*spirits* Masculine', and as above, so below. Edgar does not need a strong, conventionally masculine body, because his mastery is contained in books, wills, testaments, leases, titles, rent-rolls, documents, languages, all the paraphernalia by which patriarchal culture is transmitted from one generation to the next. Indeed, even without Nelly's designation of him as 'the master', his notable bookishness would define him as a patriarch, for he rules his house from his library as if to parody that male education in Latin and Greek, privilege and prerogative, which so infuriated Milton's daughters. As a figure in the psychodrama of Catherine's decline, then, he incarnates the education in young ladyhood that has commanded her to learn her 'place'. In Freudian terms he would no doubt be described as her superego, the internalised guardian of morality and culture, with Heathcliff, his opposite, functioning as her childish and desirous id.

But at the same time, despite Edgar's superegoistic qualities, Emily

Brontë shows that his patriarchal rule, like Thrushcross Grange itself, is based on physical as well as spiritual violence. For her, as for Blake, heaven *kills*. Thus, at a word from Thrushcross Grange, Skulker is let loose, and Edgar's magistrate father cries 'What prey, Robert?' to his manservant, explaining that he fears thieves because 'yesterday was my rent day'. Similarly, Edgar, having decided that he has 'humoured' Catherine long enough, calls for two strong men servants to support his authority and descends into the kitchen to evict Heathcliff. The patriarch, Brontë notes, needs words, not muscles, and Heathcliff's derisive language paradoxically suggests understanding of the true male power Edgar's 'soft' exterior conceals: 'Cathy, this lamb of yours threatens like a bull!' (ch. 11). Even more significant, perhaps, is the fact that when Catherine locks Edgar in alone with her and Heathcliff – once more imprisoning herself while ostensibly imprisoning the hated master – this apparently effeminate, 'milk-blooded coward' frees himself by striking Heathcliff a breathtaking blow on the throat 'that would have levelled a slighter man'.

Edgar's victory once again recapitulates that earlier victory of Thrushcross Grange over Wuthering Heights which also meant the victory of a Urizenic 'heaven' over a delightful and energetic 'hell'. At the same time, it seals Catherine's doom, locking her into her downward spiral of self-starvation. And in doing this it finally explains what is perhaps Nelly's most puzzling remark about the relationship between Edgar and Catherine. In chapter 8, noting that the lovestruck sixteen-year-old Edgar is 'doomed, and flies to his fate', the housekeeper sardonically declares that 'the soft thing [Edgar] . . . possessed the power to depart [from Catherine] as much as a cat possesses the power to leave a mouse half killed or a bird half eaten'. At that point in the novel her metaphor seems odd. Is not headstrong Catherine the hungry cat, and 'soft' Edgar the half-eaten mouse? But in fact, as we now see, Edgar all along represented the devouring force that will gnaw and worry Catherine to death, consuming flesh and spirit together. For having fallen into 'heaven', she has ultimately – to quote Sylvia Plath – 'fallen / Into the stomach of indifference', a social physiology that urgently needs her not so much for herself as for her function.[15]

When we note the significance of such imagery of devouring, as well as the all-pervasive motif of self-starvation in *Wuthering Heights*, the kitchen setting of this crucial confrontation between Edgar and Heathcliff begins to seem more than coincidental. In any case, the episode is followed closely by what C. P. Sanger calls Catherine's 'hunger strike' and by her famous mad scene.[16] Another line of Plath's describes the feelings of self-lessness that seem to accompany Catherine's realisation that she has been reduced to a role, a function, a sort of walking costume: 'I have no face, I have wanted to efface myself'.[17] For the weakening of Catherine's grasp on the world is most specifically shown by her inability to recognise her own face in the mirror during the mad scene. Explaining to Nelly that she is not mad, she notes that if she were 'I should believe you really *were* [a] withered hag, and I should think I *was* under Penistone Crag; and I'm conscious it's night and there are two candles on the table making the black press shine like jet'. Then she adds, 'It does appear odd – I see a face in it' (ch. 12). But of course, ironically, there is no 'black press' in the room, only a mirror in which Catherine sees and repudiates her own image. Her fragmentation has now gone so far beyond the psychic split betokened by her division from Heathcliff that body and image (or body and soul) have separated.

Q. D. Leavis would have us believe that this apparently gothic episode, with its allusion to 'dark superstitions about premonitions of death, about ghosts and primitive beliefs about the soul . . . is a proof of [Emily Brontë's] immaturity at the time of the original conception of *Wuthering Heights*'. Leo Bersani, on the other hand, suggests that the scene hints at 'the danger of being haunted by alien versions of the self'.[18] In a sense, however, the image Catherine sees in the mirror is neither gothic nor alien – though she is alienated from it – but hideously familiar, and further proof that her madness may really equal sanity. Catherine sees in the mirror an image of who and what she has really become in the world's terms: 'Mrs Linton, the lady of Thrushcross Grange'. And oddly enough, this image appears to be stored like an article of clothing, a trousseau-treasure, or again in Plath's words 'a featureless, fine / Jew linen',[19] in one of the cupboards of childhood, the black press from her old room at the Heights.

To escape from the horrible mirror-enclosure, then, might be to escape from all domestic enclosures, or to begin to try to escape. It is significant that in her madness Catherine tears at her pillow with her teeth, begs Nelly to open the window, and seems 'to find childish diversion in pulling the feathers from the rents she [has] just made' (ch. 12). Liberating feathers from the prison where they had been reduced to objects of social utility, she imagines them reborn as the birds they once were, whole and free, and pictures them 'wheeling over our heads in the middle of the moor', trying to get back to their nests. A moment later, standing by the window 'careless of the frosty air', she imagines her own trip back across the moor to Wuthering Heights, noting that 'it's a rough journey, and a sad heart to travel it; and we must pass by Gimmerton Kirk to go that journey! . . . But Heathcliff, if I dare you now, will you venture? . . . I won't rest till you are with me. I never will!' (ch. 12). For a 'fallen' woman, trapped in the distorting mirrors of patriarchy, the journey into death is the only way out, Brontë suggests, and the *Liebestod* is not (as it would be for a male artist, like Keats or Wagner) a mystical but a practical solution. In the presence of death, after all, 'The mirrors are sheeted', to quote Plath yet again.[20]

The masochism of this surrender to what A. Alvarez has called the 'savage god' of suicide is plain, not only from Catherine's own words and actions but also from the many thematic parallels between her speeches and Plath's poems.[21] But of course, taken together, self-starvation or anorexia nervosa, masochism, and suicide form a complex of psychoneurotic symptoms that is almost classically associated with female feelings of powerlessness and rage. Certainly the 'hunger strike' is a traditional tool of the powerless, as the history of the feminist movement (and many other movements of oppressed peoples) will attest. Anorexia nervosa, moreover, is a sort of mad corollary of the self-starvation that may be a sane strategy for survival. Clinically associated with 'a distorted concept of body size' – like Catherine Earnshaw's alienated/familiar image in the mirror – it is fed by the 'false sense of power that the faster derives from her starvation', and is associated, psychologists speculate, with 'a struggle for control, for a sense of identity, competence, and effectiveness'.

Critics never comment on this point, but the truth is that Catherine is pregnant during both the kitchen scene and the mad scene, and her death occurs at the time of (and ostensibly because of) her 'confinement'. In the light of this, her anorexia, her madness, and her masochism become even more fearsomely meaningful. Certainly, for instance, the distorted body that the anorexic imagines for herself is analogous to the distorted body that the pregnant woman really must confront. Can eating produce such a body? The question, mad as it may seem, must be inevitable. In any case, some psychoanalysts have suggested that anorexia, endemic to pubescent girls, reflects a fear of oral impregnation, to which self-starvation would be one obvious response.[22]

But even if a woman accepts, or rather concedes, that she is pregnant, an impulse toward self-starvation would seem to be an equally obvious response to the pregnant woman's inevitable fear of being monstrously inhabited, as well as to her own horror of being enslaved to the species and reduced to a tool of the life process. Birth is, after all, the ultimate fragmentation the self can undergo, just as 'confinement' is, for women, the ultimate pun on imprisonment. As if in recognition of this, Catherine's attempt to escape maternity does, if only unconsciously, subvert Milton. For Milton's Eve 'knew not eating Death'. But Brontë's does. In her refusal to be enslaved to the species, her refusal to be 'mother of human race', she closes her mouth on emptiness as, in Plath's words, 'on a communion tablet'. It is no use, of course. She breaks apart into two Catherines – the old, mad, dead Catherine fathered by Wuthering Heights, and the new, more docile and acceptable Catherine fathered by Thrushcross Grange. But nevertheless, in her defiance Emily Brontë's Eve, like her creator, is a sort of hunger artist, a point Charlotte Brontë acknowledged when she memorialised her sister in *Shirley*, that other revisionary account of the Genesis of female hunger.[23]

* * *

Catherine's fall and her resulting decline, fragmentation, and death are the obvious subjects of the first half of *Wuthering Heights*. Not quite so obviously, the second half of the novel is concerned with the larger, social consequences of Catherine's fall, which spread out in concentric circles like rings from a stone flung into a river, and which are examined in a number of parallel stories, including some that have already been set in motion at the time of Catherine's death. Isabella, Nelly, Heathcliff, and Catherine II – in one way or another all these characters' lives parallel (or even in a sense contain) Catherine's, as if Brontë were working out a series of alternative versions of the same plot.[24]

Isabella is perhaps the most striking of these parallel figures, for like Catherine she is a headstrong, impulsive 'miss' who runs away from home at adolescence. But where Catherine's fall is both fated and unconventional, a fall 'upward' from hell to heaven, Isabella's is both wilful and conventional. Falling from Thrushcross Grange to Wuthering Heights, from 'heaven' to 'hell', in exactly the opposite direction from Catherine, Isabella patently chooses her own fate, refusing to listen to Catherine's warnings against Heathcliff and carefully evading her brother's vigilance. But then Isabella has from the first functioned as Catherine's opposite, a model of the stereo-typical young lady patriarchal education is designed to produce.

Would Isabella's fate have been different if she had fallen in love with someone less problematical than Heathcliff – with a man of culture, for instance, rather than a Satanic nature figure? Would she have prospered with the love of someone like her own brother, or Heathcliff's tenant, Lockwood? Her early relationship with Edgar, together with Edgar's patriarchal rigidity, hint that she would not. Even more grimly suggestive is the story Lockwood tells in chapter 1 about his romantic encounter at the seacoast. Readers will recall that the 'fascinating creature' he admired was 'a real goddess in my eyes, as long as she took no notice of [me]'. But when she 'looked a return', her lover 'shrunk icily into myself . . . till finally the poor innocent was led to doubt her own senses . . . ' (ch. 1). Since even the most cultivated women are powerless, women are evidently at the mercy of all men, Lockwoods and Heathcliffs alike.

Nelly Dean, of course, seems to many critics to have been put into the novel to help Emily Brontë disavow such uniformly dark intentions. 'For a specimen of true benevolence and homely fidelity, look at the character of Nelly Dean', Charlotte Brontë says with what certainly appears to be conviction, trying to soften the picture of 'perverse passion and passionate perversity' Victorian readers thought her sister had produced.[25] And Charlotte Brontë 'rightly defended her sister against allegations of abnormality by pointing out that . . . Emily had created the wholesome, maternal Nelly Dean', comments Q. D. Leavis.[26] How wholesome and maternal *is* Nelly Dean, however? And if we agree that she is basically benevolent, of what does her benevolence consist? Problematic words like *wholesome* and *benevolent* suggest a point where we can start to trace the relationship between Nelly's history and Catherine's (or Isabella's). Wholesomely nurturing, she does appear to be in some sense an ideal woman, a 'general mother' – if not from Emily Brontë's point of view, then from, say, Milton's. And indeed, if we look again at the crucial passage in *Shirley* where Charlotte Brontë's Shirley/Emily criticises Milton, we find an unmistakable version of Nelly Dean. 'Milton tried to see the first woman', says Shirley, 'but, Cary, he saw her not. . . . It was his cook that he saw . . . puzzled "what choice to choose for delicacy best. . . ." '

This comment explains a great deal. For if Nelly Dean is Eve as Milton's cook – Eve, that is, as Milton (but not Brontë or Shirley) would have had her – she does not pluck apples to eat them herself; she plucks them to make apple sauce. And similarly, she does not tell stories to participate in them herself, to consume the emotional food they offer, but to create a moral meal, a didactic fare that will nourish future generations in docility. As Milton's cook, in fact, Nelly Dean is patriarchy's paradigmatic housekeeper, the man's woman who has traditionally been hired to keep men's houses in order by straightening out their parlours, their daughters, and their stories. 'My heart invariably cleaved to the master's, in preference to Catherine's side', she herself declares (ch. 10), and she expresses her preference by acting throughout the novel as a censorious agent of patriarchy.

But if Nelly parallels or comments upon Catherine by representing Eve as Milton's cook, while Isabella represents Catherine/Eve as a bourgeois literary lady, it may at first be hard to see how or why Heathcliff parallels Catherine at all. Though he is Catherine's alter ego, he certainly seems to be, in Bersani's words, 'a non-identical double'.[27] Not only is he male while she is female – implying many subtle as well as a few obvious differences, in this gender-obsessed book – but he seems to be a triumphant survivor, an insider, a power-usurper throughout most of the novel's second half, while Catherine is not only a dead failure but a wailing, outcast ghost. Heathcliff does love her and mourn her – and finally Catherine does in some sense 'kill' him – but beyond such melodramatically romantic connections, what bonds unite these one-time lovers?

Perhaps we can best begin to answer this question by examining the passionate words with which Heathcliff closes his first grief-stricken speech after Catherine's death: 'Oh, God! it is unutterable! I cannot live without my life! I cannot live without my soul!' (ch. 16). Like the metaphysical paradox embedded in Catherine's crucial adolescent speech to Nelly about Heathcliff ('He's more myself than I am'), these words have often been thought to be, on the one hand, emptily rhetorical, and on the other, severely mystical. But suppose we try to imagine what they might mean as descriptions of a psychological fact about the relationship between Heathcliff and Catherine. Catherine's assertion that Heathcliff was *herself* quite reasonably summarised, after all, her understanding that she was being transformed into a lady while Heathcliff retained the ferocity of her primordial half-savage self. Similarly, Heathcliff's exclamation that he cannot live without his soul may express, as a corollary of this idea, the 'gypsy's' own deep sense of being Catherine's whip, and his perception that he has now become merely the soulless body of a vanished passion. But to be merely a body – a whip without a mistress – is to be a sort of monster, a fleshly thing, an object of pure animal materiality like the abortive being Victor Frankenstein created. And such a monster is indeed what Heathcliff becomes.

From the first, Heathcliff has had undeniable monster potential, as many readers have observed. Isabella's questions to Nelly – 'Is Mr Heathcliff a man? If so, is he mad? And if not is he a devil?' (ch. 13) – indicate among other things Emily Brontë's cool awareness of having created an anomalous being, a sort of 'Ghoul' or 'Afreet', not (as her sister half hoped) 'despite' herself but for good reasons. Uniting human and animal traits, the skills of culture with the energies of nature, Heathcliff's character tests the boundaries between human and animal, nature and culture, and in doing so proposes a new definition of the demonic. What is more important for our purposes here, however, is the fact that, despite his outward masculinity, Heathcliff is somehow female in his monstrosity. Besides in a general way suggesting a set of questions about humanness, his existence therefore summarises a number of important points about the relationship between maleness and femaleness as, say, Milton representatively defines it.

To say that Heathcliff is 'female' may at first sound mad or absurd. As we noted earlier, his outward masculinity seems to be definitively demonstrated by his athletic build and military carriage, as well as by the Byronic sexual charisma that he has for ladylike Isabella. And though we saw that Edgar is truly patriarchal despite his apparent effeminacy, there is no real reason why Heathcliff should not simply represent an alternative version of masculinity, the maleness of the younger son, that paradigmatic outsider in patriarchy. To some extent, of course, this is true: Heathcliff is clearly just as male in his Satanic outcast way as Edgar in his angelically established way. But at the same time, on a deeper associative level, Heathcliff is 'female' – on the level where younger sons and bastards and devils unite with women in rebelling against the tyranny of heaven, the level where orphans are female and heirs are male, where flesh is female and spirit is male, earth female, sky male, monsters female, angels male. Bastardly and dastardly, a true son of the bitch goddess Nature, throughout the second half of *Wuthering Heights* Heathcliff pursues a murderous revenge against patriarchy, a revenge most appropriately expressed by *King Lear's* equally outcast Edmund: 'Well, then, / Legitimate Edgar, I must have your land'.[28] For Brontë's revisionary genius manifests itself especially in her perception of the deep connections among Shakespeare's Edmund, Milton's Satan, Mary Shelley's monster, the demon lover/animal groom figure of innumerable folktales – and Eve, the original rebellious female.

Because he unites characteristics of all these figures in a single body, Heathcliff in one way or another acts like all of them throughout the second half of *Wuthering Heights*. His general aim in this part of the novel is to wreak the revenge of nature upon culture by subverting legitimacy. Thus, like Edmund (and Edmund's female counterparts Goneril and Regan) he literally *takes* the *place* of one legitimate heir after another, supplanting both Hindley and Hareton at the Heights, and – eventually – Edgar at the Grange. Moreover, he not only replaces legitimate culture but in his rage strives like Frankenstein's monster to end it. His attempts at killing Isabella and Hindley, as well as the infanticidal tendencies expressed in his merciless abuse of his own son, indicate his desire not only to alter the ways of his world but literally to dis-continue them, to get at the heart of patriarchy by stifling the line of descent that ultimately gives culture its legitimacy.

Since Heathcliff's dark energies seem so limitless, why does his vengeful project fail? Ultimately, no doubt, it fails because in stories of the war between nature and culture nature always fails. But that point is of course a tautology. Culture tells the story (that is, the story is a cultural construct) and the story is aetiological: how culture triumphed over nature, where parsonages and tea-parties came from, how the lady got her skirts – and her deserts. Thus Edmund, Satan, Frankenstein's monster, Mr Fox, Bluebeard, Eve, and Heathcliff all must fail in one way or another, if only to explain the status quo. Significantly, however, where Heathcliff's analogues are universally destroyed by forces outside themselves, Heathcliff seems to be killed, as Catherine was, by something within himself. His death from self-starvation makes his function as Catherine's almost identical double definitively clear. Interestingly, though, when we look closely at the events leading up to his death it becomes equally clear that Heathcliff is not just killed by his own despairing desire for his vanished 'soul' but at least in part by another one of Catherine's parallels, the new and cultivated Catherine who has been reborn through the intervention of patriarchy in the form of Edgar Linton. It is no accident, certainly, that Catherine II's imprisonment at the Heights and her rapprochement with Hareton coincide with Heathcliff's perception that 'there is a strange change approaching', with his vision of the lost Catherine, and with his development of an eating disorder very much akin to Catherine's anorexia nervosa.

* * *

If Heathcliff is Catherine's almost identical double, Catherine II really is her mother's 'non-identical double'. Though he has his doubles confused, Bersani does note that Nelly's 'mild moralising' seems 'suited to the younger Catherine's playful independence'.[29] For where her headstrong mother genuinely struggled for autonomy, the more docile Catherine II merely plays at disobedience, taking make-believe journeys within the walls of her father's estate and dutifully surrendering her illicit (though equally make-believe) love letters at a word from Nelly. Indeed, in almost every way Catherine II differs from her fierce dead mother in being culture's child, a born lady. 'It's as if Emily Brontë were telling the same story twice', Bersani observes, 'and eliminating its originality the second time.'[30] But though he is right that Brontë is telling the same story over again (really for the third or fourth time), she is not repudiating her own originality. Rather, through her analysis of Catherine II's successes, she is showing how society repudiated Catherine's originality.

Where, for instance, Catherine Earnshaw rebelled against her father, Catherine II is profoundly dutiful. One of her most notable adventures occurs when she runs away from Wuthering Heights to get *back* to her father, a striking contrast to the escapes of Catherine and Isabella, both of whom ran purposefully away from the world of fathers and older brothers. Because she is a dutiful daughter, moreover, Catherine II is a cook, nurse, teacher, and housekeeper. In other words, where her mother was a heedless wild child, Catherine II promises to become an ideal Victorian woman, all of whose virtues are in some sense associated with daughterhood, wifehood, motherhood. Since Nelly Dean was her foster mother, literally replacing the original Catherine, her development of these talents is not surprising. To be mothered by Milton's cook and fathered by one of his angels is to become, inevitably, culture's child. Thus Catherine II nurses Linton (even though she dislikes him), brews tea for Heathcliff, helps Nelly prepare vegetables, teaches Hareton to read, and replaces the wild blackberries at Wuthering Heights with flowers from Thrushcross Grange. Literary as her father and her aunt Isabella, she has learned the lessons of patriarchal Christianity so well that she even piously promises Heathcliff that she will forgive both him and Linton for their sins against her: 'I know [Linton] has a bad nature ... he's your son. But I'm glad I've a better to forgive it' (ch. 29). At the same time, she has a genteel (or Urizenic) feeling for rank which comes out in her early treatment of Hareton, Zillah, and others at the Heights.

Even when she stops biblically forgiving, moreover, literary modes dominate Catherine II's character. The 'black arts' she tries to practise are essentially bookish – and plainly inauthentic. Indeed, if Heathcliff is merely impersonating a father at this point in the story, Catherine II is merely impersonating a witch. A real witch would threaten culture; but Catherine II's vocation is to serve it, for as her personality suggests, she is perfectly suited to (has been raised for) what Sherry Ortner defines as the crucial female function of mediating between nature and culture.[31] Thus it is she who finally restores order to both the Heights and the Grange by marrying Hareton Earnshaw, whom she has, significantly, prepared for his new mastery by teaching him to read. Through her intervention, therefore, he can at last recognise the name over the lintel at Wuthering Heights – the name Hareton Earnshaw – which is both his own name and the name of the founder of the house, the primordial patriarch.

It is in his triumphant legitimacy that Hareton, together with Catherine II, acts to exorcise Heathcliff from the traditionally legitimate world of the Grange and the newly legitimised world of Wuthering Heights. Fading into nature, where Catherine persists 'in every cloud, in every tree', Heathcliff can no longer eat the carefully cooked human food that Nelly offers him. While Catherine II decorates Hareton's porridge with cut flowers, the older man has irreligious fantasies of dying and being unceremoniously 'carried to the churchyard in the evening'. 'I have nearly attained *my* heaven', he tells Nelly as he fasts and fades, 'and that of others is . . . uncoveted by me' (ch. 34). Then, when he dies, the boundaries between nature and culture crack for a moment, as if to let him pass through: his window swings open, the rain drives in. 'Th' divil's harried off his soul', exclaims old Joseph, *Wuthering Heights'* mock Milton, falling to his knees and giving thanks 'that the lawful master and the ancient stock [are] restored to their rights' (ch. 34). The illegitimate Heathcliff/Catherine have finally been re-placed in nature/hell, and replaced by Hareton and Catherine II – a proper couple – just as Nelly replaced Catherine as a proper mother for Catherine II. Quite reasonably, Nelly now observes that 'The crown of all my wishes will be the union of' this new, civilised couple, and Lockwood notes of the new pair that 'together, they would brave Satan and all his legions'. Indeed, in both Milton's and Brontë's terms (it is the only point on which the two absolutely agree) they have already braved Satan, and they have triumphed. It is now 1802; the Heights – hell – has been converted into the Grange – heaven; and with patriarchal history redefined, renovated, restored, the nineteenth century can truly begin, complete with tea-parties, ministering angels, governesses, and parsonages.

* * *

Joseph's important remark about the restoration of the lawful master and the ancient stock, together with the dates – 1801/1802 – which surround Nelly's tale of a pseudo-mythic past, confirm the idea that *Wuthering Heights* is somehow aetiological. More, the famous care with which Brontë worked out the details surrounding both the novel's dates and the Earnshaw–Linton lineage suggests she herself was quite conscious that she was constructing a story of origins and renewals. Having arrived at the novel's conclusion, we can now go back to its beginning, and try to summarise the basic story *Wuthering Heights* tells. Though this may not be the book's only story, it is surely a crucial one. As the names on the windowsill indicate, *Wuthering Heights* begins and ends with Catherine and her various avatars. More specifically, it studies the evolution of Catherine Earnshaw into Catherine Heathcliff and Catherine Linton, and then her return through Catherine Linton II and Catherine Heathcliff II to her 'proper' role as Catherine Earnshaw II. More generally, what this evolution and de-evolution conveys is the following parodic, anti-Miltonic myth:

There was an Original Mother (Catherine), a daughter of nature whose motto might be 'Thou, Nature, art my goddess; to thy law / My services are bound'. But this girl fell into a decline, at least in part through eating the poisonous cooked food of culture. She fragmented herself into mad or dead selves on the one hand (Catherine, Heathcliff) and into lesser, gentler/genteeler selves on the other (Catherine II, Hareton). The fierce primordial selves disappeared into nature, the perversely hellish heaven which was their home. The more teachable and docile selves learned to read and write, and moved into the fallen cultured world of parlours and parsonages, the Miltonic heaven which, from the Original Mother's point of view, is really hell. Their passage from nature to culture was facilitated by a series of teachers, preachers, nurses, cooks, and model ladies or patriarchs (Nelly, Joseph, Frances, the Lintons), most of whom gradually disappear by the end of the story, since these lesser creations have been so well instructed that they are themselves able to become teachers or models for other generations. Indeed, so model are they that they can be identified with the founders of ancestral houses (Hareton Earnshaw, 1500) and with the original mother redefined as the patriarch's wife (Catherine Linton Heathcliff Earnshaw).

[Simultaneously, however,] the random weakening of Wuthering Heights' walls with which Brontë's novel began – symbolised by old Earnshaw's discovery of Heathcliff in Liverpool – suggests that patriarchal culture is always only precariously holding off the rebellious forces of nature. Who, after all, can say with certainty that the restored line of Hareton Earnshaw 1802 will not someday be just as vulnerable to the onslaughts of the goddess's illegitimate children as the line of Hareton Earnshaw 1500 was to Heathcliff's intrusion? And who is to say that the carving of Hareton Earnshaw 1500 was not similarly preceded by still another war between nature and culture? The fact that everyone has the same name leads inevitably to speculations like this, as though the drama itself, like its actors, simply represented a single episode in a sort of mythic infinite regress. In addition, the fact that the little shepherd boy still sees 'Heathcliff and a woman' wandering the moor hints that the powerfully disruptive possibilities they represent may some day be reincarnated at Wuthering Heights.

Emily Brontë would consider such reincarnation a consummation devoutly to be wished. [Her] outcast witch-child longs equally for the extinction of parlour fires and the rekindling of unimaginably different energies. Her creator, too, is finally the fiercest, most quenchless of Milton's daughters. Looking oppositely for the queendom of heaven, she insists, like Blake, that 'I have also the Bible of Hell, which the world shall have whether they will or no'.[32]

From Sandra Gilbert and Susan Gubar, *The Madwoman in the Attic: the Woman Writer and the Nineteenth-Century Literary Imagination* (New Haven, 1979), pp. 248, 253–5, 256–60 *passim*, 262–5 *passim*, 267, 269–74 *passim*, 276–89 *passim*, 291–4 *passim*, 296–303 *passim*, 305, 307–8, 675–7 *passim*.

NOTES

[Sandra Gilbert's essay, which is reproduced here (with her permission) in a greatly shortened form, originally appeared as chapter 8 of *The Madwoman in the Attic*, the immensely influential feminist work which she co-authored with Susan Gubar. Its theoretical position is discussed in the Introduction. References are to William M. Sale, Jr (ed.), *Wuthering Heights*, Norton Critical Editions (New York, 1972). Ed.]

1. Fannie Ratchford, *Gondal's Queen* (Austin, Texas, 1955), p. 186.

2. See Q. D. Leavis, 'A Fresh Approach to *Wuthering Heights*', in *Wuthering Heights*, ed. William M. Sale, Jr (New York, 1972), p. 313; Mark Schorer, 'Fiction and the Analogical Matrix', *Kenyon Review*, 9 (September 1949), 371; Leo Bersani, *A Future for Astyanax: Character and Desire in Literature* (Boston, 1976), p. 203; Elliot Gose, *Imagination Indulg'd* (Montreal, 1972), p. 59. [Q. D. Leavis's essay referred to here is reprinted in a shortened form in this volume – see p. 24 Ed.]

3. Robert Kiely, *The Romantic Novel in England* (Cambridge, Mass., 1972), p. 233.

4. Emily Jane Brontë, 'Often rebuked, yet always back returning', in C. W. Hatfield (ed.), *The Complete Poems of Emily Jane Brontë* (New York, 1941), pp. 255–6. Hatfield questions Emily's authorship of this poem, suggesting that Charlotte may really have written the piece to express her own 'thoughts about her sister' (ibid., p. 255), but Gérin discusses it unequivocally as a piece by Emily (Winifred Gérin, *Emily Brontë: A Biography* [Oxford, 1972], pp. 264–5).

5. Mircea Eliade, *The Myth of the Eternal Return* (New York, 1954).

6. C. W. Hatfield (ed.), *The Complete Poems of Emily Jane Brontë* (New York, 1941), pp. 255–6.

7. The realistically iconoclastic nature of Catherine's interest in riding, however, is illuminated by this comment from a nineteenth-century conduct book: '[Horseback riding] produces in ladies a coarseness of voice, a weathered complexion, and unnatural consolidation of the bones of the lower part of the body, ensuring a frightful impediment to future functions which need not here be dwelt upon; by overdevelopment of the muscles equitation produces an immense increase in the waist and is, in short, altogether masculine and unwomanly' (Donald Walker, *Exercise for Ladies* [1837], quoted in Cecil Willett Cunnington, *Feminine Attitudes in the Nineteenth Century* [London, 1935], p. 86).

8. See Leo Bersani, *A Future for Astyanax: Character and Desire in Literature* (Boston, 1976), and J. Hillis Miller, *The Disappearance of God* (Cambridge, Mass., 1963), pp. 155–211.

9. Q. D. Leavis, 'A Fresh Approach to *Wuthering Heights*', in William M. Sale, Jr (ed.), *Wuthering Heights* (New York, 1972), p. 321.

10. For a brief discussion of androgyny in *Wuthering Heights*, see Carolyn Heilbrun, *Towards a Recognition of Androgyny* (New York, 1973), pp. 80–2.

11. C. P. Sanger, 'The Structure of *Wuthering Heights*', in William M. Sale, Jr (ed.) *Wuthering Heights*, Norton Critical Editions (New York, 1972), pp. 296–8.

12. See Claude Lévi-Strauss, *The Raw and the Cooked: Introduction to a Science of Mythology*, vol. 1 (New York, 1969).

13. William Blake, *The Marriage of Heaven and Hell*, plate 5.

14. Mark Kinkead-Weeks, 'The Place of Love in *Jane Eyre* and *Wuthering Heights*', in *The Brontës: A Collection of Critical Essays*, ed. Ian Gregor (Englewood Cliffs, NJ, 1970), p. 86.

15. Sylvia Plath, 'The Stones', in *The Colossus* (New York, 1968), p. 82.

16. C. P. Sanger, 'The Structure of *Wuthering Heights*', in William M. Sale, Jr (ed.), *Wuthering Heights*, Norton Critical Editions (New York, 1972), p. 288.

17. Sylvia Plath, 'Tulips', in *Ariel* (New York, 1966), p. 11.

18. Q. D. Leavis, 'A Fresh Approach to *Wuthering Heights*', in William M. Sale, Jr (ed.), *Wuthering Heights* (New York, 1972), p. 309; Leo Bersani, *A Future for Astyanax: Character and Desire in Literature* (Boston, 1976), pp. 208–9.

19. Sylvia Plath, 'Lady Lazarus', *Ariel* (New York, 1966), p. 6.

20. Sylvia Plath, 'Contusion', ibid., p. 83.

21. See A. Alvarez, *The Savage God* (London, 1971).

22. Marlene Boskind-Lodahl, 'Cinderella's Stepsisters: A Feminist Perspective on Anorexia Nervosa and Bulimia', *Signs*, 2 (Winter 1976), 352.

23. For a comment on this phenomenon as it may really have occurred in the life of Emily's sister Charlotte, see Helene Moglen, *Charlotte Brontë: The Self Conceived* (New York, 1976), pp. 241–2.

24. To distinguish the second Catherine from the first without obliterating their similarities, we will call Catherine Earnshaw Linton's daughter Catherine II throughout this discussion.

25. Charlotte Brontë, 'Editor's Preface to the New Edition of *Wuthering Heights* (1850)', in William M. Sale, Jr (ed.) *Wuthering Heights*, Norton Critical Editions (New York, 1972), p. 11.

26. Q. D. Leavis, 'A Fresh Approach to *Wuthering Heights*', in William M. Sale, Jr (ed.), *Wuthering Heights* (New York, 1972), p. 310.

27. Leo Bersani, *A Future for Astyanax: Character and Desire in Literature* (Boston, 1976), pp. 208–9.

28. William Shakespeare, *King Lear* (I.ii.15–16).

29. Leo Bersani, *A Future for Astyanax: Character and Desire in Literature* (Boston, 1976), pp. 221–2.

30. Ibid.

31. Sherry Ortner, 'Is Female to Male as Nature Is to Culture?', in *Women, Culture, and Society*, ed. Michelle Zimbalist Rosaldo and Louise Lamphere (Stanford, 1974).

32. William Blake, *The Marriage of Heaven and Hell*, plate 24.

9

The Language of Familial Desire

STEVIE DAVIES

Bounded by silences and its own brevity, the life of Emily Brontë addressed itself exclusively inward to the intimate world of its own origins. Beyond the necessary economy of language demanded for practical purposes, she was resolute in confiding words to few outsiders, entering the world minimally, reluctantly, and nearly always with temporarily disastrous consequences to her psyche. She wrote scarcely any letters, left few recorded utterances and never shared herself in friendship.

It is a life, therefore, in which a handful of living figures made up the integrity of a complete cosmos: her father, the Reverend Patrick Brontë, her Aunt Branwell, her brother and sisters Charlotte and Anne, the servant Tabby. Confined together within the restricted space of Haworth Parsonage, these figures revealed the mirroring spectrum of human experience and passion to her, shadowed by the accompanying deaths of the other members of her family: her mother and two elder sisters, Maria and Elizabeth, who had died at the ages of 11 and 10 years. In refusing to entertain the compromise entailed by crossing the threshold from home to society, Emily Brontë preserved and declared in her art a unique integrity. Essentially, her world is the authentic theatre of childhood, interpreted non-commitally into the dialect of the elders (in the narrative voice of her fiction) or transcribed raw on to the page (in the voices of her characters). She makes literate what for most of us is prehistoric: anterior to disclosure and elucidation in the complex, explanatory and modifying composure of written language. The characters of *Wuthering Heights* teem with childhood animosities, allegiances and obsessions; they brawl, taunt, mock, manipulate, weep and play their outdoor and indoor orgiastic games within the vice of a terrible paradox. They are children liberated from the deterrent adult guardians who fence and chasten the outset of human life, but their liberation derives from the conditions that orphan and expose them.[1] Because these beings are versions of children in a child's world, they cannot be judged: the novel's tone is flat and equal, neither knowing nor casting blame or praise. Its insistent edge of asperity seems directed rather at the narrators' effort to interpret and the reader's attempt to participate, the adult voyeurs of the game played by the novel's children. The work guards its borders; it is a domain for private life, like the house at the Heights and the answering house, Thrushcross Grange, each with its different means of seclusion – shut doors and surliness on the one hand, the walled garden on the other.

Emily Brontë's work commands a unique view of childhood within our literature by exposing a language which hoarded verbatim the values, joys and pains of that state which, if not prelapsarian, presented the fall as an evolutionary sequence of stages of schism, during which process life was entered into with all one's energies in fullest vigour. *Wuthering Heights* charts a series of fractures which will end in that abeyance of vivacity which is the bondage of adult life; but the novel never enters into the language of that experience, and never fully allows its characters to grow up, nor to collude in the process. We encounter it like a problem in logic, which, having defeated generations of previous readers, introduces us to a mind forbiddingly outside the *adult* norm, either of male or female artist. Its intellectual vigour and authority invite us to reassess the apparent welter of its 'childish' raw material, as not perhaps so very vagrant: to query, in effect, what good is served by the development of consciousness, education, book-learning itself (major problematic motifs of the novel), those factors, indeed, which led us in the first place to take up *Wuthering Heights* and open it at page 1. The stages of the fall – birth, weaning into consciousness, mother-loss, father-loss, sibling-love and -rivalry, adolescence, marriage, parturition, the final split into a dead self (Catherine I) and its daughter-self – are encountered at every stage with protest by the novel's characters and as a riddle by the narrative voices. Most especially, the value of the adult culture that led to the meeting of author and reader is questioned, most memorably in the voice of Catherine in her final breakdown: 'What in the name of all that feels, has he to do with *books*, when I am dying?' (p. 122).

It is in the context of this revolutionary questioning of consensus values that we must look at the language of childhood in *Wuthering Heights*. If we examine the qualities of the protagonists' mode of utterance, we can tell from the very timbre of their voices and the manner and mode of their address that even the supposed adults (measuring by years) are only children in disguise.[2] The level of infantilism within their speech-patterns is high. At heart, the novel implies, people don't change; growth is superficial, culture is shallow and easy to erode. Edgar Linton fights his wife for the key to the room, amidst a riot of name-calling, taunts, threats and physical assaults. 'No, I'll swallow the key before you shall get it!' yells Catherine to her magistrate-husband (p. 115). In the language of her threat lies the child's spontaneous propensity for outrageous utterance: violent argument is a well-relished game of wills, in which household objects feature as pieces in the game. The infantile patterns of verbal abuse and physical threat, ridiculous as they appear out of context, will nevertheless be recognised as the merest realism by readers familiar with the rhetoric of domestic dissension in the 'real' world outside the novel. When Heathcliff first reappears at Thrushcross Grange, Linton strives to maintain a mincingly fastidious politeness in the face of his rival:

> 'Catherine, unless we are to have cold tea, please to come to the table. . . . Mr Heathcliff will have a long walk, wherever he may lodge tonight and I'm thirsty.' . . .
> The meal hardly endured ten minutes – Catherine's cup was never filled, she could neither eat nor drink. Edgar had made a slop in his saucer, and scarcely swallowed a mouthful.
>
> (pp. 96–7)

The details noted by the narrator are nursery details: the petulant 'I'm thirsty', the slop in the saucer. Like volatile children playing at tea-parties, the protagonists mime a social game as a cover for other games more explosive and disruptive.

Energy is the root of beauty, and the source of energy is the child in us: this is, I think, the unstated aesthetic of *Wuthering Heights*. The first generation of the novel stands most abundantly provided with energy, and hence makes a claim on us and has an attraction for us which subverts all consideration of ethics. The appeal is to the ego of the reader – an ego which has been rigorously starved out and stamped down since childhood, by the very process of education which has ripened the reader into a condition to assess the book. This reversal of moral and cultural norms is a major factor in what I have called Emily Brontë's 'sinistral' structuring of perception. The novel calls up and articulates a reader's vestigial nostalgia for the narcissistic mirror-vision of childhood. The ease with which we embrace the unregenerate egos of Catherine and Heathcliff (even, in a different way, Hindley, so recognisably Catherine's kin) indicates our readiness to be seduced back into the pagan hinterland of the mind's past. Amidst the welter of name-calling, fits of affection, dreams and hungers, there is a quality of pure animal vivacity which exerts a powerful pull against the learnt code of adult life which must condemn such impetuosities as anti-social. The urge of the reader is less into sympathy than into identification: 'I *am* Heathcliff' has worked on generations of readers as a personal statement to be made with and through Catherine, though – as if drugged or entranced – one very imperfectly comprehends the meaning of the affirmation. Catherine's beautiful, vagrant speech-patterns are at the centre of the novel aesthetically. They express frank, uncensored outbursts of raw egotism, unmediated by the verbal disguise by means of which we are taught to blur communication of the heart's desires. This unabashed purity of egotism is not only present but intensified at the most holy and awesome moments of the novel, to the degree that it appears to inform the very essence of the novel's value-system. At their last meeting, Heathcliff kneels to embrace Catherine, and as he attempts to rise, she 'seized his hair, and kept him down':

> I wish I could hold you . . . till we were both dead! I shouldn't care what you suffered. I care nothing for your sufferings. Why shouldn't you suffer? I do! Will you forget me – will you be happy when I am in the earth? Will you say twenty years hence, 'That's the grave of Catherine Earnshaw. I loved her long ago, and was wretched to lose her; but it is past. I've loved many others since – my children are dearer to me than she was, and, at death, I shall not rejoice that I am going to her, I shall be sorry that I must leave them!' Will you say so, Heathcliff?
>
> (pp. 158–9)

The terms of Catherine's speech indicate a childlike terror of solitude ('being laid alone') conjured up by the hectic and nervous brilliance of her localising imagery: Heathcliff as a doting paterfamilias, ambling past her twenty-year-old grave and delivering himself of a choicely spiteful epitaph is a scenario as fiercely pathetic as it is bizarrely unlikely.

More profoundly, we are moved by Catherine's panic to deeper recognitions of what it is she has to fear. She is hungrily manipulating him, as the wailing claim at the end ('Will you say so, Heathcliff?') which craves his contradiction, makes clear. She resembles a child with a horror of being left alone at night; the foundation of her security is threatened. Her fear of being buried alone while her partner wanders freely about on the face of things involves, surely, Catherine's terror that *he will grow up*. 'My children are dearer to me than she was', she has him say, her fantasy inventing alien children for him other than herself (his putative wife being no problem for jealousy, since blood-kin are the authentic objects of attachment and desire in *Wuthering Heights*. Husbands and wives are addenda to be accumulated, nobodies, strangers, necessary for procreation but not germane and primal). Catherine's hell of fear comes of her new ability to envisage Heathcliff becoming a member of another generation, betraying her to an eternity of childhood atrophied because it is unaccompanied. Later, she swerves and contradicts herself, revealing the deepest sources of her behaviour as that needy love whose code is the total allegiance of passionate dependency:

> I'm not wishing you greater torment than I have, Heathcliff! I only wish us never to be parted – and should a word of mine distress you hereafter, think I feel the same distress underground, and for my own sake, forgive me! Come here and kneel down again! You never harmed me in your life. Nay, if you nurse anger, that will be worse to remember than my harsh words! Won't you come here again? Do!
>
> (p. 159)

The driving motive of Catherine's lifetime is recorded here: *never to be parted*. Union and unanimity of sister- with foster-brother, self with other, male with and in the female, are the ground of being. Catherine's expression of tenderness, exacerbated by her mortal illness, is dictatorial – a reaching through language for power. A cajoling note has crept in – 'Won't you. . . ? Do!' *Wuthering Heights* is a unique act of search for a language which will capsize the boundaries and thresholds between self and other: a magical language which will somehow empower the creative persona to conjure that dissolution of borders into being; to run time back into itself so that early security and potency may be retrieved. It seeks to recreate the primal condition which is *never to be parted*. In this enterprise, Catherine I is always the central questor for the soul's intimate language to revoke the calamitous laws that disengage one from source.

In this work of words, Heathcliff (functioning always as a secondary aspect of Catherine)[3] participates as her double, shadow spokesman or ministering self, reminding her endlessly of the pledge (of integrity with himself) which she has broken. Each time Catherine seeks a formulation which will heal the split – between them; in herself – she fails in her invention, as language does utterly fail to alter the structure of reality. 'That is not *my* Heathcliff', Cathy goes on. 'I shall . . . take him with me – he's in my soul' (p. 160). The strategy now is to internalise a version of the beloved, to take the 'true' (i.e. desired) version into the soul in the guise of a concept and to incorporate him there, leaving the 'false' (i.e. inconvenient) version to his own devices.[4] Now there are two Heathcliffs, an inner and an outer: the effort to unify leads inevitably and ironically in the novel to division and multiplication.[5] Catherine turns away with her preferred version of reality to 'muse' on escape into 'that glorious world' beyond the enclosure of the body; but the extent to which the language's attempt to reconstruct reality dissatisfies and betrays its evanescence and duplicity in the very moment of speech is attested by her restless return to the turned back of Heathcliff: 'I *wonder* he won't be near me! . . . I thought he wished it. Heathcliff, dear! you should not be sullen now. Do come to me, Heathcliff' (p. 160). Turning him into the third person, she mediates her address through Nelly, as sulking infants may be addressed in their pointed self-exile, bargaining for their return. The petulant 'I *wonder* . . .' flounces off into a direct challenge for his obedience to her love, parentally cajoling a child assumed to be corrigible: 'Heathcliff dear! you should . . .' and modulating into that choric refrain which calls between the two from one end of the novel to the other (almost: as Heathcliff fades to a ghostly relict, he ceases to command, moves out to join her): 'Do come to me, Heathcliff'. From Lockwood's dream-ghost of Cathy: 'I'm come home' (p. 23), to Heathcliff's 'Come in! come in! . . . Cathy, do come. Oh do – ' (p. 27), to Cathy's 'I do wish he'd come. I do wish he would' (p. 83) after his departure from the Heights, to Heathcliff's delusion of her 'coming in' (p. 290) after her death. The combined pathos and force of this echoing call derives from its being levied as a compulsion upon reality to yield the object of desire to the desirer who (in the very act of utterance) clearly perceives that reality will make no concession to the language of his or her need. As Catherine addresses Heathcliff, 'Do come to me', she herself rises to fling herself toward him, to fulfil on his behalf the appeal of her own words; but this very act of fulfilment is suicidal. One final stream of words completes the process whereby the language of naked childhood emotion becomes the soul's last resort in the struggle 'never to be parted':

> He would have risen, and unfixed her fingers by the act – she clung fast, gasping; there was mad resolution in her face.
> 'No!' she shrieked. 'Oh, don't, don't go. It is the last time! Edgar will not hurt us. Heathcliff, I shall die! I shall die!'
>
> (p. 162)

Catherine proclaims the end of the world, in a detaining volley of negatives: her last word in the novel is *die*, her final articulate terror is that of separation from Heathcliff. The detail describing the threat to 'unfix her fingers' while she 'clung fast' repeats on the narrative line the burden of the speeches – figuring the will to claw back time so as to pre-empt change.

The narrative voice intervenes to soothe Heathcliff's perception of Catherine's passage out of the world. Catherine died 'Quietly as a lamb. . . . as a child reviving', she tells him (p. 166); having recognised no one after Heathcliff, 'her latest ideas wandered back to pleasant early days' (p. 167). Nelly as plainly as words can conjure images, seeks to return Catherine to that halcyon interlude which the conscious adult has to die to regain. The child in Catherine is permitted to 'revive' only as the adult dies. Her own child, the new Catherine, is to negotiate with safety the transition from adolescence into adult life: hence the first Catherine is the mother who is displaced by a child and simultaneously the mythic child who must give way to a maturing version of herself. Heathcliff throughout remains static, a fixture to replicate Catherine I's bereavement of herself. The language of search passes to him: 'Where is she? Not *there* – not in heaven – not perished – where?':

> 'Be with me always – take any form – drive me mad! only *do* not leave me in this abyss, where I cannot find you! O God! it is unutterable! I *cannot* live without my life! I cannot live without my soul!'
> He dashed his head against the knotted trunk.
>
> (p. 167)

Catherine's release from the turbulent and achingly beautiful language of desire (through disclosure of the new Catherine, the baby who appears to us as a new version of her self, calculated for survival and evolution) casts the burden of that killing language exclusively upon Heathcliff, who receives his inheritance with rage and horror. Language as a commanding and demanding prayer, a speech which derangingly knows its own tight constraints ('it is unutterable') descends on Heathcliff like a curse. He localises himself 'in this *abyss*, where I cannot find you' (emphasis added). Signs, as Hillis Miller has said, in *Wuthering Heights* codify absence, vacancy, no thing.[6] Heathcliff's 'abyss' derives from the *prima materia* from which the Creator-Spirit of Genesis divulged form and meaning, through Milton's 'wild abyss,/The womb of nature and perhaps her grave' (*Paradise Lost*, II.910–11), the abortive 'vast vacuity' (l. 932). Hence he is left stranded in a no-man's-land at once prior to and subsequent to time and space. It is an uncreated world beyond any words, which his language seeks to transform into plenitude by conjuring Catherine to declare her whereabouts. What he resists is her evacuation from reality. He does not resist, rather welcomes, his own pain as a testament to the possibility of her immanence, invoking her to haunt him. The great double assertion which consummates his rage of loss: 'I *cannot* . . . I *cannot*' demonstrates the stern literality with which Emily Brontë had contemplated the resources of language: compelling it to stand or fall by the buried metaphors which informed it. The conventional equation of another person with one's own 'life' and 'soul' is accorded by the novel's literalists the status of congruence with human actuality. But in confronting its own self-consistency, this unifying language of mutual identity breaks upon the invincible contradiction offered to it by exterior reality: the loss of Catherine. Hence the passionate repeated negatives – *cannot*, *cannot* – and the resort of the speaker to an act of expression outside the circumference of words: 'He dashed his head . . . howled, not like a man'. The language of human culture is abject before the confounding 'abyss' of hollowness in the universe to which he is committed. Heathcliff has prayed directly into the abyss and will repeat his prayer 'till my tongue stiffens', that this vast vacuity should yield up a semblance of the desired beloved. The perception that the prayer is unanswerable by the voiceless world beyond the ego is the signal for his human voice to respond by adjusting its form to the formlessness of the Abyss: to collapse into howls for what cannot be found, as the child howls for its mother in the night, *infans*, languageless. Heathcliff nowhere more profoundly than in this passage of degenerating grief incarnates a central theme of the novel – the orphaning of God's child as a cast-off in the universe.

Heathcliff's displays of spectacular excess (bruising Catherine's skin with his grip, 'grinding his teeth' [p. 160], gnashing, foaming, dashing his head against the tree [p. 167]) may be read less as extensions of Gothic convention than as the frantically untempered and inchoate reflexes of childhood.[7] Throughout its first half the novel structures itself as an escalation of uncontrolled tantrum on the part of the central protagonists, Catherine, Heathcliff, Hindley and also Edgar and Isabella Linton (whose family opposition to the children of the Heights is in some sense a spurious one, a less volcanic but equally sincere selfishness).[8] Catherine's death-scene is only one such explosion; Isabella's narrative of the communal degeneration of Hindley–Heathcliff–Isabella at the Heights in volume 2, chapter 3, is another. The staple mode of address in the novel is that of quarrel, and its structure may be shown to depend upon the evolution of one quarrel out of another, with even the more harmonious or conclusive scenes predicated upon a core of dissent. If Catherine's and Heathcliff's parting (and reconciling) discussion takes the form of a brutal and ruthless struggle of wills, so within each chapter unit action and interest tend to be generated by bad temper, verbal or physical assault, or territorial dispute. Chapter 10 as a sample yields the following structure of argument. Lockwood and Nelly began by arguing over medicine (p. 90), Edgar chides Nelly over the treatment of Catherine (p. 91), Nelly disputes with Heathcliff over his admittance (pp. 92–3), Edgar argues with Catherine over the same thing (pp. 94–5) to which she forces a conclusion by crushing their fingers together (p. 95), Heathcliff addresses Catherine with anger over her marriage (p. 96), Catherine leaves Edgar's bed after a quarrel and abuses him (p. 97), she quarrels with Isabella (pp. 101–3), a dispute which is carried on in front of Heathcliff, Isabella scratching Catherine's cheek (p. 105), and finally Heathcliff abuses Isabella (p. 106). This principle of plot construction as a tightly linked sequence of quarrels typifies in detail the novel's disintegrative tendency as a whole. Within this maelstrom, the peaceful moments seem all the more vulnerable and luminous (within this very chapter, the quiet figures of Catherine and Edgar watching the 'long line of mist winding nearly to [the] top of the valley of Gimmerton' [p. 93]; the scene in which Edgar puts on Catherine's pillow 'a handful of golden crocuses' [p. 134]). Such peaceful and

meditative times are almost always associated with strongly evoc-
ative sense of place – place as realising the image of a person long-
ago, whether exterior or interior, as for instance when Nelly broods
on the neatness of her kitchen – 'I smelt the rich scent of the heating
spices; and admired the shining kitchen utensils, the polished clock,
decked in holly, the silver mugs ranged on a tray . . .' (p. 53), and
moves to recall old Mr Earnshaw coming in and calling her 'a cant
lass', and from that 'to think of his fondness for Heathcliff, and his
dread lest he should suffer neglect' (p. 54).

But we note that these halcyon moments of meditation tend to
speak with the narrative voice and to stand abstracted from the
action itself. The velocity of the novel is provided by the state of
communal and violent tantrum which is indulged not only by the
characters against one another but also reverberates outward against
the walls of the universe, threatening the gods. Invective against the
state of things in this nether world takes the form of a feud with the
Maker, exemplified by Hindley's riposte to Nelly's injunction to
'Have mercy on your own soul!': 'Not I! on the contrary, I shall have
great pleasure in sending it to perdition, to punish its maker', drink-
ing meanwhile to his own damnation and uttering 'horrid impreca-
tions' (p. 75). Clearly, the origins of this profane verbal behaviour lie
in the dissatisfactions common to childhood with the provisions and
principles laid down by the elders. Hindley's brag has its roots in the
juvenile desire evinced in some such formulation as 'I'll make my
parents sorry they ever had me'. *Wuthering Heights* systematically
translates this vernacular into the language of religious experience,
attaching the interior situation of siblings struggling in a domestic
world to a higher register of diction which raises them to the ele-
mental status of souls exclaiming against their God. Translation
from one discourse into another also, inevitably, involves subtle
shifts within the meanings of the original material. Attitudes and
moods which within the family context may (from the outside)
appear immature take on through literary transference an heroic and
magnetic fascination and capability of universal human application,
since of course at the very centre of Christian mythology is a cosmic
story of disobedient children in mutiny against the divine Parent:
Lucifer and Eve. It is here that the authorial mythologising of the
ferocious raw material of childhood utterance derives from the latter
a genuinely religious vision which carries for the reader the 'higher'
meanings and implications of *Wuthering Heights*. From this perspective, the novel becomes a sardonic, wilful and travestying – but

perfectly logical and coherent – variation on the Calvinism with which Emily and her siblings were force-fed in childhood;[9] a vision of a reprobated universe in which God's brood, doomed from the start, chooses demonically with Him against its own election and salvation. The first Catherine is the major voice for this heresy: 'heaven did not seem to be my home' (p. 80), 'they may bury me twelve feet deep, and throw the church down over me' (p. 126), with Heathcliff playing Beelzebub to her Lucifer. It is focused within speeches and carried by the narrative line during certain phases of the action in a joint proclamation of what amounts to extreme Protestant defiance. The novel nails its *Theses* to the church door with relish and acrimony.

At the same time, it locates an alternative area of the divine to that of the Father–God. Deep in its own experience of lack, absence and loss, the psyche in *Wuthering Heights* perceives a spiritual home identifiable with the mother. A void in the communal life of the characters (the first generation of mothers, Catherine and Frances, die in or just after childbirth) is wistfully transferred, and thence to some degree filled, to a new location in the created and suffering universe itself. Beneath the action of the novel, readers are impressed by their intuition of the attending and waiting presence of the moor, despite the seldom-noted fact that it is barely described in physical terms during the crucial first half of the novel. It receives, endorses and forgives; or rather, endorses the fact that there is nothing to forgive. It is the realm of silence and retreat, a playground for children; the mythic ground of action. Beyond the human focus of desire (Catherine's love for Heathcliff) is implied the larger object of desire (Catherine's love for the heath). On the psychological level, the children's refusal of control in *Wuthering Heights* is also a mute demand for the embrace that gathers the child in to himself, providing the limit to his ire and destructiveness. The voices exhibit the combined relish and terror of the uncontrolled idiom that distorts the face of childhood into that of a monster, magnifying its angers into a demonic threat to existence itself. The means of such embrace (the mother) is almost wholly absent from the text, though its children rage and wail loudly enough to wake the dead. Nelly, rocking on her knee the motherless Hareton, hums a snatch of a ballad from Scott: 'It was far in the night, and the bairnies grat,/The mither beneath the mools heard that' (p. 76). In the song, as I have shown elsewhere,[10] the natural mother awakens in her grave at the keening of her orphaned children tortured by their stepmother. Her corpse trespasses across the barrier of mortality, impelled by the fiat of their grief, to remedy their situation. The motherless author of *Wuthering Heights* releases the voices of her characters as a universal cry of need. The novel records both the potency of that need and its absolute failure to register or to obtain the satisfaction of a reply. Yet each time we reread, this fearful hope is freshly aroused, and the novel with profound artfulness never denies that either the dead may walk with us or we sleep with them, in the fullest reunion.

The familial world is controlled at best by a foster-mother (Nelly) together with a kind father (the elder Mr Earnshaw, Edgar Linton), at worst by 'Devil Daddy' (Hindley, Heathcliff). Nelly's prose style, with its curious nullity and blankness of emotional response, neutralises and frustrates the hysterical compulsions recorded in direct speech. Hence the novel's language of desire is constantly being absorbed into a thick, muffling wall of incomprehension:

> She paused, and hid her face in the folds of my gown; but I jerked it forcibly away. I was out of patience with her folly!
>
> (p. 82)

> She rung the bell till it broke with a twang: I entered leisurely. It was enough to try the temper of a saint, such senseless, wicked rages!
>
> (p. 118)

> He began to pace the room, muttering terrible things to himself; till I was inclined to believe, as he said Joseph did, that conscience had turned his heart to an earthly hell – I wondered greatly how it would end.
>
> (p. 325)

As narrator, Nelly's cool management of domestic affairs on the page is ambivalent, distanced and unwittingly implicated. Narrative and direct speech are frequently at odds. The aim of the censorious, censoring narrative is to mute and suppress the raw emotions indulged by the direct speech; to obscure its meaning as consciousness seals the unconscious into inscrutability. In the second half of the novel, the language of desire is displaced by a general rise in the 'dream-material' toward consciousness and synthesis with the narrative voice: a transformation of prehistory into history, or dream-matter into conscious thought, as if a sleeper gradually awakened. The exception to this rule is Heathcliff, in whose accounts of his state of mind to Nelly the original language of desire endures but tends to shift into a brilliant and scintillating language of marvellous dissatisfaction such as characterises much of Emily Brontë's lyric poetry. Heathcliff's 'My soul's bliss kills my body, but does not satisfy itself' (p. 333), for instance, recalls the visionary prisoner of 'Julian M. and A. G. Rochelle': 'visions rise and change which kill me with desire' (l. 72). Death as a release from this galled and excoriated nervous condition is apprehended by the novel as rest and succour in a mother-world which resolves the conflicts of the upper world in a completion born not of settling scores by bargain or forgiveness, nor of reaching adjustment with things as they are (that is, by growing up), but by entering into the being of the beloved, in shared sleep. Heathcliff's 'transformation' (p. 289) into the substance of Catherine underground, to which he looks forward with famishing eagerness, is the falling asleep of a lifelong insomniac, entering into the balm of the subliminal world, which gives entire permission to his every desire by abolishing in its entirety the wordy, needy self. Language and desire cease simultaneously; the heath, clambering over the low church wall on to the threefold graves of Catherine, Edgar Linton and Heathcliff, is finally observed to be occupied in the process of erasing the writing which signs their presence to the upper world: the names on the headstones. Burying their individualities in itself, the moor takes its children home.

From Stevie Davies, *Emily Brontë* (Hemel Hempstead, 1988), pp. 42–57 *passim*, 58–66, 165–7 *passim*.

NOTES

[This essay is taken from the first chapter of the second of Stevie Davies's two books on Emily Brontë. Although both have a feminist perspective, they contest the view (best represented by *The Madwoman in the Attic*) of Brontë as suffering from the cultural marginalisation of nineteenth-century women, stressing instead the freedom and power of Emily Brontë's work.

As a practising novelist, Davies sees herself as 'kicking off from' rather than engaging with the academic debate. Her first book, *Emily Brontë: The Artist as a Free Woman* (Carcanet, 1983), substitutes a psychological model based on modern studies of left-hand/right-hand brain orientations for the more usual Freudian model in order to free her analysis from what she regards as a patriarchal belief in psychosexual determinism.

Where this earlier book focuses on the 'tenderness' of *Wuthering Heights*, *Emily Brontë* (Hemel Hempstead, 1988) focuses on its power. Where Gilbert sees Brontë as banished to the wilderness by 'Milton's bogey', Davies sees her engaging in a 'joyous literary feud' which substitutes for 'Father God, Mother Earth' (the title of the last chapter).

Stevie Davies's chapter appears here, with her permission, in a shortened form. References are to *Wuthering Heights*, ed. Ian Jack (Oxford, 1985). Ed.]

1. See Leo Bersani, *A Future for Astyanax: Character and Desire in Literature* (Boston, 1976), p. 203, for an acute analysis of the familial complex explored by *Wuthering Heights*.

2. For the childish basis of personality and behaviour in *Wuthering Heights*, see Jane Miller, *Women Writing about Men* (London, 1986), p. 82; Irving H. Buchen, 'Emily Brontë and the Metaphysic of Childhood and Love', *Nineteenth-Century Fiction*, 22 (June 1967), 63–70.

3. See C. F. Keppler, *The Literature of the Second Self* (Tucson, Arizona, 1972), p. 135, for Heathcliff as a type of the secondary self.

4. See Adrienne Rich, *On Lies, Secrets, and Silence: Selected Prose, 1966– 78* (New York, 1979), p. 90: 'The bond between Catherine and Heathcliff is the archetypal bond between the split fragments of the psyche, the masculine and feminine elements ripped apart and longing for reunion.'

5. J. Hillis Miller, *Fiction and Repetition* (Oxford, 1982), p. 62, gives a helpful account of this frantic procedure of duplication.

6. Ibid., p. 67.

7. See D. P. Varma, *The Gothic Flame* (London, 1957).

8. See Leo Bersani, *A Future for Astyanax: Character and Desire in Literature* (Boston, 1976), p. 201.

9. On the Brontës' Calvinist inheritance, see Valentine Cunningham, *Everywhere Spoken Against: Dissent in the Victorian Novel* (Oxford, 1975). Cunningham makes the important point that it is not the Methodism in the Brontës' background (Tabby was a Methodist, and Patrick Brontë had strong Wesleyan sympathies and connection) which accounts for the Calvinist influence, but the Cornish Calvinistic Methodism imported by Aunt Branwell in combination with the hellfire theology indigenous in the region.

    [Students should be aware, however, that other scholars do not accept the evidence for Aunt Branwell's 'Calvinism' (which rests on the reconstruction of a single deleted word in one of Charlotte's letters) and that the colony of Methodists still surviving in Cornwall are *Arminian* (non-Calvinist) Methodists. See Grace Elsie Harrison, *The Clue to the Brontës* (London, 1948), p. 12; Tom Winnifrith, *The Brontës and Their Background* (London, 1973), ch. 3; Arthur Pollard, 'The Brontës and their Father's Faith', *Essays and Studies*, new series 37 (1984), 48; Valerie Grosvenor Myer, *Charlotte Brontë: Truculent Spirit* (London and

Totowa, NJ, 1987), p. 59; Edward Chitham, *A Life of Emily Brontë* (Oxford, 1987), p. 26; Tom Winnifrith and Edward Chitham, *Charlotte and Emily Brontë* (Basingstoke and London, 1989), p. 30. Ed.]

10. In Stevie Davies, *Emily Brontë: The Artist as a Free Woman* (Manchester, 1983), pp. 156–7. See also Stevie Davies, *Emily Brontë* (Hemel Hempstead, 1988), pp. 36–41.

10

The (Self-)Identity of the Literary Text: Property, Proper Place, and Proper Name in 'Wuthering Heights'

PATRICIA PARKER

I

> The end of linear writing is indeed the end of the book.
> (Jacques Derrida, *Of Grammatology*)

In 1957, Ian Watt began *The Rise of the Novel* by tracing the parallels between the growing popularity of the novel form and a number of contemporary Enlightenment phenomena – the realist epistemology of Bacon, Descartes, Hobbes, and Locke; the growth of Protestantism with its fondness for personal inventory and for measuring time and progress in the sequential form of the journal or diary; economic individualism, with its division of labour and private property; and the 'principle of individuation' enunciated by Locke:

> The 'principle of individuation' accepted by Locke was that of existence at a particular locus in space and time: since, as he wrote, 'ideas become general by separating them from the circumstances of time and place', so they become particular only when both these circumstances are specified. In the same way the characters of the novel can

only be individualised if they are set in a background of particularised time and place.[1]

This principle is connected in Locke – who also wrote a defence of private property – with the differentiating function of proper names, the very indicators of individual identity, since, as Hobbes maintained, a 'Proper Name' is 'singular to one only thing'.[2] Locke, whose work everywhere pervades the eighteenth century, established a principle in which individuality is linked to definitive placing – a place marked by the proper or 'appropriated' name which designates an individual identity and prevents its being confused with another (*Essay*, III.3.4). In literature, argues Watt, 'this function of proper names was first fully established in the novel', with its attention to names as designating 'completely individualised entities' so as to 'suggest that they were to be regarded as particular individuals in the contemporary social environment'. Names point a finger, or single out, as Foucault observes in his discussion of the primacy of naming or denomination in the Enlightenment; they say, as the preacher does to Lockwood in his first dream at Wuthering Heights, '*Thou art the man!*'[3]

More recently than Watt, Patricia Drechsel Tobin, in *Time and the Novel*, has extended this exploration of the relation between the novel and the phenomenon of linearity in all its Enlightenment forms – the line of time, of language, of narrative, and of thought, the model which informs the linear structure of Puritan diary and capitalist ledger-book, of genealogy and chronological history. Derrida, in his discussion of the line and the book in *De la grammatologie*, describes this linearity as 'the repression of pluri-dimensional symbolic thought' and makes a connection between linear writing, logic, scientific and philosophical analysis, and history understood as a line or irreversible progress. Foucault characterises it as a shift from a Renaissance fondness for resemblance to a preference for classification and sequential or causal reasoning, from metaphor's paradigmatic verticality to metonymy – the syntagmatic and sequential. Discourse, he observes, is understood in the classical *episteme* as 'a sequence of verbal signs', a spacing out of the simultaneous into the successive, into a 'linear order' whose parts 'must be traversed *one after* the other'. It is the linear model which produces what Foucault calls the 'reciprocal kinship' between the 'chain of discourse' (Hobbes), epistemology as 'the chain of knowledge', the conception of time as chronology or irreversible sequence, and the Enlightenment preoccupation with progress. And it is this linear logic, combined with the conception of time as chronological sequence, which informs the novel as well, linked so closely with chronology as to be arguably 'chronomorph', even when it appears to be transgressing that order.[4]

Wuthering Heights is crucially situated within this history, not only because of its own preoccupation with proper name and proper place, but because in so many ways it recapitulates both the linear Enlightenment grid and its exclusions, the 'rise of the novel' and its potential unmaking. It may therefore be approached as one of those nineteenth-century texts which call into question – long before contemporary interest in this problem, which may be itself an after-effect of the disruption of the classical *episteme* – precisely the identity, or self-identity, of the text, by the simultaneous demonstration and undoing of the epistemological claims and ordering structures of the novel form.[5] In *Wuthering Heights* this undoing involves both nature, which is placed outside the orderly 'house of fiction' in the binary opposition of nature and culture on which Lockwood's narrative partly depends, and the *unheimlich*, or uncanny, mobility of tropes such as metaphor traditionally described as 'alien', part of the excluded which threatens the identity of that which seeks to control or master it.

II

> We're dismal enough without conjuring up ghosts and visions to perplex us.
>
> (Nelly Dean, *Wuthering Heights*)

> the authoritarian demands put pressure on a narrative voice to turn into a narratorial voice and to bring about [*donner lieu à*] a narrative that would be identifiable.
>
> (Derrida, 'LIVING ON: Border Lines')

Wuthering Heights would seem to present us with a quintessential Enlightenment narrative in its preoccupation with the claims of superstition and reason, primitive and civilised, and in the ambivalent middle position occupied by its secondary narrator, Nelly Dean, between belief in the supernatural and her own housekeeper's sense of order and proper place. The novel opens with a date (1801) inaugurating the text of a narrator who identifies himself in the opening line ('I have just returned from a visit to my landlord – the solitary neighbour that I shall be troubled with'), very soon after records his own proper name ('Mr Lockwood, your new tenant, sir'), and then provides a second date (1802) at the beginning of chapter XXXII. The generic identity of the text would appear to be that of the diary or journal – that sequential ordering of time and narrative that allies the novel with the linearity of chronology, genealogy, or history. Lockwood himself seems to belong on the side of enlightenment, as the master narrator whose distance from the superstitious and supernatural phenomena he encounters gives the novel, in the view of some of its readers, a reassuring sense both of progress and of closure. The question of the identity of the literary text, then, when raised with regard to *Wuthering Heights*, involves at least two related issues: its generic identity, the novel form, with its dependence on chronology, spacing, the principle of individuation, and the designating function of proper names; and the identity, or self-identity, of a text which appears from the beginning to be the unified production of a single hand – authorised by the conferring of his narrative signature or proper name.

In approaching the question of the identity or self-identity of *Wuthering Heights*, we might have recourse to a distinction from Maurice Blanchot, taken up again in a recent essay by Derrida which has precisely to do with the question of identity, and with the relationship between identity and placing. Blanchot distinguishes the 'narrative voice' from the 'narratorial voice', which in *Wuthering Heights* would be that of Lockwood himself, 'the voice of a subject recounting something, remembering an event or a historical sequence, knowing who he is, where he is, and what he is talking about'. The 'narrative voice', by contrast, is, in Blanchot's phrase, 'a neutral voice that utters the work from the placeless place where the work is silent'. The narratorial voice can be located and identified – it has, says Derrida, and confers on the work, 'une carte d'identité'. But the narrative voice has no fixed place: it is both atopical and hypertopical, nowhere and everywhere at once. In Blanchot's terms, the neutral narrative voice is 'ghostlike', a spectre which haunts the narratorial text and, itself without centre, placing, or closure, disrupts and dislocates the work, not permitting it to exist as finally completed or closed.[6]

This ghostlike atopicality and hypertopicality of something which resists definitive placing or closure may remind us in *Wuthering Heights* of its own principal ghost, that 'Catherine' who haunts Heathcliff after her death, overrunning all boundaries by being at

once everywhere ('I am surrounded with her image! . . . The entire
world is a dreadful collection of memoranda that she did exist, and
that I have lost her!') and in no single, definable place ('Where is she?
Not *there* – not in heaven – not perished – where?'). The novel is full
of ghosts, demons, and uncanny presences, from the 'Catherine'
Heathcliff begs to 'haunt' him (ch. XVI, 204) to the 'ghostly Catherine'
Linton (ch. IV, 75) of Lockwood's second dream in the room at the
Heights he describes as 'swarming with ghosts and goblins' (ch. III,
68); from Catherine's evocation of Gimmerton Kirk ('We've braved
its ghosts often together, and dared each other to stand among the
graves and ask them to come'; ch. XII, 164) to Heathcliff's affirmation of his belief in ghosts (ch. XXIX, 320), and his warning of the
consequences of not burying him next to the open side of Catherine's
coffin ('if you neglect it, you shall prove, practically, that the dead
are not annihilated!'; ch. XXXIV, 363). This repeated reference to
ghosts in the novel is also countered, however, by their denial, from
Isabella Linton's 'It's well people don't *really* rise from their grave'
(ch. XVII, 216) to Lockwood's concluding assurance against the
superstition that the dead Catherine and Heathcliff 'walk', when he
visits their graves in the closing lines of the text ('I lingered round
them, under the benign sky; watched the moths fluttering among the
heath and harebells; listened to the soft wind breathing through the
grass; and wondered how anyone could ever imagine unquiet slumbers, for the sleepers in that quiet earth'). The exercise of closure
itself, by the master narrator who confers on the text his own
unifying identity and proper name, is linked with the laying, or
denial, of ghosts, a forestalling of an uncanny return or 'advent', a
term the narrative several times repeats.

Wuthering Heights, then, offers the reader both the possibility of
ghosts and the denial of them. But there is also in the novel a textual
ghost, in Blanchot's terms, which inhabits and dislocates the identity
conferred by Lockwood's narratorial order and its Enlightenment
preoccupation with linearity, propriety, and proper place. All we
have is Lockwood's text, but inscribed within it as its own uncanny
other is an 'alien' text inhabiting it and disrupting its ordering
structures – Lockwood's diary, Nelly Dean's genealogical history,
and the very sequential process of reading which the novel form
invites. Derrida speaks, in his discussion of the 'linear norm' and the
'form of the book', of the undoing of the linear which takes place in
the margins and 'between the lines'.[7] *Wuthering Heights*, with its

own emphasis on marginal, competing, and heterogeneous texts – Catherine's manuscript writing, for example, inserted into the 'margins' or 'blanks' of 'good books' (ch. III) – itself provokes a double reading in which the text begins to lose the sense of coherent order or unified identity its organisation under a single identifiable narratorial voice would confer upon the book. Not insignificantly, it is to books that Edgar Linton repairs in the midst of his wife's delirious ravings (ch. XII), and books that Lockwood piles up in a 'pyramid' to keep out a ghostly alien or 'changeling' who seeks to re-enter the house (ch. III). Reading itself – in the proper left-to-right order in which Hareton Earnshaw learns to decipher the inscription which will restore him to his property and rightful place – is part of the process, in this novel, of civilisation and enlightenment. But, in Derrida's terms, the 'text' – like Heathcliff, both 'orphan' and 'alien' – works against the order and identity of the 'book', and that which is in the margins or between the lines becomes part of the text's own 'subversive dislocation of identity in general'.[8]

Readers of *Wuthering Heights* have frequently commented on its apparent binary oppositions – nature and culture, good and evil, heaven and hell, primitive and civilised – and less frequently on the way in which it undermines this division in the very process of calling attention to it, as Shelley does in *The Witch of Atlas*, with its opening reference to the Enlightenment division into 'those cruel Twins', Error and Truth. Both logic and the logic of identity are founded, for Derrida, on the opposition of inside and outside which inaugurates all binary opposition – where each of the terms is 'simply external to the other'. The expulsion of one involves a domination or mastery, like naming itself, which Nietzsche (speaking precisely of the opposition of 'good' and 'evil') links with a taking of possession or appropriation. But, once expelled, the 'outside' functions as a ghost: the identical is haunted, as Foucault says of the Enlightenment table or grid, by what it excludes. The principal story in *Wuthering Heights* involves the usurpation of a house, or property, by a 'houseless' (ch. IV, 78) outsider or alien. Heathcliff, in a language the novel itself employs, is the 'guest' who becomes the 'master' of the house. What I will suggest is that Lockwood's own Enlightenment narrative – with the sense of unified identity it confers upon the book – is inhabited by a textual guest which threatens to become host, two terms used together in chapter III (p. 68) at precisely the point where it is a question of Lockwood's having penetrated to the centre of the house and encountered a 'ghost'.[9] To look for the identity of the literary text may in this, as in other nineteenth-century narratives, be finally to discover a Ghost Story.

III

> Thrushcross Grange is my own, sir.
>
> (Heathcliff)

For Derrida, the self-identity of the text is intimately linked to *propriété* in its widest sense. What must be emphasised, however, is that the complex of terms related to the 'proper', a complex to which recent criticism has again called our attention, also engaged the Enlightenment, precisely in connection with the problem of identity. By considering the relation of property, proper place, and proper name in Lockwood's text to the question of its unified identity, we return to the context with which we began – the Lockean principle of individuation, its relation to discrete chronological sequence or line and to the boundary-marking of individual identity through what Locke termed the 'appropriation' of the proper name. In the process, I shall suggest that the two sides of the debate over *Wuthering Heights* – between formalist critics who emphasise its narrative structures and Marxist or sociological critics who emphasise its involvement with the laws of private property – converge in this novel precisely on the question of 'property' in its most radical or fundamental sense.[10]

Property and proper name are connected, first, in the figure of Lockwood himself: it is he who owns or masters his own text – as Hobbes says of the connection between Author and Owner (*Leviathan*, I.xvi) – and lends his name as the single unifying presence of a narrative which repeatedly calls attention to the importance of proper place, property, propriety, and proper name. The emphasis on place or position in Lockwood's text is everywhere: in the plot founded on the relation between the two houses, Wuthering Heights and Thrushcross Grange; in the sense of speech as placing characters by region or social class; and in Joseph's pharisaical insistence on the Sabbath as an inviolable place in time. This is joined by a more specific focus on ownership, possession, and property, from Heathcliff's opening 'Thrushcross Grange is my own, sir' (ch. I, 45), his reference to his own son as 'property' (ch. XX, 242), Lockwood's uncertainty about who is the 'favoured possessor' of the female figure he encounters at the Heights (ch. II, 55), and Earnshaw's finding the orphan Heathcliff without an 'owner' (ch. IV), to the principal exchange of the plot, in which Heathcliff acquires the very property from which he had been excluded. Private property and its dividing lines are reduced to an extreme in the scene in which the 'divided' Linton children (ch. VI, 89) almost rend a pet dog 'in two' in their struggle for possession – a sacrifice of whole for part which recalls the judgement of Solomon and its revelation of the logic, and limits, of property. The careful guarding of the Linton property at Thrushcross Grange against all trespass is epitomised in the elder Linton's charge to the little 'outlaws' Catherine and Heathcliff – 'To beard a magistrate in his stronghold, and on the Sabbath, too!' (ch. VI, 90). The biblical resonance of the charge recalls both Christ's trespass of the Sabbath and his breaking down of all barriers or partition walls (2 Corinthians 10:4: 'For the weapons of our warfare are not carnal, but mighty through God to the pulling down of strong holds').

'Property' in the sense of the establishment of boundaries – and the prohibition of trespass fundamental to a society based on the laws of private possession – appears as well in the frequency in the novel of images such as windows, thresholds, and gates which mark the boundaries between places, or between inside and outside. From the opening chapter, the novel's establishment of boundaries or dividing walls is intimately linked with the language of its narrator, whose syntax raises barriers even as he pushes through the gate which keeps him from the Heights ('I do myself the honour of calling as soon as possible, after my arrival, to express the hope that I have not inconvenienced you by my perseverance in soliciting the occupation of Thrushcross Grange'), and whose convoluted speech contrasts pointedly with the abruptness of Heathcliff's replies and the Height's own unmediated entrance ('One step brought us into the family sitting-room, *without any introductory lobby, or passage*'). Lockwood, indeed, presents himself in a series of episodes involving the interposition of barriers: his rebuffing of the young girl whose attentions he had initially encouraged, his interposing of a 'table' between himself and the dog whose fury he himself provoked (ch. I), his piling up of books to keep out a ghostly 'Catherine Linton' (ch. III) and rubbing her wrist against the broken glass of a partition which no longer divides. These apotropaic gestures provide our first introduction to the narrator who will both request and relate the housekeeper's story from the framed and mediated distance of

Thrushcross Grange. In the midst of the chaos he himself has caused by baiting the dogs, Lockwood assimilates them to the biblical 'herd of possessed swine', and his hastening to interpose a table between himself and the fury he has raised proleptically enacts the function of the narrative which ensues, the casting out or distancing of demons too menacing to the enlightened mind, in a novel whose mediating perspectives and multiple narrations themselves both conjure and frame.

Lockwood's text, however, is remarkable for its emphasis not only on proper place, property, and boundary lines but also on trespass, transgression, or crossing, or on boundary lines which themselves become thresholds. Heathcliff, the figure through whom Earnshaw will pass into Linton and back again, is pictured frequently at doorways or other places of crossing. And the novel is filled with crossings or exchanges of place which are frequently also reversals of position. Edgar and Isabella Linton's arrival at the Heights reverses the direction of Catherine and Heathcliff's trespass. Catherine and Isabella exchange places through marriage, the former moving from Heights to Grange when she marries Edgar and the latter, in her elopement with Heathcliff, moving in the opposite direction. The subsequent longing of each to return would map another crossing: Catherine in her delirium in chapter XII imagines a return to the Heights; Isabella in the very next chapter writes 'My heart returned to Thrushcross Grange in twenty-four hours after I left it' (ch. XIII, 173). Heathcliff and Hindley change places as oppressor and oppressed; and the transformation of oppressed child into oppressive father which Kettle and others see as the central reversal of the novel is part of the general sense within it of things turning into their opposites or taking on the spirit of the place they exchange for another. Nelly remarks on the way in which Isabella and Heathcliff seem, after their marriage, to change positions ('So much had circumstances altered their positions, that he would certainly have struck a stranger as a born and bred gentleman, and his wife as a thorough little slattern!'; ch. XIV, 184). 'Crossing' is insisted on even at the purely verbal level – Nelly Dean's unsettling vision (ch. XI) and Hindley's threatened burial (ch. XVII, 221) at 'crossroads'; characters repeatedly responding 'crossly', not bearing 'crossing', or described as 'cross' (ch. IX, 128; ch. X, 134, 137); Nelly's warning Heathcliff, regarding Catherine, to 'shun crossing her way again' (ch. XIV, 184); and even the name of Thrushcross Grange. The trope which is figured as a cross (*chi*, χ) is the figure of crossing known as chiasmus, the trope which Scaliger described as creating 'a scissor formation in the sentence',[11] and this kind of scissor formation frequently provides the closest diagrammatic form for the exchange or reversals of place in the plot itself.

We could go on listing the novel's various forms of crossing or transgression, from the undercurrent of incest which would undermine the sequential authority of the genealogical line, to the crossing of boundaries between animal and human, nature and culture, responsible for the heightened intensity of the novel's language.[12] When Catherine's brow is described as suddenly 'clouded', a dead metaphor comes once again to life, loosed from the tomb of the banal or familiarly 'proper', and she becomes for a moment a novelistic Lucy, wrapped up in rocks and stones and trees. Language which should be dead – if we think of the Enlightenment strictures against the improper crossings of tropes – becomes in this novel alive and even violent; and the air swarming with 'Catherines' as Lockwood reads in chapter III may have its counterpart for the reader in the unsettling mobility of words which refuse to stay fixed in their single, or proper, meaning. 'Bridle' in the scene in which Nelly sees Isabella's dog suspended where 'a bridle hook is driven into the wall' (ch. XII, 166) contaminates 'bridal', as it stands as a menacing sign of Heathcliff and Isabella's elopement. Joseph's apparently peripheral and unreadable dialect is central to this kind of crossing, his 'goood-for-nowt madling' (ch. XIII, 180) combining both 'maid' and 'mad', just as his earlier 'marred' (p. 180) crosses 'married' and 'marred'. Readers of the novel soon learn to translate these dialect forms into standard English, as part of the accommodation of 'primitive' speech to the civilised mind. But for a moment the words resist this standardisation, and their very ambiguity, blurring the line between dialect and the lexicon of civilised speech, contributes to the novel's sense of menace, of something undermining the boundaries of the age both of Enlightenment and of the Dictionary.

IV

Die Namen individualisieren nur zum Schein.
(Stempel)

The narrative of *Wuthering Heights*, then, combines proper place and property on the one hand and transgression or crossing on the other, in a way which suggests that it is the very erection of boundary lines which creates the possibility of trespass. It also calls attention to the activity of proper names – those names which in Hobbes and Locke distinguish individual identities and in Watt's description are inseparable from the principle of individuation integral to the novel form itself. And it does so in a way which would enable us to suggest how this crossing of boundaries undermines the identity of the text, the very partitions which Lockwood needs in order to produce a satisfying Enlightenment narrative or 'good book'. An interest in names and their relation to identities already marks the dizzying series of aliases or multiple designations in the Gondal saga, whose profusion of names or initials capable of reference to several different characters suggests the accommodation involved for Brontë in moving to the more Lockean assumptions of the novel form – each name in its place and a proper place for every name. *Wuthering Heights* seems to be alerting the reader to the function but also to the potential autonomy of proper names by its insistence on their detachability, their application to more than one person, or the several names by which a single character may be called. If the function of proper names is to be the boundary markers of individual identity and thus to contribute to the coherence and readability of the narrative,[13] these very instruments of order and identity are in this text unreliable instruments. The confusion which makes Lockwood feel 'unmistakably out of place' (ch. II, 56) in the opening chapters results partly from the ambiguity of proper names as indicators of place or property – of who belongs to whom – or of position in the genealogical grid, since 'Mrs Heathcliff' cold be both Heathcliff's wife and his daughter-in-law (ch. II), the 'Catherine Linton' of Lockwood's second dream (ch. III), either mother or daughter. Names in these opening chapters – including the 'Hareton Earnshaw' whose appearance as inscription on the Heights prompts Lockwood to desire 'a short history of the place' (ch. I, 46) – are detached from clear or unambiguous reference and call out for histories, or explications.

Lockwood's confusion over names, identities, and proper placement reaches a climax in chapter III, which has itself strikingly to do with proper names and proper place, with both the establishment of boundary lines and their transgression. He finds on the window ledge of his room at the Heights writing which is 'nothing but a name repeated in all kinds of characters, large and small – *Catherine Earnshaw*; here and there varied to *Catherine Heathcliff*, and then again to *Catherine Linton*':

> In vapid listlessness I leant my head against the window, and contin-
> ued spelling over Catherine Earnshaw – Heathcliff – Linton, till my
> eyes closed; but they had not rested five minutes when a glare of white
> letters started from the dark, as vivid as spectres – the air swarmed
> with Catherines.
>
> (ch. III, 6)

When he rouses himself 'to dispel the obstrusive name' (p. 62), he
finds yet another name ('Catherine Earnshaw, her book') introducing the marginal script – itself not in its proper place – which tells of
the Sunday when Catherine and Heathcliff, compelled to 'square'
their 'positions' for the appropriate Sabbath reading, throw the
compulsory 'good books' (p. 63) into the dog-kennel, are threatened
by Joseph with being 'laced . . . properly' for it, and then 'appropriate
the dairy woman's cloak' for that crossing to the Grange which
leaves a gap in the writing, taken up again only after the pair's crucial
partition and Hindley's swearing to reduce Heathcliff to his 'right
place' (p. 64). This pivotal chapter is virtually obsessed with names:
the proliferating and disturbingly mobile 'Catherines'; the ghostly
'Catherine Linton', called by Lockwood an '*appellation* . . . *which
personified itself* when I had no longer my imagination under control' (p. 69, my emphasis); the name 'Jabes', like 'Zillah', taken from
a biblical genealogy (1 Chronicles 4:9) or list of 'Scripture names'
like the one Catherine and Heathcliff are threatened with having to
learn 'if they don't answer properly' (ch. VI, 88); the cudgel 'denom-
inated' a pilgrim's staff. But it is also preoccupied with the problems
of proper place and with the erection, and crossing, of dividing lines
or partitions: the blurring of the boundaries between real world and
dream ('I began to dream, almost before I ceased to be sensible of my
locality'); the pilgrim's staff as a sign of displacement, of not being in
a proper place; the ironic echo of Christ's 'breaking down the wall of
partition', making the 'two' into 'one' (Ephesians 2:14) in the clergy-
man's 'house with two rooms, threatening speedily to determine into
one'; the multiplication of the sequential 'partitions of discourse' in
the '*four hundred and ninety* parts' of Branderham's sermon, each
devoted to different 'odd transgressions'; and the linear partition of
time, since the partitions of the Puritan sermon traditionally corres-
pond to the ages of history between Creation and Apocalypse (an
association which may explain why, in the dream, reaching the final
'head' or partition brings on eschatological echoes).

The sermon itself, on the 'Seventy Times Seven, and the first of the
Seventy-first', is a virtual *reductio ad absurdum* of sequential parti-

tion, in which something beyond accounting – the forgiveness of trespasses not 'seven times, but until seventy times seven' (Matthew 18:22) – is reduced to sheer enumeration:

> Oh, how weary I grew! How I writhed, and yawned, and nodded, and revived! How I pinched and pricked myself, and rubbed my eyes, and stood up, and sat down again, and nudged Joseph to inform me if he would *ever* have done. I was condemned to hear all out: finally, he reached the '*First of the Seventy-first*'. At that crisis, a sudden inspiration descended on me; I was moved to rise and denounce Jabes Branderham as the sinner of the sin that no Christian need pardon.
>
> 'Sir', I exclaimed, 'sitting here within these four walls, at one stretch, I have endured and forgiven the four hundred and ninety heads of your discourse. Seventy times seven times have I plucked up my hat and been about to depart – Seventy times seven times have you preposterously forced me to resume my seat. The four hundred and ninety-first is too much. Fellow-martyrs, have at him! Drag him down, and crush him to atoms, that the place which knows him may know him no more!

The rhetorically divided sermon picks up the image of the divided house through its own partition, what Blair, passing on the tradition in his *Lectures*, called the 'method of dividing a Sermon into heads', the 'formal partitions' the art of preaching shares with all 'Discourse' (*Lectures*, xxxi).[14] But it also contravenes the traditional warning, echoed in Blair, against unnecessary 'multiplication into heads', against dividing the subject into 'minute parts' and so fatiguing the listener.

Arrival at the sermon's final partition leads in the dream to figures for biblical Endtime and for the upsetting of sequential order. The boundary between dreamer and dreamed here, however, is also one of the partitions which threatens to break down. Branderham's accusation of Lockwood ('*Thou art the Man!*'; p. 66) recalls both a New Testament violation of a partition wall (Acts 21:28) and an Old Testament application of a parable to its hearer (2 Samuel 2:7). Lockwood and the preacher become increasingly hard to distinguish as the dream moves towards mutual violence and Jabes' accusatory 'Thou' – echoing an address to a hearer unexpectedly inscribed within a story he had thought himself outside (2 Samuel) – turns the focus back on Lockwood himself, as nomination becomes virtually inseparable from accusation.[15] The Lockwood who objects to the multiplied partitions of Branderham's divided sermon himself scrambles to erect a partition or dividing wall of books in his second dream, when the ghostly child threatens to enter the house through a window which no longer keeps the outside out. And the multiplication of the partitions of discourse, which Lockwood objects to in that first dream, has its counterpart in Lockwood's own preference as narrator for the sequential narrative partitions which keep names, times, and events in their proper place after this unsettling night.

It is significant that it is after this night that Lockwood both loses his way in the snow when it removes the indicative function of signs ('the swells and falls not indicating corresponding rises and depressions in the ground'; p. 73) and blots out the 'chart' in his mind with the 'line of upright stones' that formerly served as 'guides'. But it is also after this night that he requests the housekeeper's explanatory 'history', which begins with a sorting out of proper names and, as in Foucault's description of classical discourse, 'sorts out' the simultaneous into the successive, into a 'linear order' whose parts 'must be traversed *one after* the other'.[16] Mrs Dean begins by describing Heathcliff as 'very near' – and then hastens to eliminate the ambiguity by adding that she means not 'close' but 'close-handed'. But the parsimoniousness of Heathcliff and the parsimony which is one of the senses of 'near' are joined by the extreme economy of names themselves ('Heathcliff' serving 'parsimoniously', as Frank Kermode puts it, as both Christian name and surname),[17] a paucity emphasised by the novel's own striking juxtapositions. 'Catherine, Mrs Linton Heathcliff now' (ch. XXVIII, 316), for example, contains the names of both rivals for this *second* Catherine's mother. The swarming and disembodied names of chapter III, beyond Lockwood's control and endowed with an unsettling mobility, are themselves too compressed or 'near' – sheer parataxis or juxtaposition, without explanatory syntax or reference, and with a power of combination neither logical nor chronological. It is only in the history provided by Mrs Dean, who presents herself as 'a steady, reasonable kind of body', distinguished both by her housekeeping and by her familiarity with books (ch. VII, 103), that the names are given their proper place within a genealogical line. Her history – which Lockwood insists should proceed 'minutely', and which is accompanied by such emblems of *chronos* as the clock on the wall (ch. VII, 102; ch. X, 129) – moves in reassuring Enlightenment fashion in a single, irreversible direction from beginning to end, from the passionate Catherine and Heathcliff to the tamer, book-reading Cathy and Hareton, and imparts a sense of progress to the text as it moves to its ending. And yet, because Lockwood's request comes immediately after his disturbing night, the very linearity of the narrative, told from the Linton property at Thrushcross Grange, links the mode of narration – the establishment of its boundaries or narratorial partitions, the assigning of a proper place to each proper name – with the boundary-marking of property, and creates thereby the specifically narrative possibility of trespass, of something which transgresses both the linearity and the identity of Lockwood's text, even as it calls attention to his narrative *as* narrative, as both demand and need, a spacing or *espacement* of the unbearably 'near' into an order more accommodated to the civilised and enlightened – or novel-reading – mind. Logical and chronological are here inseparable; and what Barthes calls 'the chronological illusion' is part of the function of logic itself, the overcoming of repetition through syntax or narrative.[18] Sequence struggles to master repetition in order, as we say, to get somewhere. And what in chapter III is called 'nothing but a name repeated in all kinds of characters, large and small' is spread out over the characters of a housekeeper's history frequently read as a story both of progress and of enlightenment.

Nelly's tale performs its function, and the two characters who could embody the obtrusive 'Catherines' are distanced by a generation. But there remains even in Ellen Dean's sequential narrative a sense of something which will not be accommodated to *chronos* or its logic – in the uncanny crossings, conflations, or reversals which transgress the categories of chronological time and sequence and, even more strikingly, within the activity of proper names themselves, the very markers of discrete identity. The novel's powerful, and disturbing, images of something that cannot be accommodated or contained – the 'oak in the flower-pot' and 'sea' in a 'horse-trough' (ch. XIV) – have their counterpart in the sense of something resisting Lockwood's ordered narratorial frame. Even after Nelly begins her story, proper names are not wholly reliable boundary lines. Northrop Frye observes that the word 'identity' has a double aspect, identity *with* and identity *as*. The problem with proper names in this text is that they participate in this duplicity, disrupting by their repetition over several possible referents the very principle of individuation they exist to designate or mark.

The text's adherence to social conventions of naming – proper names in this society as indicators not only of identity but of proper social place – is as strict as its adherence to chronology or to property law: Heathcliff, for example, is degraded by a pointed distinction in the mode of naming ('You may come and wish Miss Catherine welcome, like the other servants'; ch. VII, 94) and later ridicules his son for calling his own cousin '*Miss* Catherine' (ch. XXI, 251). But, if this novel observes the carefully articulated system of naming in which the form of address reflects distinctions of position, it also calls attention, even after chapter III, to the multiple names a single character can be called and conversely to the potential for ambiguity when, as with the 'Mrs Heathcliff' Lockwood erroneously places in chapter II, more than a single character can be identified by the same name. In chapter VI, for example, Hindley is called variously 'Mr Hindley', 'young Earnshaw', and simply 'Hindley', depending on the socially appropriate form of address. But the first time he is called 'Mr Earnshaw' ('I threw a shawl over my head and ran to prevent them from waking Mr Earnshaw by knocking'; p. 88), the reader may receive a shock, since the former 'Mr Earnshaw', called in the previous chapter 'by name' (ch. V, 85) in order to wake him, before they realise that he is not sleeping but dead, is now dead and his name, as in all forms of genealogical succession, now transferred to his son. The identity of the name momentarily effaces the boundaries of individual identity which the proper name should properly preserve.

The ambiguity of proper names is joined by the possible detaching of name from person or proper place, as in the spectral rising of disembodied 'Catherines' (ch. III), the suggestion that the first Catherine's 'name' might be a substitute for her presence or 'voice' (ch. XII, 158), or in the moment when that Catherine stares at her reflection ('Is that Catherine Linton?'; p. 159) and the name – hers in any case only by marriage – is, as it were, detached from her person even before it is transferred to a second 'Catherine Linton' at her death. When Heathcliff says to Cathy, 'I swear Linton is dying' (ch. XXII, 266), the context, or narrative placing, indicates that he refers to his son. But that context's own references to a transferred name – 'Catherine Linton (the very name warms me)' – and to exchange of place ('Just imagine your father in my place, and Linton in yours') make it possible to note that 'Linton is dying' could, out of its proper place, also refer to Catherine's father or to the progressive effacement of the Linton name. Names in this text frequently appear as a place or space to be filled, as the alien Heathcliff takes the name left vacant by an earlier, legitimate son, as the second Catherine Linton gets her name on the death of the first and fills the place of 'Miss Linton' after it has been vacated by Isabella's marriage, or as the initials 'C.' and 'H.' on the balls Catherine Linton and Linton

Heathcliff find in a cupboard at the Heights (ch. XXIV, 280) could as easily be filled by them as by 'Catherine' and 'Heathcliff', or later by 'Catherine' and 'Hareton', a possibility which would work against the narrative's carefully separated identities and times.

Names also participate in this text's transgressions or crossings. The curious mode of naming Hareton when he is first placed by Nelly on the genealogical grid – as 'the late Mrs Linton's nephew' (ch. IV, 75), rather than as the late Mr Earnshaw's son – subtly allies him with 'the house on which his name is *not* carved',[19] just as the inscription 'Hareton Earnshaw' on the lintel or, in northern dialect, 'linton' of Wuthering Heights may suggest a crossing of families which will in the narrative be achieved only after Hareton's marriage to Catherine Linton and their removal to the Grange. The potential chaos of sheer naming or categorisation is part of the oppressive weight of Lockwood's first dream; but a similar chaos may be conjured from the alliances and associations that names make independently of persons, almost as if they were engaged in a shadow play of combinations not permitted on the novel's more civilised surface, a mobility and transportability unsettling to the Enlightenment order or grid. Incest – the primal social trespass or crossing of boundaries – may be present not only in the uncertain relationship of Heathcliff and Catherine but in the promiscuous combination or confusion which remains open to names themselves, independent of genealogical or social placement.

Let us choose, for illustration, the most outrageous example. The female characters in the novel are variously called by their first and their family names, so that Isabella, for example, is also referred to simply as 'Miss Linton'. When she elopes with Heathcliff, Edgar Linton proclaims that she is to be thereafter 'only [his] sister in name' (ch. XII, 170). At the only level which makes any logical sense, this phrase 'in name' is simply a formula for her disowning – a severing of a family tie in which the name will remain as the only trace of a former connection. But the other character who is, in the literal sense, his 'sister in name' is his daughter, a 'Miss Linton' who will also become, like Isabella, a 'Mrs Heathcliff'. This might hardly be noticed if it were not for the novel's insistent reference to names as virtually autonomous entities, a reference, however, wholly plausible in the marrying and giving in marriage which form the principal exchange of the plot. When Isabella says in chapter XIII, 'My name *was* Isabella Linton' (p. 175), the phrase suggests what for a woman in a society where property relations extend to marriage is the repeated experience of detaching person from name, an exchanging of one name for another which Nelly reminds Heathcliff may involve a more radical change in identity ('I'll inform you Catherine Linton is as different now, from your old friend Catherine Earnshaw, as that young lady is different from me'; ch. XIV, 185).

Frank Kermode points out that the three names Lockwood finds etched on the window ledge in chapter III – *Catherine Earnshaw, Catherine Heathcliff,* and *Catherine Linton* – map in their textual order the novel's principal crossing or exchange, from left to right the story of the first Catherine and in reverse that of the second, a reading of the text supported, I would add, by the housekeeper's own reference to 'retracing the course of Catherine Linton' (ch. XVI, 202) after her death, by Lockwood's striking textual metaphor of the daughter as a potential 'second edition of the mother' (ch. XIV, 191), and by Nelly's calling attention to the reverse order in which both Lockwood and the reader have been introduced to the two female figures who share the same name ('About twelve o'clock, that night, was born the Catherine you saw at Wuthering Heights'; ch. XVI, 201). This plotting of the history through the names is possible only through a reversal, a reading first in one direction and then in the other. The reader aware of the way in which things in this novel change places or seem to turn into one another – human into animal, civilised into violent, ghost into person, and person into ghost – might even perceive a lurking palindrome or verbal reversal in the name of the housekeeper herself, variously called 'Ellen' and 'Nelly', a suggestion outrageous to readers of the naturalised *Wuthering Heights* preferred by Q. D. Leavis and others, but perhaps not entirely inappropriate for a character who, as go-between, meddler, and even 'double-dealer' (ch. XX, 266) in the plot, also mediates as a kind of boundary figure between superstition and enlightenment and moves as narrator in two directions, in towards the story in which she is involved, and out towards her civilised listener.

V

It is, indeed, in the literal sense of the word, preposterous.
(Coleridge, 'The Friend')

Retracing or reversing the left-to-right order of reading involves an upsetting of the simple linear sequence of diary, chronology, or genealogy and calls into question the Lockwoodian text and its relation both to enlightenment and to the very idea of progress. The narrative itself is for the most part preposterous, in the still-current nineteenth-century sense of a reversal of proper order: it begins with the second Catherine and proceeds to the first. The dominating influence of mere sequence creates the illusion of proceeding away from the opening scene, when in fact, or in chronology, it proceeds *to* it: the shock of hearing at the beginning of chapter XXV, 'These things happened last winter, sir' is the shock of the revelation that things which had seemed, in the familiar spatial metaphor, before us, are now just behind us, not distanced but close enough to overtake the present time. Even Nelly's carefully sequential 'history' includes episodes which upset its own partitions between discrete identities and times, disrupting both the linear order of the text and the certainty of chronological placing. In chapter XI, for example, Nelly tells of the apparition or uncanny return ('all at once, a gush of child's sensations flowed into my heart') at a crossroads pillar – itself inscribed with the initials of three possible directions – of Hindley himself as a child; then of finding when she hastens to the Heights that the apparition has preceded her, that what she thought was behind her now stands before her very eyes ('looking through the gate'), before she reflects that this child must be not Hindley but his son Hareton; and finally of her panic when, after her request to Hareton to fetch his father, Heathcliff appears. Hindley (the grown man whose apparition as a child conflates the intervening twenty years), Hareton (the child whom Heathcliff later describes as 'a personification of my youth, not a human being' and who has already appeared to the reader as a man), and Heathcliff (the figure who is, like Hareton, an oppressed child and, like Hindley, an oppressive father), are in this supernatural incident too 'near', as the boundaries which should separate child from man, a child from his father, and individuals or discrete chronological times from each other here forsake even the housekeeper and send her back to the 'guide-post' ('feeling as scared as if I had raised a goblin'; p. 149), before the apparition, 'on further reflection', fades into the light of common day. The scene is virtually the narrativisation of a preposterous Wordsworthian copula – 'The Child is father of the Man' – a metaphor whose conflation of times and identities shocks, before the mind accommodates it logically and chronologically as a condensed analogy, and the conflation of times is spread out, or spaced, over what is called the 'natural' life of a single individual.

Yet another conflation of times, or separate parts of the text itself, occurs in chapter XII, where a delirious Catherine Linton experiences a collapse of the distancing space of time ('the whole last seven years of my life grew a blank! . . . I was a child'), in which the years between the crossing of the moors which first separated her from Heathcliff and her marriage at nineteen to Edgar Linton drop away ('supposing at twelve years old, I had been wrenched from the Heights, and . . . converted, at a stroke, into Mrs Linton, the lady of Thrushcross Grange, and the wife of a stranger'; p. 163). These identifications of historically separated times may remind us of the aberrant 'identity with' of metaphor – a transgression of the boundaries of both logic and chronology which would provide the temporal counterpart of Catherine's own radical copula 'I *am* Heathcliff' (ch. IX, 122).[20] But what is even more upsetting to both is this chapter's 'preposterous' textual recalls, its repeated echoes of Lockwood's encounters in chapter III: the snowy down plucked by a 'wandering' Catherine recalls Lockwood's 'wandering' in the 'snow'; the 'blank' of the disappearing space of years recalls the 'blank' filled by Catherine's marginal script; the 'oak-panelled bed', 'wind sounding in the firs', and opened 'casement' of Catherine's delirium (ch. XII, 162–3) recall Lockwood's enclosure in the same bed at the Heights, the 'fir-tree' moved by the 'gusty wind' and the terrifyingly open casement window (ch. III, 66–7). These echoes create the uncanny sense that the 'Catherine Linton' who in chapter XII is 'no better than a wailing child' (p. 162), sees herself as the 'exiled' and 'outcast' twelve-year-old of the crossing Lockwood reads about in chapter III, and imagines a return to the Heights through the graveyard 'ghosts' of Gimmerton Kirk, *is* the 'wailing child' ('still it wailed'; ch. III, 67) or ghostly 'Catherine Linton' of Lockwood's second dream, who attempts to return to her 'home' after wandering on the moors for 'twenty years'. The two chapters, on rereading, contaminate each other preposterously, upsetting the ordered linearity of the narratorial text. The recalling of chapter III in chapter XII – a phenomenon common enough in the sequential process of reading in which a later chapter may recall an earlier one – here involves an uncanny, or preposterous, reversal, since the earlier chapter which the later one recalls has its place, chronologically, almost twenty years after it.

The sense of fixed and inviolable place in time is also shaken by the uncanny sense of repetition in the return of the first Catherine in the second (whom Edgar Linton distinguishes from her mother by a difference in name) or by Joseph's calling Isabella (recently converted from a 'Miss Linton' to a 'Mrs Heathcliff') 'Miss Cathy', and saying that 'Hathecliff' will rebuke her for her tantrum (ch. XIII, 180). The mind can accommodate the crossing by reference to Joseph's age or confusion; but the only character who is both 'Miss Cathy' and one whose tantrums will be punished not by Hindley but by Heathcliff is the *second* Catherine, a Miss Linton who will also become a Mrs Heathcliff, a character who has already appeared to the reader and to Lockwood but who, in the story's chronology, is at this point not even born. Chronos in the myth devoured his children; the disruption of chronology in this novel allows children to come again.

Wuthering Heights refuses to let the reader forget that both the chronological sense of time and the linear habit of reading depend upon sequence, on events maintaining a syntax, or proper sense of place. But Lockwood's encounter with the swarming and spectral 'letters', the undercutting of the rational explanation of his first dream (merely a 'fir-tree') in the uncanny return of the second, Nelly's crossroads apparition, chapter XII's preposterous recalls, and Joseph's curious mistake are all episodes in which things refuse to keep their proper place. Tropes such as metaphor (Catherine's defiant 'I *am* Heathcliff' or the sheer parataxis of the juxtaposed 'Catherines') and *hysteron proteron* (the figure of reversal which Puttenham called 'The Preposterous')[21] unsettle the careful boundaries and spaced linearity of Lockwood's text and reveal its own strategies of closure or enclosure as precisely that. The impulse to enclose is finally so intimately connected with the psychology of the narrator whose diary it is that all forms of closure, of shutting off or containing – including the narrative itself – become suspect or inadequate to their task, like the coffins of gothic fiction which refuse to stay shut. A neutral and 'ghostlike' narrative voice inhabits and dislocates even Lockwood's final lines, which seem to promise a final forestalling of repetition, or uncanny return. What Foucault calls the return of both nature and tropes undermines the narrator's closing refusal to 'imagine unquiet slumbers, for the sleepers in that quiet earth': nature, in the 'soft wind breathing through the grass' and the 'moths fluttering among the heath and hare-bells'; and writing, or tropes, in the appearance there of buried names, 'Heathcliff' and 'Hareton', the two oppressed children of the text itself. The curious absence of names in the description of the returning 'ramblers' Lockwood hastens at this ending to 'escape' creates, if only for a moment, the illogical possibility that these ramblers are not the solid, second-generation Cathy and Hareton but the ghostly Catherine and Heathcliff, whom the country folk insist still 'walk'.

The endless debate over whether the novel's second generation constitutes a progress or decline in relation to the first may be precisely endless because the two sides are simply the opposite faces of a single coin – two possibilities within the model of the line. The second generation only approximately repeats the first; and it is this difference within repetition which constitutes both 'spacing' and the possibility of 'progress'. The novel proffers in familial and genealogical terms the twinned questions of progress and enlightenment which so preoccupied eighteenth-century discourse. 'Reading' is part of the achievement of both enlightenment and progress in *Wuthering Heights*. But it is difficult to banish the suspicion that Cathy's civilising of Hareton by teaching him to read is at least partly a project to forestall boredom, a way, as we say, of filling the time. The second-generation couple, who get together over the pages of an 'accepted book' (ch. XXXII, 345), and whose domesticating of the Heights Lockwood approves, are still shadowed by the 'contrary' (ch. XXXII, 338) activity of the first, if only in the margins which disrupt the 'good book' provided in this ending by Lockwood himself. W. J. Harvey writes that it is precisely the 'muting' of intratextual conflations or echoes 'by the intervening mass of the novel' which makes the difference, in *Wuthering Heights*, between it and the 'intolerable' or 'gothic' reverberations which would have resulted if the echoes of one part of the text in another – the repetitions, for example, of that casement window from chapter III – had been 'more closely juxtaposed'.[22] But *Wuthering Heights* manages to reveal this very spacing as a strategy of the novel form itself, an accommodation to its 'civilised' (Kermode) or 'bourgeois' (Macherey) reading public.

We have, finally, to honour both the naturalised novel – or the sense of naturalising or of 'life' it produces by means of such spacing – and the uncanny conflations which disrupt both its unified identity and its linear structures. Lockwood is, as several readers suggest, a surrogate for the reader, and even Kermode's linear ordering is a form of Lockwoodian analysis – an ordering in sequence of the simple profusion of names in chapter III, which fill the air like the snowy feathers of chapter XII. The very binary oppositions by which readers traditionally structure meaning are in this text both generated and undermined. The difference between Earnshaw and Linton, salvation and damnation, nature and culture, primitive and civilised, or (paradoxically) graves that join and windows that divide, is finally a partition or dividing wall which does not really divide but is instead constantly crossed or transgressed by the novel's literal exchanges or by tropes such as metaphor which are 'beyond good and evil', which appear amoral because as in any purely verbal exchange they proceed by a more, or less, than human logic. But, at the same time as it undermines these partitions, the text does not allow any satisfying or simple identity *with*: Catherine's copular 'I *am* Heathcliff' suggests a unity beyond partition which in the novel nowhere appears. Metaphor itself involves a transgression of the boundaries of 'property', but its radical union is, as Derrida would say, always already inhabited by difference. There is always 'partition': the binary oppositions in this text both break down and are regenerated, as the revolt against the proliferating partitions of discourse in Lockwood's first dream moves to the reintroduction of a partition in the second. Even the text's uncanny conflations – or the potential identification of one part with another – cannot be conscripted to a conclusive identity. The distance between Catherine's delirium in chapter XII and Lockwood's second dream in chapter III is almost, but not quite, the twenty years of the ghost child's exile on the moors. The connection – neither logical nor chronological – remains and militates against logic, chronology, and the sense in both of progress, but cannot finally be forced to 'make sense'.

The identity of the literary text, both as unity and as a self-identity, guaranteed by the narratorial subject who offers the novel we read as his book, is in *Wuthering Heights* radically undermined: the text remains perpetually, and frustratingly, other to itself, forever inhabited by its own ghosts. The haunting of the narratorial text by something which escapes both identification and placing cannot simply be explained by recourse to the distinction between narrator and effaced author, to the substitution of one proper name – or one kind of mastery – for another. Indeed, we feel in reading Emily Brontë's novel the pertinence of at least one of her sister's prefatory remarks: 'the writer who possesses the creative gift owns something of which he [sic] is not always master – something that at times strangely wills and works for itself'.[23] Critics of *Wuthering Heights* as diverse as Fredric Jameson and Frank Kermode have remarked on its unsettling sense of automism, a staple feature of the gothic as a mode which foregrounds the unsettling mobility of *things*. Brontë's novel, whose 'characters' are both the embodiments of a genealogical history and the unsettling graphic letters of chapter III, suggests that something as apparently modern as the notion of a text writing itself may have a peculiarly gothic pedigree. And the recurrence of the figure of the 'spectre' or 'ghost' in contemporary narrative theory may return us to the ghost narratives of the period we call post-Enlightenment – if we understand that 'post', as we now do that of 'post'-structuralist, as still caught within the very structures it dismantles or undermines. *Wuthering Heights* calls into question not only private property but the very idea of the 'proper'; its violation is not only of moral proprieties but of novelistic ones. In the terms of one of its own most persistent figures, it demands a reading which seeks to raise more demons than it casts out.

From Patricia Parker, *Literary Fat Ladies: Rhetoric, Gender, Property* (London and New York, 1987), pp. 155–6 *passim*, 158–77 *passim*, 260–4 *passim*.

NOTES

[This essay has evolved through various previous versions. In 'The Metaphorical Plot', in *Metaphor: Problems and Perspectives*, ed. David S. Miall (Sussex: Harvester, 1982), pp. 133–57, Patricia Parker argues that the plot of *Wuthering Heights* functions by *substitutions* of place, property and name, just as metaphor puts 'one thing in place of another', and that this 'metaphorical plot' is related to the violence of the novel's outrage to propriety.

Two other essays by Patricia Parker – 'The (Self-)Identity of the Literary Text: Property, Propriety, Proper Place, and Proper Name in *Wuthering Heights*', in O. J. Miller and Mario Valdés (eds), *The Identity of the Literary Text* (Toronto, 1985), and 'Anagogic Metaphor: Breaking Down the Wall of Partition', in Eleanor Cook *et al.* (eds), *Centre and Labyrinth: Essays in Honor of Northrop Frye* (Toronto, 1983) – have also contributed to the essay reprinted here.

In the 'Retrospective Introduction' to *Literary Fat Ladies*, Patricia Parker explains that the earliest of these essays dealt with 'the relation between the unsettling mobility of tropes such as metaphor and the boundary markers of private property', while the more recent essays 'move explicitly toward questions of gender and genre as well as of property, and the entanglements of rhetorical questions with questions of ideological framing and political consequence' (p. 1).

Parker's use of modern literary theory is individual in several ways. Firstly, her immense erudition enables her to argue that 'the relation between the text of something called (for better or for worse) "literature" and something called (for better or for worse) "theory" is anything but a *sens unique* [one-way process]' (p. 7); the theories now being elaborated are anticipated by the older texts which they claim to elucidate, and may even be built upon them. Secondly, she brings together 'names often wielded by opposing camps' – such as Foucault and Derrida – because, thirdly, she uses theory 'heuristically' – in order to find things out for herself (pp. 5–6).

'The (Self-)Identity of the Literary Text' as it appears here has been slightly shortened with the publisher's permission. References are to *Wuthering Heights*, ed. David Daiches (Harmondsworth, 1965). Ed.]

1. Ian Watt, *The Rise of the Novel* (1957; reprinted Harmondsworth, 1963), p. 22, citing Locke's *Essay Concerning Human Understanding*, Book III, ch. 3, section 6.

2. See Locke, *Essay*, II, 3, pp. 2–5; Hobbes, *Leviathan*, part I, ch. 4; and C. B. Macpherson, *The Political Theory of Possessive Individualism: Hobbes to Locke* (Oxford, 1962).

3. Ian Watt, *The Rise of the Novel* (1957; reprinted Harmondsworth, 1963), pp. 18–19; Michel Foucault, *Les Mots et les choses*, trans. as *The Order of Things* (New York, 1973), especially pp. 104 ff.; Emily Brontë, *Wuthering Heights*, ed. David Daiches (Harmondsworth, 1965), ch. III, p. 66. All subsequent parenthetical references to the novel are to chapter and page in this edition.

4. See Patricia Drechsel Tobin, *Time and the Novel* (Princeton, 1978), introduction; Roland Barthes, 'An Introduction to the Structural Analysis of Narrative', trans. Lionel Duisit, *New Literary History*, 6 (Winter 1975), 237–72; Jacques Derrida, *Of Grammatology*, trans. Gayatri Spivak (Baltimore, 1976), pp. 85, 332; Michel Foucault, *The Order of Things* (New York, 1973), pp. 82–92; Eleanor N. Hutchens, 'The Novel as Chronomorph', *Novel* (Spring, 1972), 215–24; and Harold Toliver on 'Linear Logic' in *Animate Illusions* (Lincoln, Neb., 1974). See also, on the ideological implications of form, Pierre Macherey, *A Theory of Literary Production*, trans. Geoffrey Wall (London, 1978). The description of this 'linear logic' does not imply unawareness of writing in the Enlightenment which parodies or undermines it (the case of Sterne or Swift, for example). For a critique of the Foucauldian characterisation of an earlier Renaissance *episteme* and assertion of a rupture with it, see Patricia Parker, 'Retrospective Introduction', *Literary Fat Ladies: Rhetoric, Gender, Property* (London and New York, 1987), p. 6.

5. On identity understood as 'self-identity', see the discussion of two differing conceptions of identity (as permanence amid change and as unity amid diversity) in Paul Edwards (ed.), *An Encyclopedia of Philosophy* (New York, 1967), under 'Identity'; 'Almost all the writers of the period under discussion, from Descartes to Kant, took the term "identity" to mean that an object "is the same with itself" (Hume).' The more particular sense of self-identity (*identité à soi*) as used by Derrida involves as well the notion of self-presence. For readings of other

nineteenth-century texts in relation to the question of a unified identity and narratorial mastery, see, for example, Shoshana Felman on Henry James's *The Turn of the Screw* in 'Turning the Screw of Interpretation', and Peter Brooks's 'Freud's Masterplot: Question of Narrative', *Yale French Studies*, nos 55–6 (1977); Cynthia Chase, 'The Decomposition of the Elephants: Double-Reading *Daniel Deronda*', *PMLA*, 93 (March 1978), 215–27; J. Hillis Miller, *Fiction and Repetition* (Cambridge, Mass., 1982); and Maria M. Tatar, 'The Houses of Fiction: Toward a Definition of the Uncanny', *Comparative Literature*, 33 (Spring 1981), 167–82.

6. Maurice Blanchot, 'L'Absence de livre', in *L'Entretien infini* (Paris, 1969), pp. 564–6. The translations from it here are taken from Derrida's discussion of Blanchot's terms in 'LIVING ON: Border Lines', in Harold Bloom *et al.* (eds), *Deconstruction and Criticism* (New York, 1979), pp. 104–7.

7. Jacques Derrida, *Of Grammatology*, trans. Gayatri Spivak (Baltimore, 1976), p. 86.

8. Jacques Derrida, *Dissemination*, trans. Barbara Johnson (Chicago, 1981), p. 86. See also pp. 103–4.

9. See respectively Derrida, *Dissemination*, p. 103; Nietzsche, *Zur Genealogie der Moral*, First Essay, II; and, on ghost/host/guest, J. Hillis Miller, 'The Critic as Host', in Harold Bloom *et al.* (eds), *Deconstruction and Criticism*, pp. 220 ff. In addition to the juxtaposition of 'guest', 'host' and 'ghost' in chapter III, we are told at the end of chapter XVII, 'The *guest* was now the *master* of Wuthering Heights' (p. 222; my emphasis).

10. For the complex of terms related to 'proper', see, *inter alia*, Jacques Derrida, *Of Grammatology*, trans. Gayatri Spivak (Baltimore, 1976), pp. 26, 107–12, 244, and Derrida's long footnote on Marx's critique of the linguistic association of 'proper' and 'property' in *The German Ideology*, in 'White Mythology: Metaphor in the Text of Philosophy', trans. F. C. T. Moore, *New Literary History*, 6 (Autumn 1974), p. 15. For a survey of Marxist criticism of Brontë's novel, including the work of Arnold Kettle, Raymond Williams, and Terry Eagleton, see Ronald Frankenberg, 'Styles of Marxism: Styles of Criticism. *Wuthering Heights*: A Case Study', in Diana Laurenson (ed.), *The Sociology of Literature* (Keele, 1978). This survey necessarily omits Fredric Jameson's provocative short discussion in *The Political Unconscious* (Ithaca, NY, 1981), pp. 126–9.

11. Joseph J. Scaliger, *Poetices Libri Septem* (Lyon, 1561), IV, xxxviii.

12. These have been discussed in, respectively, Patricia Tobin, *Time and the Novel* (Princeton, 1978), p. 41, and Mark Schorer, 'Fiction and the "Analogical Matrix"', *Kenyon Review*, 11 (Autumn 1949).

13. See the discussions of proper names in, for example, Michel Butor, *Répertoire: Études et conférences 1948–59* (Paris, 1960), p. 252; Jacques Lacan, 'L'instance de la lettre dans l'inconscient', *Écrits*, I (Paris, 1966), p. 252; Charles Grivel, *Production de l'intéret romanesque* (Paris, 1973), pp. 128–44; and Jacques Derrida, *Of Grammatology*, trans. Gayatri Spivak (Baltimore, 1976), pp. 107–13.

14. Hugh Blair, *Lectures on Rhetoric and Belles Lettres* (1783).

15. On nominative and accusative, see Geoffrey Hartman, 'Psychoanalysis: The French Connection', in Geoffrey Hartman (ed.), *Psychoanalysis and the Question of the Text* (Baltimore, 1978), pp. 94ff.

16. Michel Foucault, *The Order of Things* (New York, 1973), pp. 82–3.

17. Frank Kermode, *The Classic* (New York, 1975), p. 123. [Reprinted above, p. 39 Ed.]

18. Roland Barthes, 'An Introduction to the Structural Analysis of Narrative', trans. Lionel Duisit, *New Literary History*, 6 (Winter 1975), 251–4. We might remember, in relation to this markedly genealogical novel, the characterisation of genealogy itself as a form of spacing in Nietzsche's *Zur Genealogie der Moral*.

19. Frank Kermode, *The Classic* (New York, 1975), p. 120. Other readings which have contributed to my argument here include, in addition to those of Hillis Miller and Fredric Jameson already noted, Dorothy Van Ghent's pioneering study in *The English Novel* (New York, 1953); Terry Eagleton's in *Myths of Power: A Marxist Study of the Brontës* (London, 1975), pp. 97–121 [reprinted above, p. 118 Ed.]; Carol Jacobs's '*Wuthering Heights*: At the Threshold of Interpretation', *boundary 2*, 7 (1979), 49–71; David Musselwhite, '*Wuthering Heights*: The Unacceptable Text', in Francis Barker *et al.* (eds), *Literature, Society and the Sociology of Literature*, Proceedings of the Conference held at the University of Essex (July 1976), pp. 154–60; and Margaret Homans, 'Repetition and Sublimation of Nature in *Wuthering Heights*', *PMLA*, 93 (January 1978), 9–19. Musselwhite speaks of the 'bracketing of Lockwood' which characterises readings as otherwise divergent as those of Q. D. Leavis, 'A Fresh Approach to *Wuthering Heights*', in *Lectures in America* (New York, 1969) [reprinted here, p. 24 above. Ed.], and Eagleton's chapter. We might add to this the reading of the ending of the novel as Brontë's capitulation to the conventional 'novelistic tradition' in Leo Bersani's *A Future for Astyanax* (Boston, 1976), p. 221.

20. For this temporal form of copular metaphor ('A *is* B'), see Northrop Frye, *Anatomy of Criticism* (1957; reprinted New York, 1966), p. 124, on the phenomenon of the grown man's feeling 'identical' with himself as a child. The Wordsworthian atmosphere of an episode such as Nelly's experience in chapter 11 also brings to mind Wordsworth's preoccupation with those fearful 'vertical' moments when the bound-

aries vanish and a distancing 'space' of years drops away. The late Paul de Man once remarked in conversation that what he referred to as 'aberrance' in *The Prelude* was like a grown man's saying of a picture of himself as a child, 'That's me' (or 'I') – Frye's principal instance of this copula.

21. George Puttenham, *The Arte of English Poesie* (1589), ch. 12. See also Derrida on the '*hysteron proteron* of the generations' in Freud's *Beyond the Pleasure Principle*, in his 'Coming into One's Own', in Geoffrey Hartman (ed.), *Psychoanalysis and the Question of the Text* (Baltimore, 1978), pp. 136–46.

22. W. J. Harvey, *Character and the Novel* (London, 1965), p. 187.

23. See Charlotte Brontë's Preface to the 1850 edition of *Wuthering Heights*, reprinted in the Daiches edition, p. 40.

Further Reading

One of the aims of this book is to give a sense of how criticism of *Wuthering Heights* has developed during the twenty years since the first Casebook. Although I have grouped my suggestions for further reading in sections such as editions, introductory guides etc., I have tried to preserve something of the sense of development by listing works chronologically within each group in order to stress how criticism itself has a history.

EDITIONS

There are a number of excellent editions of *Wuthering Heights*. The most scholarly of these is

Wuthering Heights, ed. Hilda Marsden and Ian Jack (Oxford: The Clarendon Press, 1976)

but all the following have useful introductions and notes. The Critical Editions edited by William Sale and Linda Peterson include a number of reprinted critical essays (hardly overlapping with this collection), and Heather Glen's Introduction and Afterword provide an extremely intelligent critical overview.

David Daiches (ed.), *Wuthering Heights* (Harmondsworth: Penguin, 1965).
William M. Sale, Jr (ed.), *Wuthering Heights*, Norton Critical Editions (New York, 1972).
Ian Jack (ed.), *Wuthering Heights*, World's Classics Series (Oxford: Oxford University Press, 1981).
Heather Glen (ed.), *Wuthering Heights*, Routledge English Texts (London: Routledge, 1988).
Linda H. Peterson (ed.), *Wuthering Heights*, Case Studies in Contemporary Criticism Series (New York: Bedford Books of St. Martin's Press; Basingstoke and London: Macmillan, 1992).

BIOGRAPHY AND OTHER WRITINGS BY EMILY BRONTË

One of Emily Brontë's many peculiarities as a writer was that she left so little information about herself. Even the manuscript of *Wuthering Heights* has disappeared, and there are no letters or essays in which she describes its writing or reception. Edward Chitham has written both a full-length, authoritative biography and a brief biographical introduction from this unpromising material:

Edward Chitham, *A Life of Emily Brontë* (Oxford: Basil Blackwell, 1987).
Tom Winnifrith and Edward Chitham, *Charlotte and Emily Brontë: Literary Lives* (Basingstoke and London: Macmillan, 1989).

Emily did, however, leave a large body of poetry. For many years the 'definitive' edition has been:

C. W. Hatfield (ed.), *The Complete Poems of Emily Jane Brontë* (New York: Columbia University Press, 1941).

There is now, however, a completely new edition:

Janet Gezari (ed.), *Emily Jane Brontë: The Complete Poems* (Harmondsworth, Penguin, 1992).

CRITICAL ANTHOLOGIES

There is probably as much criticism written about *Wuthering Heights* as any other literary text. An annotated bibliography and four carefully edited collections will help to give a sense of the scope of this criticism up to 1970; Harold Bloom's more recent collection has only two items in common with mine:

Janet Barclay, *Emily Brontë Criticism 1900–1980: An Annotated Check List* (Westport, Conn.: Meckler Publishing, 1983).
Miriam Allott (ed.), *The Brontës: The Critical Heritage* (London: Routledge & Kegan Paul, 1974) [covers criticism up to 1900].
Richard Lettis and William E. Morris (eds), *A Wuthering Heights Handbook* (New York: The Odyssey Press, 1961).
Miriam Allott (ed.), *Wuthering Heights*, The Casebook Series (London: Macmillan, 1970; revised edn 1992).
J.-P. Petit (ed.), *Emily Brontë*, Penguin Critical Anthologies Series (Harmondsworth, 1973).
Harold Bloom (ed.), *Emily Brontë's Wuthering Heights*, Modern Critical Interpretations Series (New York: Chelsea, 1987).

INTRODUCTORY GUIDES

There are a number of helpful introductory guides to the novel and its critics:

Graham Holderness, *Wuthering Heights*, Open Guides to Literature Series (London: Open University Press, 1973).
Rod Mengham, *Emily Brontë: Wuthering Heights*, Penguin Critical Studies Series (Harmondsworth: Penguin, 1988).
Hilda D. Spear, *Wuthering Heights by Emily Brontë*, Macmillan Master Guides (Basingstoke and London: Macmillan, 1985, 1987).
Felicia Gordon, *A Preface to the Brontës* (London and New York: Longman, 1989).

U. C. Knoepflmacher, *Emily Brontë: Wuthering Heights*, Landmarks of World Literature Series (Cambridge: Cambridge University Press, 1989).

Lyn Pykett, *Emily Brontë*, Women Writers Series (Basingstoke and London: Macmillan, 1989).

Peter Miles, *Wuthering Heights*, The Critics Debate Series (London and Basingstoke: Macmillan, 1990).

TEXT AND HISTORY

The following group of critics is concerned in different ways with the relationship between history and textuality in the novel; Bakhtinian dialogism is combined with feminist/psychoanalytic insights in Patricia Yaeger's article, while David Musselwhite's article argues for the impact of Emily Brontë's reading of near-contemporary history in Brussels:

Patsy Stoneman, 'The Brontës and Death: Alternatives to Revolution?', in *The Sociology of Literature: 1848*, ed. Francis Barker *et al.* (Colchester: University of Essex, 1976).

Patricia Dreschel Tobin, '*Wuthering Heights*: Myth and History, Repetition and Alliance', in *Time and the Novel: the Genealogical Imperative* (Princeton: Princeton University Press, 1978), pp. 38–42.

Carol Senf, 'Emily Brontë's Version of Feminist History: *Wuthering Heights*', *Essays in Literature*, 12 (Autumn 1985), 204–14.

James Kavanagh, *Emily Brontë*, Rereading Literature Series (Oxford: Blackwell, 1985).

David Musselwhite, '*Wuthering Heights*: The Unacceptable Texts', in *Partings Welded Together: Politics and Desire in the Nineteenth-Century English Novel* (London: Methuen, 1987).

Patricia Yaeger, 'Violence in the Sitting Room: *Wuthering Heights* and the Woman's Novel', *Genre*, 21 (1988), 203–29.

MARXISM

Marxism, like feminism, is much less homogeneous than is often thought (compare Kavanagh and Musselwhite – both Marxists – in the previous section, for instance). A useful summary of varieties is found in:

Ronald Frankenberg, 'Styles of Marxism, Styles of Criticism: *Wuthering Heights*: A Case Study', in *The Sociology of Literature: Applied Studies*, ed. Diana Laurenson, Monograph No. 26 (Keele, Staffs: University of Keele Press, 1978), pp. 109–44.

FEMINISM

It is worth noting that neither Lettis and Morris's anthology of *Wuthering Heights* criticism, published in 1961, nor Miriam Allott's original Casebook (1970) has any feminist content. Feminist criticism is largely a phenomenon of the last twenty years. It is all the more surprising, therefore, that there is now not only a large amount of feminist criticism (by no means over-represented in this collection), but also a wide variety of feminist viewpoints. The first book listed in this group serves as an introduction to the varieties of feminist criticism and uses *Wuthering Heights* as an example in several chapters:

Sara Mills *et al.* (eds), *Feminist Readings/Feminists Reading* (Sussex: Harvester, 1989).

Carol Ohmann, 'Emily Brontë in the Hands of Male Critics', *College English*, 32 (1971), 906–13.

Ellen Moers, *Literary Women* (1977, reprinted London: Women's Press, 1978), pp. 99–110.

Nina Auerbach, 'This Changeful Life: Emily Brontë's Anti-Romance', in *Shakespeare's Sisters*, ed. Sandra M. Gilbert and Susan Gubar (Bloomington, Indiana: Indiana University Press, 1979).

Margaret Homans, 'The Name of the Mother in *Wuthering Heights*', in *Bearing the Word* (Chicago: University of Chicago Press, 1986), pp. 68–83.

Andrea Dworkin, '*Wuthering Heights*', in *Letters from a War Zone* (Secker and Warburg, 1987).

Stevie Davies, *Emily Brontë: the Artist as a Free Woman* (Manchester: Carcanet, 1983); and *Emily Brontë*, Key Women Writers Series (Sussex: Harvester, 1988).

Patsy Stoneman, 'Feminist Criticism of *Wuthering Heights*', *Critical Survey* (June 1992), 147–53.

PSYCHOANALYSIS

Psychoanalytic studies have become a great deal more sophisticated since Thomas S. Moser's patronising study, 'What is the Matter With Emily Jane?' (*Nineteenth-Century Fiction*, 17 [1962], 1–19). Leo Bersani's is the most difficult of these, while the last two derive from a variety of psychoanalysis called 'object relations theory'.

Juliet Mitchell, '*Wuthering Heights*: Romanticism and Rationality', in *Women, the Longest Revolution* (1966, reprinted London: Virago, 1984), 127–44.

Helen Moglen, 'The Double Vision of *Wuthering Heights*: A Clarifying View of Female Development', *Centennial Review*, 15 (Fall 1971), 391–405.

Leo Bersani, *A Future for Astyanax: Character and Desire in Literature* (Boston: Little Brown, 1976).

Margaret Homans, 'Repression and Sublimation of Nature in *Wuthering Heights*', *PMLA*, 93 (January 1978), 9–19.

Philip Wion, 'The Absent Mother in Emily Brontë's *Wuthering Heights*', *American Imago*, 42 (1985), 143–64.

Barbara Schapiro, 'The Rebirth of Catherine Earnshaw: Splitting and Reintegration of Self in *Wuthering Heights*', *Nineteenth-Century Studies*, 3 (1989), 37–51.

STRUCTURALISM

Crudely speaking, the difference between structuralism and poststructuralism is that structuralists looked for universal 'keys' to human culture, whereas poststructuralists recognise historical and cultural specificity. Goetz's article

gives an unusually straightforward structuralist reading based on Claude
Lévi-Strauss's distinctions between 'nature' and 'culture', 'the raw' and 'the
cooked':

William R. Goetz, 'Genealogy and Incest in *Wuthering Heights*', *SNNTS:
Studies in the Novel* (North Texas State University), 14 (Winter 1982),
359–76.

DECONSTRUCTION

The textual complexity of *Wuthering Heights* has offered scope for the most
sophisticated of poststructuralist and deconstructive readings:

Carol Jacobs, '*Wuthering Heights*: At the Threshold of Interpretation',
boundary 2, 7 (Spring 1979), 49–71.

J. Hillis Miller, '*Wuthering Heights*', in *Fiction and Repetition in Seven
English Novels* (Cambridge, Mass.: Harvard University Press, 1982),
42–72.

Eve Kosofsky Sedgwick, 'Immediacy, Doubleness, and the Unspeakable:
Wuthering Heights and *Villette*', in *The Coherence of Gothic Conventions*
(1980; reprinted New York and London: Methuen, 1986).

Notes on Contributors

Stevie Davies taught English Literature at Manchester University 1971–84, leaving to become a full-time novelist and literary critic. Her publications include *Emily Brontë: The Artist as a Free Woman* (Manchester, 1983); *Virginia Woolf's 'To The Lighthouse'* (Harmondsworth, 1989); *John Milton* (Sussex, 1991); and three novels, *Boy Blue* (London, 1987); *Primavera* (1990); and *Arms and the Girl* (1992).

Terry Eagleton is Warton Professor of English Literature and Fellow of St Catherine's College, University of Oxford. His publications include *Criticism and Ideology* (London, 1976); *Literary Theory: An Introduction* (Oxford, 1983); and *The Ideology of the Aesthetic* (Cambridge, Mass., 1990).

Sandra Gilbert is Professor of English, University of California, Davis. With Susan Gubar she has co-authored *The Madwoman in the Attic* (New Haven and London, 1979); and *No Man's Land: The Place of the Woman Writer in the Twentieth Century*, 2 vols (New Haven and London, 1988–9); and has co-edited *The Norton Anthology of Literature By Women: The Tradition in English* (New York and London, 1985). She has also published four volumes of poetry, most recently *Blood Pressure* (New York and London, 1988).

Naomi Jacobs is Associate Professor of English, University of Maine. She is the author of *The Character of Truth: Historical Figures in Contemporary Fiction* (Illinois, 1990) and of articles on utopian literature, pedagogy, Aphra Behn, Dickens and the Brontës. She is currently writing a book entitled *When Silence Speaks: Dialogue and the Brontës*.

Frank Kermode, KB, FBA is an Hon. Fellow of King's College Cambridge; sometime King Edward VII Professor of English at Cambridge. He is the author of *Romantic Image* (London, 1957); *The Sense of an Ending* (New York, 1967); *The Classic* (London, 1975); *The Genesis of Secrecy* (Cambridge, Mass., 1979); *Forms of Attention* (Chicago, 1987); and *An Appetite for Poetry* (Cambridge, Mass., 1989).

Q. D. Leavis taught at Cambridge University, although she never held a formal post. Her major publications are *Fiction and the Reading Public*

(1932), and her *Collected Essays*, edited in three volumes by G. Singh (1983–9). She collaborated with her husband, F. R. Leavis, on the journal *Scrutiny* (1932–53) and *Lectures in America* (1969).

Michael Macovski is Associate Professor of English at Fordham University in New York City. He is the author of *Dialogue and Literature: Apostrophe, Auditors and the Collapse of Romantic Discourse* (Oxford, 1992), and *Dialogue and Critical Discourse: Literature, Linguistics, Literary Theory*. He is currently working on cultural attitudes to linguistic crimes in Regency England.

John T. Matthews is Associate Professor of English, Boston University. He is author of *The Play of Faulkner's Language* (Ithaca, 1982); and '*The Sound and the Fury': Faulkner and the Lost Cause* (Boston, 1990). He is editor of *The Faulkner Journal* and his present project is a book on frame narrative in the American South.

Patricia Parker is Professor of Comparative Literature and English, Stanford University, California. She is author of *Literary Fat Ladies: Rhetoric, Gender, Property* (1987), and has co-edited *Shakespeare and the Question of Theory* (with Geoffrey Hartman, London, 1986), *Literary Theory – Renaissance Texts* (with David Quint, Baltimore, 1986) and *Lyric Poetry: Beyond New Criticism* (with Chaviva Hosek, New York, 1985).

Lyn Pykett is Senior Lecturer in English at the University of Wales, Aberystwyth. In addition to the book on Emily Brontë, she is the author of *The Improper Feminine: the Women's Sensation Novel and the New Woman Writing* (London, 1992) and other works on nineteenth- and twentieth-century fiction, popular fiction, and the nineteenth-century periodical press.

Index